Advance Praise for
Public Displays of Affectation

Haurin's skillful use of language in this collection of stories makes familiar subjects—new love, old love, faithful and unfaithful love—seem vivid, strange, and exciting. This is a book I genuinely enjoyed reading.

> - Liz Moore, author of *The Words of Every Song* and *Heft*

With a keen eye for the telling detail and a well-tuned ear for dialogue, Shaun Haurin explores the myriad shades of gray that shroud adulthood and haunt the contemporary heart. A compelling and emotionally intelligent collection.

> - Marc Schuster, author of *The Grievers*

PUBLIC DISPLAYS OF AFFECTATION

stories by SHAUN HAURIN

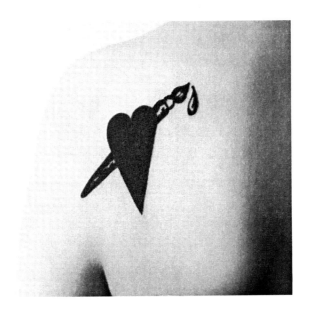

photographs by
ALYSSA ROBB

Cover Star: Shay Kretowicz
Bobo Lazarus illustration by Enrico Botta

PS Books
Philadelphia, Pennsylvania

Public Displays of Affectation
by Shaun Haurin

Public Displays of Affectation Copyright 2012
Published by PS Books, a division of Philadelphia Stories, Inc.

ISBN 13: 978-1-105-86962-4

"Dream Girl" appeared in Philadelphia Stories; a much shorter
version of "Me, Tarzan" appeared in The Ledge (as "Tarzan in
Training"); "Big Game" and "The Front" appeared in The Baltimore
Review

Cover and interior images by Alyssa Robb.
Bobo Lazarus image by Enrico Botta.
Used with permission.

PS Books
93 Old York Road
Ste. 1/#1-753
Jenkintown, PA 19046
www.psbookspublishing.org

PUBLIC DISPLAYS OF AFFECTATION

9.20.12

PSB13

To Maureen,
The odds are getting fatter by the minute

Your body, an open book of revelation
  and public displays of affectation
                    - Walter Ego, 'New Taboo"

Talent is more erotic when it's wasted.
                    - Don DeLillo, *Cosmopolis*

Contents

He was busy thinking of all the pop songs
associated with bison. . .

Big Game

Gabriel trailed Jana's muscular truck to her favorite bar, a big corner property within walking distance, coincidentally, of the trinity row house in which he'd been raised. The bar was lit up like the inside of a refrigerator, and seemingly under attack by a gigantic mutant crab from outer space. The fake crustacean looked as if it were about to bore a hole through the poorly shingled roof and, as if in retribution for scores of atrocities perpetrated against its kind—vats of boiling water, carapace-crunching nut-crackers, Agent Orangesque Old Bay—devour the horde of heedless patrons partying hard inside.

But vengeful alien seafood, it struck Gabriel, was the least of his problems. He was about to enter a working-class watering hole, in what was arguably the least tolerant neighborhood in a famously intolerant city, to watch a football game with the sort of woman who didn't so much as draw attention to herself as hijack it at knifepoint. Jana had tabby hair and perfect skin and eyes of Windex blue. She also had the kind of screen-goddess seductive power to which even Gabriel, a decidedly gay man, wasn't wholly immune.

"Follow me," Jana called, and for a heartbeat it actually seemed possible not to. For a heartbeat Gabriel, in the kind of wildly delusional moment he most often associated

3

with really good sex, thought to himself *No way, uh-uh. Catch you on the rebound.*

He locked eyes with the lightless orbs of the rooftop shellfish and considered taking his chances with the crab.

"I need a beer," Jana said, that skilled motivator of men. She turned in the doorway and shot Gabriel a phony little-girl frown to emphasize her need.

Gabriel was a bartender by trade, a kind of patron saint of parched throats. But even without the online mixology degree and a steady gig slinging drinks at Bella Luna, the upscale pizzeria where he and Jana worked, he would've felt obliged to fetch this eternally thirsty woman a drink.

Inside, the bar was standing room only, but Jana knew a waiter, a vanilla-haired musclehead, Richie Rich on steroids. He led them upstairs and showed them to a slab of Formica the size of a large cutting board. The football game was on in every sense of the term: on the ubiquitous TV screens orbiting the bar like stalled satellites; on the conspicuous team hats, jackets and jerseys management seemed to be handing out gratis at the door; on the wagging BBQ- and ranch-tinged tongues of the sort of diehard fans who weren't so diehard that they could score tickets to the game. Jana, too, was on. She seemed to feed off the charged atmosphere. Some people got high on drugs or booze or sex or sports or art or religion or sex or food or sex. Jana Browne was addicted to attention. She got high on simply being seen.

"What?" she asked in response to Gabriel's undivided attention. "See something you don't like?"

"On the contrary, you look great," he said. "Every guy in this bar knows your coordinates."

Jana glanced down at the twin mounds of her jersey, ample even beneath her oversized, unsexy sports attire.

"Wow, I've never heard them called *that* before." She laughed her silent laugh, rolled her eyes, and showed her unlikely companion too many teeth to count. "First rule of being a woman," she said, suddenly serious—or mock-serious, Gabriel couldn't tell, "is don't let 'em fool you. Every guy in this bar knows nothing but what down it is and how many inches there are to a fresh four. But I appreciate the compliment."

Another waiter appeared, empty-faced and out of breath. Gabriel had expected college girls in skimpy outfits, not aging frat boys in polo shirts and Gap khakis. The guy was clean-cut, All-American, borderline invisible. A looming tabula rasa toting a blank tablet.

Jana ordered poppers and crab fries and mussels marinara. The waiter Frisbeed them CD-size paper plates like he was dealing a deck of cards. The beer selection was as provincial as the neighborhood: three of the five brews on tap were variations—Lite, Genuine, Ice—of the same tasteless brand.

The food arrived faster than it should have.

"I can't believe Matt," Jana said, biting into a tiny meteor of breaded pepper and cream cheese. A dollop of white decorated a corner of her lovely mouth before a tentacular pink tongue appeared and carried it away. "Such a wuss."

Matt had bailed, received a text message from Laura, his off-again, on-again girlfriend, just as the three of them were walking out the door of Bella Luna. The message insinuated—as only truncated, Tarzan-inflected text messages can—that if Matt dropped whatever he was doing and ran right over, he could have his way with her. For once. Of course it was all baloney, the wicked manipulations of a woman who had dumped him three times in as many months and had no idea what she wanted from her Pavlovian dog-man. (Matt visibly salivated every time Laura's number appeared on the tiny green screen of his phone.) Jana had told him on more than one occasion to grow some balls. Still Matt clung. Some men were gluttons for a very specific brand of punishment.

"He's in love," Gabriel countered. "We can't hold that against him." He swallowed a mouthful of watery beer. "Can we?"

Jana shot him a pained expression through the steam of red broth and obsidian shellfish.

"Right," he said. "My bad."

"I can't stand guys like that," she hissed. "It's so unattractive."

Gabriel screwed up his face. "What? Guys who show their emotions? Guys who care?"

"Guys who *dote*," Jana clarified, chewing on a gummy mussel. "Promise me you'll never be a guy who dotes."

"You have my word." He plucked a few orange-dusted fries from their paper boat and plunged them into a soufflé cup of melted cheese. "And here I thought you had a thing for him."

"Who? Matt?"

Gabriel nodded.

Jana shook her head. "Don't get me wrong, he's totally hot and all. But I tend to need a little more than pimped-out rims and a pretty face. Not to mention a really cute ass." Eyes on him, Jana scooped up some marinara with half of a stray shell and slurped the blood-red sauce with all the élan of someone drinking champagne from a shoe. Some of it missed her mouth, however, and streamed down her chin, making her look like she'd been sucker punched. "Not that a guy would notice," she said, smiling evilly.

Gabriel still wasn't sure what had tipped Jana off, if tipped off she was. There was little that was overtly "gay" or even feminine about him, minus the manicured hands and ridiculously feline eyes. In fact it always surprised him how most people, many of them gay, assumed he was straight. Gabriel passed, with flying colors. If anything, he was a straight-man stereotype, a downright slob: he had shirts with missing buttons he kept held together with twist ties and had been known, in a moment of desperation, to staple cuffs onto a pair of pants with unfinished hems. Oblivious women routinely threw themselves at him. Not just artsy women, who imagined he was creative (which he wasn't) or sophisticated women, who assumed—despite or precisely because of his thrift—that he had money (which he didn't). But shop girls and waitresses, working-class stock who should've been trained to spot if not stone the queer from a mile away.

His sexuality, by all accounts, was a well-kept secret. So why was Jana going out of her way to imply otherwise?

"I notice everything," Gabriel said. "I'm a bartender. It's my job."

Jana ignored this comment. Something painful had just happened to the fans of the home team. An underage girl seated at the bar put her head in her hands and appeared to sob. Her underage girlfriend draped a comforting arm around her shoulder and breathed tender words like "They just got lucky" and "There's plenty of time" in her multiply pierced ear.

When Jana finally trained her bluish-green eyes on him they were clear as the Caribbean. "Sorry this didn't work out the way you planned."

He shrugged. "I don't know what you're talking about. I hadn't planned anything."

"Good," said Jana. "I don't believe you, but good. We're here to have some fun." She nodded toward the nearest TV screen. "Despite what happens up there." She lifted her dainty, girl-shaped glass to her lips and drained what was left of her beer. "No more Kool-Aid," she pronounced. "I want some hard stuff."

"Yoo-hoo?" Gabriel joked.

"You wish."

No sooner had Jana lifted a finger to summon the waiter than he appeared, spaniel-like, by her side. "Two shots of Goose," she said, not bothering to ask Gabriel what he preferred. "No, scratch that. Make it whiskey." Then, to Gabriel: "We'll replace pretty boy Matt Lowell with rough-and-tumble Jack Daniel's."

"A toast," said Gabriel, when the miniature drinks arrived.

Unbidden, Jana came around to his side of the table and plopped herself down on his lap. Gabriel was vaguely aware of heads turning, of whispers being passed around the bar like those of huddled-up amateur athletes guarding plays.

"To Bella Luna," Jana cooed. "The beautiful moon." Her breath was hot on his neck; her tiger-striped hair smelled edible, like something he could sink his teeth into and swallow. "Our illustrious place of employ."

Gabriel grimaced; she sounded like him. "To football," he countered.

"Ah, to football," echoed Jana. "And men in tight pants."

Gabriel was still sober enough to suspect Jana of baiting him, so instead he said, "To splitting the uprights" and waggled his mother's eyebrows.

Jana whooped. "I'll drink to that!"

They drank. When Gabriel opened his eyes again, he found Jana making a sour face at him. It took him a minute to realize that her dancing features comprised a mirror image of the face he was making at her. They weren't whiskey drinkers, that much was clear.

"Jack just kicked my ass, Jellybean," Jana said. "But that's okay. I like it rough."

Jana had nicknamed him Jellybean simply because one slow night at Bella Luna, Gabriel had recited all the lyrics to Jellybean Benitez's "Sidewalk Talk." But then Gabriel knew the words to scores of silly pop songs. It could've been worse. She could've dubbed him Scritti Politti or Kajagoogoo or Orchestral Manoeuvres in the Dark.

Gabriel put his empty shot glass on the table. When he glanced over his shoulder at the nearest TV screen, he saw that he and Jana were being watched.

Truth be told, Gabriel wasn't attracted to many different kinds of men. Unlike his friend, Roger, whose only prerequisite was that a potential lover have a penis (and preferably an American Express gold card-carrying penis), Gabriel couldn't just tumble into bed with someone simply because that someone seemed willing, if not eager, to tumble into bed with him. Of course there were always exceptions. Gabriel was thirty-three, had first slept with a man—a man about the age he was now—back when he was nineteen. Regrets, he had a few. But given the choice Gabriel preferred to be drawn to his lovers. *Yeah, as in drawn and quartered* Roger would say.

The man making eyes at him from clear across the bar was a cliché: Seven-o'-clock shadow. Shoulders broad as a buffalo's. Hands like catcher's mitts. As a rule Gabriel liked lanky guys, sinewy yet strong-limbed; very short hair; smooth chests; compact asses (with a pang he realized he had the same taste in men as Matt Lowell's sometime girlfriend).

Gabriel wasn't a big believer in "gaydar." Barring flamboyant behavior, he couldn't tell much from a person's hair or clothes or supposed body language. But he rarely even needed to. A person—man or woman, straight or gay—looks you in the eye the way this man was looking at Gabriel and you just *knew*.

Jana nudged him. "Looks like somebody's got an admirer." She lifted her chin toward the bar, where the man Gabriel had secretly dubbed Buffalo Bill was holding court. He'd turned back to his beer buddies, who were engaged in a series of intricate hand-slaps and head butts in celebration of some favored call or another.

"You think so?"

"I don't know much," Jana smirked, "but I know when a man wants me." She eyed Gabriel. "Chalk it up to women's intuition."

Gabriel was confused. "Who?" he said, only half-feigning ignorance. "With the tattoo?"

One of Bill's buddies was an exceptionally loud guy—loud even for these human foghorns. Bald and prodigiously goateed, he resembled nothing so much as an overfed walrus barking for another pound of fish. There was some sort of tattoo crawling up or down the back of what should've been his neck. Even cold-sober Gabriel's eyes weren't the best, and he was too far away to unscramble the image.

"Eeewww. No way. Not with *your* junk." Jana got more mileage out of foul language than most men Gabriel knew. It wasn't unappealing. "The one next to him. The lumberjock."

It was a reference to Bill's plaid flannel and thermal

undershirt combo.

"You mean jack."

"You know him!" squealed Jana.

"No, no," he clarified. "Lumberjack. You said jock."

Jana's eyes narrowed to non-existence. Gabriel had seen them do this before, in response to a disrespectful diner or a certain ass-grabbing busboy, and had always been thankful that he wasn't the cause. "I meant jock," Jana hissed. "It's called a pun. I thought you studied lit."

"Oh," he said. "A long time ago."

Could Jana be right? Could Buffalo Bill's X-ray vision really have been meant for her? She was still perched on his lap, after all, where the bar flavors of beer, cigarettes and Old Bay mingled sickeningly with Jana's fruity perfume.

"Fill me up, Gabe," Jana said. "I feel a man-size thirst coming on."

Gabriel did as he was told, tipping the fresh pitcher—when had it arrived?—and filling Jana's miniature pilsner with too much beer.

"Easy, Stud," she advised, damming the impromptu river with a bulwark of coarse brown napkins. "You trying to get me drunk or what?"

"Or what," joked Gabriel, smiling gamely. He glanced at Buffalo Bill just as Bill glanced away.

Suddenly Gabriel wanted this man more than he should have, more than he felt he had any right to. By rights Bill belonged to Jana. This was her man, at her bar, in her world. If the man wasn't gay and Jana wanted him, there was nothing Gabriel could do about it, short of throwing himself at the guy, which more likely than not would land him in the hospital. But if Gabriel was right and Bill was gay—or at least open to exploring his sexuality—didn't he have every right to stake his claim, so to speak? His cock seemed to think so. But his cock, Gabriel reminded himself, was blind. Jana's rump was fitted snugly against his groin, with the usual results, but his eyes were on Bill.

Jana looked lovingly over her shoulder at Gabriel and applied a bit more pressure to his lap. "Hmmm, that's nice," she whispered boozily in his ear. "That means a lot to me, Gabe."

Gabriel had played this game before (though admittedly never with so tempting an opponent) and alcohol was always involved; it made things so much simpler, the way booze filtered a prism of infinite, consciousness-expanding colors into a single, manageable monochrome. Still, he didn't trust it: not the booze, not Jana's boobs, and certainly not flannel-happy Mr. Machismo, who for all Gabriel knew was in on the whole sorry pseudo-seduction.

Gabriel didn't want Bill simply because Jana wanted him; it wasn't as catty as all that. But he had to admit that Jana's interest in the man put pursuing this rather tenuous attraction more on the scale of a military offensive.

Jana rasped something in his ear about Gabriel having his way with her, but he hardly heard her. He was busy thinking of all the pop songs associated with bison: "Buffalo Soldier." "Buffalo Stance." The U2 video for "One," in which a herd of stampeding buffalo runs over the edge of a cliff and, perhaps not incongruously, the band members appear in drag. Not one of them—not even pretty boy Larry Mullen—made very convincing women.

"Did you hear what I said, Gabe?"

"Sorry."

"You should be." Jana tossed her fragrant hair in his face and leveled her heavy-lidded eyes at him. It was a look meant to convey that the always beautiful and infinitely charming Ms. Browne would not suffer another slight. She would commit hari-kari with her crab fork first. "I asked whether or not you were ever going to kiss me."

All at once the deafening noise in the room seemed to drain away. Gabriel had no choice but to blame it on the booze. The former English major in him kicked in and he was reminded of a few favored lines by Wallace Stevens: "It may be that in all her phrases stirred / The grinding water and the gasping wind; / But it was she and not the sea we heard." As house siren, Jana's may have been the only song capable of drowning out the bar's din. But her range was hopelessly limited from a closeted gay man's point of view. Although Gabriel's desire was palpable—so palpable that he drunkenly feared it would puncture his pants—it also happened to be grossly beside the point. What Gabriel wanted Jana Browne couldn't give him. In fact all the woman could really do was take.

Still, what harm was there in a kiss?

"Clock's ticking, Gabe. What do they say? 'For a limited time only.'"

Jana's face widened; she seemed to have multiple rows of teeth, like a shark. Gabriel wished he could say that the alcohol blunted her features, made her enviably angular face sag a bit, her greenish-blue eyes bulge, her lovely mouth go slack, but none of this was true. If anything the booze brought Jana's beauty into sharper focus. She never seemed more in control of a situation than when there was a very real threat she might lose it. Some people were turned on by surrender in a lover. Not Gabriel. As far as he was concerned, surrendering was his job.

Jana, sensing as much, placed a warm hand on his thigh.

"Does this help?"

Without waiting for a response, Jana took Gabriel's face

in her hands and pressed her mouth urgently against his, roughly parting his teeth with her tongue. She tasted pretty much the way she smelled: like a well-tended woman in a neighborhood bar. Gabriel's own tongue, that lousy host, had curled toward his throat when Jana Browne finally came to call, where it seemed intent on hiding until the unannounced guest got the hint and went away. Gabriel heard a collective cry of anguish and thought for a second that every fiber of his being was calling out in protest, if not in pain. Something, somehow, had gone horribly wrong.

He opened his eyes in time to catch the replay. The home team had blown not one but two easy tackles, allowing its opponent to run thirty-five yards for a touchdown. He watched a shoeless player kick the ball through a huge yellow tuning fork and saw that the score was 14-3. The game clock read late in the fourth quarter.

"Goddamn bums!" someone hollered in Gabriel's ear. "He should be shot for missing that tackle!"

"Shot twice!" someone seconded.

"Hold up, lemme go get my gun," joked another, sending a ripple of uneasy laughter around the bar.

"I'll be right back," cooed Jana. She slid off Gabriel's lap and straightened her short denim skirt. She was impossibly pleased with herself for someone who had just won a game of tonsil tennis by forfeit. "Time to drain the pool."

Jana wriggled her way toward the restroom. More than a few heads swiveled like spotlights in her direction. The largest and shaggiest of these heads, Gabriel couldn't help noticing, belonged to Buffalo Bill.

Gabriel watched the massive man watch Jana slink past him. She didn't so much as glance at him—didn't acknowledge Bill at all, as far as he could tell—and yet the very pulse of her body, from the slight sway of her arms to the easy swivel of her considerable hips to the alternating steps of her oddly shod, cowboy-booted feet seemed engineered to put her on display, to signal her as a woman designed to be devoured with one's eyes. Gabriel envied Jana's inebriated grace, the way she turned a crowded bar into a catwalk simply by setting her fluid body in motion.

Gabriel considered leaving right then and there; he couldn't honor the devil's deal struck between his teeth and Jana's tongue, couldn't go through with whatever it was—marriage, kids, more consciousness-killing ménage à trois with throat-scorching Jack Daniel's—Jana expected of him. He attempted to stand but couldn't find the floor. His head felt like a flushed toilet. How could he make a seamless escape with the room rattling along like the Market-Frankford El?

Rather than go anywhere, Gabriel sought Buffalo Bill's problematic gaze, resolved to make some telepathic point, no matter how misinformed or obscure. But Bill wasn't where he was supposed to be. Maybe he too had needed to drain the pool. Maybe he was draining and drilling it right into Jana, her chlorine-streaked mane visible above the stall door, her gleaming legs hugging his mid-section like a snug-fitting floatation device. Bill was gone. In his stead Gabriel locked eyes with his buddy, The Walrus. And The Walrus was not impressed by what he saw.

A moment later the small mountain of a man loomed over Gabriel's café table, heaving. The trek across the packed bar had done him in. He pointed an accusative finger at Gabriel. He might as well have been aiming a gun.

"That shirt's purple, pal."

Gabriel was speechless. He glanced down at what he was wearing and found that, indeed, his shirt was purple. The

Walrus knew his color chart. But could the creature be objecting to what he perceived as a feminine color—and, by extension, an effete man—in such an undisputedly masculine environment? Did people overtly object to such things anymore? Gabriel's shirt wasn't made of silk, after all. It was neither blousy nor clingy, neither frilly nor sheer. It wasn't lavender or orchid or even legitimately plum. It was a purple shirt. Plain purple. He'd bought it secondhand.

"So what?" Gabriel said. The syllables came out sounding more defiant than he'd intended. Everyone within earshot translated them as *En garde!*

The Walrus raised a paddle-flat flipper—for what purpose Gabriel did not know—but suddenly stopped short, for Jana was beside him now, lovely, glowing, unhappy Jana, with her boobs and her hair and her sluttish, double-edged smile. Gabriel smelled her before he felt her physical presence, her damp hand on his shoulder, her hip warm against his arm. The Walrus's eyes widened in pure childlike wonder. Gabriel's assailant hadn't noticed Jana before. His eyes had been glued to the game. The dope.

"It's not the same purple," Gabriel heard Jana say in his defense, though in comparison to what he still didn't know.

Ah, Jana to the rescue! Jana, like manna, falling from heaven. Instant babe in a box, just add beer. Gabriel's very own goddess from a machine...

Jana glanced up at the nearest screen, which displayed two team emblems on either side of a chart of statistics. It was then Gabriel realized that it wasn't the color The Walrus objected to—though he seriously doubted the guy had a closet full of purple, unless it appeared in tandem with silver or black, on his various hockey, football and basketball jerseys—so much as where he'd seen the offending shade and when. On this particular night, in this particular game, purple was the color of the enemy.

The Walrus gave Jana the once-over and somehow still mustered the courage to grumble, "Close enough." He wasn't a hopelessly dumb beast, for experience had taught him that the only reaction he would be capable of getting from a woman like Jana was a violent one. But that's okay. Violence was his forte.

Gabriel saw Jana's hand close around the long handle of her two-pronged shellfish fork. The old instincts were kicking in, the instincts Gabriel couldn't help finding simultaneously thrilling and disconcerting. My god, he thought, in the slang of B-movie gang-bangers, she's going to stick the guy. A faint smile played upon his lips.

"Go back to the bar," Jana ordered. "He's not bothering anybody. Leave us alone."

The Walrus expelled a sour cloud of air in lieu of a laugh.

Jana brandished her pathetic weapon. "I said fuck off!"

"Whoa, whoa. There's no need to get *physical.*" His emphasis made the word sound blue. "I'll make a deal with you," The Walrus said. "If he takes off the shirt he can stay." He regarded buxom, short-skirted, cowboy-booted Jana Browne not unlike the way a toddler regards a chocolate Easter bunny. "Scratch that, sweetness. If *you* take off your shirt, he can stay."

Jana bit her freshly painted lip. She seemed to be considering the proposal.

"Jimmy," said a voice from behind Gabriel. It was deep and even, radio-smooth.

Gabriel turned and saw the kind eyes, easy smile and muscle-stuffed farmland flannel of Buffalo Bill.

"You're embarrassing yourself, Jimmy. Go sit down."

"Fuck no," said The Walrus, whose tattoo Gabriel now noticed resembled some sort of snake with legs. "You see what this guy's wearing?"

Bill said nothing, simply placed a brown paw on The Walrus's shoulder. "Go sit down, Jimmy," he repeated. "For me." Bill made it sound as though The Walrus would be doing him a favor by honoring his request, though clearly it was the other way around. If anybody was being done a favor it was The Walrus, and he knew it.

Still, he looked from Jana to Gabriel and back again. What, with her pronounced face paint, roller coaster curves and homespun sugar hair, the woman was a human amusement park. The Walrus seemed to think he was being robbed of at least one good ride. "You're a lucky motherfucker," he hissed at Gabriel. Then, as emasculated as his favorite football team, he suavely blew Jana a parting kiss and waddled away.

"Sorry about that," said Bill. "Jimmy takes sports far too seriously."

"Apparently," snorted Jana. "You should keep that guy on a leash."

Bill smiled knowingly. "He'd only chew through it."

Jana laughed, the sound of one seduction replacing another. Seducing Gabriel had been a challenge, a lark. But seducing Buffalo Bill was her stock-in-trade. "Have a seat," she said, pulling up an empty chair. "You don't want to miss the rest of the game."

Bill sat down. "The game's over," he said, catching Gabriel's eye. As if in extrasensory support of this pronouncement, the opposing team intercepted the ball. Within seconds they were up another seven points.

The bar crowd bawled and beat their breasts. Bill casually pulled a lighter from his flannel pocket and lit the cigarette that had magically appeared between Jana's lips. Then he lit one of his own.

Jana exhaled dramatically. "Okay, now I'm bummed," she said through a puff of smoke. She looked far from bummed to Gabriel. She looked like the birthday girl, homecoming queen and bride-to-be all rolled into one.

Again Bill smiled at Jana as one might smile at a lovingly crafted piece of furniture. More than his bulk or his easy banter or his obvious brains, it was the man's confidence that disarmed Gabriel. Self-assurance looked good on the guy; like his Paul Bunyan get-up, he wore it well.

"I'm going to need to be consoled," Jana said, glancing back and forth between the two men. "By somebody," she teased when neither one of them raised a hand, "or some*bodies.*"

Buffalo Bill lifted his eyebrows at Gabriel, who responded with a shrug. Gabriel meant the gesture as *Who needs her* but Bill seemed to interpret it as *Be my guest.*

Bill peered over his shoulder at his buddies at the bar. The game was still on but all eyes were on him. The Walrus in particular appeared to be wondering what could be keeping the reluctant leader of their unsavory pack.

"Sure," Bill finally said to Jana, seeming to avoid her companion's gaze. "I'll console you."

"One for one," said Jana, utterly unsurprised. The guy could've torn open his shirt to reveal her initials shaved into his chest hair, and Gabriel's unfazed coworker would've kept her legendary cool. "How about you, Jellybean?"

It wasn't the first time Gabriel had been presented with such an offer, and something in Jana's eyes implied she didn't expect to be turned down. Her staggering presumptuousness—about her allure, about Bill's preference, about Gabriel's sexuality—rankled him. That, and the ostensibly mindless way her hand had strayed to Bill's Popeye-like forearm, a wayward pet returning home.

"I'm going to finish this beer, wait out the rest of the game," he lied. "See you at work."

It was refreshing to see Jana look flustered. She glanced from Gabriel to Bill and back again, as though the two men had secretly decided something that had nothing at all to do with the fabulous female specimen seated between them. She nodded, once, as if to say *Your loss* and left the bar without saying goodbye.

Gabriel had an inkling Bill wouldn't actually go through with it; this was just an elaborate game some people played. The object was to see how far one was willing to go in order to dupe others and oneself. The more radical the extreme, the larger the score, though it became increasingly difficult, round to round, to keep an accurate tally. But Gabriel had underestimated his opponent; sadly, Bill proved to be quite skilled at the game. He was likely the local champ.

Bill rose and threw two twenties onto the rickety, beer-ringed table. He glanced resignedly at the empty beer cans lining the walls like so many unread books and presented a thick hand for Gabriel to take, or not take, it was his call. Only it wasn't Gabriel's call, not really. And it was beginning to look like it never would be.

Gabriel took the man's hand in his and couldn't resist giving it a light squeeze. It seemed to him, in the mild euphoria that surrounds and precipitates such risks, that Bill squeezed back. But maybe he was mistaken. Maybe Gabriel, desperate for evidence and half in love, only imagined the sensation, the way an amputee is said to imagine sensation in a limb that, despite what feels real, simply does not exist.

Bill shot Gabriel a sad half-smile before letting go. "Cool shirt," he teased. He turned and followed tipsy Jana Browne out to her truck, where, like fair-weather football fans and diehards alike, they would spend what was left of the cold, hopeless night—or at least what remained of the big game—trying to console each other.

The eyes have it.

Best Man

The birthday girl's a born flirt, strutting the length of the living room floor to the strangled chords of the Sex Pistols, her two-toned hair artfully tousled, her silly striped dress and battered jack boots radiating as many mixed signals as a wartime sub. They don't know what to make of her, the half-soused thirty-somethings positioned like star-struck movie extras amid the whimsical, hand-me-down decor. Daniel decides it's her willingness to play the fool that makes thirty-five-year-old Kristina Kolakowski such a catch. Dancing on the sofa, out-whining even Johnny Rotten, she's simultaneously attainable and safely out of reach. Hester Prynne for beginners. Madame Bovary-lite.

"Don't know what I want but I know how to get it," Kristina sings before spotting Daniel and squealing his name into the karaoke mic: "Danny!"

No one calls him Danny anymore—they're not allowed. Even Daniel's mother, arguably the only woman with any right or reason to infantalize him, doesn't dare try it. ("Mama's boy" is a tag he's had some trouble shaking.)

Kristina clears the living room in one long stride—she's a tall woman, with a Brobdingnagian gait—and kisses Daniel hard on the cheek. "I'm so happy you're here," she whispers in his ear.

Daniel hands over the bottle and book he's brought in her honor. "I said no presents," Kristina mildly chastises as she takes Daniel by the hand. Her palms are surprisingly dry, considering she's been hamming it up, her shoulders laid bare by the strapless, iridescent New Wave number Daniel is finding himself hard-pressed to ignore. He wants to taste Kristina's shoulders, to bite into them like chunks of white chocolate and have them turn to syrup in his mouth.

Chez Kolakowski is warm and dark, not unlike the birthday girl's bespectacled, wide-set eyes. Kristina has done her best to transform the sober suburban manor into a cozy opium den; candles burn on every surface, and patterned silk throw pillows the size of kindergarteners squish underfoot. A few faux-exotic tapestries have been pinned up over the requisite MoMA prints and cloying family photos. The lone lamp's regular bulb has been replaced with a scarlet one. The overall effect is that of a DIY red light district smack-dab in the middle of White Bread, U.S.A.

"Charlie?" Kristina calls, leading Daniel through the house. "Has anyone seen my husband? He's about yay big, with pious blue eyes and hair like Morrissey? Oh, Char-*lie*?"

Kristina introduces Daniel round as a writer. The capital-W implied by her tone makes him uncomfortable, almost apologetic. The genial, respectably employed guests smile and ask him what he writes, exactly. "His story's just won a prize!" Kristina whisper-squeals. And for once it's true. A thousand dollars from a contest listed in an industry magazine. It's a small fortune to Daniel, but scant evidence he's not wasting his life. *Congratulations*, they say. *Good for you. Nice going.* No one seems interested in reading it.

A pair of massive hands descends on Daniel's shoulders, gripping them like the talons of some prehistoric bird of prey. "Happy belated New Year, stranger."

"Hey, Chazz. How are you?"

Charlie thumps his chest, Tarzan-style. "Picture of health. You?"

"Good," Daniel says, as Charlie leads him away from the living room, and away from his wife.

"Bye, Danny," coos Kristina.

"Then not-so-good," Daniel adds. "Then good again."

Charlie looks at him for a long time; his gaze is unwavering. He has no qualms about looking another man directly in the eye, and for quite a few beats longer than what's considered customary. Daniel admires this about Charlie, the man's inherent comfort in his own skin. "So I read," Charlie says.

He's referring to the long letter Daniel addressed to the "Kolakowski clan" but wrote primarily to Kristina. In it, he detailed the long, slow descent into pseudo-madness and sexual depravity that ultimately led to the end of his affair with Kara, a woman with a sadistic streak as long and disconcerting as her well-toned legs. The letter ran to some twenty-two pages and didn't skimp on the details. In many ways it was the most honest thing Daniel had ever written. Too honest, maybe. He wanted it back.

"You know," Charlie says, "mail from you gets my wife buzzing for a week. Should I be worried?"

"Of course," Daniel says with a grin.

"You should write more often," Charlie half-kids. "Getting the missus all hot and bothered usually works in my favor."

Daniel nods, though he never considered this.

"And I don't mean witty little e-mails," Charlie continues. "She likes the look of your *penmanship*, for Christ's sake. She tells me this. You know that line in "Famous Blue Raincoat" about taking the trouble from her eyes? That's you and Kristina. Sometimes I think she married the wrong man."

"I don't know," Daniel replies, instinctively scanning the room for Kristina. "I still see an inkling of trouble there."

Charlie laughs a bit too loudly. "That's only her allergies acting up."

Daniel still isn't sure whether Charlie knows it, but there came a point during the courtship of his wife when Kristina came to Daniel for advice. At the time Charlie was the lead singer of a mildly successful band of shameless anglophiles disastrously named English Breakfast. It was at an English Breakfast show—their last show, as it would turn out, held at the old Kasbah—that Kristina led Daniel out back and confronted him in the alleyway.

"What should I do?" she wanted to know, a question Daniel, in his supreme egotism, had interpreted as "What do you want me to do?" He and Kristina had never been an item—they shared a drunken kiss once, before she'd started dating Charlie, which he suspected neither of them would ever forget—yet there had always been this almost intuitive understanding that they were meant for each other. *What do you want me to do?* Kristina essentially asked him, her Technicolor hair short and alive at the time, framing her inquisitive feline eyes with a buzzing nimbus of red. Daniel should've just kissed her. The scene, at least, was begging for it, and he had never been the kind of man who could let a dramatic moment go by essentially undramatized. He should've kissed her and let the proverbial cards fall where they may. Instead he said,

"Charlie's the best man I know," effectively sabotaging any chance they had of ever being together.

Kristina, too, had a weakness for high drama, and she's unused to being rejected. She knitted her brow, stuck out her tongue—another image etched onto his memory—and stalked back into the bar. He and Kristina spent the rest of English Breakfast's set at opposite ends of the club. She accepted Charlie's proposal the second he came off stage.

"She married the man who proposed to her, Chazz."

Charlie wags an accusatory finger at him. "And don't you forget it. That's the real reason I had you stand as my best man, you know. To make it more real for you."

Charlie escorts him into the kitchen, where there are more new faces, mostly female, huddled around the butcher-block table Kristina salvaged from someone's trash on Hudson Street a decade ago. Daniel spies homemade hummus and pita bread; ink-blue corn chips and salsa; sesame sticks and whole-wheat pretzels and toasted goat cheese. He follows Charlie through the crowded room, past the ceramic LOVE sign replica balancing atop the stove; past the kitschy bull's horns hanging high above the sink; past the Sub-Zero festooned with underage artwork.

"Where are the kids?"

"My mother's," Charlie says with a grin. "Kristina wanted an 'adult party' for once. I don't know what she expects to happen. My wife has a rather inflated view of other people's capacity to transgress. Largely thanks to your fiction."

Smiling politely at polite people as they move through a sliding glass door and onto the deck, Daniel finds that his host, The Gentle Giant, has fashioned a kind of igloo out of the leftover snow and therein stashed a couple of beers.

"Heineken, Yeungling, how about a Sasquatch Brew?"

"Lager."

It's cold out here, but Charlie isn't in a hurry to get back inside. He pulls a cigarette and pack of matches from his pants pocket as surreptitiously as if he'd produced a twisted stick of marijuana. Kristina loathes cigarettes. Daniel knows ahead of time that Charlie will blame his old friend for the way his clothes smell, to say nothing of his breath and fingers.

"We didn't think you were going to show," Charlie says, lighting up. "Well, *I* didn't. Kristina kept the faith."

"Oh yeah?"

"'Danny'll be here,' she said. 'Danny's the best. He wouldn't miss my party for the world.'"

"She's right," admits Daniel. "I am the best."

"But you had second thoughts," Charlie presses, exhaling smoke through his nostrils. "Come on, admit it. I won't say anything. It's not always easy being close to a woman like my wife. Even when you have the luxury of leaving her behind."

The comment confuses Daniel, in part because it's such an un-Charlie thing to say. He lets it go by, chalks the baiting up to one-too-many gin and tonics. "The thought never entered my mind," he lies.

"Yeah, well it's sure entered mine."

"Charlie," Daniel says, feeling as though he's missed something, "what are we talking about?"

"Nothing, nothing," Charlie waves at imaginary gnats. He squashes out what's left of his cigarette in the snow along the railing. "Let's go in. It's colder out here than I thought."

Back inside, Kristina's got Black Flag going full-tilt. More than a few guests have disapprovingly plugged their ears.

Daniel wonders if this isn't a dig at Charlie. The music, coupled with the man's bizarre comment outside, alert him to the possibility of some very real tension between his friends, two people who have always outwardly adored each other.

"That's my wife," Charlie says with a wry grin, "Resident anarchist. Punk rock and play dates."

"Little Miss Subversive," Daniel chimes in.

"Yeah. She's a regular Mata Hari of the Main Line."

"Can I use that?" he asks.

Suddenly Charlie looks exhausted, ghostlike. Daniel always supposed he could see right through the guy, but this is different, this almost seems literal. For a split second he is actually shaken. But then Charlie places a heavy, sweaty hand on his shoulder to steady himself—he's had more to drink than he's let on—and Casper the Tipsy Ghost is a flesh-and-blood numbers-cruncher again. "Who am I to stop you?" Charlie murmurs, and then like any good ghost quickly disappears.

"So you're the writer."

There's a diminutive blonde woman at Daniel's elbow, a pair of startling blue eyes beneath a clipped head of incandescent hair.

"Yes," he says, because there's no getting around it. Kristina has long-since exposed him.

"What do you write?" the guileless blue eyes want to know. She's swathed in black—ankle boots, flared slacks, scoop-neck tee—but with a multi-colored, serpentine scarf wrapped twice around her neck. It looks as though she's trying to strangle herself with a rainbow, and it strikes Daniel that this woman, whether consciously or not, is sending out a few mixed signals of her own.

"Oh, lies," he says, his standard reply. "Nothing but lies."

"Lies? I don't understand." There's the faintest trace of an accent. A glint of mischief swims into those twin pools of blue and she says, "Where I come from, writers tell the truth."

"Really? Where do you come from?"

"Jersey," she says. They laugh.

"Your accent sounds slightly more exotic."

"Sorry: Joizy." She sips her wine. "Denmark, originally. The home of Hamlet."

"Rotten place," quips Daniel.

"Oh yes, yes," she says, making an obscure gesture with her hands. Her nails are practically non-existent, bitten down to the quick. "You've been there? Rotten to the core."

"Do all Danish women look like you?" he wonders aloud.

"Oh, no," she smiles again, a tinge of crimson coloring her flawless butter rum complexion. "I'm the ugly duck of the family. You should meet my sister. Twice my size and breasts out to here." She pulls on her top to show Daniel how well-endowed she might've been had the birth order been reversed.

"Boobs are overrated," he offers, playing devil's advocate, all the while taking the woman's candidness as a surprisingly good omen.

"Bah, you like boobs, I can tell. You're a boob man."

A boob man? No, Daniel's not a boob man. He's not *not* a boob man, of course. He's a boob man, an ass man, a leg, eye and mouth man…

"Who's a boob man?" Kristina says, rudely inserting herself between them. "Danny?" She gives him an accusatory look, like he's the one responsible for the flat tire she had the other morning, or the fact that a mouse has taken up residence beneath their stove. "Say it ain't so," she pouts, painfully aware that, as breasts go, her pubescent nubs are pretty darn skimpy.

"Breasts are nice," he confesses. "But what I really go for are overdeveloped earlobes."

"Me too!" squeals the Danish rainbow woman.

"I was worried for a second there," Kristina says, brightening. "Thought you'd turned into a beer swilling alpha-male like my husband."

"Charlie is the alpha *and* the omega," says Daniel.

"His blood's as red as it gets," admits Kristina, glancing at the blonde. "I see you've met Marja. Marja, this is Danny Mancuso. My oldest crush."

Kristina gushes at Daniel, making the kind of face most often employed by "barely legal" girls on late-night television spots for chat lines. Kristina's been legal for exactly seventeen years now. But the youthful glimmer in her artfully framed eyes has Daniel picking up the phone.

"Marja is Roy's wife," Kristina adds, not without relish.

"Oh?"

Marja nods. "Eleven years with that fine specimen over there." She nods toward a stocky guy who has taken the bull's horns from the kitchen wall and is threatening to charge at a woman in a slinky red dress. Marja puts her hand to her head in mock-desperation. Or is it? "God help me."

"God help the woman in red," Daniel says.

"Charles and I are going on seven," Kristina chimes in, as though it's some sort of competition. Daniel she persists in calling Danny; her husband she brands Charles. "It's not always this…punk rock."

"No, at this late date it's much more *pet* rock," says Marja, cracking up.

Roy charges into the kitchen, his path diverted by his wife's very distinctive laughter, a sound not unlike that of a full recycling can being toppled by a raccoon.

"What's so funny?" Roy inquires with a smile, handing the horns over to Kristina. What he really wants to know is who's responsible for tickling his wife's adorably foreign funny-bone.

Whereas Charlie is rectangular and Daniel downright octagonal (a fellow grad student once described him as a "man of angles"), Roy is all circles: shaved head, silver spectacles, second-trimester paunch. Like many a bald man's response to hair loss, he sports an overgrown goatee. He's dressed well, if conservatively, in an expensive black blazer, designer jeans and shiny black loafers with tassels. Beneath the blazer he bucks convention (or at least thumbs his nose at it) with a band collar. There are rings—some gleaming with Jolly Rancher jewels, some unadorned bands of silver or white gold—on half of his ten fingers, and, if Daniel's not mistaken, a tiny square of gold stuck like a kernel of corn between two teeth.

Eleven years, Daniel muses. *Marja and the Human Marshmallow.*

"We're talking about how boring married life can be," explains Marja, wrapping her arms around Roy's considerable waist.

"Nature of the beast," he says. Then, to Daniel, "Married?"

Kristina laughs. "That's like asking Rush Limbaugh if he subscribes to *Mother Jones*."

Daniel shakes his head and holds Kristina's gaze. "Haven't found the right woman," he says, sounding lame and unconvincing.

"I'll say," seconds Kristina. "But you've found plenty of wrong ones."

Marja raises her eyebrows.

"My hero," Roy says.

"Let's change the subject."

"Oh, come on," objects The Human Marshmallow. "Tell us about the wrong ones. Don't hold back."

"Rachel," Kristina says, smirking as if she's guessing at a secret password or casting a forbidden spell. "Elysia. Teena. Jeni-with-an-i."

"Jeni-with-an-i," repeats Roy. "Yesss."

"Katie One, Katie Two. Star Anise."

"Star Anise?"

"Ooooh, I know," Kristina says with glee, her eyes widening. "*Kara.*"

There is a pause. Marja and her gelatinous hubby regard Daniel, awaiting a very specific brand of entertainment.

"Hey, I've got a steady girlfriend," blurts Daniel. "We're practically engaged."

Kristina isn't buying it. "Really," she says. "What's her name?"

Someone begins belting out a Mariah Carey tune in the living room, and Kristina is noticeably torn between getting the scoop from Daniel and silencing the offensive Mimi impersonator with the deadly bull's horns.

"Just a name, Danny," Kristina teases. "Give us a name."

"Glitter," suggests Roy.

"Esmeralda," Marja chimes in.

"Wanda-Jane."

"What's the game?" Charlie wants to know as he wanders into the room. He looks much better now, flushed and full of life, corporeal in the best sense of the word.

"Guess Danny's Girlfriend," Kristina tells him.

Charlie looks straight at Kristina and, feigning confusion, says, "I thought *you* were Daniel's girlfriend."

Silence, save for the yowling living room chanteuse.

"Wow," Roy deadpans. "Who knew?"

"Don't be an ass," Kristina says to Charlie. She foists the horns on him and stalks away.

Roy tries to catch his wife's eye, but Marja turns away from him and heads out of the kitchen. What can the Human Marshmallow do but follow?

Daniel turns to Charlie. "What was all that about?"

"Oh, she had it coming." He regards his friend semi-suspiciously. "And so did you, if you don't mind my saying."

"Me?"

"Serves you right, leading her on like you do."

"Charlie—"

Charlie displays his massive palm in protest. "Save it. I've got bigger fish to fry." He glances over his shoulder. "What do you think of Marja?"

"Marja?" Daniel shrugs.

"Oh, come on, *Danny*, don't play coy with me. You'd bang her in a heartbeat."

"Except she's married."

Charlie does his best to look surprised. "When has that ever stopped you?"

This is unfair. Daniel slept with a married woman once, way back when he was still in school. He'd see her at the same lunch truck every day, ordering the same tuna salad on rye and apple juice, which for some reason he found adorable. She was carrying a book by Alberto Moravia, which certainly didn't hurt. Her name was Diane, she worked in the Admissions Office, and her marriage was falling apart. They took advantage of each other for a few weeks—he capitalizing on her vulnerable emotional state; she preying upon a much younger man and a student—until her guilty conscience got the better of her. He only mentioned it to Charlie at the time because he happened to bump into them, canoodling in an off-campus bar. Daniel claimed Diane was already divorced, but Charlie called him on it. Her wedding ring was in plain sight.

"Look, I'm not condemning you," Charlie says.

"Good."

"Far from it," he adds.

"Meaning?"

A big goofy grin unfurls like a flag across Charlie's all-American face.

"Marja," he says.

The name is all Daniel needs. Charlie Kolakowski, his moral superior, husband to Kristina, father to Nancy and Max, is fucking another man's wife.

"Since when?" Daniel asks.

Charlie takes a long pull on his beer and shrugs. "Couple of weeks."

"And you're okay with this?"

"Shouldn't I be?"

"I don't know," Daniel admits. "I've never been married."

"Good point." Charlie claps him sympathetically on the back. "You had your eye on her, didn't you?"

"What? No."

"Sure you did. Daniel Mancuso walks into a party and all the pretty girls are supposed to swoon."

There's an unfamiliar edge to Charlie's voice that Daniel finds disconcerting. "Cut it out, man."

"I don't blame you, though," Charlie says.

Kristina materializes beside Daniel and slips her long, lily-white arm through his. Charlie looks from Daniel to his blatantly flirtatious wife, then back again. He smiles. "I blame the pretty girls," he says, moving off.

"What was that about pretty girls?" Kristina wants to know. "You boys weren't comparing notes, were you?"

"Yes," he says. "As a matter of fact we were."

"Oh yeah? What did Lurch say about me? Did he say I like it from behind?"

Daniel nearly does a spit take. "Thanks for the visual."

Kristina shoots him a mischievous look, even for her. "C'mon," she says.

"C'mon what?"

She takes Daniel by the hand. "Follow me," she says. "If anyone asks, I'm giving you a tour."

The Kolakowskis' bedroom is large, dark and schizophrenic, haunted by unassuming Scandinavian furniture, an ornate full-length mirror and an anemic weeping ficus that's shedding like a pet. A very large pine bed befitting a couple of giants is heaped with dark leather coats, and flashes of down-stuffed parkas appearing like heat lightning in a stormy summer sky. Kristina—crazy, creative Kristina—has hung a homemade mobile of shards of colored glass in front of one window, and decorated the opposite wall with the many different styles of eyewear she's donned over the years; at least twenty pairs of glasses hang on painted nails above the bed. In addition to a number of frames that fall into the Horny Librarian category, Daniel spies one gold-rimmed Oppenheimer, a few flashy, rhinestone-studded Cat's Eyes, and at least half a dozen Clark Kents, some mottled tortoise-shell but most death-black, as popularized by the likes of Elvis Costello and mid-eighties Morrissey.

"The eyes have it," he says.

"I'm not a collector," Kristina says. "Not by any stretch. But I've kept every pair of glasses I've worn since I was sixteen."

"Are you really blind without them?"

Kristina takes off her glasses, squints and makes a squirrel-like motion with her mouth. "Ever see a naked mole rat?"

"No," he admits.

"You're better off," she laughs. "They're ugly little fuckers."

Kristina clears a spot on the bed and sits down. She lays her glass of shiraz on the bedside table next to a strategically-placed copy of *The Bumblefuck Review*, where Daniel's most recently published story has appeared. She pats the space beside her.

Daniel sits. Kristina puts a hand on his thigh.

DontknowwhatIwantbutIknowhowtogetit.

"Kristina," he says.

"Yes?"

Their faces are as close as two faces can get without actually touching; he can practically feel the heat radiating from Kristina's myopic, semi-woozy gaze. Daniel's never wanted to kiss a woman more. Of course, he's never wanted to kiss a woman more on more than a few previous occasions, with all kinds of other women. Kristina knows this. In fact she's banking on it. She's staged this whole phony seduction—been staging it for years—on the not unproven theory that Daniel Mancuso is a supremely weak man. But unlike the first one, there's really nowhere they can go after this kiss. Kristina knows this too. Why even bother, then, with the temptation? Because for Kristina—who, despite the name-calling, Daniel's convinced is still madly in love with her husband—temptation is the whole point. Without at least the threat of transgression, the wo-man would simply cease to exist.

"How are you?"

"How am I?" Kristina smirks her knowing smirk and moves in closer; Daniel didn't think it was possible. She takes his hand and places it on her left breast. Then, with her hand covering his own, she gives herself a gentle squeeze. When she speaks again, her breath is wine-scented and thrillingly warm against his face. "You tell me."

"Charlie," Daniel manages to croak, and somehow musters the courage to withdraw his hand.

Kristina pulls a face and looks away. "Screw Charlie."

They're quiet for some time. Downstairs, the sounds of shrill laughter and Prince's "Little Red Corvette." It takes Daniel a minute to realize that it's Charlie singing, if singing is even the right word.

Daniel laughs, and then so does Kristina.

"I put that song on there for you," she says. "And he has to go and ruin it like that."

"Oh, I don't know. He's not half bad."

"No, he's not half bad," Kristina agrees, only it doesn't sound like a compliment. "And he's certainly not *all* bad, like you." She looks Daniel in the eye and smiles. "God help me, Danny, I married a good man."

So she doesn't know. She might suspect, but she doesn't know for sure. And if it's Daniel's duty to school her, he doesn't feel especially obliged to do so.

"You did," he says, vaguely wondering what it might be like to have Marja whisper tender obscenities to him in her underwear. "You married the best man I know." It's still the truth.

There's a pause while each of them considers the shining tower of goodness that is Charlie Kolakowski.

"Ever get the feeling you're being watched?" he jokes, glancing up at the wall of faceless eyewear.

"Yes," answers Kristina, and for once her voice is not a whisper. She stands and offers Daniel a hand. "But I like that feeling."

When they descend the stairs they find that Roy is the most vocal member of a small band of mostly male guests who are making a drunken, albeit intriguing case for a game of Spin the Bottle.

"What?" he's saying to his wife. "If married life's so 'boring,' why not spice it up with a grade school kissing game. Huh? Look, no tongue, okay? We'll have a rule about tongue."

"Stop making a fool of yourself," Marja hisses at him. "We're not swingers."

"No tongue and no touching," Roy adds, inspired. "And no kiss over five seconds."

"Five seconds and no tongue," someone snorts. "Have fun."

"It's a modest house," says Charlie, as he refills his wife's empty wineglass. "A converted attic, three bedrooms, two baths. Hardly warrants a twenty-minute tour."

"We broke for lunch," Kristina says. "Get over it."

"Forget the bottles," Roy is saying. "How about Twister? You have Twister, don't you? Everybody has Twister."

"Truth or Dare," someone suggests, and Roy hops on that train.

"Yes, Truth or Dare. Perfect!" He glances at his rainbow-choked wife. "We'll play Truth or Dare."

"You might have to play by yourself," Kristina admits, looking around at the remaining guests.

"Or *with* yourself," Marja giggles evilly.

"Wouldn't be the first time," counters Roy.

"Or the last," Charlie chimes in.

The Human Marshmallow's smile quickly fades. "I guess with a wife like yours, you don't have to play with yourself much, eh Charlie?"

Charlie's face goes white for the second time that night.

"That's enough," says Marja. "You're drunk. We're going home."

"Enough?" Roy says the word as though learning it for the first time. "I haven't even started yet—"

"Hey, guys, come on," Kristina says. "This is supposed to be a party."

"That's right," Roy says, not without malice. "That's why I'm drunk. That's why I showed up drunk. So as not to disappoint the Party Girl and her Good Time Charlie!"

"Stop it!" shouts Marja.

"Oh, for fuck's sake," huffs Kristina.

"I guess if I had a wife like yours," Roy goes on, "I wouldn't need to fantasize about fucking a wife like mine!"

Suddenly the whole room goes quiet, not counting the sound of Marja's palm connecting with the gelatinous flesh of her impudent husband's face.

Marja momentarily looks even more stunned than Roy. She turns toward Kristina. "I'm sorry about your birthday," she says matter-of-factly. She goes, coatless, out into the snow.

"Your coat—" Charlie starts to say, then stops short.

"Keep it," Roy sneers, his round face red with the imprint of his wife's hand. "A souvenir." He looks at Kristina, shakes his head and leaves.

For once nobody feigns an offer to help clean up, and within minutes the house is empty—the remaining guests claiming sleepless kids, pricey sitters, Sunday plans involving all sorts of strenuous activity. Daniel, whose life involves none of these things and likely never will, hangs back at Kristina's request. He, rather than Charlie, retrieves the various coats and handbags from the voyeuristic master bedroom, thanks everyone for coming, bids the guests goodnight. Following Marja and Roy's dramatic departure, Charlie quickly disappeared upstairs, citing too much gin. Daniel pictures his old friend desperately constructing some elaborate story behind the flimsy defense of the locked bathroom door. At least that's what he would be doing, if their roles were reversed. But Charlie is better than that. Surely a man like Charlie Kolakowski would be preparing to tell his wife the truth.

Kristina remains upstairs for a long time. More than once Daniel starts to leave, but stops himself, in part because he's already promised her he'll stay but mostly because, despite everything that's happened, he's looking forward to one of Kristina's cleaving goodbye hugs. He's had his hand on this woman's breast, and can still recall the long-ago, beer-and-bubblegum-flavored taste of her tongue in his mouth, but it's the promise of that hug—her lithe back beneath his hands; her organic shampoo filling his nose; her husky, purposefully misleading voice tickling his ear—that has him hanging around like some neglected third wheel, and at the risk of wearing out his welcome, cardinal sin of vagabonds and aging playboys the whole world over.

Kristina finally comes downstairs and joins Daniel on the couch, where he's reading a months-old music magazine. The flimsy mock-designer dress is gone, as are the evil black boots; she's replaced them with an ancient Penn sweatshirt, yoga pants and dingy bunny slippers.

"Kristina—"

"Just tell me, Danny." She takes his hand. "For real. Do you know about this, whatever 'this' is?"

If he says *Go ask Charlie*, she'll simply reply *I just did. Now I'm asking you*. If he asks to be left out of it, she'll assume he's been privy to secret information all along. Charlie is one of his oldest friends in the world, but Daniel has always been closer to Kristina.

Daniel takes a breath and shrugs. "He hasn't said anything to me."

Kristina stares him down. Her expression is almost comically serious, her face alarmingly pale, even for her. The perennial playful light in her eyes has dimmed. It suddenly hits Daniel how dependent upon the rosy cheeks and twinkling eyes and sly smile he's become, how he's always taken Kristina's time-defying youthfulness for granted. The woman looks her age, for once.

"Okay," she concludes, still searching his face.

"Okay?"

She smirks at him and, just like that, the antsy, ageless Kristina returns with a flourish. It's scary. "Okay, Danny, okay. I'll leave you alone now."

"Well, you don't have to *leave me alone*, exactly."

"I'm sorry about upstairs. About making you touch me."

"You didn't *make* me do anything."

"Still, it wasn't right."

"I'll live," he half lies. But something's wrong. That is, something in addition to having just found out her husband is having an affair with the lovely Danish woman who lives across the street. "I shouldn't leave you like this," he says.

"No, it's okay. It's better if you go."

After a moment he rises, reluctantly, from the impossibly cozy couch. Pointing at the stairs, Daniel says, "Tell Chazz I said goodbye."

She nods.

"Go easy on him," Daniel says. "He's still a good man."

Kristina stands too. After all this time the woman's height still takes him by surprise. "Well, whatever kind of man he is, he's the only one I've got." She looks around at the remains of her bash, and sighs. "God knows I've had happier birthdays, Daniel."

On Kristina's tongue his given name sounds stranger than usual, a borderline insult. He feels implicated, and he knows why.

"You already knew, didn't you."

Kristina nods again. "He just came clean. But I've known for a while. When you live with someone long enough, it's impossible not to know certain things."

Daniel thinks of Kara, how when she took up with another woman he knew about the betrayal almost without knowing. She sat there reading Bataille or chewing on a cereal bar or cranking up her beloved Tool in the jeep, and all Daniel could do was seethe. For a long time he didn't even know why. Then one day, just like that, he understood. But the understanding only made things worse.

"I didn't want to see you get hurt."

"Oh no?" Kristina says, strangely, and begins to cry. She daubs at her tears with a sweatshirt sleeve. "Don't worry, I'll be fine. *We'll* be fine. It's not like I'm going to divorce him or anything." She looks at Daniel. "Oh, I'll make him suffer, all right," she snorts. "But no way am I breaking up this family."

Daniel's instinct is to hold Kristina, to give his old, upset friend a hug. But his instincts, he remembers, aren't to be trusted.

"Good," he says, in lieu of touching her. Then lamely repeats the word: "Good."

They move to the door and Kristina opens it wide. At the bottom of the uneven steps, Daniel turns to say goodbye. The bedraggled birthday girl cocks her head slightly to one side, as if to imply that Daniel's face, though familiar, has become oddly difficult to identify. He kicks at a stone like a schoolboy and mutters an apology. Kristina starts to say something, stops herself, and looks off toward the well-lit house across the street. She shuts off the porch light. When she turns back to Daniel her eternally shielded eyes show little sign of recognition, let alone any semblance of friendship or flirtation.

Daniel watches without comment as Kristina steps silently into the house. She offers him neither kiss nor cleaving goodbye hug, only the polite, practiced smile she normally reserves for strangers.

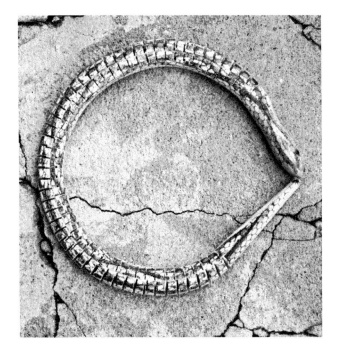

It was easy enough to get lost in one's own head.

Other Woman

If not for the glasses, I never would've recognized her. The iridescent hair was largely to blame for my confusion—somehow Gina had managed to stuff her shoulder-length mane of coffee-brown curls under a cropped blonde wig. The strapless black dress, too—snug as shrink-wrap and patterned with writhing Chinese dragons—was worlds away from the shimmery track suits and funnel-cuffed yoga pants she usually favored. I knew the woman—her sibilant snore and hyena-laugh; the soup-like scent of her sweat and sun-baked taste of her skin; the pointed nevus decorating her navel like a tongue of flame hovering above a disciple's head—as well as I knew the proverbial back of my hand. But it wasn't until Gina shifted in her seat and turned away from the bar, affording me a good look at her elliptical eyewear, that I finally recognized the flashy woman as my wife.

"Is this seat taken?" I said, wondering what to make of the intriguing, inexplicable costume but determined not to make any cracks about an early Halloween. I had two older sisters, expert attention-getters who in their adolescence had been prone to all sorts of unexplainable behavior—one had walked around with her head half-shaved and the word PROTOTYPE scrawled in Sharpie on her scalp; the other had eaten nothing but malted milk balls for three days straight—and I didn't scare easily when it came to women. Plus, Gina's tight black dress was already making the backs of my knees sweat.

Gina shrugged a shoulder, which I interpreted as permission to join her.

"I'm Frank," I said, extending a hand.

"Hi Frank!" Gina giggled, waving at me as though across a crowded room. "Pleased to meet you!"

This wasn't like Gina; making a spectacle of herself wasn't her style. She had an enviable, uncanny ability to blend in. She didn't favor make-up, and typically her hair was what any seasoned salon girl wouldn't hesitate to call a mess. I happened to find her beautiful, but even I recognized that Gina's brand of beauty was like a food stain on a busy shirt: it was easy to miss, but once you noticed it, it was pretty much all you noticed.

I thought she might be drunk, until I realized she was merely drinking mineral water. It was cold comfort: Gina's behavior would've made a lot more sense with a half-empty bottle of Beaujolais on the table. Without the wine, I was doubly confused.

"And you are?" I said.

Gina paused before answering. Her blank expression implied I'd just asked her the social security number of the guy washing dishes in the back. "I'm Melinda," she said finally.

This shut me up. A woman with whom I'd had a precursor to a fling had disparagingly dubbed my wife Melinda, after a shady character in a Bob Dylan song. I knew this must be Gina's idea of a joke, however unfunny. But I also knew that any reference to my transgression didn't bode well.

"Right," I said. "Melinda."

She nodded. "Something wrong?"

"If you're Melinda…" I said, trailing off. A more cynical man might say that while playing dress-up was one thing, taking on an emotionally charged alias and adopting a persona to go along with it smacked of something worse. But Gina had gone to the considerable trouble of pretending to be someone else, and the least I could do was to pretend—or at least pretend to pretend—right along with her. "I'm just trying to figure out who I'm supposed to be." I waited a beat before adding, "Tom Thumb?"

Gina didn't blink. "You're Frank," she said, smiling inscrutably. "You said so yourself."

Good, so I was still Frank. I didn't relish the notion of having to become someone else at this late date. I wouldn't know where to start.

"Well, I'm glad we got that straightened out." I glanced around at the plush, amniotic décor: the glorified beanbags that passed for dining room chairs; the great, heavy swaths of room-dividing fabric, gathered like the wings of some majestic, mythical bird. The floor was covered in what appeared to be the pelt of a hundred flayed Muppets. Kismet wasn't a restaurant Gina and I had ever set foot in, though we'd driven past it a million times on our way to the Ben Franklin Bridge. But I guess never having set foot inside the place was sort of the point. "Can I get you a drink, *Melinda*?"

"And how," she said, vigorously nodding.

I signaled to the bartender and ordered two glasses of merlot. "Excuse me," my date said, correcting me. "I'll have a Long Island Iced Tea, please."

I couldn't hide my surprise. At dinner, one glass of good red wine was usually Gina's limit. But what did I know about this woman's likes and dislikes, her chemical makeup or behavioral history? We'd only just met.

"So tell me about yourself," I said, leaning in close. "Is this a favorite *haunt* of yours?" I sounded like some pretentious pick-up artist and I knew it. But I was having trouble getting my bearings. Despite Gina's reassurance, I was finding it easier to play at egghead lounge lizard than attempt to be myself. Besides, when faced with the brevity and boldness of that little black dress, what choice did I have?

Gina knitted her brow. "Are you seriously asking me if I come here often? In the interest of full disclosure, I'm Aquarian, it's 7:45, and, yes, this little doohickey on my wrist is my only tattoo." She looked at me slyly over her eyeglasses. "For now."

Gina had an ouroboros inked round her left wrist like a bracelet. It had been her college graduation present to herself, the result of a brief, youthful infatuation with Theosophy. She hated it now, of course, its glaring obviousness and diminished significance. More than once I'd suggested she have it removed, if it bothered her so much. But I knew she couldn't imagine the rest of her arm without it, and the truth was neither could I.

"Cheers," I said when our drinks arrived, and unwisely gulped my wine. Dispensing with her straw, Gina took a healthy swallow of her own misleadingly named cocktail.

"So you've really never been here before?" I said. She shook her head no. "And yet you seem to fit right in."

Gina narrowed her eyes at me, but only slightly. I could see her trying to decide whether she'd just been insulted. To hear her tell it, I had this bad habit of phrasing compliments so that they doubled nicely as slurs. It was all about tone, and I usually preferred to keep mine tricky to pin down. Gina, on the other hand, favored a more blue-collar brand of insult. "I'm not crazy about that shirt," she said, out of the blue.

I instinctively glanced down at the blood-red button-up Gina had bought me for Christmas. The shirt was too flashy for me—the material was overly decadent and tended to drape funny—but I couldn't tell her that.

"An old friend gave me this shirt," I said.

"An old fuck-buddy, you mean."

"No, no, more than a fuck-buddy. Much more."

"Ah, I get it now," Gina said, smiling. "The love of your life bought you that shirt, just before you callously broke her heart and she disappeared forever."

This was not the kind of turn I was hoping the conversation would take. "I'd rather not talk about old friends, Melinda. I'd rather talk about new ones."

"I bet you would." Gina raised her glass and took another unladylike swallow. "I bet talking's not all you'd rather do."

When I'd gotten home from work earlier that evening, I'd found a note taped to the refrigerator door. KISMET, 8:00. KEEP AN OPEN MIND. Gina was by nature a homebody. We both were. We were content to sit in on a Saturday night playing board games or watching episode after self-defeating episode on The Food Network. Yet all those hours of culinary TV did nothing to inspire us to concoct any meal more elaborate than Sunday gravy. And all those board games were beginning to leave me, well, bored. I was eager to see what I might have to keep an open mind about—had Gina switched nail polish? was the restaurant run by children?—and had been so efficient at showering and getting dressed that I arrived at Kismet twenty minutes early. To kill time I went next-door to a shop called Brute and pretended to inspect intimidating objects of outsider art.

"So, what do you do for a living?" I said. "Or are you already doing it?"

"I'm a designer," Gina said, ignoring the implied insult.

"Really? Fashion?"

She shook her head. I could see she hadn't thought this far ahead. I was relieved to find that, for all her verbal acrobatics, she too was performing without a net.

"You know those things that some people put up on their property in order to keep other people out," Gina said, "or their kids and animals in?"

I looked at her. "Fences?"

"Yes!" she squealed, as though I'd invented the word. "I design *fences*."

"Fascinating," I said, feigning fascination. "'Good fences make good neighbors.'"

"That's our tag line!"

I looked at her. "That's Frost."

Gina glared at me. "No kidding, Frank."

Chastened, I decided to stick to the script. "But aren't most fences pretty much the same?"

"Oh, no," she said. "There's the lattice fence, and the picket fence, and the cyclone fence. Those are pretty simplistic, I admit. But then there are all kinds of specialty fences, like the basket-weave or the spooky wrought-iron fence with the points on top." Gina sipped her drink, buying time. "That's actually what we call it in our catalogue: Spooky Wrought-Iron Fence with Points on Top."

"There's a catalogue?"

"Of course there's a catalogue. Would you like to see it?"

"You have one on you?"

"Not in this dress, I don't!" And she was right: her skin-tight dragon dress left very little to the imagination. Which was fine by me, because lately my imagination had been getting the better of me. She'd be hard-pressed to stow a pamphlet somewhere on her person, let alone a magazine with actual pages. "But if you play your cards right..."

"You'll invite me back for a nightcap!" I said, rubbing my hands together like the mustachioed sicko who ties the screaming damsel to the track.

Gina's face changed. "Um, no," she said. "Boy, are you out of practice." I shrugged, as if to say *You win some, you lose some.* "I only meant that I could have one sent to your home, upon request."

"Sorry."

"Apology accepted." She frowned. "So what do you do, Frank?"

I considered saying something fanciful like professional groomsman or world champion bubble-gum blower, but in the end opted for the truth. "I'm an electrician."

"Oh." Gina didn't seem very impressed. "That sounds, sort of... dangerous."

"Oh, it is," I assured her. "You really have to know what you're doing. Otherwise..." I mimed sticking my finger in a wall outlet and getting zapped. Gina didn't laugh. I was worried that I might be bombing. But then I remembered that, wig or no wig, this woman was actually my wife, and no matter how badly I bombed, eventually we would end up in the same place, if not the same bed.

I glanced around the bar and noticed a trio of overgrown teenagers stealing peeks at my wife's modest but unavoidable cleavage. Some guys would be flattered to find their spouse the object of this sort of primitive male approval. I was not one of those guys.

"Why don't we get out of here?" I said, again leaning across the table, smarmy as you please.

Gina's eyes flashed behind her owlish, overpriced spectacles. "Jeez Louise, it's only our first date, Frank. What did you have in mind?"

"I've got this great little place over at 2nd and Greenwich. And a pricey bottle of Prosecco left over from Valentine's Day."

Gina held my gaze and, to my surprise, my heart flitted like a canary in its brittle bone cage. "Okay," she said.

"Really? Just like that?"

"Just like that," she said, sliding off her barstool.

"Don't you think that's a little risky? Remember, you barely even know me. We only just met."

"I like to live dangerously." Gina tugged shyly at the hem of her slinky strapless dress and her triumvirate of admirers across the bar elbowed each other like horny hockey players. "C'mon, Frank the Electrician," she said, taking me by the hand. "Let's try something shocking."

When Gina woke me the next morning, she had her plaid grandpa pajamas on and her brown hair down. "Rise and shine," she said, raising the shades. The room resembled an overexposed photograph. "No rest for the wicked."

I sat up in bed. "What time is it?"

"Time to get up," she said.

The tiny dragon dress wasn't flung over the chair, where we'd left it. The glowing blonde wig was nowhere to be seen. "Where'd she go?" I said, making a show of searching the bedclothes for Melinda.

"Where'd who go?"

"My date," I said. "The platinum-blonde minx I took home last night."

"Maybe she turned back into a pumpkin," Gina snorted. "Or maybe you dreamt it."

"In that case I can't wait to go back to sleep." I shut my eyes and pretended to snore. When I opened them again, Gina was the epitome of patience worn thin.

"I take it you had fun," she said, "with this 'platinum-blonde minx'?"

"Fun is an understatement. I think I'm in love."

"Whoa, down boy," she said. "Aren't you putting the cart before the horse?"

"Now there's a position I'd like to try!"

She ignored me. "Don't you have to ask her out on a second date? Assuming she was real."

"I was sort of hoping she would just appear out of thin air," I said. "Assuming she was real."

Gina plopped next to me on the bed. "Try calling her instead. It's a safer bet."

"I never got her number," I said. "I don't even know her last name."

Gina patted my back as if she cared. "Then I'd say you're out of luck, Stud."

But contrary to Gina's prediction, my luck held. A little over a week later, Melinda sent me an email. The subject heading read DATE # 2: ELECTRIC BOOGALOO, and in it Melinda claimed that she would be in my "neck of the woods" on Saturday night and asked if it would be "kosher" for her to deliver my catalogue of fences "by hand." In short, she was inviting herself over. Fortunately Gina had plans to go dancing with some friends from work. This took some serious suspending of disbelief on my part: Gina had no friends at work. As for dancing, we'd both gone on the record as considering it beneath us.

"Next time we should try your place," I said, tangled up in the sheets like some meticulous arachnid's midnight snack. Melinda had conveniently forgotten the fence catalogue but remembered the condoms, which I thought was a nice touch.

"My place is no good," Melinda said. "Assuming there's a next time."

"Why's that?"

She held my gaze. "I'm married, Frank. Remember?" Fact was I didn't remember because Melinda hadn't mentioned it. By all accounts she was concocting an autobiography as she went along.

"I'm married too," I pointed out. "I manage to work around it."

Melinda rose and began hunting for her clothes. "I can't have you in my home," she said. "I *won't* have you in my home. I may insult my husband in a myriad of ways, but I won't insult him like that."

"What a gal," I said.

She stopped rooting around and glared at me. "I'm not a big fan of sarcasm."

"I'm not a big fan of hypocrisy." For some reason this made her laugh. "Where are you going?"

Melinda pulled on her jeans—a tight, pricey pair I'd never seen before. "Home," she said.

"It's two in the morning," I said, clutching the alarm clock for added effect. I left out the part about this being her home, about me being her husband. Although I didn't want her leaving the house at this hour and going who knows where, I also didn't want to ruin the freaky faux-affair we had going by calling her out. "Is this trip really necessary?" I said, echoing the Looney Tunes I still watched on occasion over heaping bowls of cereal or untoasted Pop-Tarts.

Melinda didn't miss a beat. "Th-th-th-that's all folks," she said, heading for the door.

Gina got home half an hour later, smelling of the diner down the street.

"Dance with any strange men?" I asked, propped up in bed. Ever since she left, I hadn't stopped thinking about Melinda.

"As many as I could," Gina said. "But they were more like strange bearded boys." She went down the hall, as was her custom, to change into her Depression-era pjs. "How was your night?" she called from the bathroom.

"Okay, I guess."

"Okay?" she said, coming into the bedroom. She got under the covers and turned off the lamp. "Just okay?"

"I missed you," I said, wishing it were true.

Gina took so long to respond that at first I thought she hadn't heard me. I couldn't tell whether she doubted the veracity of my statement or was debating the wisdom of responding in kind. Maybe both. "I missed you too," she said finally, before drifting off to sleep.

This strange charade of infidelity went on for a few weeks more, with us meeting semi-secretly behind Gina's back, my wife and her untrustworthy husband in effect plotting against her. Typically we met at some out-of-the-way place, some shadowy taproom or café I, for one, had never set foot in. We were incognito, or at least Gina was, and sneaking around the city like a couple of code-named double agents—like a couple of actual *adulterers*—was supposed to be part of the fun. We smooched in carports and vestibules; in department store dressing rooms and the backs of bouncing taxis; in basement stairwells and shoddy fire escapes and the fragrant entranceways to subterranean transit. Once, we entered the Comcast Building and amorously rode the elevator up and down the endless length of the building until Security got suspicious and directed us to the hotel down the street. And one oppressively gray, gratuitously sinful afternoon, we were depraved enough to fuck in an empty confessional of St. Patrick's Church, around the corner from rain-plagued Rittenhouse Park. (After twelve years of plaid skirts and mnemonic prayers, Gina was no fan of the Catholic Church, but Melinda downright despised it, labeling the sacrament of Confession "masochistic gossip-mongering" and Holy Communion "codified cannibalism.") Both women were pushing my buttons, I knew, and were anxious to see just how far I'd go, to what degree I'd cheat on my wife with the woman I'd married. I told myself I'd go at least as far as they would, if not farther. I'd call every bluff, regardless of whether there actually were any.

Then, a month or so after Melinda had first entered our life, Gina stormed into the kitchen while I was having lunch and tossed something soft at my face.

"What the fuck is this?" she said.

"Huh?" She'd hit me in the side of the head with a pair of panties. I picked them up off my plate and recognized them as Melinda's underwear, the black, web-fine fabric I'd come to associate with my wife's sultry alter-ego. Gina had worn underwear like this, not so very long ago. But she couldn't be bothered with hand washing, and the Whirlpool had torn the gossamer undergarments to shreds. "You're kidding me, right?" I said.

"Do I look like I'm kidding?" Amazingly, she did not. In fact Gina was livid, her face flushed the color of my beloved capicola. "I found them in the bedroom behind the radiator," she said without a trace of irony or concealed mirth or mischief-making. Nothing in our shared history suggested that Gina could be such a believable actress. The wild success of her Melinda routine depended heavily on her audience's willingness to overlook certain inconsistencies of character in exchange for raw passion and an eagerness to disrobe. If I hadn't known better, I would've thought I'd done something wrong, perhaps irremediably wrong, and had just gotten caught red-handed. "Who is she?" Gina demanded.

"This is crazy," I said, my mouth full of fatty Italian meats. "You know exactly who she is."

Gina's eyes widened. "I do? You say that like it's a good thing. That makes it worse, asshole, not better."

I glared at her. "She's you, Gina."

"What's that supposed to mean?"

"I mean you and Melinda. You're the same person."

She waved away the notion as if shooing a stingless insect. "You said I know her, Frank. But I don't know anybody named Melinda. Of all fucking things," she snorted.

How was I supposed to take her seriously? Barring mental illness on a grand scale, there was no way Gina was telling the truth. She was putting me on, of course, and very close to putting me off. "And the Oscar goes to…"

This stopped Gina cold. "What's she like?" she said, taking a different tack.

"Melinda? She's totally hot," I said, feeling spiteful. "The platinum hair, the sexy clothes, the kamikaze confidence. It's a real turn-on."

Gina nodded, slowly to herself at first, but then more emphatically, as though some odd, longstanding notion of hers had finally been confirmed. She leveled her cold, bespectacled eyes at me. "Does she turn you on like Teresa turned you on?"

Teresa Pellegrino was co-owner and schmoozer extraordinaire of Morpheus, a dimly-lit den on the southwest corner of our block. The place was heavy on Nina Simone and year-round Christmas lights. We dined there once or twice a month by default. Most often a wispy young man wearing his much younger brother's clothes served our drinks while we waited for a table to open up. But occasionally we entered the restaurant and found Teresa tending bar.

I wasn't imagining there was chemistry between us—Teresa told me so herself. The woman was the personification of the phrase "no uncertain terms."

"What is it with us?" she asked me one night, right in front of a trio of old-timers, three Morpheus regulars dressed so identically in two-tone bowling shirts and tweed Jeff caps they could've been each other's body doubles. Gina hadn't been feeling well, and had practically thrown me out of the house rather than have to smell me cooking a meal.

"What do you mean?" I said, one eye on the look-alikes.

Teresa frowned. "You know exactly what I mean," she said, slicing a lime. "But it's probably better for all involved if you continue to act like you don't."

We hadn't broached the subject again until the night, some months later, when I'd entered Morpheus in the middle of a snowstorm. I had every reason to believe the place would be closed, or at least closing, when I got there. I was half right. I hadn't known Teresa was alone in the restaurant when she'd unlocked the door for me. I hadn't known, but that didn't mean I hadn't been hoping.

"I don't want to talk about Teresa," I told Gina, hiding behind my half-eaten sandwich. "I haven't set foot in that place in over a year."

"Am I supposed to be grateful?"

"No," I said. "But you're supposed to have forgiven me. Those are your words, not mine."

"Forgiveness I can handle. But forgetting…"

"It wasn't what you think it was."

"What I think is that my husband stuck his tongue in another woman's mouth, a neighbor, no less. Something tells me it wasn't the first time."

"That's bullshit and you know it."

"Oh, do I?"

I know plenty of women—tire-slashing, window-smashing women—who would've marched right into Morpheus smack-dab in the middle of the Saturday night dinner rush and pulled its husband-hijacking proprietor out into the street by her hair. I used to admire those women. That was before I had reason to fear them.

"If it wasn't for the booze," I said.

"Her boobs!"

"*Booze*, Gina. Jesus. I said booze."

"Oh," Gina said. "Sure, blame the booze." But I knew what was coming next. "Teresa's got great boobs, though, you have to admit. And because she wear clothes two sizes two small, they're really hard to miss. People say she had them done, but I think they're wrong. She should get her money back if she did. I mean they're pretty impressive, as is, but they're far from perfect. And people should only pay for perfection." Gina glanced down at her own adorable but modest God-given breasts. "What's wrong with these?"

"Not a damn thing," I said.

But she wasn't listening. She knitted her brow and cupped her tits as if offering them for my examination. "If you tell me what's wrong, maybe I can fix it."

"There's nothing wrong," I said. "They're perfect."

"So it's the rest of me that's substandard."

"Cut it out, will you? We shouldn't even be having this conversation."

"We're not having it," Gina said, smiling creepily and snatching up her alter ego's underwear. "See, I'm walking away. End of boob non-conversation."

"Table for one?" Teresa had said to me that snowy night from behind the bar. Her gang of gorgeous, black-clad wait-staff, I couldn't help noticing, were all gone.

"Sorry," I said. "I thought you might still be open."

"Technically we are open," Teresa said. "Even though I just sent everybody home." She came out from behind the bar and locked the door behind me. "You just squeaked in before closing time," she said. "Lucky you." She followed my gaze to an overhead chalkboard advertising the day's specials. "Regrettably, there are a few items on the menu that aren't available tonight, due to the fact that the chef knocked off early."

I nodded. "Which items?"

"All of them," Teresa smiled. She shifted her weight and seemed to relax a bit. That's when I noticed the opened bottle of Chianti on the bar. "What's it like out there?"

I glanced over my shoulder as though I'd forgotten what heavy snow looked like and was in need of a visual aid. "It's lovely," I said, and instantly wished I'd chosen a blunter, more utilitarian word, something we could both sink our teeth into. Teresa Pellegrino had grown up in a two-story row house not three blocks away, though she now owned a small building, a piece of impossibly priced real estate, in uber-hip Old City. Neighborhood men didn't use words like "lovely," unless it was in reference to a game-saving catch or the shape of a woman's ass.

"Lovely," Teresa laughed, sizing me up. "I didn't figure you for a poet, Frank."

"What did you figure me for?"

Teresa sighed heavily. "Oh, I don't know," she said, eyeing me. "Just a regular guy, I guess. A regular guy whose reach has always exceeded his grasp."

"Robert Frost," I said, surprising her. "Now who's the poet?"

I could see skeptical, streetwise Teresa beginning to regret her decision to let me in. All working-class women are wired this way. Still, she took pity on me—hospitality has always trumped skepticism in hardscrabble South Philly—and gestured for me to take a seat at the bar. "Where's the Goddess of Gloom?" she said.

"You mean Gina?"

Teresa shrugged as if to say *Call her whatever you want.*

"On the other side of the city," I said, sitting down and shaking out of my coat. "Waiting for the snow to let up."

"Haven't you heard, it's not supposed to let up. At least not any time soon."

Now it was my turn to shrug.

"You don't seem overly concerned."

She was right. My wife and I had been out of synch all day, if not all that week, and our phones contained an essay's worth of snide, if not outright hostile text messages to confirm this sad fact. I was glad to be rid of her for a while. "Gina is safe and warm," I said. "She can spend the night on her sister's couch, if need be."

"Spoken like a true gent." Teresa went back behind the bar and poured me a beer. We toasted the supposedly bad weather and drank our respective poisons.

"You don't strike me as a Dylan fan," I said. Teresa knitted her brow. "That line you used a minute ago, calling my wife the Goddess of Gloom."

"Oh, that's just something I picked up from the jukebox. Don't let the short hair and tight clothes fool you—the kids today love hippie music. Bob Dylan, Janis Joplin, Jefferson Airplane. I hear 'White Rabbit' half a dozen times a week." She came out from behind the bar. "Should I play it?"

"Go ask Alice," I said, trying to be smart.

But instead of Grace Slick, after a moment it was Bob Dylan's nasal, unorthodox voice I heard singing about Eastertime in Juarez. Dylan's words were in my ears and, seconds later, Teresa's hands were on my back. "Dance with me," she said.

I should've said no, of course. Married men don't dance with half-drunk women in empty neighborhood bars, especially at the height of a snowstorm.

"I wonder about you," Teresa said, once we were in each other's arms and swaying, slightly, to the music. I smiled politely but thought it best to ignore her comment. Instead I focused on the narrow gap between Teresa's front teeth, wondering if it was wide enough to slip a dime through.

"Who would you be if you could be anybody else?" she asked out of the blue.

"Bob Dylan," I said.

Teresa shuddered. "He's hideous."

"He's a legend," I said. "And a poet."

"I hate to tell you, hon, if you're shooting for legendary you're in the wrong business."

The obviousness of her remark made me laugh. "Tell me something I don't know," I said.

Teresa tightened her grip and leaned in close. I felt her fingernails through my shirt. "How about if I just show you?" she said.

"You live in a fantasy world, you know that?" Gina had said to me a few days after I told her about Teresa. "Like a little boy. What did you think, that some slutty bar owner was going to swoop down and save you from a disappointing life, like some big-titted, cocktail-shaking superhero?" She straightened her back and adopted a robotic anchorman voice. "Faster than premature ejaculation. Able to leap massive egos in a single bound! Look, up in the sky—it's a bird, it's a plane, it's… it's…Other Woman to the rescue!"

"Very funny," I said, barely suppressing a smile. "How long have you been rehearsing your routine?"

"Not as long as you, babe," Gina snorted. "Nowhere near as long as you."

A week after our kitchen confrontation, I received a text message from a number I didn't recognize. "Winterspring-summerfall," it read. "Rm 314."

I needed to put an end to this business with Melinda. It had been fun for a while, but it had never been as fun as it should've been: two consenting adults spicing up their sex life with a little harmless roleplaying. An undercurrent of malice tainted my dealings with my bogus mistress. She wasn't a character Gina had created so much as an identity she'd adopted, a second person she had become. Lately,

Gina put me in mind of one of those actresses who don't break character for days after filming has stopped, so closely do they identify with the person they've portrayed. Only Gina wasn't an actress. This was neither her job nor her art—this was our life. Melinda was an escape, but she was also the personification of Gina's pain. Of course Gina hid behind her alter ego, that's what alter egos were for. But whatever else I wanted—the Phils to win the pennant; a better paying job; the occasional drink with a pretty stranger still capable of adoring me—I didn't want my wife to feel pressured to hide.

Thirty minutes later I entered the lobby of the posh hotel on Logan Circle. We'd spent our wedding night here, a gift from Gina's parents. Maybe it was meant as a grim joke, this ultra-expensive evening rendezvous. Or maybe, on some level, Gina wanted to replay our wedding night. Back then, too exhausted to do much else than scarf shrimp cocktail and count our loot, we fell asleep in our clothes, with horseradish-heavy ketchup stinging our tongues and stiff hundred-dollar bills in our hands.

Melinda answered the door in a shimmering kimono emblazoned with the requisite Chinese dragons. Her lips were the color of a schoolyard crush; her eyeliner, alluringly Egyptian. She wasn't wearing glasses.

"What's with all the dragons?" I said. "And where are your glasses?"

Melinda shrugged a shoulder. "Dragons rock," she said, without further explanation. "And I switched to contacts."

My wife had a longstanding hate-hate relationship with her eyewear. For her own good, I'd been trying to get her to switch to contacts for years. But she was squeamish about, as she put it, sticking things in her eyes. I, for one, preferred her in glasses. Without them she looked like a pencil sketch of herself, and vulnerable in a way I often couldn't handle.

"What's this?" she said, nodding toward the package in my hand.

I'd been raised to never show up anywhere empty-handed, even, apparently, luxury hotel rooms in which one was meeting one's pretend mistress. But it wasn't better-than-average breeding that prompted me to stop on my way over and purchase *Highway 61 Revisited*. For weeks now I'd had to contend with my wife's disconcerting doppelganger routine. Gina claimed to have no knowledge of "this Melinda bitch"; Melinda, for her part, referred to my wife only in the abstract. Things were getting out of hand. It might seem cruel, but I was hoping to use this gift—as smelling salts, as finger snap, as spell-breaking magic word—to call Gina's rather flamboyant bluff once and for all.

"A present," I said, handing it over. Melinda studied the package for a long moment before gingerly unwrapping her gift. When she saw what it was, a shadow passed over her face, but only briefly. "There's a song on there I think you'll really like," I said, by way of explanation.

Melinda narrowed her pretty blackened eyes at me. I saw that callously referencing my infidelity this way was the wrong thing to do. She'd referenced it herself, of course, by christening her alter ego with Teresa's catty nickname. But that wasn't the same thing.

"My dad's a huge Dylan fan," she said, admirably, frustratingly, sticking to the script. I may've betrayed her, but she wasn't about to betray herself.

My father-in-law had been dead for the last eight years, the too-young victim of a coronary. As far as I could tell, the only music he'd listened to while alive was made by svelte, alliteratively named men in lightweight cardigans the color of Easter eggs.

"He plays the harmonica," she added.

"Dylan?" I said. "Of course."

Melinda crisply shook her head. "My dad, bozo."

"Oh." I followed her more deeply into the room, which had the beguiling distinction of seeming both boundless and overly intimate. "Sorry I'm late," I said.

"Having second thoughts?"

"Just the opposite. I wanted to give *you* a chance to back out."

Melinda put the CD on the bureau and moved to the bed. "I have a rule about backing out," she said, sitting down. "The rule is, I don't do it."

"Even with a married man?"

"An unhappily married man," she specified.

"Who says I'm unhappy?"

This made her laugh. "You wouldn't be here if you weren't. You'd be off with your four-eyed bride, playing Scrabble on a Saturday night or learning how to make...*paella*."

She was making fun of me—making fun of us both—but I didn't mind. Her lips were glistening like a well-licked lollipop. Her legs were luminous as her fake white hair. I moved toward her, smiling despite myself. "Maybe I'm just curious," I said. I took off my coat and tossed it onto a chair. "Maybe I have no intention of doing what you expect me to do."

"Well if that's the case, Frank, and this is all about pure *curiosity*, I'd say you're even unhappier than I thought." Melinda took hold of my belt buckle and pulled me toward her. When her robe slipped off her shoulder, I saw that her upper arm was branded with some semi-scabbed private symbol, an indecipherable glyph.

"What's this?" I said.

Melinda didn't flinch. "What's it look like?"

"It looks like you got another tattoo," I said, uninterested in what it might mean. "After all your talk about getting rid of the ouroboros. 'Tats are so cliché,' you said. 'They're more like corporate logos now.' I can't believe you'd do this."

Melinda frowned. "You can believe—or not believe—whatever you want." She undid my buckle, unzipped my pants. "I would've gotten a Chinese dragon, if that book hadn't ruined it for everybody."

"I don't know about this," I said.

"This, my new tattoo," Melinda said, "or this, my pretty red mouth so close to your very hard cock?"

I stared down at her. "Any of it," I said.

"Gee, how can I convince you?" Without waiting for a response, she buried her face in my boxers.

Within seconds the blankets were rent from the bed, pillows cast aside like so much dead weight over the stern of a sinking ship. But midway through our romp I decided I wanted my wife back. *Enough of this half-assed masquerade*, I thought while taking one of Melinda's shell-pink nipples between my teeth. *Enough playacting.* I was suddenly desperate for something, anything, real.

I took a fistful of iridescent hair in my hand and tugged on Melinda's wig.

"Ouch!" she yelped, slapping my hand away. "What the fuck, Frank?"

"I'm sorry," I said, momentarily flustered. "It's real? You cut your hair too?"

"Of course it's real! And for future reference, I don't get off on having it ripped out of my scalp."

"But it took you years to grow it out. I can't believe you'd just cut it all off."

"I cut my hair a long time ago, Frank, not that it's any of your business." She sat up and straddled me now, swaying like an Eskimo steadying a kayak. "Ugh, people kept comparing me to Julia Louis-Dreyfus."

"I know. I was one of those people."

There was an evil glint in her eye. "Let's see how you like it," she hissed, yanking on my hair.

"Ow!"

"But why stop there?" She balled her fists.

"Don't get crazy, Gina…"

"Stop calling me that! I'm not your fucking wife!"

"Okay, I'm sorry. *Melinda*…"

"Your wife lets you dick around with the neighbors and doesn't have the guts to make you pay!" She took hold of my wrists and began beating herself with my hands as best she could. "Well I'll make you pay!"

"Cut it out," I shouted. "You're going to hurt yourself."

"I don't think so, Frank," she sneered, and continued to batter her naked body with my captured hands. "I think *you're* hurting me! I think you couldn't stop hurting me if you tried!"

Without warning Melinda freed my wrists and rolled off me. I knew she was upset, but I didn't think she was upset enough to do either one of us any more harm. I'd begun to pull on my pants when something sharp struck me in the eye. "Fuck!" I shouted, clutching my face. With my good eye I saw Dylan—his poufy hair and busy black shirt—staring up at me from the bed. He looked mildly disappointed in me, as if I'd failed to see all this coming and had only myself to blame for any injuries I sustained. "You hit me in the eye!"

But my attacker was in the bathroom, frantically getting dressed. The satin dragon robe was pooled on the floor like a puddle of my own blood.

"You asked for this," Melinda spat as she came back into the room. She went to my coat and fished my car keys from the pocket. "Whether or not you're man enough to admit it to yourself, Frank, I'm giving you exactly what you want." She hefted a duffel bag much too big to be billed as "overnight" and, intent on not meeting my blurry gaze, stalked to the door, undid the lock and shut it behind her with the opposite of a slam.

I didn't go after her. I'd be lying if I said I wasn't relieved, at least initially, to find myself alone. But it wasn't a sudden desire for solitude that kept me in the ritzy hotel room, my pants shackling my ankles, my eye already beginning to swell like a soufflé. Everybody was always going on about how small Philly was, how homey and overfamiliar it felt, especially in relation to its overachieving big brother, New York. But it's a city nonetheless, a place people can easily get lost in, if they're so inclined. It was easy enough to get lost in one's own head. No, I knew better than to chase after Gina—or Melinda, or some brave new combination of the two—because, one way or another, regardless of whether I ever saw either of them again, the woman I'd married was gone.

Twin Peter Cottontails gone bad.

Carpe Diem Disease

Dexter stood over Alison's crouched form, his father's golf umbrella in hand, an expression of exaggerated disgust distorting his face. The expression was bogus, a flimsy defense. Alison looked feral, wolf-raised, pawing through the dirt, and beautiful in a way Dexter wasn't prepared for. She'd never had any qualms about getting her hands dirty; it never bothered her to have food or dirt—or later, paint and clay—jammed beneath her fingernails. Dexter was the fastidious one, the clean freak, the prude. He kept his distance, telling himself he didn't want mud on his clothes. But if Alison Croft so much as nodded toward the mire, there was little doubt Dexter would join her there.

"Nice night for a funeral," Dexter said.

"Fuck, Dex!" Alison started. "You scared the shit out of me." She didn't get up.

"And I wasn't even trying," he lied. "Need a hand?"

"No thanks."

"Um, this might sound like a dumb question—"

"Digging," Alison said, cutting him off.

"Ahhh," Dex said, mock-enlightened. Evidently she was going to make him work for it. And why not? Dexter was nothing if not an over-achiever when it came to Alison Croft. He'd stayed up late studying her for years. "What are you even doing *home*?" he said. "What are you digging *for*?"

Without pausing in her messy work, Alison replied, "None of your fucking business."

She was up to her elbows in mud, her mythological hair matted with rain, her boxy grandpa pajamas clinging to her body like Saran Wrap. It was the middle of the night; it'd been raining steadily for hours now, a driving rain accompanied by the kind of wind that lent larger trees the sound of passing trains. It was no time for gardening, though she couldn't have been doing that, could she? Dex had spotted Alison from his bedroom window and instinctively began snapping pictures. But no sooner had he made himself comfortable by his rain-splattered window, trusty Nikon in hand, than he was struck by the worrisome notion that Alison could disappear from her parents' back yard as magically as she had appeared, and what's more (being Alison) probably would. Sick of keeping his distance, Dexter quit the clandestine photo shoot, walked right off the set. He might as well be out there in the miserable weather with his crazed neighbor, busy either digging something up or burying it deep. He might as well be crazy Alison's even crazier accomplice, for once.

"Wait. You're out here in the middle of the night, in the pouring rain, dressed like somebody's Pop-pop, and I'm not supposed to ask questions?"

"Can you believe it?" scoffed Alison. She straightened up and pointlessly began wiping water away from her face. When she glanced down at her soaked clothes, she was treated to the same display of soft porn as Dexter.

"You want to know what I'm doing out here?" She smiled unforgivably and arched her back. "Waiting for you, Stud."

Dexter knew when he was being fucked with. "Not my style," he said, channeling buckets of nonchalance from his notoriously blasé neighbor. But his mind's eye was working overtime to visualize Pudding Night at an old age home in order to discourage one headstrong erection. "It's cold out here," he said. "And in case you haven't noticed, really, really wet."

"'April is the cruelest month, breeding lilacs out of the dead land, mixing memory and desire, stirring dull roots with spring rain.'"

"Wow, okay," conceded Dex. "I thought you were a painting major."

Alison ignored him. As usual, Dexter couldn't help feeling accused, though of what he wasn't sure. It wasn't merely that Alison was judgmental—she was judge, jury and executioner. She'd long ago cruelly condemned her mother to solitary confinement, based on evidence that was circumstantial at best. Dexter himself was serving a life sentence for a crime he might even have admitted to, had he any idea what it was. It couldn't have been a reluctant, off-the-cuff rejection, administered half a decade ago, could it?

In fact it was exactly five years ago today that Alison had presented Dexter with the opportunity to mess up his life a little, or at least give it that hard-to-fake "lived-in" look. It was no secret that she'd headlined many of his post-pubescent erotic fantasies. Even today Alison continued to make guest appearances, a big name boosting the viewership of a sitcom with a flagging fan base. At the time Dexter had made the mistake of confiding this semi-taboo information to his best friend and Alison's brother, a boy well versed in the realm of public humiliation. So his crush was common knowledge. Thus, the sleeveless boat neck shift dress Alison had fashioned from Sesame Street wrapping paper, the smiling likes of Elmo and Big Bird and Oscar the Grouch regarding him like the mocking members of some cartoon bestiary, by turns daring Dex to rend the crinkly garment from her supple seventeen-year-old torso and warning him not to. The back door was unlocked, as usual. Alison had surprised him in the kitchen, sampling the stucco-like butter cream icing on his birthday cake. Her freckled face was dusted with silver glitter, her lipstick, iridescent orange. Atop her burnished head sat a pretty green bow, big as a bowler.

Alison was naked underneath. Dexter knew this without having to ask. Besides, she'd told him, point-blank, "I'm naked underneath." She was as good as her word. Dexter smiled nervously, lowered the Liz Phair, asked her to repeat that, please. When she did, he took a tentative step toward her, then another. He was inches away from working a finger beneath the main seam of Alison's makeshift dress, of undoing the tabs of sticky Scotch tape clasps, when without so much as a mayday Dexter felt the nose of the single engine plane that was his chutzpah begin to dip. What followed was a rapid and dramatic drop in altitude, a free-fall culminating with Dex being tossed from one end of his desire to the other like so much unsecured cargo. He muttered some excuse about this not being a good idea, warning that certain people—specifically the balding chiropractor and prim, uber-practical cake-maker with whom he lived—would be home soon. He didn't try to straighten the plane, didn't so much as glance at the gears. Dexter just bailed.

To her credit, adolescent Alison responded to the rejection in typical Croft fashion: She laughed in his face, called him a fool, and stormed through the living room and out the front door, sounding every bit like a birthday gift Dexter would never get to unwrap.

He knew it was pointless (and kind of pathetic) to berate himself over a years-old botched seduction, but berate himself he did. Sometimes he thought *So what, I screwed up. I was just a kid.* But this was not the norm. The norm was Dexter consoling himself with the knowledge that over the last five years he'd managed to do just fine for himself in the area of seduction, even without Alison Croft's help, even despite (or precisely because of) his failure with the teenage girl all his future lovers would dub, with varying degrees of hostility and insecurity and admiration: The One Who Got Away (Caitlin); The Bane of My Existence (Suz); Party Girl in a Paper Dress (Dana); Glitter (Jeni-Leigh); The Ghost of Birthday Past (Jane). Because he never stopped talking about Alison Croft. Because no matter with whom he happened to be involved, Dexter never stopped willing himself back into that moment when the girl had offered herself to him as the gift she truly was. If nothing else it was a terrific story, even if he came out looking, to quote Alison, like a fool. But Dexter was banking on there being *degrees* of foolishness; in truth, it was his only hope. After all, how many men even in their prime inspire that kind of behavior? How many of his lady-killing contemporaries could say they knowingly shot down the girl of their dreams?

And yet, ever since the fateful morning of his twentieth birthday, there had been something standoffish about Alison, a transparent barrier that even today Dexter wasn't sure he'd attempt to traverse even if he were equipped with the appropriate tools: a rope to secure himself; a pick axe to chip away at her icy exterior; a descrambler to penetrate Alison's vaguely familiar, semi-secret code. Dexter had long since determined that Alison wasn't unattainable—just too damn hard to locate underneath her many strata of sarcasm and all that hair. At times she seemed to exist under glass, or, again, in keeping with the drenched pjs, beneath a film of plastic wrap (her windfall good moods could spoil easily). And even though they were neighbors, had lived next door to each other at the far end of Elysian Fields' lone cul-de-sac for some fifteen years, on certain occasions—namely her brother's twenty-first birthday party; the time he caught her toking in his father's shed; Homecoming, 2005—it was as though Dexter didn't know Alison Croft at all. Or worse: Alison didn't know Dex.

Dexter gestured toward the house with his umbrella. For a moment Alison looked as if she might actually follow him. Then she looked away.

"C'mon," he said, prompting her. "Exhume Xena's bones some other time." Xena had been Alison's parakeet. She'd died years ago, and was buried out here somewhere. Dexter had read a few words—Rossetti's "Sleeping at Last"—at the funeral. "Preferably when it's dry."

He took her arm. Alison took it back.

"Funny you mention Xena. I just came across her coffin, compliments of her Uncle Bryan's size eleven Air Jordans." They'd buried the bird in an old sneaker, in what at the time seemed an edgy if pungent sarcophagus.

Dexter was confused. "Isn't that what you're out here looking for?"

Alison glared at him over her shoulder. "Why the fuck would I want to dig up a sneaker full of bird bones?"

"Dunno," he admitted. "Mixed media project? Suspicion of foul play?" He paused. "Making room for baby?"

Alison's face changed, and not for the better. "You're sick."

"Sorry. That wasn't funny."

"No, it wasn't. And you're sick." Alison stood up. To Dexter's astonishment, she pushed under his umbrella. "How'd you hear about that?" she asked, wringing out her hair. "We're under strict orders around here to keep our mouths shut. Loose lips, according to Molly. As if Queen Jabber-jaws has any room to talk."

Dexter knew that referring to her mother by her first name was one of the many ways Alison disassociated herself from what she saw as maternal incompetence. She'd done it since she was twelve.

He knitted his brow in an expression of profound disappointment.

"Right, I almost forgot," said Alison. "Bad news travels fast around the tenth circle of hell."

"Is it?" he said. "Bad news?"

Alison looked away and kicked at a pile of mud with her filthy slippered foot. "Beats me," she said. "I don't have an opinion one way or the other."

Dexter grinned. "I'll mark my calendar."

"Ha-ha." Alison looked at him for what felt like the first time. Her big blue-green eyes resembled precious stones in the glare of the floodlight, making him think of that famous Miles Davis composition, the one his father had played for him once as a kid, after explaining to his very young son how colors are made. "I'm blue, your mom's yellow. Together we make green. That's you, Dexie. You're green."

Alison glanced up at Dexter's bedroom window and grinned at him as if she were harboring a concealed weapon, which in some sense he supposed she was. In one swift motion she hauled off and fired her first loaded question. "Couldn't sleep?"

It was true that sleep didn't come easily to Dexter these days, though he'd never put much stock in unconsciousness. Even as a kid his mother had referred to her "Dexie Cup" as a night owl, her lovely, husky voice tempered by that by-now-heartbreaking mix of adult confusion and concern. Back in college, when all his buddies were cuddling up for naps with fleece-swathed coeds on rainy November afternoons, Dexter was over in the library pumping out some term paper or another, or holed up in the campus coffee shop, surfing the Net. It was a bona fide sickness, this Herrick's Malaise, an irreversible condition he'd apparently been born with but whose symptoms, like most illnesses, became more pronounced and unavoidable with age. Informally, it was known as Seize the Day Syndrome (SDS) and, in its advanced stages, Carpe Diem Disease (CDD). No sooner would his head hit the pillow than at Dexter's back he was sure to hear time's winged chariot hurrying near. Not surprisingly, CDD's leading symptom was an acute awareness of one's own mediocrity, often manifesting itself in near-constant insomnia and self-destructive delusions of grandeur. Long-time sufferers tended to take risks, to live life as they would live it during, say, the final, feverish days of their corporeal existence.

But what of Alison? Other than insomnia, what was *she* suffering from? Nobody in her right mind should be out at this hour, dressed for bed but instead farming some ungodly crop, in the bone-chilling, supposedly spring rain. But what really made her look as if she'd lost it, what truly gave the scene that suburban-noir seal of approval, were Alison's feet, which—rather than the red Chucks or checkerboard Vans or shit-kicking Doc Martens Dexter was used to seeing her in—were stuffed into the disemboweled hides of once-fuzzy bunny slippers, the synthetic fur soaked and stained brown, twin Peter Cottontails gone bad.

The juxtaposition of bunnies and burial, foul weather and flimsy attire, was jarring but somehow suited Alison, a paradoxical girl Dex could never quite peg. He took a mental photograph (he'd left the F1 up in his room. Part of what made Dexter a lousy photographer was his inability to see the camera as an extension of himself; he was always leaving it places, which would've been improbable had he ever learned to think of the apparatus as a third eye or extra limb) and titled the composition *Alison in Elysia, Burying Dead Pets*, then cut it to just *Dead Pets*. It sounded like a neo-goth band name, or something he'd read, growing up, on one of his neighbor's inscrutable self-made slogan-tees. (*Wanker* had been one. So had *Jock Tease*, *Vegetable Love*, *Brilliant Mistake*.) It struck Dexter that the name "Alison Croft" was for him itself a slogan, one of those pseudo-philosophical catch-phrases all kids cling to, one that, at three a.m. on the morning of his twenty-fifth birthday, he'd never quite understood nor had fully outgrown.

Dex was vaguely aware that catching Alison thus engaged might've sent a better man running to her aid—or running the other way—if aid was in fact what the girl needed, a pair of galoshes slung around his neck like a barrel of warm brandy, the outsized golf umbrella held aloft like a black parachute to slow and soften her fall. Instead it made Dexter strangely immobile, like an audience member. Now that he thought about it, Alison Croft was always stopping him in his tracks, forcing him to reassess any given situation, making him think. She was that kind of girl. Granted, sometimes what Dexter thought was *Nice try* or *You're a loon* (other times, simply, *Fuck you*). But think he did, often at length, and to the benefit, he chose to believe, of his development as an interesting human being.

Alison nodded knowingly. "Once a perv, always a perv."

"We're neighbors," he lamely offered. "I'm not a perv."

"What!" Alison cackled. "You're King Perv. Oedipus Dex, Dexter the Deviant." She edged a bit closer to him under the umbrella; her hair smelled like a passing storm. "It's kind of flattering." She yanked on Dex's own hair and then, without warning, left the protection of his umbrella and turned back to her bizarre chore. Without looking at him she said, "It was nice of you to drop by and all, but I'm kind of busy here."

"Yeah, sure. I understand." This was patently untrue. Wasn't that part of the attraction?

"By the way," Dexter blurted, eager to deliver some killer parting line, desperate to get the last word with a woman adept at creating new ones. "How's he doing, Lord Bryan?"

Enquiring after Bryan was like commenting on the weather: a telltale sign that he had nothing new or original to say.

"Fine," Alison said, "considering. He'll be okay. Bryan's resilient. He's like a toddler that way—accident-prone." She guffawed. "Only his accidents tend to ruin people's lives."

"As if I didn't know."

"Oh, get over it already," she huffed. "You and the dentist's wet dream were all wrong for each other."

The Betrayal, as Dexter liked to think of it, had happened a good three years ago. That's when his best friend by default—professedly amoral and ultra-horny to begin with—had begun putting the moves on Dex's then-girlfriend, a budding dental hygienist at the junior college in neighboring Hampton Township. Bryan desiring whatever had been earmarked as Dexter's wasn't exactly a new phenomenon: over the years he'd wanted (and sometimes gained possession of) everything from his Pogs to his Playstation to the plaid sports coat Dexter had worn to the Senior Prom. At one point in their very early twenties—a heady time, a veritable Golden Age of nameless girls and surprisingly good, North Philly-grown ganja—Bryan had even expressed interest in Dex's already-ancient Volvo, if sneaking over in the middle of the night and re-parking the car in a secret spot half a mile away could be seen as simply expressing interest. The car meant everything to Dex, and Bryan knew it. And if he didn't know it, he should have. Bryan had the frustrating and remarkably ballsy habit of pleading ignorance where his selfish, often insulting behavior was concerned, and, even though nobody believed him when he claimed to have no knowledge of setting the Antrims' baby spruce on fire or grabbing Jenny Krumpholz's amazing left breast in the eat-in-kitchen of her Pine Street apartment, he got away with it all. Bryan Croft, Elysian Fields' very own Teflon Don.

Dexter was a trusting soul—some might say trusting to a fault—but he was no dummy. He was well aware of his buddy's desperate attempts to bed his girl; more than one person, including Dana herself, had alerted him to the threat. Dexter told her, rather pointedly he thought, to do whatever she liked with Bryan Croft, despite the fact that Dana following this advice was sure to destroy Dex (which it had for weeks afterwards, a dark time during which he'd done little more than swallow Tastykakes, binge on Walter

Ego's *Absence of Light*, and ritualistically burn every single photo, from grade school Confirmation to Mardi Gras semi-nudes, of his treacherous, teeth-cleaning ex). Dexter wasn't one to make demands on the people he loved, though it would've been nice if this particular person had been intuitive enough to realize she was being delivered an ultimatum, and responded accordingly. Instead she chose to interpret Dexter's pitiful defense mechanism as indifference. Dana Ort, too, was a skilled table-turner.

Dexter wasn't as innocent in all this as he let on. In an admittedly weird way, the jilted lover was curious to see just how far Bryan Croft was prepared to go with his girl. By then it was pretty clear that Dexter's girl was prepared to go all the way with Bryan, three thousand miles in a notoriously combustible Tempo, a pile of old grunge cassettes—Soundgarden, Mudhoney, Screaming Trees—on the back seat and a sack of Science Diet in the trunk for Butterscotch, the orange tabby Dana couldn't leave behind. To hear Bryan tell it, he drove while Dana massaged various parts of his road-weary body. They stopped only to pick up provisions, change the litter box and make use of gas station rest rooms (the last two of which smelled the same). They didn't rent motel rooms. They were short on time and short of cash. Dana slept in the car, curled up with Butterscotch on the back seat. As a rule Bryan didn't believe in sleep. And as for sex, well, luckily Bryan had spared Dex the gruesome details, although he did claim that the open road had had a powerful, almost pharmaceutical effect on his cock; with a sly grin he likened his erect member to the Ford in which they hurled themselves across this brutal, insanely beautiful country: BUILT TO LAST.

The happy couple actually got hitched in Vegas, beginning a karma-killing life together by destroying a decade-plus friendship in the process.

Three years later, word around Elysian Fields' lone cul-de-sac was that Bryan and Dana had recently called it quits. The break-up was over a baby Dana didn't want born.

"Are you saying your brother did me a favor by first stealing and then marrying my girlfriend?"

"Admit it," Alison said, "with Dana you were only after one thing. Correction: two things."

Dexter played dumb, but blushed despite himself. After all, his neighbor's pajama top was practically transparent. "Laughing gas and free teeth cleanings?"

Alison bent down and picked up her plastic beach shovel. "Close," she said, and again began to dig.

After a few minutes Alison squealed with satisfaction and turned toward Dexter, a besmirched Tupperware container in her hands. "Found it," she said, beaming. "Finally." She eyed her neighbor cagily. "Not that this hasn't been fun."

"What is it?" asked Dexter.

Alison sat down on the mound of mud she'd created. She tilted the container this way and that, peering through the translucent plastic at the mysterious objects rolling around inside. "I got really freaked out after 9-11," she said. "I didn't think we'd be here five years later, let alone fifty. But I buried this thing anyway, just in case."

"And here we are," Dex said.

"Yeah," agreed Alison, "here we are." She sighed heavily. "Lucky us."

Over the years Dex had logged more hours watching Alison—or simply staring at her bedroom window when he knew she was home, waiting for her to appear—than watching television or surfing the Net. He'd missed the second tower's collapse because he'd caught Alison standing wide-eyed before her own bedroom TV in gym shorts and a heartbreaking training bra. She had no qualms about leaving her bedroom light on after sundown, so that all through his tortured adolescence Dexter was afforded a clear view as his neighbor not-so-obliviously chatted on her chunky rotary phone, blow-dried her shrouding Godiva-locks, perfected her uninspiring high school art projects. More than a few times she caught him looking, but on these occasions rather than curse him out or call his mother—or even draw the blinds—Alison simply waved. Smiled and waved as if across a crowded cafeteria and went about the business of torturing Dex until it was time for bed, in effect robbing a born voyeur of his cherished anonymity.

"So why dig it up? And why now?" Dexter smiled. "I mean, why rob the future residents of Elysian Fields these insights into the warped, mysterious mind of Alison Croft?"

Alison just shrugged and got to her feet. "I want my stuff back, is all."

Dexter wasn't buying it. Still, he was far from ready to walk out of Alison's pricey, well-appointed shop.

"Speaking of warped minds," she said, "what brings you back to Lesion Fields? Baby Jane kick you out?"

Jane was the woman Dexter had been living with for the past eighteen months. Living with, that is, until a week before, when she'd tried to wake him from uneasy dreams and he'd unconsciously called her by another's name. Jane was a disproportionately proud woman. The heated conversation that followed snowballed into a full-blown argument about where Dexter's allegiances lay. (The dream wasn't anything new—it involved his former neighbor, some second string Muppets, a birthday cake the size of a Volkswagen.) The dream was merely the final straw. The split, at least according to the camel, was a long time coming.

Alison was wrong about one thing, though: Jane hadn't kicked Dexter out. She'd politely asked him to leave. There was a difference.

When Dexter didn't respond Alison stood and faced him. "Oops, sorry," she nearly giggled. "Lucky guess."

"It's for the best," Dexter said. "We were doomed from the get-go." It could've been true. "She was an incorrigible litter bug," he continued, unbidden. "I just can't be *intimate* with somebody who throws gum wrappers on the ground."

Alison smiled, genuinely this time. She retrieved her plastic beach shovel from the mud. "I hear you."

Dexter's last significant conversation with Alison, the brick-solid foundation of the tenuous twig-and-straw friendship he'd built with the elder Croft, had taken place about a month after her brother's transgression, during which Alison had played the peacekeeper to decidedly mixed reviews. Her frustratingly bipartisan take was, Yeah, my brother's an asshole, but what can you do? *What you can do is kiss me*, Dex remembered thinking. *Kiss me full on the mouth or leave my life forever.* Twenty-two had been an emotional age for him. Besides, Alison had worn that kitschy terrycloth tennis dress she looked so goddamned privileged in, her fawn-colored freckles set off against anemic butter cream skin, like a photographic negative of the night sky. The suffocating humidity had done insanely chic things to her hair. Superhumanly intuitive Alison Croft had once again read Dexter's mind. Read it like the

Surgeon General's warning to quit smoking and then blew a cloud of carcinogens in the boy's face.

Dexter hadn't spoken to Alison since, not in any sense that mattered. In the years following his rift and subsequent semi-reconciliation with Bryan, he'd occasionally caught her in the drive, getting in or out of her ice cream-colored car, preceding or following a rare family visit; he'd "coincidentally" run into her at the mall, where for about a week during the summer before she moved to the city Alison had worked at Paper Trail, a stationary-slash-arts supply store; he'd even sat behind her at an Ani DiFranco show the previous fall without her knowing—though the wolfish brunette Alison was with had turned and apologized to Dexter for dancing into him during a heart-pumping rendition of "Shameless." But he and his former neighbor hadn't exchanged an interesting word or meaningful look in three whole years. They were the strangest of strangers; once, they'd been friends.

The rain had slowed to a drizzle, but the wind had picked up. It whipped around them, edging them this way and that, like a couple of big, disobedient dogs.

"What's he going to do?" said Dexter.

"He who?"

"Bryan."

Alison knitted her brow.

"I mean, what's he *want* to do?"

"Who knows," she said. "He says one thing one day, another thing the next. Tomorrow it'll be something different. Bryan doesn't know what he wants any more than I do. That's why it's hard for me to blame Dana. Ultimately, it's her decision. You know as well as anybody that my brother isn't exactly dad material." She snorted. "Despite what Molly and her Christian Coalition think."

"People change," he offered.

Alison got in his face, brandishing the dime store shovel like a switchblade. "No, they don't. Everybody keeps saying that, but in the end people don't change. Situations change, circumstances change, not people." She backed off. "You have to respect a girl who makes a difficult decision and sticks by it. Whatever the cost." She tucked her treasure under her arm like a schoolbook. The rain started up again. "I'm going in," Alison said over her shoulder. "See you around."

"C'mon," Dex said, moving toward her. "I'm curious. What's in there?"

"Curiosity killed the cat, King Perv."

As if he didn't know. Dexter did a quick tally and discovered he was currently burning through his seventh or eighth life, by conservative estimation.

"No way I'm telling you," Alison said.

"Why not?"

"Partly because it's none of your business. But mostly because I can tell you really, really want to know."

"That's twisted," he told her.

Alison shrugged, and trudged toward the house without further comment. When she reached the sliding glass doors she paused, turned, and shuffled back to the garden. Almost as an afterthought, she kicked off her corroded bunny slippers and gingerly presented them to Dexter as though passing him twin newborns.

"Happy birthday," she said, by way of goodbye.

"Wait," Dex said, once again grabbing hold of Alison's arm. Something told him that glancing into that cruddy Tupperware container would be like being given a guided tour of the girl's very soul. "Let me look inside."

Alison regarded Dexter's hand and smiled. For a second he was sure she'd relent and grant him this modest birthday wish. Still, when Alison nodded, the affirming gesture threw Dex a moment, until he saw that it was born of some stark realization, possibly about him but more probably and rewardingly about herself. Alison was the center of this shoddy suburban universe, lest anybody need reminding. They were standing on a flooded cul-de-sac where, as usual, all roads led maddeningly back to unknowable Alison Croft.

"Some other time," Alison lied, leaving Dexter little choice but to loosen his grip. She turned and headed back toward the lightless house, her secret, self-made treasure safely in hand.

As for censorship, this was a first.

The F-Word

"Is it risqué?" Lauren asked, using a word DeMarco associated with burlesque, with fleshy retro strippers named Candy or Bubbles, not with literature, not high art. Her tarblack hair was down for once, her lips shellacked a disarming, visceral shade of red. Enveloped in a stinky bubble of smoke—apparently the owners of neighborhood dives like this could afford to snub their noses at antismoking legislation—the woman still smelled like fresh fruit salad. "You seem like the kind of guy whose work might raise eyebrows, all buttoned up and battened down. Like some prim Victorian with a basement full of corseted sex slaves."

"My basement's full of boxes of old books," DeMarco said.

"I bet."

In lieu of social consciousness DeMarco would settle for raising eyebrows. "Eyebrows are underrated," he explained. "These days everybody's having them plucked away, like those little old ladies you see riding the subway at all hours, muttering into the collar of their fake fur coats. They draw them on with conte crayon, it seems. Makes mostly real people look like mannequins."

"Mostly real," snorted Lauren. "Nice."

"I'm all for Brooke Shields and Jennifer Connelly—Irish women, by the way, tend to have amazing eyebrows, reminiscent of turf. It's one of the things I miss most about the eighties—women's eyebrows."

Lauren smiled and took a contemplative drag on her cigarette. DeMarco resisted an urge to compliment her on her own eyebrows, which were full and defiantly unshaped, giving her otherwise cheerful face a look of perpetual disdain. A casual observer might interpret that look as the stock expression of someone who patently didn't care. But her esteemed professor had observed her for weeks now, and DeMarco knew better. Luckily for him, Lauren Martinez happened to care about a variety of things, failed fiction writers not least among them.

DeMarco tore his eyes away from Lauren long enough to survey his surroundings, the way he'd always heard writers are supposed to do. His token returning student considered the bar a dive, and her brusque, ironclad assessment wasn't far from the truth. The place sure couldn't flaunt the literary street cred of the 92nd Street Y, and it wasn't remotely as posh as the oak-paneled halls of the prestigious liberal arts colleges in which he'd heard quote-unquote celebrity writers give their famed readings. The management didn't bother to card here, and any band with a semi-ironic name—PRE-SHRUNK, he'd read on the Xeroxed calendar of dates taped to the men's room wall, SOLVE FOR X, THE DISGRUNTLED SPEEDBUMPS—could easily schedule a gig. But calling it a dive, he decided, was doing it a disservice. O'Hooligan's was a dive; Skeezy Pete's was a dive. This place, with its cruddy mosaic floor and dusty deco light fixtures and encyclopedic beer selection, was the watering-hole equivalent of a dive's lower-middle-class cousin.

DeMarco glanced up at the television and saw George Costanza lying face down on the floor of Jerry's apartment in his underwear. "A former friend of mine used to call me Stuffy," he admitted. "Capital S." He left out the part about calling the friend Buffy, a Lycra-clad slayer in her own right, an elementary school teacher who took her clothes off for extra cash at a real dive-bar down in Essington. The only demons Zoe had set out to slay after sundown were her own.

Lauren gave him the once-over. "That's sad," she decided.

"Uh-huh," he agreed, laughing, which in turn made Lauren laugh too. He saw her teeth, perfect as a white picket fence. Good teeth had always turned him on. Good teeth and bushy eyebrows—God, he was stuffy!

She was no kid, this candid, idiosyncratically attractive student of his, and neither was he. DeMarco wondered to what extent her age alone accounted for the attraction. Lately he found himself drawn to older women, women with a little life behind them, women with laugh lines and crow's feet and stories to tell. Only Lauren wasn't a storyteller; she tended to keep her mouth shut, at least when she wasn't busy making inspired wisecracks or bitching about her ex. (This subterranean sense of decorum, so beguiling in a tough-minded, working-class woman, had fueled Lauren's loathing of the confessional poets they'd recently covered in class.) The woman was the living, breathing rep-resentation of "show, don't tell." If she were a short story, her author might be Hemingway: sharp, solid, concise. But not without beauty, not without a certain measured grace.

What Lauren had shown him so far was a rather self-conscious, closed-mouth kiss, administered the previous week, in the front seat of her beat-up SUV. It was a kiss with purpose, a kiss with promise. A harbinger, as they say, of things to come.

Or was he reading too much into it, the tragic flaw of English majors the whole world over? Lauren must've had to pull some considerable strings to be here. But she was far from throwing herself at him. Did he even want her to? Of course the chase was infinitely better than the kill, as Billy Bragg, via the bar's surprisingly eclectic jukebox, had a few minutes ago so eloquently expounded. But courting Lauren Martinez, if a courtship this was, had all the earmarks of a S.W.A.T.-team standoff.

"Well, try not to shock us too much," she said, nodding at the crowd. "There are children in the audience."

Then, as if on cue, one of his "children" was by his side.

"Hello, Dr. D," Brett said. (DeMarco's students were forever making this mistake, assuming he had a Ph.D. simply because he taught upper-level courses. For a while he continued to correct them, but then he'd just given up. The initials LOL and BFF meant far more to them than Ph.D.) "Oh, excuse me. I didn't see you had company."

Brett wore a chic polka dot halter-top and pressed low-riding jeans. DeMarco had tried to buy Maya a pair of those same jeans once, but when she got wind of the price she took them right back to the store, a funkier-than-thou designer boutique off Rittenhouse Square. "What's wrong with them?" asked the incredulous, tsunami-coiffed sales clerk, sounding as though she'd given birth to the very bleach-creased pants his then-wife was in the process of disowning. "They cost too much," straight-shooting Maya told the girl. "Plus my husband's insane."

Brett, like Lauren, had also managed to get her story told, although the younger woman had taken a more scenic, circuitous route. DeMarco knew she came from money. She'd intimated this, in that charming, intentionally casual (or was it casually intentional?) way she had, during the student-teacher conference, which had begun in class and continued over taco salads at an off-campus Mexican restaurant. But he'd already guessed her pedigree: the professionally groomed hair, the good shoes, the perennially buffed and buttered look were dead giveaways. You couldn't judge a book by its cover, but by and large you could judge college kids. Most of DeMarco's students came to class hiding their post-adolescent insecurities beneath frumpy sweats and "performance" fleece. Not Brett. Brett was ready for her close-up, and probably had been since birth. Her well-tended body was an open secret. It whispered to him in his sleep.

"We've reached a decision, Herr Doktor," Brett said, an homage to Sylvia Plath, her favorite poet.

"Oh really? Who's 'we'?"

Brett swung away from him toward the dance floor—or what DeMarco imagined served as the dance floor when the likes of The Disgruntled Speedbumps were in town—her wealth of half-curled blonde-brown hair nearly toppling his lager in the process. She inclined her head toward two girls in knock-offs of her own designer jeans and candy-colored T-shirts two sizes too small. "You know. Fitzy, V and me."

"Fitzy" was Sarah Fitzwater, a dead-ringer for a famous pop music diva, minus the pug nose; "V" was Victoria Moog, a plump, cheerful girl who, when drunk, pretended to "service" her kitschy life-size poster of white-suited Tony Manero (this info via Brett, who wasn't as careful as she might have been with other people's secrets).

"We've decided no more beating around the bush," continued Brett, all business. "We came all this way, with finals and everything. V's practically on her deathbed, she's been coughing so much." V made a horrendous big dog sound, for emphasis. "She may hack up a lung, before the night's out. You simply have to read." She fixed him with her startling blue eyes, so reminiscent of a child's and, at the same time, so very not. "No is not an option, Herr Doktor."

It was nearing the end of the semester and many of DeMarco's students were in danger of what he only half-jokingly referred to as the f-word: failing. He wasn't nearly as old as they'd expected him to be on that bitterly cold afternoon in the very new year when he'd first made their acquaintance. Despite the sports coat and sweater-vest and closely shorn beard, they failed to take him (and his participation policy) as seriously as they might a professor twice his age. Now they were scrambling, Proust-like, to make up for lost time. "Grade us on a curve!" they cried. "What about extra-credit?" they whined. Finally DeMarco had relented and offered attendance at this reading—which he attended every month, without ever sharing his own work—as extra-credit.

Brett was different. Brett was an across-the-board A-student. She, like Lauren, didn't need to be here. Yet here she was.

DeMarco had every intention of reading. Still, he told Brett he wasn't going to, told his stylish A-student that he'd forgotten the pages, that someone had apparently replaced his printer's cartridge with invisible ink, that in effect his dog had eaten his homework. To his surprise she'd taken him seriously, her lovely, fawn-speckled face crumpling like wet cardboard.

"Oh, come off it," said Lauren, who'd been busying herself with the loose change on the bar, engaged in the kind of three-coin air-hockey DeMarco had thought only eighth-grade boys played.

"Come off what?" DeMarco asked dumbly.

Lauren shot him an admiring, mildly derisive sidelong glance. "You know damn-well you're going to read. Don't tease the girl." She turned to face Brett and patted her reassuringly on the shoulder. The condescension was palpable. "He likes you, honest. He's just really, really good at being a jackass."

DeMarco didn't know what offended Brett more: being condescended to by a woman twice her age and, judging by her comments in class, nowhere near her intellectual equal or hearing her favorite professor being insulted.

"I repeat," Brett said to him, some of the playfulness but none of the game gone from her voice, "no is not an option."

She turned on her heel—high heels and designer jeans, something else DeMarco missed about the eighties—and started back toward her friends.

He watched her go. Someone behind him was reciting Byron: "'She walks in beauty, like the night / Of cloudless climes and starry skies; / And all that's best of dark and bright / Meet in her *ass*-pect and her eyes.' Emphasis mine," Lauren said.

DeMarco started to turn toward her but stopped short; he couldn't bear to see the derisive expression on Lauren's face. What's more, he didn't deserve it. Who could blame him for flirting with Brett? And who could blame Brett, in turn, for flirting back? Why, it was the most natural thing in the world, this student-teacher erotic tension. Lauren knew this better than anybody. After all, she was a student too.

Without turning to acknowledge Lauren's comment, DeMarco called Brett back and told her, in effect, that he was at her service, her wish was his command. Despite her usual reserve Brett tittered and turned an irresistible shade of red. He thought of the Joan Jett cover of that terrific old song, "Crimson and Clover." Was there more to Brett Eames than met the eye? She seemed a composite of contradictions: sensuous but reserved, bookish but naive, serious-minded but infinitely sweet. Something about the young woman—some shadow moving behind those streak-free windowpane eyes—suggested there was a limit to the sweetness, a point at which Brett would shed the stylish clothes and cute comments and reveal a far more private, if not primal, self.

Brett glanced at Lauren, who'd been mesmerized by the smoldering tip of her near-dead cigarette. There was no love lost between them. They weren't enemies, exactly. But they were far from friends.

"Order me a drink, already," Brett told DeMarco. "I'm not in the habit of buying my students drinks."

Insulted, Brett smiled evilly and brandished her festive designer clutch as though it were the deed on a house on which she was finally about to foreclose. "You order," she told him. "I'll buy." She reached into the overpriced envelope and retrieved a brand-new fifty-dollar bill. Then she waved over the bartender, who seemed suspiciously unfazed by his fetching, well-heeled patron, and proceeded to order a round for her aging classmate and their esteemed professor.

"They'll have another," she said, nodding toward DeMarco and Lauren with obvious amusement. "And a Long Island iced tea for me."

"Number three," the bartender said.

"But who's counting?"

To his credit, the man shot her a parental look. "Me."

Brett rolled her eyes. "I'll take baby sips," she said, flirting now. "Promise." She turned to her instructor, beaming. Her prematurely tanned shoulder gleamed like a brass newel, while her too-blue eyes buzzed like the perennial holiday lights haphazardly strung above the bar. "On me," she said.

On Brett… under Brett… off to one side…

"Thanks, Dad," Brett said to the bartender as the man delivered their booze and moved away.

"I'm not in the habit of letting students buy *my* drinks, either," DeMarco told her.

Brett regarded him as one might regard an ornate but overly familiar piece of furniture. There wasn't a trace of innuendo in her voice when she asked, "What *are* you in the habit of letting your students do?"

He imagined Lauren doing a spit-take, spraying the artfully disheveled hipsters nearest her with tepid, half-swallowed beer.

Perhaps feeling she'd overstepped her bounds, Brett didn't wait around for a reply. Instead she gently removed the straw from her drink, took a big gulp of the innocuously named concoction and rejoined her friends on the other side of the bar.

"She's adorable," Lauren said, exhaling an anemic plume of smoke in lieu of the regurgitated lager. "And she clearly adores you."

"And you?" DeMarco asked.

Lauren smiled but didn't seem all that surprised by the question. She certainly wasn't flustered, which was his intention. "Me what?"

She was playing hard to get, or at least hard to get a handle on. Apparently she wanted to see him squirm. (See Stuffy. See Stuffy squirm. See Stuffy, against his better judgment, fall for all the wrong kinds of women.) Rather than respond to his admittedly tactless question with a tactless comment of her own, she'd called his bluff by feigning ignorance and asking him to be specific. But in life, if not in art, specifics came hard for DeMarco—just ask Maya, who'd left him a long, angry goodbye letter claiming, among a host of other tragic flaws and generally bad behavior, that he was "chronically wishy-washy" and "ultimately unknowable." He couldn't make a joke out of it. Or worse, clam up, say nothing and suffer through the ensuing silence. Everywhere he turned he found there was no turning back. "Do you adore me, too?"

Lauren didn't flinch. "Adoration is a strong word. It implies some sort of hero-worship. Aside from my daughter and that guy over there pouring the drinks, I'm too old to have heroes."

She took his hand in her much warmer one. "Let's settle for boat-loads of admiration and great respect."

DeMarco nodded assent, and gently clanked his beer against hers. "Ditto."

They drank.

From where they sat at the bar they could see Brett and her friends. Evan Rook, a big presumptuous kid cut from American Idol cloth, brazenly approached the trio and whispered something in Brett's ear. DeMarco saw the boy put out his hand and Brett shaking her pretty head no, I'm sorry, I can't. Was he asking her to dance? To bum a cigarette? To go smoke a bone in the alley behind the bar? Brett caught Herr Doktor's eye. Herr Doktor shrugged and looked away.

"You know she's named for the Hemingway character," Lauren said, "I forget which book."

"*The Sun Also Rises.*"

"Right."

"Lady Brett Ashley."

"How perfect," Lauren whispered. "Another?"

"Allow me, Doc." Evan said, tossing a twenty onto the bar and winking at him. Evan was wearing his tight frat T-shirt what appeared to be inside-out. He also had boundary issues, and not merely when it came to his embarrassingly curvaceous classmates. DeMarco, too, repeatedly found himself fending off Evan's invitations to various keg parties and happy hours and sports rallies. The young man seemed determined to cast his instructor in a rebellious uncle light. DeMarco didn't mind the attention, in theory; Evan was likeable enough, if woefully misguided and overly impressed with himself—a reckless combination, the very hallmarks of youth. But being pegged as one of the boys by a much younger male student made DeMarco look bad.

"No thanks, Evan." He pushed his empty bottle away. "That's my limit."

"Ah," said Evan, pointing a finger, "you don't fool me, Doc. I bet you could drink us all under the table." Evan glanced over his shoulder at a cluster of his classmates, who for the most part had been keeping their distance. In class they were an animated, downright chatty bunch, at least prior to class discussion. But out in public with each other, and their English professor in unheard-of jeans and sneakers—their world, in effect, turned upside-down—they became shy and withdrawn. Shy and withdrawn, except for suave Mr. Rook. "How about you, Lauren? Can I get you anything?"

"I'm good." Lauren wasn't fond of Evan. She called him Evan the Terrible right to his face; the boy took it in stride, took it as a compliment.

Evan held Lauren's gaze a beat longer than was customary, even for a well-built charmer with nothing to lose. It seemed to DeMarco that the younger man would've liked to stay in their company a bit longer, but deferred to his professor—after all, a grade was at stake—and what he correctly sensed was a seduction-in-the-making. He grabbed his order of beers. "Be good," Evan said, winking at his professor as he left.

"You don't like him," DeMarco said to Lauren once the boy was out of earshot.

"Please," she groaned. "The kid's a sadist in sheep's clothing. I've seen his kind before. Hell, I married his kind, remember."

Lauren took a long pull on her beer. She seemed defiantly self-sufficient, and so very alone in the world—basically how DeMarco wanted to appear to others, though never quite could. She wasn't his idea of an ideal mate; she wasn't even his idea of a worthy risk. Middle-aged mom or no, a student was a student. So said the university's recently revised sexual harassment policy. But DeMarco had kissed her just the same, and ever since had been counting the days until he would kiss her again.

Despite the me-against–the-world persona, Lauren wasn't really all that alone. There was that cloying, reluctant ex-husband, figurative paterfamilias of Evan the Terrible and his cryptically silk-screened ilk; a cloying five-year-old daughter named Rose; a dog, no doubt cloying as well.

"What's your dog's name?"

Slightly taken aback, she told him.

"*Hard Times*," he recognized. Then, in Sleary's pronounced lisp, "Thissy Jupe's father's thircus dog."

Lauren paid the bartender and smiled. "I've always loved Dickens."

"A critical and a commercial success."

"A man who knew how to toe the line," she said significantly. She handed DeMarco a fresh bottle of beer despite what he'd told Evan and lifted her own tumbler of Scotch. "I switched."

"I see."

"To Dickens," she said, lifting her glass.

"To toeing the line."

She smiled slyly. "Hear, hear."

DeMarco wasn't a big drinker. If he didn't want to actually sound like Sleary up there on stage, this would have to be it. His bloodstream welcomed this extra hit of booze, though. Reading his work aloud to a roomful of strangers could be nerve-racking (unlike teaching, which didn't force him to bide his time or require him to bare his soul in quite the same fashion). Once he got up there and got going he would be fine. It was the getting up there that rattled him.

"May I see it," Lauren asked, "your manuscript?"

He pulled from the back pocket of his jeans a folded sheaf of paper, the title story of his new, never-to-be-published book. To add to the other two unpublished books he'd written.

"It's not the final draft," he said, in an effort to lower her expectations.

"It never is." She looked it over. "I like the title."

The story, about a recently divorced mother of three who returns to college years after having dropped out, was called "Return to Me." He'd written it for Lauren. Scratch that; strictly speaking everything he wrote he wrote primarily for himself (Maya had been ever-so-helpful in pointing this out). But he'd had Ms. Martinez in mind when he created the main character. Or at least the woman he imagined Ms. Martinez to be.

Lauren's eyes roved over the opening page. Almost immediately her face changed.

"What's the matter?"

"Nothing," she lied.

"I saw that, you know. The way your nose crinkled. C'mon, I'm a grown man. I can take it."

Lauren shrugged. "Awful lot of f-bombs," she said. "For somebody so...sophisticated."

DeMarco made a show of widening his eyes and took a step back. "Aghast" was the look he was going for. "You're kidding," he said.

She wasn't. "This is what you're going to read to these kids?"

"You have something against the word—"

"Stop," she said. "Don't say it."

"But it's a fine word, it's a lovely word. It's the truest word there is."

"Please," she told him, "I'm not some kid."

"That, I can see. And that's exactly why I find your reaction so hard to believe."

"It's not what you think. Of course I'm no stranger to bad language. My father was a big fan of the f-word in particular."

The f-word.

"And, perhaps not coincidentally, so was my ex-husband," she added. "I'm sick of it, that's all. Even though everyone else can't seem to get enough of it."

"Including me."

She looked him in the eye. "You're an authority figure. You shouldn't be reading it aloud to these kids."

"There are no kids here," he said evenly. "Everyone here is an adult."

"Chronologically, yes. Legally, ok. But not emotionally, not psychologically."

"Psychologically?"

"Look, I get it. I know why you do what you do."

"You do?" DeMarco said, unsure of what exactly she was getting at. "Could you fill me in, then?"

Something behind Lauren's caramel-colored eyes changed; he could almost see her going into her wind-up. "OK, since you asked. How many have there been, for argument's sake?"

Strike one: Got caught looking.

"Pardon?" he said.

"How many Bretts?"

Strike two: Bad call. A bit low.

"That's unfair."

"Damn straight—unfair to them."

Strike three: Swing-and-a-miss. The woman has one helluva fastball.

"I thought we were talking about my story here, about the 'f-word'?"

"We were, we are. It's all related."

"I don't see how."

"You don't see how one abuse leads to another?"

"Whoa, what 'abuse'?" DeMarco said. "What are you even talking about?"

"Oh, come on. Don't play dumb. I was there, remember, when you kissed me. Don't think I flatter myself by thinking I'm the first."

Lauren wasn't the first, but neither was she the tenth, or twentieth, or ten-thousandth, as she seemed to be implying. DeMarco had only ever kissed one other coed, and at the time even she had been a *former* student, a Slavic platinum blonde who'd come to his office for a recommendation and left without a trace of her sugary pink lipstick. (Like her lank, baby-fine hair, DeMarco's review of Martina's academic performance had been glowing.) But he'd never slept with a student, or really even tried. In that respect he was kind of hoping Lauren *would* be the first.

"Just do me a favor," she said. "Don't read this." She tapped the pages as though ordering another card at the blackjack table. "At the very least leave out the foul language."

DeMarco didn't know what to say. No one had ever tried to censor his work before. Edit it, yes. Reject it, of course. But as for censorship, this was a first.

"You don't think they hear worse than this on the radio?" he said. "Worse even than this on TV? Which world do you live in?"

"The same world as my five-year-old daughter."

DeMarco gestured dramatically to his students, many of whom seemed to have at least one ear cocked toward their professor's heated conversation. "But these people are not five years old. Far from it." He wanted to solicit driver's licenses, to prove dates of birth. But there was no need—the girls' barely clothed bodies were proof enough. The short skirts and tight jeans and teensy tees were exhibits A, B and 36C. Far cry from five years old! Huh, far cry from fifteen!

"I'm not DeSade," he offered. "I'm not even Philip Roth. There's more offensive fiction to be found in fifteen minutes of a Fox News broadcast than in anything I ever wrote."

"That's not the point," Lauren said. "In fact all the more reason not to read it. If they hear it on TV, as you say, they sure don't need to hear it from you. I wonder…"

"You wonder what? Don't stop now."

"I just realized it's not about them needing to hear it, is it? It's about you needing to tell it to them."

She was right, DeMarco did need to "tell it to them." (This, like Prufrock, and so much more.) But not for the reasons Lauren believed. He knew what she was getting at, the metaphorical deflowering, art, if not exactly imitating life, then at least doing a pretty good job of temporarily standing in. Wish fulfillment, wishful thinking, if wishes were trees… DeMarco would never properly seduce any of his flirtatious, seemingly eager-to-be-seduced students, that magnificent human sacrifice, Brett Eames, included. He was much bolder on paper than he was in person. And although sex with some of these girls—"girls" now instead of "women"?—would no doubt be time well spent, making the stuff up would always be infinitely more fun. Not to mention more permanent.

"This isn't about 'them,'" he said. "It's about Brett."

"I couldn't care less about Brett," snorted Lauren.

"No, but I could. And that bothers you more than you're willing to admit."

The heavily bespectacled woman in charge of announcing the readers brushed past him on her way to the podium and gave DeMarco's shoulder a light squeeze, indicating the reading was about to start. She was dressed like Churchill's famous description of Russia, with a short black skirt slung over her flared slacks, a clerical cardigan buttoned to the neck.

"Well?" It was Brett. She was standing before him now, beaming. For DeMarco? For his work? Was there even a difference?

"I'm next," DeMarco heard himself say. Then, rather stiffly to Lauren, "If you'll excuse me..."

"Don't go yet, Dr. D." Brett was barring his way. She was tipsy. "Good luck kiss," she said, puckering up and pressing herself against him. "Just a peck, I promise. No tongue."

Be careful, Herr Doktor, what you wish for.

Brett was more than tipsy; on the slippery, single-lane highway leading to Oblivion, Brett had passed the charming village of Tipsy miles ago, and was coming up fast on the derelict town of Wasted, PA. *Gee, your hair smells terrific*, DeMarco couldn't help thinking, with a shampooed shammy of it shoved under his nose. He placed a hand, lightly, on each of her newel-smooth shoulders with the intention of easing her away. She felt weightless and watery; his own head was swimming. "Please, Herr Doktor," she whined. "One little baby-kiss. To keep the bad dreams away."

"Christ, stop calling him that," snapped Lauren. She turned on her stool to face Brett; if the younger woman had been wearing lapels, hard-boiled Lauren would've grabbed her by them and pulled her close. "He doesn't have his doctorate and you're no Sylvia Plath."

"What should I call you then?" Brett whispered to him, all but ignoring her cranky classmate.

From the stage DeMarco heard the owlish Iron Curtain announce his name.

"I could call you that," she offered. "If you'll let me."

"I have to go, Brett." DeMarco scanned the crowd for Fitzy and V, but Fitzy and V were nowhere to be seen. He cleared a place for her at the bar. "Sit here. Lauren will look after you. Won't you, Lauren."

"You betcha," Lauren said.

"Oh, god," groaned Brett, getting to her feet. "I feel sick. Where's the bathroom?"

"Back that way," he said. "Lauren will show you. I have to go now. They're calling my name."

"I need the bathroom," DeMarco heard Brett whine as he made his way to the stage. "Like, right now..."

Wherever the bathroom was, it wouldn't have been close enough for Brett to reach in time. Fortunately she had her designer clutch in hand. One receptacle was as good as another when one's stomach decided to revolt.

It was dark up on stage, and noisier than DeMarco expected. He had to hold his sheaf of typewritten pages at an odd angle just to make out his own words. He made a crack about the lighting, or lack thereof—something about this not exactly being what James had had in mind, when he said that writers "work in the dark." A few people chuckled, but no one really laughed.

He saw Brett, wiping vaguely at her mouth with a cocktail napkin. Fitzy and V walked out of the shadows and took their friend by the hand, leading her toward the bathroom—the blind leading the blind—for all the good it would do either Brett's designer bag or her wobbly self-esteem. He took it they would be in there for a while, hiding. They might even consider sneaking out the back. Either way, they would miss their esteemed professor's reading.

In Brett's stead DeMarco saw Lauren, somewhat vindicated, defiantly perched on her bar stool, waiting for him to get on with it. She wasn't going anywhere. On the contrary, the woman wouldn't move a muscle until he'd finished reading, or at least until he'd finished the first page. Until then, her posture seemed to say, whatever existed between them in the way of "erotic tension"—whatever existed in the way of that kiss—hung in   the   balance.

DeMarco didn't owe her anything, other than an impartial grade. So why did he feel so much in the woman's debt? And what's more, why was he reluctant to let her down, so reluctant, in fact, that he was actually considering taking the literary equivalent of a late-round dive? Despite the tough exterior, he knew Lauren often thought of herself as a failed wife and mother; DeMarco often thought of himself as a failed husband and writer and, now, in light of Lauren's accusations, a failed teacher too. Two wrongs didn't make a right, but what did two aging maybes make?

DeMarco took a deep breath and began to read, his eyes anxiously skipping ahead to every word his tongue was loath to delete.

My dad dreamt of cartoons.

Me, Tarzan

"Johnny's back," my mother announced one muggy summer night over a steaming plate of baked ziti. My dad hadn't been paying particular attention to her, which was a shame, because even I'd noticed she had her hair done differently—nothing dramatic, just a fresh cut, adding extra bounce to her bob—and was cruising for a compliment. But Gabriel Hayes was a preternaturally distracted man, one step ahead of himself and two steps behind everyone else. He routinely walked around with his fly open and got into fender-benders with parked cars. Some men, the lucky ones, were preoccupied with sports teams, or car parts, or with defiling their barely-legal babysitters. Others, the doomed, the walking wounded, were slaves to a dream that, due to bad timing or poor life choices or a debilitating tragic flaw, would always remain just out of reach. My dad dreamt of cartoons. He was a working-class Walt Disney in search of his million-dollar mouse.

"Johnny's back," my mother repeated. "Who knows for how long?" She clearly considered this her trump card, the only one in her entire deck sure to make her oft-unreadable husband's face fold.

"Johnny?" my dad said, more to himself than to any of us seated at the table. He was busily doodling on a pad of plain white paper, which he often did during meals, and

119

while in the bathroom, and in front of the TV. He even kept a pad of paper in the glove compartment and doodled during red lights. To hear him tell it, he was on the verge of perfecting his newest character, one that would take the Saturday morning cartoon establishment by storm, to say nothing of buried-trinket cereal boxes and mood-enhancing Happy Meals. It seemed he was forever on the verge of some animation breakthrough or other. He'd already run through a menagerie of tuxedo-wearing mice and punk rock rabbits. More recently he'd become obsessed with a dachshund named Bobo Lazarus who suffered from an identity crisis: Bobo woke up one morning and couldn't remember how to bark. "Johnny who?" he said.

My mother smirked and silently watched him squirm. Granted, it was hard to be civil in the record-degree heat, let alone lovey-dovey. But lovey-dovey was what I was used to. For days now I'd convinced myself that the intense heat was responsible for drying up whatever superhuman adhesive had, for almost a third of their lives, held my clingy parents together. But I was only fourteen at the time, and had no real idea why their marriage might be coming unglued.

"Para-*dis*-ee," my mother said breathily, just to get on his nerves.

My dad delivered mail for a living. It was stressful, backbreaking work, a job he was in no way cut out for. He couldn't handle the constant ribbing and locker room mentality of most of his fellow mail carriers any more than he could handle being out in the hot sun for hours at a stretch, wearing polyester pants and lugging a Santa sack full of junk mail. As a boy he'd dreamt of becoming an animator, of driving out to California and getting a job working for Disney. As he got older, the prospect of traveling to the Magic Kingdom dwindled and then disappeared completely. At twenty-two he'd met my mother—or re-met her, since they'd known each other pretty much all their lives—at a funeral for a mutual acquaintance who'd been killed in a car crash. They began dating, and before he knew it he had a wife to support, two squawking mouths to feed. He took the test for the post office out of sheer desperation—it was good pay, with excellent benefits—and reluctantly accepted the job "on a trial basis." Here he was, thirteen years later, still schlepping mail.

"There goes the neighborhood," he said, ignoring his wife's theatrics. He frowned and turned back to his art.

But she wasn't finished with him yet. My mother had grown up the only daughter out of eight children, and as such was a seasoned card-player (as well as a skilled tire-changer, TV-fixer and toy-assembler). She had another ace up her sleeve—or in this case tucked, like a secret wad of cash, inside a cup of her brassiere. "He thinks he's Tarzan, apparently," she said.

This got my dad's attention. "What?"

"He stands out on Millie's front porch and screams like Tarzan," she said. "Ask Sammy. I half-expect a herd of elephants to come storming through the schoolyard when he does it."

He looked at me, his elder son, for confirmation, and I nodded. Whoever this Johnny guy was, he seemed to be someone my parents could agree upon. They were actually being civil to each other. This was the longest conversation they'd had in days, certainly the longest they'd had without raising their voices. Could it last?

"I saw him too," I said.

I'd been out back when Tarzan came to call, halfheartedly shooting hoops on the freestanding basketball net my dad had recently erected. Gabriel Hayes was not a handy man, and the private ball court was far from his idea. My mother had sweet-talked him into it, back when sweet talk wasn't an oxymoron. Ever since The Beating a few weeks before, she'd prohibited my brother Geno and me from hanging out in Comstock Playground, where she couldn't keep an eye on us or, more particularly, on the marauding gang of Puerto Ricans who were said to have taken a battalion of taped broomsticks and baseball bats to Jimmy Duncan's luckless body, working it over like a piñata. Word on the street was that Dunc had it coming, that he'd danced with the wrong girl at Electric Playground and paid for it with his life. But the word on the street was wrong. Jimmy Duncan had been the sixteen-year-old equivalent of beige wallpaper—he was that adamantly ignored. He'd never set foot inside any playground that I could recall, electric or otherwise. And if Dunc danced at all it was in the privacy of his own bedroom, with the door locked and the blinds tightly drawn.

My disinclined dad had dug a hole, filled it with cement, and did his best to clear the questionable ball court of patchy grass and natural debris. Months later, we were still waiting for the blacktop. It's not much fun dribbling a big rubber ball on uneven, rock-plagued terrain. But I was out there anyway, like some Spalding-obsessed lunatic, attempting a series of thwarted lay-ups under the sadistic early-summer sun.

I watched, amazed, from my makeshift Madison Square Garden as Tarzan came out onto Millie's front porch, beat his chest with his free hand—in his other hand he strangled a plastic bottle of half-drunk orange juice—and sang his wordless song. It was prophetic and poetic, simultaneously nonsensical and sublime. Music to a discerning pair of adolescent ears, for sure, but like no song I had ever heard played on my trusty boom box or piped over the PA system in the musty church basement during school dances. And no wonder: Tarzan was a front porch pop star, a born performer who just happened to keep time on his chest. He had the sun for a spotlight, a cupped hand for a microphone, a bottle of Tropicana in lieu of the jug of Carlo Rossi a more generous performer might partake of and kindly pass around. His back-up band consisted of buzzing air conditioners and barking dogs and honking car horns. The concert itself didn't cost a dime, but that's not to say the show was exactly free.

Finished with his performance, I fully expected Tarzan to swing away on some improvised vine—a downed telephone wire, say, or dysfunctional clothesline. At the very least I figured he'd scale the modest row house from which he'd emerged and do a full-blown Rocky Balboa, mouth thrown open, arms in the air. The untranslatable noise he'd made sounded like a prelude to something, a warning to take heed and watch what this fearsome and seemingly fearless man might do next. But Tarzan did nothing next, or at least nothing worth noting. He simply stretched, downed what was left of the o.j. and lumbered back inside.

My dad shrugged, and I got the feeling that people had been shrugging at Tarzan's behavior all his life. "It could be worse," he said. "He could think he was the Wolfman, and keep us up with his howling all night long."

"Is he crazy?" Geno wanted to know.

"Yes," my dad said, without looking up from his flipbook.

"Gabe."

He looked at his wife. "He's not crazy the way you think," he said, resuming his doodling, his eyes fastened on a bouquet of daisies a red-faced Bobo was presenting to the object of his canine affections, a prissy cocker spaniel named Desiree. "He's done some pretty crazy things, even your Mom would have to admit." He shot my mother a knowing glance and, to my surprise, she didn't look away. "I want you guys to stay clear of him, okay?"

"Why?" I said. "He seems harmless to me."

"Listen to your Dad, Sam," my mother broke in. "He knows a little something about crazies."

"He's far from harmless, Sammy. I grew up with the guy. Your Mom and I both did. Just do me a favor and trust me on this, okay?"

While I thought it over my dad turned to a fresh sheet of paper and sketched a cartoon likeness of my face superimposed on the body of a chimp swinging on a vine. Underneath it he wrote "Sammartino Hayes, stop monkeying around!"

He handed me the drawing. "Okay?" he repeated, lovingly pinching my cheek.

"Okay, okay," I said.

Tarzan was a big guy, as you might expect, barrel-chested and overly bronzed, with faded tattoos illustrating his thick arms like the cheaply silk-screened T-shirts sold down the shore. His hair was dark and perennially damp, slicked back and styled away from his face like some latter-day greaser, a T-bird wannabe. His hands were big as catcher's mitts; his eyes hidden behind green-glassed tortoiseshell shades. With his beer gut, flip-flops and EZ-Bake tan, he put me in mind of a lifeguard gone to seed, an aging

Kahuna-type for whom summer begins in April and ends, with a whimper rather than a pyrotechnic Labor Day bang, just shy of Halloween.

For a while I managed to keep my distance. Whenever Tarzan—it was impossible for me to think of him as "Johnny"—appeared on Millie's front porch, I watched silently from my bedroom window or just inside the kitchen screen door and took it all in. Gradually I became obsessed with the guy, or to be more specific, with his brazen, bizarre jungle yodel. I had to know why he did it, whether he'd lost a bet or was trying to impress some girl or was totally out of his mind. I just had to know, though at the time I didn't know why.

"That guy, like, seriously scares me," Natalie admitted one prematurely sweltering afternoon. *Girlfriend* is probably too strong a term for the secret smiles and sustained glances and incessant handholding that comprised the romantic life of our month-old relationship. We had yet to swap spit, mostly because Natalie thought it sounded disgusting, like something you'd be forced to do in the event of an emergency, and even then reluctantly.

Natalie was slender and smart. She had tar-black Cleopatra bangs and brown eyes a size too big for her face. I liked the way her mouth twisted when she got excited. I liked the freckles—twenty-seven by mid-June—marching like a formation of ants across the bridge of her pert nose. I even liked her name: Natalie Elizabeth Cole. Nat Queen Cole, my dad called her.

"What's so scary about him?" I asked.

Natalie shrugged. "My dad says he's, like, shell-shocked."

"I think the term *shell-shocked* only applies to people who've actually fought in a war," I said.

"Not true. Some people get it from just, like, y'know,

whatever," she said, rather unconvincingly. "Life."

"Says who?"

"My dad, for one. But he gets it from watching the news."

Seemingly all Natalie's dad did was watch the news. At the dinner table he referred to anchormen by their first names and did his best to imitate their gratingly enunciated, hyper-responsible patter. He'd spent the previous winter converting their basement into a bomb shelter, complete with a stack of *Copious Crosswords*, a drawer full of can openers and every conceivable flavor of Campbell's soup, in triplicate.

"Well, I guess your dad is an authority on craziness," I said, echoing my mother.

Natalie wrinkled her nose, a gesture she employed to indicate that she found something offensive or disgusting or just plain stupid. "Not funny," she said.

But I couldn't stop. "Hell, he practically holds a PhD in lunacy! He could teach a course at Penn!"

"You're an ass." She took my hand. "What about the drugs?" she said, sotto voce.

"What drugs?"

"I don't know. Everyone says he's on something."

"Did your loopy dad tell you that too?"

Natalie wrinkled her nose so vehemently I thought it would fly off her face and poke me in the eye. She rose to go. "He didn't have to," she said, her tone implying that one of us was helplessly, hopelessly clueless. "It's called common knowledge."

Moments later I found myself standing on Millie Paradise's front porch. Millie was a toy-like woman who cooked in her basement and zipped her head into a puckered bubble of plastic when it rained. I'd never seen a son, or grandson—or anybody, for that matter—visit her, and my first thought upon spotting Tarzan was that the woman had died and this strung-out, shirtless goofball moved in. Millie occasionally delivered chilled Pyrex pans of "ice-box cake"—a scrumptious concoction of graham crackers and chocolate pudding—and I was invariably dispatched to her cramped, cave-like abode to buy a Mass card whenever an ancient neighbor or teenage junkie kicked the bucket. Other than that, my family's dealings with the dowdy, dusty artifact of a woman were virtually non-existent.

Clearly I couldn't rely on Natalie for sound information, and my parents, predisposed against our odd, prodigal neighbor for their own reasons, weren't much help either. I had questions—or one question, rather, and I desperately wanted it answered. It never entered my mind that Tarzan might plead the Fifth. If nothing else, he seemed like a straightforward kind of guy.

I rapped lightly on the storm door, which for some odd reason was decorated with the silhouette of a century-old horse and buggy. Nevertheless my knock sounded like homemade thunder at a high school play, and Tarzan answered right away.

He came outside, or halfway outside, and stood there, his foot propping open the storm door, staring down at me. "Yeah?" was all he said.

He was huge. Even bigger than I'd thought. It took me a minute to find my voice.

"I live next-door," I stammered.

Though he donned his trademark sunglasses, I got the feeling Tarzan was squinting at me as if into the sun. "The Boyles live next-door," he barked. "You a Boyle?" His tone implied he already knew the answer.

"I mean behind you, next-door." I pointed toward the gaping patch of overgrown grass where another row house should've been. The mower was on the fritz again, and my dad had neither the time nor the inclination to get it fixed. Buying a new one was out of the question. He talked a big game about wild flowers and tomato plants and fragrant bushes of mint, basil and parsley, but every spare minute the man had was spent doodling cartoons. "That's my yard."

Tarzan's features didn't budge. He whipped off the sunglasses and I saw that, despite his obvious fatigue and an apparent hangover, his eyes were as clear as a cloudless summer's day.

"You're the Hayes boy. The mailman's kid."

"Yeah," I said.

"I remember when you were yay big," Tarzan said, lowering his paw-like hand to his knee. His mood was lightening. "You used to sit out here for hours chalking up that street. I drew you a dinosaur once, though it looked more like a dog." He shrugged. "I'm no artist. Like your dad." There was an edge to his voice that made this simple statement of fact sound like a slur. He leaned in closer and put a conspiratorial hand—the hand he yodeled with—up to his mouth. "How's yer mom?"

"Not bad," I said. It wasn't exactly a lie.

"Your dad's a lucky man," Tarzan whispered, looking off toward our house. Then, he repeated under his breath, "Lucky man."

I didn't like what he was getting at. I was only fourteen, but I wasn't completely ignorant of adult matters. It was bad enough when my dad got that leering, primitive look in his eye whenever my mother darted from the bathroom to her bedroom in nothing but a towel. I couldn't bear seeing it in a stranger.

"How's *your* mom?" I said.

Millie, who suffered from Alzheimer's, had moved in with her sister and brother-in-law a few neighborhoods away, only days, not coincidentally, before her eldest troublemaking chicken had come home to roost. The woman's illness explained her having recently shown up at our door, disheveled and disoriented, looking for someone named Lulu. Lucia, my mother later informed me, had been Millie's sister. She'd died from some vague illness back in Italy when they were both little girls.

Tarzan looked out across the schoolyard and shook his head sadly. "Not too good, cuz." He placed a meaty paw on my shoulder. I felt the weight of his bulk. "But thanks for asking."

A ghost appeared in the gloom behind him, a soft, curvy shape that eventually took the form of a girl. Or woman, rather, because this person bore little resemblance to the objects of my pubescent affection, the pony-tailed, plaid-skirted schoolgirls who paid me little or no mind. She too wore plaid—a roofer's padded shirt-jacket, thrown over her naked torso—but that's where the similarities ended. She sighed, and raked her fingers through her hair, which was too bright and badly mussed. I caught a glimpse of one perfect, beckoning white breast.

"Who's the kid?" she said, and sneered. "Shit, don't tell me you got another one."

"Relax, hon," Tarzan cooed. "He ain't mine. He's a neighbor. His name's—" here he turned back to me with two raised eyebrows forming boldfaced circumflex. "What's your name, buddy?"

"Buddy," I lied. "Everybody calls me 'Buddy.'"

Tarzan grinned. It was as though the left side of his stubbly face had decided to smile without informing the right. "How about that," he said. He didn't buy it, I could tell, but he was too disinterested to care.

"Buddy, meet Cyndi," he said, formally introducing the blond, who'd already begun to slink away.

"Cynthia," she corrected him, without coming any closer to the door. "Got any coffee?"

"Well, she was Cyndi last night," he confided in a chummy tone. "Emphasis on the Cyn—know what I mean?"

I didn't, not exactly, but I didn't tell Tarzan.

"So," he said, clearly anxious to get back inside and his hands on his semi-clad houseguest, or just on a fresh cup of joe. His amusement with me had already run its course. "What can I do for you? You selling candy for school?"

"School's out for the summer."

Tarzan checked an imaginary watch. "So it is." Again the grin, the raised eyebrows. "What then? Chop-chop. Time is money, cuz."

This from a man who rose at noon.

I wasn't even sure myself what I was doing here, what I hoped to gain by knocking on this supposedly dangerous man's door. I did have that one question, though, which I eventually managed to form. "Why do you do that?"

Tarzan knitted his brows. He looked confused, or mock-confused, like he'd just missed something. He shot a comical glance—one, two—over each shoulder. "Do what?" A mischievous look swam into the placid blueness of his eyes. "Do *Cyndi?*"

I shook my head no, even though that particular question was no less dire and its answer, however muddled or misunderstood, far more intriguing. "That, like, y'know," I said, sounding just like Natalie. "That scream you do."

"Oh, you mean this." And here he took a deep breath and let rip one of the strangest, and most strangely satisfying, sounds I'd ever heard.

I checked the schoolyard for a stampede of elephants and nodded.

Tarzan considered. It didn't appear as though he'd ever given it much thought. Certainly no one had ever asked him about it. He had a reputation for being wacko, a reputation he was well aware of and probably fostered. He shrugged. "Some people go jogging, some people zone out with Jane Pauley on the Today show. Some people guzzle a pot of coffee." He shrugged again, his signature gesture. "I yodel like the Lord of the Apes. It's just how I start my day."

"You do it at twelve noon," I pointed out.

Again he leaned in close, like a man with more than a few secrets to share. I smelled the familiar scents of hair mousse and orange juice and Polo cologne. "My day starts later than yours," he said with a smirk, "because it ends a whole lot later." He waggled his eyebrows again and I laughed. "Should I stop?" he said. "Does it bug you? Did your lovely mother send you over to complain?"

"No, no. Nothing like that," I assured him. "We don't mind."

Tarzan smiled widely and I saw that the man was missing a tooth. "Good," he grunted. "I'm glad."

His polite way of saying get used to it.

"Where've you been?" my mother asked from behind a surgical mask. The woman was a clean freak, but her compulsiveness didn't come naturally to her: she had a host of bizarre, largely unidentifiable allergies, foremost among them furniture polish, which made her break out in

a horrible snakeskin rash. (My dad called her Reptilia, and
not always as lovingly as he might. He'd even created a
mini-comic book for her birthday once, in which a snake-
skinned superwoman with a forked tongue slithered into
the bad guys' lair and secretly straightened up—bad guys
were such slobs!—before injecting them with her
paralyzing venom.) What, with her headscarf and facemask
and iridescent rubber gloves, she looked as though she
were disposing of bio-hazardous material rather than
simply dusting her recently dusted living room. Spring
cleaning, once a week, every week, for as long as I could
remember. "It's not like you to just disappear."

She was right. Geno was the magician of the family, the
kind of kid who got up in the morning, poured himself a
heaping bowl of cereal and was neither seen nor heard
from again until dinner, at which time he'd appear, all
sticky fingers and scraped knees, with just enough time to
wash his hands and take a leak—usually in that
order—before the baked ziti hit the table.

"Next-door," I told her, only half-intending to.

"Next-door? At Clara's?"

I shook my head. It was impossible to lie to my mother.
To hear her tell it, her seventh oldest brother—the uncle
for whom I was named—was a shamelessly compulsive
liar. She'd learned early on to recognize all the signs, right
down to increased pulse rate and dilated pupils. Uncle Sam
was famous for being sent to the corner store for a loaf of
bread or carton of eggs, swiping the groceries while the
shop-owner was busy appeasing a disgruntled senior
citizen or flirting with a young mother, and keeping the
money for himself. "Uh-uh. At Millie's," I said.

"What were you doing over there?" she said after a
moment.

I shrugged. "Talking," I said, and added with what must have seemed a defiant grin, "to the Lord of the Apes."

My mother didn't smile. "To that no-good Johnny, you mean." She put down her perennial dust rag, one of my dad's old Hanes undershirts, cut into quarters. "I don't believe you, Sam. After everything your Dad said about him. He's got a screw loose, that one. He's a bad influence. Not to mention a lousy human being." I was surprised to hear her talk so harshly. For the most part my parents weren't judgmental people. They had their prejudices, for sure, most of them bequeathed to them by their wildly superstitious immigrant parents. But, consciously or not, they did a pretty good job of keeping these prejudices to themselves. If you weren't paying very close attention—or, say, if you happened to be fourteen—it wasn't hard to mistake my provincial yet unprepossessing parents for citizens of the world.

"Why does everybody say that? What's he done, exactly? Maybe if I knew—"

"You're just a kid!" she snapped. "You don't need to know anything more than your parents tell you." She was being unreasonable, which I was unused to, and which, even more than the screaming and vaguely spooky get-up, scared me a little. She caught a glimpse of herself in the large mirror over the couch and softened a bit, adding, "You don't know him like we do, Doll."

But I didn't care to know Tarzan the way my parents knew him. I wanted to know Tarzan for myself.

When my dad got home from work later that day, my mother told him about where I'd been, and with whom I'd spoken, even though I'd begged her not to. They were barely speaking to each other, but when it came to their kids they always found a way to communicate. He found me alone in my room, with my sketchbook opened on my lap, and sat down, cross-legged, next to me on the flimsy rag-rug.

"Mind if I take a look?" he asked.

"It's no good," I said. "Not like yours. Besides, you won't like it."

"I don't have to like it, Sam. It's your personal sketchbook. You don't need my approval."

"That's not what I mean." Reluctantly, I showed him the picture of Tarzan I'd been doodling, complete with Wayfarers and Hawaiian-print jams. I'd transformed his uninspiring brick home into a leafy tree house, the oblivious teenage boy outside the storm door, into Cheetah. There was even a glimpse of Cyndi in the background, in an off-the-shoulder jungle print dress, looking more like a lascivious Wilma Flintstone than Jane, with her lip curled and her staticky hair askew.

"Hmmm," my dad said, half smiling to himself.

"I told you it was no good."

"You're right," he began. "It's not good, it's great. The facial expressions, the shading, the proportions... Remember how much trouble you used to have with foreshortening?" I nodded. "You're a talented kid."

I took the book from him and blushed despite myself. Praise from Gabriel Hayes was hard to come by, but not because he was an unfeeling man. On the contrary, sometimes it seemed he felt too much. Often he just forgot.

"You're a bright kid, too. That's why your behavior today confuses me."

I shifted uneasily on the rug. "I only wanted to ask him a question—"

"You're not using your head here, Bud," he cut me off.

My dad had a habit of doing that. Like a lot of dreamers, he wasn't the most patient person. "You're just not being smart."

I didn't know what to say to this. The conversation had begun so promisingly, with him complimenting my drawing, that I was a bit shocked to find, in the end, I'd only disappointed him.

"We're only trying to protect you."

"From what? Is he a druggie? Is that why you don't want me over there?"

My dad looked flabbergasted, like I'd just puked up rose petals or spoken fluent Japanese.

"Why do you say that?"

I shrugged. "It sorta makes sense."

He started to say something, but stopped short and filled the void with a sigh instead. The man was a prolific sigher. The Eskimos may have a dozen different words for "snow," but Gabriel Hayes had a hundred different types of sigh, all of which expressed some subtle variation of dissatisfaction, ranging from mild physical fatigue to all-out disgruntlement and utter exasperation.

"I don't know about any drugs, Sam. But I do know the guy's a wacko, always has been. He's done some things in the past…." He trailed off, shaking his head. "Drugs," he snorted. "Drugs would be redundant."

He waited for me to meet his gaze. "Sam," he said, pointing to the sketchbook. "This Johnny Paradise is nobody's role model."

"He does what he wants," I offered.

This made my dad laugh. "That he does."

"He doesn't answer to anybody, I mean. What's wrong with that?"

"Nothing, I guess. As long as he doesn't hurt any of the

people he doesn't answer to."

We sat in silence. I knew even then that my dad wasn't telling me everything, partly because his, just like mine, was a limited perspective. Still, Tarzan must've done something to turn my parents against him; they weren't unreasonable people, and the evidence, circumstantial though it may have been—the bravado, the hangovers, the socially unacceptable jungle yodel—was certainly against him. But I couldn't help wondering whether the guy had ever been given a fair trial.

"Does Mom want you to stop drawing cartoons?" I said. "Is that what you've been fighting about?"

"We're not fighting."

"No," I said. "You don't talk to each other long enough to fight."

My dad turned away from me. "She doesn't want me to stop, exactly. She just thinks it's time I faced certain…realities." He turned back toward me, his ears burning red. "Let's face it, chances are Bobo Lazarus and his ilk won't be paying my mortgage any time soon. That deadbeat dog doesn't even have a job!" He shook his head, but whether at Bobo's disappointing performance or his own, it was difficult to tell. "I'm not having much luck as a part-time cartoonist. For whatever reasons."

"I'm one of those reasons," I said, as if the thought had just occurred to me. "Geno too."

"No," he said distantly. "Not really."

"You sure?"

He smiled sadly, and mussed my center-parted, too-long hair. He seemed very tired all of a sudden, like someone who'd spent all day going door-to-door lugging a sack stuffed with utility bills and supermarket coupons in the scorching summer heat. "Yes, Sam-I-Am," he said. "I'm sure."

I wanted more than anything in the world to believe him. I wanted to believe him so badly, in fact, that for the rest of that night and on into the next morning, that's exactly what I did. Then Tarzan called at noon, like some zoological lunchtime whistle, and the primitive, pre-verbal song he sang made the more familiar man's ingenuous words sound manipulative, contrived, patently untrue. I knew then that my dad had looked me straight in the eye and told me a big fat lie. But I couldn't hold it against him. After all, it was the exact same lie he continually told himself.

"Check it out," Bobby McShane said, waving a brown paper bag in my face. The boy's lightless eyes weren't quite level, his sunburned nose comically askew.

"What's in the bag?" I asked.

"What's in the bag?" Bobby repeated. He had a habit of doing this. He also had a habit of creeping me out. I should've ignored him, of course, should've kept walking. But you could no more ignore a brute like Bobby McShane than you could ignore a violent gastro-intestinal reaction to bad shellfish. "Guess, rookie," he said, slapping the brim of my ball cap. "Guess what's in the bag."

I shrugged and, knowing Bobby, said, "A decapitated cat."

"A decapitated cat," he gurgled. "I wish." He watched me and waited. "Guess again."

"A wingless pigeon," I said, beginning to enjoy myself. "Snakes and snails and puppy dog tails."

"Not even close, dick-wad. Look."

Bobby dumped the contents of the bag onto the dead grass between us. I was amazed despite myself. Out tumbled firecrackers and jumping jacks, bottle rockets and pocket bombs, a few Roman candles. July 4th was a couple of weeks away, but neighborhood boys like Bobby were prepping early. After all, fireworks were synonymous with summer. They may've been illegal, but they weren't unavailable. You just had to know where to look. Clearly, Bobby McShane had had his big, canine eyes wide open.

"Wow," I said.

"Wow," Bobby repeated. "How about holy-fucking-Jesus-H-Christ. How about admitting you'd suck my rock-hard mega-dong horse dick for a lousy pack of jumping jacks, let alone the whole goddamn stash."

Bobby McShane was a boisterous, bullying kid, a boy with a pronounced forehead and worrisome sadistic streak, a streak that often played itself out, in gruesome and elaborate ways, upon a host of unfortunate birds and bugs, or the odd luckless squirrel. I'd never liked him, but girls flocked to the guy like gulls to a goldfish cracker. I could never understand it. Bobby was a strange-looking boy by anybody's standards. His blunt, disparate features put me in mind of a puzzle whose pieces, though not quite plumb, could be made to fit together with some effort. It was only when you stepped back and surveyed the image as a whole that you realized the thing made virtually no visual sense.

One of the girls Bobby had under his thick, grimy thumb was Tina Garzone, who entered the ball field on that broiling June day wearing a tight black dress, vaguely Egyptian espadrilles and an outrageous amount of make-up, even for the teenage daughter of an Italian-American beautician. To my dismay, Tina's hair was piled high atop her head, as if daring someone—anyone—to tug on it like a booby trap and pull it crashing down. Elaborate bridesmaid coifs like these, it struck me, were erected purely to taunt and tease uneasy wrecking balls made of twitching male fingers.

"How was the funeral?" Bobby asked her, too preoccupied with his pyrotechnic stash to pay Tina much attention, let alone a direct compliment. As a fourteen-year-old boy, I too was a slave to the obvious allure—the din and senseless destruction, to say nothing of the potential danger—of a makeshift fireworks display. But even I wasn't foolish enough to favor the dime-store explosives over the flesh-and-blood firecracker in the form-fitting dress.

"Think about what you just said," teased Tina. She didn't seem the least bit slighted by her boyfriend's disinterest, probably because her expectations were nil. It was hard to disappoint a girl like Tina Garzone, although Bobby was certainly up to the challenge, and never tired of trying. She caught me staring. "Hey Sam."

"Hey." Tina was a junior in high school. She'd been two years ahead of me at Mother of Sublime Grace; I was surprised and flattered that she even knew my name. Of course, on her lips it sounded more like an aria, sung by a wood nymph, beneath a light spring rain...

"C'mon, Sammy, stop flirting with my girl," Bobby half warned. "Hold it steady." He nodded toward my house. "Pretend you're up in your room and Tina's down here in a bikini, sunbathing."

"Bobby," Tina said.

He leaned in closer. His breath smelled of the cheese fries he'd wolfed down ten minutes before. "Picture her topless, man. Tits out, nipples hard—the whole nine yards."

Unbeknownst to Bobby, I didn't have to work very hard to imagine Tina topless—she and Bobby were playground regulars. On more than one occasion I'd spied them pawing each other, or rather Bobby pawing Tina, a drunken man searching for the light switch on an unfamiliar wall. It was also a little like watching an armed robbery in progress, and out of respect for the victim I'd almost looked away. But when Bobby's groping fingers suddenly got lucky, respect—along with my bulging eyeballs—went out the window. A secret latch had been sprung, and out popped one of Tina's magnificent, chocolate-brown breasts, which her sweet-toothed boyfriend appeared to mistake for a generous scoop of ice cream.

"Pig!" Tina cuffed him on the head. "You're a sex maniac."

"Hey, slut," yelped Bobby. "Hit me again and I'll return the favor."

"Yeah, right," said Tina, unfazed. "Remember what happened when I fell off your handlebars."

"That wasn't even my fault!" Bobby said, sounding like a scavenging sea bird. He tugged on a wayward curl, but, to my disappointment, Tina's frozen wave of hair stayed put. "No way I could see that pothole with this fucking rat's nest in the way."

Tina laughed evilly. It was a rich, sinful, womanly laugh. It made me blush on the spot, as if I'd overheard a lover's quarrel or a foul-mouthed comedy routine.

"Tommy kicked your ass."

Tommy was Tina's older brother. He was built like Grandma Hayes's ancient Frigidaire and was twice as cold. Still, to say that Tommy Garzone had a short fuse was to exaggerate the depths of the man's patience.

"Bad-ass motherfucker," Bobby said, shaking his head. His admiration, even at the cost of his own physical well-being, was obvious.

"What are you straps doing, anyway?"

Bobby flashed his Joker-grin. "Sammy here wants to be an astronaut when he grows up, right Sammy? He's just practicing."

"Fucking pyromaniac," she said to Bobby, unable to keep the admiration out of her voice. I wondered what kind of maniac I'd have to be in order to get Tina to look at me that way. Fourteen-year-old cartoon maniac wasn't going to cut it.

"Don't do it," Tina said to me, slowly shaking her towering head of hair. But I could tell from her tone of voice and the expectant look in her eye that she was as curious as her boyfriend to see what would happen. Their eyes locked, and I was just naïve enough to confuse this look with curiosity about *me*.

"Now or never," Bobby said.

What would Tarzan do?

"Well?" he said. I nodded, and bullying Bobby McShane lit the fuse.

Nothing happened. The firework was a dud. We tried another, and another still. Apparently all the roman candles were duds. Possibly they'd gotten wet somehow, left out in the rain, were dried out and sold cheap to Bobby, who despite what big eyes he had, couldn't tell a potent firecracker from a birthday candle.

"Back so soon?" Tina said. "Tell me, is the moon really made of cheese?"

"What the fuck?" Bobby said.

"Stick to setting fires in garbage cans, babe. You're not cut out for astrophysics." Tina shot me an appraising, inquisitive look, the equivalent of that age-old loaded question *Who is more foolish, the fool or the fool who follows him?*

"I'm going home to get changed," she said, ostensibly to Bobby. Her eyes were on me. "Come around when you get bored of not blowing things up." She pinched her boyfriend on the cheek, and I made the mistake of laughing.

"What the fuck's so funny?" Bobby snapped. "This shit wasn't cheap."

"Live and learn," I said, trying not to sound too much like a smart-ass. "You could always resell it."

"Yeah, you're right," Bobby said, a sinister look slithering into his eyes like a tattooed serpent sliding through the sockets of a skull. "How much you willing to give me for it?"

"Me?" I said. "Stick it up your ass." I was of a mind that if you didn't talk tough with a bully like Bobby, you were doomed to a life of wedgies and masochistic KICK ME signs and a perennial wet head, compliments of the nearest toilet bowl.

"I've got a better idea," Bobby said, grabbing me by the collar. I glanced over my shoulder, but Tina was nowhere to be seen. My assailant tightened his grip while with his other hand he brandished the baton-like, formerly worthless firework. I finally understood just how much of a maniac Bobby McShane really was. "How about I shove it up *your* ass instead?"

"Whoa, whoa," came a vaguely familiar, slightly hoarse voice from behind us. "If anybody's sticking anything up anybody's ass, it's gonna be the Trans Am of my right foot up the Hershey Highway of Maggie McShame's bastard son."

We turned, Bobby still clutching me by the shirt, and found Tarzan cradling two gargantuan slices of what smelled like Ernie's extra-anchovy pizza in one hand, a vase-size Styrofoam fountain soda in the other. By the look of it he'd already started in on his pungent lunch on the way back from the pizzeria; his stubbly cheek bulged with what could easily have passed for chewing tobacco, and his substantial chin glistened with translucent orange grease. He must've left the Wayfarers at home.

"You OK, Buddy?"

I tried to nod even though I was far from OK. But Bobby's Vader-grip made moving my head up and down problematic.

It took him a minute, but Bobby finally caught on. "Who's Buddy?" he said.

Tarzan's face instantly changed as though he'd just gotten word that someone had sideswiped his beloved Firebird or that Cyndi, despite her rough-and-tumble, devil-may-care demeanor, didn't really enjoy their down-time together. "Who's talking to you, McShame?" he snapped, employing a familiar familial nickname that I, for all my talk of standing up to bullies, would never dare employ.

At the second mention of the wholly unflattering nickname, Bobby seemed to shrink a little, like a cotton shirt left in the dryer too long.

"You wanna take your grimy mitts off my cousin?" Tarzan said. He phrased it in the form of a question, the gent.

Bobby loosened his grip, then let go of me completely.

"I was just kidding around," he stammered, though it came out sounding more like *There, there. Easy, boy.*

Tarzan winked at me when Bobby turned away. "What's Maggie up to?" he asked the older boy, his mood lightening. "Christ, last time I saw Maggie McShame I was counting the curls on the top of her bobbing orange head…"

Bobby turned a shade of red to rival his mother's lusty Irish lips. He wasn't used to biting his tongue, though he was making a veritable meal out of it now. Part of me felt bad for the bully. But the other part—the Tarzan part—felt like asking him if I should pass him the ketchup.

"Tell her Johnny says hi, will ya?" Tarzan widened his eyes in surprise and made an O shape with his stinky fish-filled mouth. "Silly me," he said, as though he'd made a serious faux pas. "Johnny Paradise," he added for clarification. "Junior."

"Thanks," I said, once Bobby was out of earshot.

"My pleasure," Tarzan chewed. "I can't stand that little prick." He presented me with the half-eaten pizza, the oil of which had begun to soak through the flimsy paper plate. The smell alone was borderline unbearable. The brownish, leech-like anchovies really did look hairy, even though my mother often put them in tossed salads and had repeatedly explained to her sons that what could pass for parallel strands of hair were in reality edible, follicle-thin fish bones. "Wanna bite?"

I shook my head no even though I was hungry. Talking to Tarzan was one thing. But sharing a meal with the man—and especially a meal as unappetizing as this—was a transgression I was in no way prepared for. And yet if this was somebody's idea of forbidden fruit, why shouldn't I take my neighbor up on the offer? If I truly wanted to be like Tarzan, or at least Tarzan-like, I had to start somewhere. Anchovy pizza was as good a place as any.

"On second thought," I said, "maybe just a little."

"Good man."

Tarzan bent toward me, holding the gooey slice aloft. I bit down, worked the very strong flavors around my mouth for a minute, and then forced the whole half-masticated mess, with mixed results, down my tightening throat.

"Well?"

"Salty," I said, trying not to gag. "But not bad."

"But not good either," he read my mind.

"An acquired taste."

"That it is, cuz," Tarzan replied in his vague fashion, amused, as usual, at his own private jokes. "That it is."

"Bobby's mom," I said, initiating a conversation I wasn't convinced I had any right or reason, really, to initiate.

"That kid doesn't have a mom," interrupted Tarzan. "Rumor has it he fell out of the sky, tossed out the window of a passing U.F.O."

"Ha-ha. That's pretty funny."

He nodded in agreement.

"Um, why do they call her McShame?"

Tarzan craned his neck to indicate disbelief, disappointment, even. "It's called a pun, Buddy, a play on words. McShane? McShame? Get it?"

"I get it," I said, a little insulted.

"You mean how did she get that nickname? You're a bright boy," Tarzan said, sizing me up. "Do the math."

Math, of course, wasn't the problem. Although it wasn't my favorite subject, when forced to I could add and subtract, multiply and divide. I could convert decimals to fractions, measure angles, solve for x. It was xxx I had trouble coming up with answers for.

Tarzan took pity on me. "You know how some people are given nicknames opposite of what you might expect?"

"Like naming a big guy Tiny," I said, "or a short guy Stretch."

"Precisely!" shouted Tarzan, adopting a twitty British accent. "Now let us consider the peculiar case of Ms. Maggie McShame."

I thought this over. "She has no shame," I offered.

"None that I know of," admitted Tarzan. We'd reached the corner of our block, the point at which our paths were forced to diverge. But I wasn't ready, just yet, to leave the Lord of the Ape's company, and anxious to impress a man it wouldn't necessarily be in my best interest to impress.

"But it works the other way too."

Tarzan slurped his oversized soda and regarded me warily, or mock-warily, since it was always difficult to tell where the man stood, emotionally speaking. Even his rare expressions of seemingly genuine emotion had an edge of sarcasm about them. And this, rather than the badder-than-thou attitude or marathon skirt chasing, was the man's true talent: despite all the smoke and mirrors, despite having the psychological profile of a set of Russian nesting dolls, he came across as a run-o'-the-mill-what-you-see-is-what-you-get-tell-it-like-it-is blue-collar guy. My hero.

"How so?" he smiled, obviously pleased with his young protégé's progress, and chewed ice.

"Her actions are shameful," I said, "so the name McShame actually fits."

Tarzan folded the paper plate in half and neatly stuffed it into the now-empty Styrofoam cup. Not for the first time he put his hand on my shoulder, and made a point of fixing me with his oceanic blue eyes. "There's nothing shameful about a blow-job, Buddy," he said, and for once I was almost certain he might be serious. Then he smiled his near-perfect "gotcha" smile, the sporadic gaps intimating a flawed human being behind an otherwise movie star-mouth. "But I like the way you think."

The spare back bedroom of our house doubled as my dad's studio. This is where he kept his drafting board and drawing supplies: tomato cans full of magic markers and colored pencils; a T-square that doubled nicely as Thor's hammer when Geno and I played superheroes; a sickly-pink eraser big as a block of cheese. Headshots of various dogs, both real and imagined, decorated the walls, the likes of Snoopy and Odie and Underdog and Zeke. Bobo Lazarus was there, by turns angry and surprised, shamefaced and confused, happy and sad. My dad had two tiers of milk cartons full of cassettes—he rarely worked without music—and a mini-fridge in one corner, where he kept chocolate milk and mini-cereal boxes, the odd ham sandwich. He'd dubbed it his Fortress of Solitude, though in darker moods my mother was known to refer to it as Fantasyland. The aspiring animator could be found here on Sunday mornings and most nights during the week, working under a merciless retractable desk lamp, interrogating his elusive cartoons as if they were privy to secret information he would never uncover on his own. He'd sworn them off more times than I, for one, cared to count. No matter what he told his family, Gabriel Hayes could no more stop doodling cartoons than Bobby McShane could stop bullying smaller kids or Johnny Paradise stop performing his mid-day Tarzan routine.

"Sammy-boy!" my dad called to me as I passed by his studio on my way downstairs. "Let me show you something."

Entering the room, I heard Daryl Hall on the radio lamenting the fact that someone had his body and now wanted his soul. My dad reached into his portfolio and retrieved a small stack of storyboards. As he arranged them on his drafting table, I saw that they portrayed the misadventures of a certain working-class canine I'd come to think of as a sort of two-dimensional pet.

"Well?" he said, trying not to beam. "What do you think?"

At first glance I thought they were terrific, and told him so. I'd always been a big fan of my dad's work—maybe his biggest fan. But even to my inexperienced eye the man seemed to have outdone himself with these latest drawings: both more artistically adept and yet simpler somehow, more direct. Distilled.

"I thought Bobo was on his way out," I said, smiling.

I can't go for that, no can do…

My dad nodded, as though his star canine was the one who made these sorts of decisions and he had little say in the matter. "So did I. But you know Bobo as well as I do. The dog has a mind of his own." He put down the storyboards but continued to study them, clearly awed by their polish even as he continued to search the panels for telltale imperfections. "I guess a part of me still believes I can do it all—support a family and make my art and…" he trailed off.

"And what?"

"And not ignore your mom," he said. He looked at me. "Or my boys."

"Yeah, but what if you can't?" I said, surprising myself. No sooner had I spoken the words than I wished I could take them back, show up at the Speech Store, receipt in hand, and exchange them for something less emotionally dear.

"Huh?" To look at the man you wouldn't think the downside of his plan had ever crossed his mind. He seemed annoyed with me now, as though I'd purposely breathed the decidedly un-magic word that would break the spell that enabled him to create his all-too-ephemeral art. He smiled wanly at me but I could see him shutting down, a carnival whose festive lights were extinguished in stages, ride by blazing, dark-defying ride.

"Then I guess I'd just have to turn in my mail bag," he said with a grin. "Good riddance."

That's when the weight of what he was saying—and the crux of my parents' unsettling estrangement—began to sink in.

"You mean quit?" The notion that my dad might stop being a mailman and focus full-time on his cartoons both frightened and yet somehow excited me. Would he actually do it? After all this time, would my hyper-responsible father finally take that exhilarating, near-suicidal step off the edge of the cliff? I wanted so much for him. But I was only fourteen, and wanted even more for myself.

"Don't worry," he said, catching the distressed look on my face. "It won't ever come to that."

But what if it does? I couldn't help thinking. The double life my dad was leading was beginning to take its toll, and he was threatening to quit his job. At the very least he was entertaining the possibility. Which to him must've seemed like the artistic equivalent of a prison break, but would mean nothing less than financial ruin for the rest of us. No wonder my mother was worried.

I stood silently at my dad's elbow, watching him work. There was no denying that the man was happiest when immersed in the creation of some new cartoon. His eyes were keen, his smile, fixed and broad. He was hunched over his comatose cartoon dog like a local hero about to successfully administer mouth-to-mouth. How could something that made him so undeniably happy threaten to make the rest of us so irreparably sad?

My desire to right the unwitting wrong I'd committed outweighed my ambivalence about my dad quitting his job. The last thing I wanted to be was an obstacle, yet another hurdle in need of being cleared on the long and winding road to artistic fulfillment. Besides, it was a flippant threat, nothing more, made mostly in jest. I was almost sure of it.

"Go for it," I said. But my dad didn't acknowledge the comment—he'd already turned back to his drafting table and was avidly exploring the brave new world of Bobo Lazarus. The Fortress of Solitude was meant to be just that. As usual, I'd worn out my welcome.

The next day the temperature had dipped into the low nineties, and I again found myself accidentally-on-purpose hanging out with the one person I was forbidden to see. The funny thing about living next-door to Tarzan was that I didn't have to be standing next to the man to feel his influence. I heard it every day, at high noon, and secretly, silently responded to the sound of his voice like any obedient jungle animal, a monkeyboy in the making, a Tarzan in training. Gabriel Hayes' life was not his own. He was a slave to a well-paying but mind-numbing job, a job that was killing him, a job he'd always hated, and with good reason. He was a slave to his family, to a pretty if hyper-practical woman and two good kids, but kids nonetheless, kids with needs and demands and all kinds of problems that required solving on an almost hourly basis. He was a slave to his art as well, though here, at least, he didn't seem so much to mind, in fact preferred it this way. By contrast, Tarzan had sole ownership of his life; his fate was in his own massive, sun-colored hands.

"My dad doesn't like you," I blurted.

We were in Millie Paradise's back yard, where Tarzan had

set up a Mr. Turtle pool and, pinned to the clothesline above it, a vinyl tablecloth emblazoned with silver bells, bow-tied candy canes and Christmas wreaths. The pool into which he'd sunk his big, sloth-clawed toes, was for his twin nieces Anna and Vanna, who were four. They rarely visited—in fact he hadn't seen them in months—but according to Tarzan it was good to be prepared. In the way of said preparation, he had a six-pack of Budweiser in a Playmate cooler on one side of his beach chair, a boom box blaring Bruce Springsteen on an overturned milk crate on the other. Atop his head teetered a paper crown which he'd charmed out of the "busty chica" who'd sold him his cellophaned, flame-broiled lunch. He looked ridiculous, of course, like working-class royalty on his folding madras throne. But when Tarzan pointed out that there were worse ways to spend a lazy summer afternoon, I was inclined to agree.

"Your dad doesn't like me?" he said, feigning hurt feelings. "No shit, Sherlock. Gabriel Hayes ain't exactly named in my will either."

"You've got a will?" I said.

"A will and a way," he said vaguely.

"Well, I mean he doesn't know you, right?"

Tarzan took a long pull on his Bud and shrugged. "We grew up together."

"Yeah, but you guys were never really friends. You never hung out."

"No. Your dad was a…what's the word for a guy who keeps to himself?"

"Loner?" I suggested, though it was hard to picture my dad in a leather jacket and motorcycle boots.

Tarzan shot me a tolerant smile. "Not exactly, Buddy. Fancier than that."

"Introvert."

"Yeah, that's it. Your dad was an introvert."

"You mean he was a nerd."

"No. Yeah. Sort of. Hold on," he said, "I love this line."

I waited for him to finish singing along with the Boss about heroes and redemption and dirty hoods. "Sort of?"

He drank some more beer, waving away a bee that'd been buzzing around the top of the can, apparently angling for a swig. "Nerds get teased, nerds get picked on. Your dad was smart and kept his distance. He didn't get beaten up on a routine basis—ow! Fucker!" The bee had stung Tarzan on the back of his hand, and paid for it. "Now," he continued, "that was partly because of your Pop-pop, out of fear."

I'd never really known my paternal grandfather. I'd heard stories, of course, most of them not good. One of the few photographs my parents had of the man showed him and my dad, age seven, standing beside a set of Lionel trains. They stood at opposite ends of a basement platform, my Pop-pop forcing what, technically, would be classified as a smile, my pint-sized paterfamilias holding his own hand and looking as though he'd just been caught touching something he may or may not have been told not to touch.

"My Pop-pop was a crazy old man when he died," I said.

"Yeah, well he was an even crazier young man when I was a kid. Hothead, too. He used to hurl trashcans at the alley cats for pissing on his tomato plants. And the older he got, the crazier he seemed. Even the younger guys made a point of staying on his good side. Not that he even had one. Shit, he wasn't much bigger than you are now. But size doesn't matter." Tarzan laughed, inexplicably. "Even when they tell you it matters, cuz, it don't. Remember that."

"Who's they?"

He laughed again, at my expense, I was sure. "You'll find out soon enough." He crushed the can between his palms like a superhero squashing a bomb. "Bull—you know his nickname was Bull?" I nodded. "Bull didn't take shit from nobody. Crazy beats strong every time." Tarzan's belch was soulful, saxophonic and synchronous with the end of "Thunder Road"—in short everything you'd expect from a beast reared on bananas and beer. "Remember that, too."

"Crazy beats strong," I repeated.

"Right. Take a deck of cards. Everybody looks for an ace. And the Ace of Spades has this reputation as the 'death card'—oooh. Nobody cheats death, right? People forget the most powerful card is the joker. And why?"

"The joker's wild," I said.

"Bingo, right again," Tarzan beamed, sounding like a half-soused game show host. "A joker's capable of anything. He can be whatever he wants."

I thought about what he said. "So you never picked on my dad because my Pop-pop was crazy?"

"Hey, I never picked on nobody."

"That's a double negative," I piped, mimicking Sister Margaret-Mary. "It means just the opposite."

Tarzan glared at me. Clearly he was taken aback, but just how far back was anybody's guess, least of all mine. It seemed I'd offended him, which up till now hadn't been an especially easy thing to do. "I stand corrected," he said. "I never picked on *anybody*." He made a fey gesture with his hand and said, "I'm a lover not a fighter" in a high-pitched voice. "Believe it or not, I never started a single fight in my entire life. You saw what happened with that bee—totally unprovoked." Another sly smile, followed by a fresh swig of beer. "Now, I've been known to finish a few fights."

"So other people never picked on him because of my Pop-pop."

"Look, Buddy, your dad was always a little different. Not in a bad way, exactly. At least he could draw, which was a plus. Most kids think drawing's cool."

"If you say so."

"I mean, the guy's no Michael Angelo. He's a cartoonist, for crying out loud."

"Not even."

"But he's got talent," Tarzan insisted, poking me in the chest more roughly, I hoped, than he'd intended. "That's obvious."

He was being generous now, and I wasn't sure why. Maybe Tarzan was trying to shame me. If so, it'd worked. "I guess," I admitted.

"One more," he said, consulting his oft-checked, non-existent wristwatch. "For the road."

"Big plans tonight?"

"The biggest." I raised my eyebrows to show that I was all ears. "Well, aside from being Saturday night—which in my book is reason enough to celebrate—I got a wedding."

"Yeah? Whose? Yours?"

"Ha, ha. Not in this lifetime, cuz."

Tarzan seemed convinced, but I wasn't so sure. He was a confirmed bachelor, but it wasn't hard to see him ten years down the road, tethered to a wife and kids, growing fat and gray with a Cyndi or a Julie or an Ann-Marie. How long could he keep it up, anyway, this eternal Endless Summer routine? What happens to a guy like Tarzan after the temperature plummets and the trees go bare?

"An old friend," he said. "Very old friend, in fact. Neighborhood guy. Your dad would know him. Jackie Cassady."

The name rang some distant warning bell. Was Jackie Cassady the guy who flooded a police cruiser—soaking the dozing officer inside—by turning on a nearby fire hydrant? Or was he the guy who hijacked the iceman's truck on a lark and unloaded its arctic cargo into the neighborhood swimming pool? Could they be one and the same person? Could they *not* be one and the same person?

"They used to call us Butch Cassady and the Sundance Kid," Tarzan said. I couldn't see his eyes, but I would've bet a month's allowance that they sported one of those nostalgic "faraway" looks.

"Which one were you?" I joked.

"Funny, Buddy. You must get that from your mom. Razor-tongued."

I wasn't about to discuss my mother's tongue, on any level, with Tarzan. Whenever he brought her up, I did my best to steer the conversation away from that hazardous stretch of road. I was reluctant to fuel any long-burning fires that might still be smoldering in her honor beneath Tarzan's brawny barrel chest. "I guess you're going to have a pretty good time tonight, huh," I said, lamely changing the subject.

"Shit, I sure hope so, Buddy. I'm the best man."

There was a moment of silence, presumably while we both considered the phrase "best man." Was Tarzan, in fact, the best man for the job? He was skilled at a lot of the things you might expect a working class man-child to be skilled at. But even at fourteen the irony of Tarzan, a man for whom pledging life-long allegiance to one woman seemed not merely foolish but the telltale sign of some sinister, largely self-willed form of insanity, standing mute witness to the Sacrament of Holy Matrimony wasn't wasted on me.

"Well, I'm going to see *E.T.*," I piped up, adding, "With a girl."

I understandably had trouble referring to Natalie as my girlfriend in the company of this man who seemed to see most human relationships—at least relationships between the sexes—as drawbacks, liabilities, incomprehensible self-sabotage. "Don't bring sand to the beach" might've been his advice, had he ever left the shore in the first place. If a girlfriend at his age seemed borderline masochistic, having one at my age was downright suicidal.

"Space aliens," Tarzan scoffed, deciding, for once, not to take the bait.

"You don't believe there's life on other planets?"

"Nah," he said. "If there was, and they had half a brain, they would've knocked us off a long time ago."

"Maybe they're just waiting for the right time," I said, thinking of the End Times, the approaching millennium, the likelihood of the world being reduced to rubble by invaders from another galaxy, if not our very own Milky Way.

"Or maybe the little green men are already here, and have been all along."

I didn't get it, not at first. "What does that mean?"

"The enemy within," Tarzan said dreamily, staring off into space.

"Well one way or another, I think the world's in a lot of trouble," I said, which happened to be a very real fear of mine, though it was the first time I'd actually said it aloud, in the presence of another human being. It felt good.

Tarzan snorted again; this time it rankled me.

"What, you don't think the world needs saving?"

Tarzan looked at me as though I had just blown him a kiss. "The world's always needed saving, Buddy, and it always will." He angled his movie star mug toward the raging sun and chuckled condescendingly to himself. "But not from egg-headed space aliens or homicidal robots."

"Okay," I said. "What then?"

I expected him—a la Sister Margaret-Mary, a la Natalie's dad—to conjure up images of warhead-stocked silos, of power-crazed madmen with blinking panic buttons. In short, I thought he'd philosophize that humans needed saving from nobody or nothing so much as themselves.

Instead Tarzan smiled. "Ain't it obvious?" he said, standing up and straightening his silly paper crown. He drew a deep breath and began to beat his massive chest. Then he launched into his still-impressive Tarzan impersonation, undermining the Boss' authority and scaring a small flock of pigeons off a nearby roof.

He sat back down and looked right through me.

"The world needs saving from guys like me."

When I got home I called Natalie and asked her to meet me at the playground after dinner, a full two hours before the movie, and as such our first real date was due to begin. I'd suddenly decided it wasn't working out, this fledgling, pre-adolescent love affair between our fingers, and resolved to put an end to it, extra-terrestrials be damned. All through dinner, mechanically scarfing my mother's tuna ronis, I kept thinking that Tarzan wouldn't settle for an unpopular nose-wrinkler with a crazy dad, Tarzan wouldn't waste his time holding hands. I was kidding myself, of course, but suddenly I longed for a girl with frosted hair, a smart-mouthed, sleepy-eyed girl who wore too much mascara and walked around half-naked, looking for coffee. Natalie was never going to be that girl. The girl guzzled nothing but Yoo-hoos.

Natalie surprised me by showing up in a clingy cotton dress, a striped off-the-shoulder number that accentuated her long legs and exposed part of her pretty, dimpled clavicle. There were purple Jellies and baby doll socks on feet that once sported only Converse All-Stars. Her hair, formerly flat, black and glossy as a wet chalkboard, was now twice its size, teased-out with plum highlights. There was a trace of very adult mascara inked onto her doll-like eyes. All this for a wayward space alien with a penchant for Reese's Pieces?

At the astonishing sight of my soon-to-be-ex-girlfriend, I forgot what I'd so desperately wanted to tell her. Luckily, Natalie confessed to already knowing.

"You do?" I said, amazed.

She nodded. "I'm, like, ready when you are."

"You are?"

Natalie nodded again, lowered the lids of her eyes and inexplicably leaned her suddenly strange face into mine.

We stood this way for a few seconds, until it dawned on me that ultra-squeamish Natalie was waiting for a kiss. This was a breakthrough in our relationship, a relationship I had rashly all but written off. I'd never actually tried to kiss Natalie before, mostly because she'd made it painfully clear that kissing not only didn't interest her, it kind of turned her stomach. "Think about it," she'd said. "The kinds of stuff people put into their mouths." Just when or why she'd had a change of heart was hard to say. But her heart, along with her boyish clothes and blasé countenance, certainly had changed.

"Hey!" she squealed, reeling backwards when our lips finally touched. "First things first," she giggled. Then, glancing at my hands, Natalie stopped giggling. "Where is it?" she asked.

"Where's what?"

"Duh, Sammy. Where's the ring?"

"The wha—"

"Hey buddy," I heard someone call, and promptly ignored it. Then I realized that I was Buddy, and Tarzan the guy doing the calling.

"C'mere," he said, waving me over. "Make it snappy."

I could smell the Polo on him from clear across the schoolyard. In fact, if it weren't for Tarzan's signature scent, with which he'd baptized himself liberally, I might not have recognized him. His hair was slick and swept back, as always. But gone were the pineapple-printed shorts he'd worn when first we'd met, and the grimy jeans and Dickies I'd spotted Tarzan returning home from work in, when the man bothered to work at all. In their place was a swanky double-breasted tuxedo and gleaming spectator shoes. Sans socks.

"Cool shoes."

Tarzan peered down at his feet as though the Shoe Fairy had surreptitiously swapped his down-and-out work boots with Michael Jackson's very own two-toned beauties. "Yeah, they are pretty cool," he admitted.

"Won't you get blisters like that?"

"Blisters!" he guffawed. "Gee, Buddy, I don't know. What I do know is James Bond never wears socks." He grinned. "Tarzan the Ape-Man sure didn't wear any friggin' socks!"

I laughed. "James Bond never wears socks?"

"Not in the sack," he said, as though he had it on good authority.

"Nice monkey suit, too," I joked, though Tarzan didn't seem to get it.

"You mean this?" he said, pulling proudly on his lapels.

"A best man has to look his best, cuz. Part of the job description."

"Ah. Where's Cyndi?" I asked, peering over a huge, black shoulder, anxious to see what the sleepy sex kitten would look like in taffeta and high heels.

Tarzan reached inside his jacket and whipped out his trademark tortoiseshell Wayfarers. "How can I put this? Cyndi's not the kind of girl you take to a wedding."

"She's not?"

"I'm flying solo tonight, Stud." He lightly beat his giant Oreo cookie of a chest. "Me, Tarzan," he grunted. "No Jane."

No Jane? What did he mean "No Jane"? Wasn't Jane the whole point?

"Who's the little piece of tail?" Tarzan nodded toward the playground, where Natalie stood impatiently tapping a plastic-slippered foot. She looked the epitome of the scorned woman, even though I hadn't quite scorned her, and full-blown womanhood was still a few years away.

"That's my fiancée. Or so I'm told."

"Listen, kid," Tarzan said, ignoring my comment and crouching down next to me. "I thought some more about your question, about why I do…what I do. I gave you a shitty answer before. We're buddies—ha—and you deserve better."

"Wow," I said, excited despite myself. "Okay."

"So, you want to know the real reason why I scream like Tarzan? You remember why Tarzan—the real Tarzan—screamed like that?"

"The real Tarzan," I said, pretending to be a smart-ass.

Silence.

"Not exactly," I admitted.

"Well I do. See, he screamed whenever he needed space.

How would you feel, shut up in that tree house all day with only Jane and that crazy chimp to talk to. The point is, Tarzan screamed that way whenever he wanted to *party*."

That was it. Tarzan, the ultimate party animal. My smile headed south. I felt gypped.

"Don't do it," Tarzan said, folding himself into his sleek Firebird before I could demand a better answer.

"Huh?"

"Take my advice," he said, sounding suspiciously like the kind of used car salesman who says *Trust me*. But with the sunglasses and the monkey suit and the slicked-back hair, the stubble and the purring ride and the five-hundred-thousand-dollar smile, how could a fourteen-year-old boy not take this man's advice? "You're too young to get hitched."

Then Tarzan, a.k.a. Johnny Paradise, pumped up the jungle rhythms emanating from his overgrown Matchbox car and flashed an unforgivable smile. "Trust me," he actually said, and sped away.

The look on Natalie's face when I returned to the schoolyard told me I wouldn't get to sit next to her in a darkened movie theatre any time soon, let alone get another shot at a kiss.

A gust of frigid air enveloped me as I entered the Richtown library, a half-frozen ghost pausing to wrap me in its icy embrace before passing through my sweaty flesh and dissolving in the heat. Modest though it was—but boasting an imposing iron gate and fancifully medieval façade—the library was cozy and inviting in winter, what with the abundance of dusty holiday decorations and the whole place smelling of tea water and the radiators pinging back and forth like conversing wartime subs. But I liked it best in summer, when the air conditioning was cranked up to arctic BTU's and the stacks were all but empty.

I slipped past Mrs. Dunbar, in her pink-and-green Fair Isle cardigan; she was too busy drawing her bony finger through the butterscotch icing stuck to a cellophane Tastykake wrapper to say hello. Mrs. Dunbar had a mouth full of sweet teeth, and there was always a plastic bowl of complimentary hard candy or bite-size chocolate bars at the checkout. Today it was silver, coin-sized Peppermint Patties, one of my favorites. The thought of walking home with a creamy piece of candy melting in my mouth put an involuntary smile on my face.

I went to the stacks thinking I would peruse a few books on homemade Halloween costumes. It was a little early to be dreaming of October, but it was hard not to, considering how the library sat catty-corner from a massive abandoned church the neighborhood kids called St. Nobody's. St. Nobody's was a famous Richtown ruin, the kind of place kids instinctively led their visiting cousins to, in the hopes of lending a little local myth or mystery to what was essentially a rather dull and depressing working class river ward. The destruction was pervasive: over the years, vandals had carted off all the external statuary; the semi-shingled roof, which looked to have borne more than its fair share of twisters, was torn off or collapsed in places; the grass was more yellow than green, wildly overgrown; many of the stained glass windows were shattered or marred by baseball- or stone-sized holes. In a few months the long-dead place would come alive, like some hastily sewn golem, with autumnal adolescent dares and secret midnight séances. Come Mischief Night, the shamelessly vandalized church would be briefly resurrected only to be subjected to even further victimization. But now, on a broiling afternoon in June, it just looked forlorn and forgotten, like a huge broken toy God hadn't played with in years.

I often tried to picture St. Nobody's in its heyday, but even with the roof repaired and the ivy cut back and the smashed kaleidoscopic windows made whole, it seemed far from inviting. The pitifully dilapidated place had always reminded me of a television spot for a haunted castle on the boardwalk in Brigantine. Whenever I peered up at one of the long lancet windows, I saw a sun-shy vampire shrink from view.

I was hoping to go all-out this year, and resolved to scare the pants off anybody and everybody who crossed my path. Instead I was distracted by a table full of *Cracked* magazines, the covers of which displayed dead-on caricatures of Coco and Leroy, Detectives Cagney and Lacey, select members of the conniving Ewing clan. To hear my dad tell it, the artwork wasn't as polished as that of its rival, *Mad*, but it was good enough for me. I settled in with half a dozen ratty magazines and hardly noticed any imperfections.

"Not exactly Shakespeare," I heard a familiar raspy voice half-giggle over my shoulder. I turned and saw Tina Garzone, in a raspberry tank top and white denim shorts, smiling like she'd just gobbled the sort of satisfying summer dessert she so temptingly resembled. "I wish comic books were on *my* summer reading list," she said, brandishing a black, cloth-bound book.

Strictly speaking, *Cracked* wasn't a comic. But I wasn't about to split hairs with a girl as remarkably coiffed as Tina.

"And you, Sammartino Hayes," she grinned even as she knitted her brow. "I expected more from the Michelangelo of MSG."

I looked away and shrugged, painfully aware that my ears had just turned an unfortunate shade of red.

"What can I say? You caught me. I'm a closet comic book junkie."

Tina shrugged back and sat down beside me. She smelled of garlic and pink lemonade. "To hear Bobby tell it, you're a closet a lot of things."

I didn't know what to say to this, so I said nothing. I'd learned at a very young age that most people are happy to talk whenever someone is willing to just sit back and listen.

Tina smiled slyly and moved closer to me on the bench. "Is what Bobby said true?" she whispered, a glint of evil—a glint of her boyfriend, it struck me—in her mesmerizing, burnt-sugar brown eyes. "Do you have a *bodyguard?*"

"We're friends," I said, supposing she meant Tarzan.

"He's old enough to be your dad," she snorted.

"Well he's not my bodyguard."

Tina smiled and moved her heavily bangled hand to my leg. "I get it," she said, giving me a squeeze. I wondered whether, if I were a form of produce, Tina would find me fresh enough to buy and bring home. She shot me a look I immediately understood was meant to cure me, on the spot, of any trendy fey afflictions. "Do you think I'm pretty?" she asked out of the blue.

"Definitely," I said, though it was hard to meet her gaze.

Apparently an unqualified affirmation wasn't good enough for Tina Garzone. "I don't mean, y'know, objectively," she said, squeezing my thigh a second time. She glanced over her edible brown shoulder. Mrs. Dunbar was asleep at the reception desk, doubled over as if in pain. The butterscotch Krimpets had done her in. I could hear her snoring from clear across the room, even above the collective drone of the air conditioners, to say nothing of the amped-up beating of my hyperventilating heart.

"If you think I'm pretty," Tina said, "you need to prove it."

Was kissing Tina Garzone worth a bloody nose or black eye—or worse—courtesy of homicidal Bobby McShane? Because of course Bobby would find out. One way or another, eventually word would leak out. Word always does.

So I had to ask myself how many bones, how many pints of iron-rich blood a boy my unremarkable size could afford to spare in the name of adolescent lust.

Tina leaned in close and, keeping her eyes on mine, casually lapped at the palm of her right hand with her pretty pink tongue. Quite a few bones, was my naïve, knee-jerk response. A paramedical six-pack of plasma, give or take a plastic-handcuffed can.

It turned out that kissing Tina Garzone wasn't an option. She already had her proof, seeing as how her saliva-slick hand had surreptitiously found its way inside my red gym shorts.

"Oh," I said.

"A-haaa," Tina giggled. "Surprise, surprise. Sammartino Hayes thinks I'm pretty."

"What are you doing?" I asked, stupidly, as though there might be a perfectly legitimate reason for Bobby McShane's girl to be tugging on me like the knob of a defiantly locked door.

She didn't answer; she was too engrossed in her work. I couldn't help noticing how blatantly Tina looked her age, how surprisingly unsure of herself and suspiciously young in light of the rather adult motion she was making with her hand.

"This isn't a good idea," I eventually croaked, even as I decided that Tina's slippery one-handed massage trumped the squaring of the circle and the invention of the wheel and, quite possibly, my Nonna Dellapenna's sugar-coated fried dough. Try as I might, I couldn't keep from worrying what might happen if the slumbering librarian were to catch Tina red-handed, whacking poetic, and Richtown Library's most faithful patron with his dorky short pants down.

"If Mrs. Dunbar wakes up—"

"Shut up!" hissed Tina. "Forget about ancient Mrs. Dumbbell!" She was perspiring now along her hairline, damp, dark curls like little cursive letters clinging to her scalp. Maybe, taken altogether and arranged a certain way, they would spell out a warning to high tail it back home. Maybe not. Either way, the air was on full-tilt but Tina was losing her cool. "What's taking so long?"

"Nerves, I guess."

Tina made an unkind face, and it seemed the less charitable she grew the sexier she became to me. "Shit, Sam, if you had any *nerves* at all, this would've been over and done with ten minutes ago."

She had a point. But I was hopelessly distracted by the fact that we were in a very public place doing a very private thing, where any moment the librarian could be roused from her cake-fueled catnap by the involuntary noises I was trying desperately not to make. Either that or an unsuspecting mom and her wide-eyed toddler would wander through the front door, and we'd scar the kid for life.

"Focus," growled Tina.

"Ouch!" I yelped. "That kinda hurts."

"Whaddya expect?" she snarled, clearly offended that I had called into question her foolproof squeeze-tug-release technique. "I'm all out of spit. There's no *lubrication*."

Unbelievably, the raspberry tank top and caramel-colored eyes were no longer doing it for me; the stress was displacing the sheer joy of sex. So I closed my eyes and followed the advice dispensed by Bobby McShane a few days before, conjuring the image of his top-heavy girlfriend in her infamous zebra-striped bikini. But the bikini alone didn't work either, or at least wasn't working fast enough. That's when I telepathically instructed dream-Tina to reach behind her back, unhook the jungle-print bra, and slowly, slowly, let the gaudy thing fall...

"Jackpot!" Tina shouted as my stubborn slot machine finally paid off.

This startled Mrs. Dunbar out of her sleep. "What's that?" she called. "Is everything okay over there, kids?"

"Well?" Tina asked teasingly, her back to the front desk, her head glistening with sweat. I got the feeling she would've offered a high-five or hauled off and slapped me on the back, if not for the soiled hand she was hiding under the table. "Everything okay, Sammy?"

"Uh, yeah," I said, like a man regaining consciousness. "Everything's great. I'll be right back."

I slunk off to the bathroom, where I immediately set about convincing myself that what had just happened hadn't happened at all, and I wasn't, in essence, a dead man. It was no small feat. I had better luck disposing of the evidence, right down to the conspicuously gleeful expression plastered across my neon-flushed face.

Tina must've been thinking the same thing. When like a good criminal I returned to the scene of the crime, I found that my brazen, sticky-fingered accomplice was nowhere to be seen. It seemed Bonnie had made her getaway without telling Clyde. And here I thought we were a team.

She'd left a soiled *Cracked* magazine behind, though, like a crumpled calling card. But she'd forgotten her own book. I read the title and took it with me to the front desk, thinking it best to make a quick exit and that I owed Tina a favor.

"*Othello*," Mrs. Dunbar said, tsking her tongue while she stamped the return date onto the card at the back of the book. She looked me over. "What a stupid little man," she added unsympathetically.

I just assumed she meant the Moor.

Later that night I woke with a start, sweaty and disoriented and semi-aroused. Apparently the power had gone out in the middle of the night, because the hieroglyphic digits on my clock radio were blinking 12:39. Thunder was rumbling off in the distance; the good people of Camden were in for a round of wild weather. A welcome breeze blew through the window and I was momentarily bathed in the fecund smell of summer rain. I went to the window and, sure enough, the kitchen roof was puddled with water. The night air had turned cooler with the passing storm, so I turned down the box-fan and climbed back into bed.

I'd almost fallen back to sleep when I heard a strange noise above the hunger-pang din of distant thunder: it was directly beneath me, coming from the kitchen...

I tiptoed down the hall to my parents' bedroom and found the door open wide. The radio was on and their own fan was going full-tilt, but the bed was empty. Huh. Maybe Deanna and Gabe had finally made up and were celebrating with a late-night snack. Or maybe some crazed meth-head had broken in, dragged them both from their bed and had them tied to kitchen chairs with a steak knife to their throats…

"Where's Dad?" I found my mother alone in the kitchen ransacking the fridge, the knives all neatly lined up in their slab of blonde wood, no murderous meth-heads in sight. Jars of condiments and bottles of various beverages crowded the Formica counter. The woman often had trouble sleeping, and it wasn't unheard of for her to while away the wee hours engaged in some tedious domestic chore or other. Rather than swallowing pills or drinking a glass of wine—or lamely counting sheep—she preferred to combat her insomnia with late-night cleaning sprees. Once, I'd awoken with stomach cramps at three a.m. to find her doggedly scrubbing the toilet—a truly Sisyphean exercise in a house containing three boys with very bad aim.

"Ssshhh," she said, putting her finger up to her nose and smiling. "He's crashed out on the couch."

I glanced over my shoulder and, sure enough, spied a lone bare foot slung over the sofa arm. "What are you doing?" I asked, even though I already knew, or thought I did: there was a carton of milk on the floor, and a white puddle of the stuff pooling around my mother's bare feet.

"Hungry," she said, turning her attention back to the gaping fridge.

"It's one in the morning. You're standing in a puddle of milk."

"Oh, hey, I'm sorry, hon. Did I wake you?"

Something wasn't right. Spills this size normally didn't stand a chance against Deanna Hayes. Even minor table messes drove her mad. Where was her mop? Where were her trusty bucket and sponge?

"Aren't you going to clean that up?" I asked.

"Huh?" she said, following my gaze to the floor. "Oh,

yeah. In a minute." She shrugged. "No use crying over spilt milk," she giggled.

I frowned and scanned the kitchen for a napkin or dishrag, anything with which to clean up the spreading white mess.

"I'm *really* in the mood for some macaroni salad," my mother said more to herself than to me. "Now, where did I put that Tupperware container?"

"What's wrong with you?" I said.

My mother took her head out of the fridge and straightened up. "What do you mean?"

Her hair and clothes were damp, and not with milk. The backdoor, I noticed, was ajar.

"Why are you all wet? And why's the back door open? We you *outside*?"

"I went for a walk," she said vaguely, shooting the door a dirty look for betraying her. "Just to get some air."

"In a thunderstorm?"

"It wasn't raining when I left," she said, as if that explained anything.

"Where did you go?"

"I told you, hon. For a walk."

"By yourself?"

"Do you see anybody else here?" She shrugged and giggled again, something I was by no means used to. Partly for this reason it rubbed me the wrong way. At this unsettling moment, alone with my uncharacteristically giddy mother in the kitchen at one a.m., it seemed to me that women could be divided into two admittedly reductive categories: those who giggle and those who do not. Deanna Hayes did not giggle. She did not titter or twitter, gurgle or guffaw. In fact her laughter was of such a sober, subdued variety as to sound, from a short distance or over the phone, like nothing so much as crying.

The other reason my mother's giggling irked me was because it implied she'd found something funny, something I couldn't figure out on my own or might not understand. If a joke had been made, I'd missed it. Maybe the joke was on me.

"You look weird," I accused, my face flushed. It was meant as an insult, but my mother actually looked younger to me somehow, her severe features more relaxed, her eyes—though glassy and red-rimmed—sort of highlighted and hyper-alert. Then it hit me: she's happy. The realization made me sad. Whatever had brought about this dramatic change in her appearance, whatever had brightened her smile and lightened her eyes and effectively shorn years off her age, like an ice sculptor sharpening and specifying a statue by means of an electric saw, existed outside the home. It had nothing to do with the gifted, oblivious man slumbering on the couch. And it had even less to do with me.

My mother sighed, and just like that she was a thirtysomething mother of two. "Go back to bed, Sam," she said coldly. "I'll be a few minutes cleaning this up."

"I'll help," I said, moving toward a roll of paper towels.

"No!" she snapped. "Just, please. Go to bed."

I looked at her. "Okay, okay, for shit's sake."

"And watch the mouth, bud."

I did as I was told and went back to bed. But of course I couldn't sleep. After a while, I heard my mother down in the kitchen, humming to herself. I could've been wrong—there was a floor between us, after all, and she was chewing on mushy macaroni salad, making all sorts of other noises while she ate—but the mood-enhancing tune on her lips sounded an awful lot like "Thunder Road."

The next day I didn't waste any time heading over to Tarzan's. Lately my reality—Dunc's heinous murder; my parents' estrangement; a man who jungle-yodeled like some novelty horn or Amazonian noon-time whistle—had proved more surreal than any cut-and-paste collage work or whimsical found poem my subconscious might conjure up. By all accounts I was an imaginative kid. But my extraordinary encounter with Tina Garzone was something I would've been hard-pressed to dream up all on my own. And as far as secrets went, it was just too fantastic to keep.

Tarzan, with his legendary appetites, would love it. He was an eternally famished man, and this was just the sort of stuff he devoured as greedily as a six-pack of his beloved Bud or Millie's cement-mix pasta fagioli. Tina's inexplicable but self-proclaimed status as Bobby's property—she actually had a sleeveless, wide-necked iridescent sweatshirt that read, in stenciled, faux-collegiate font, PROPERTY OF BOBBY MCSHANE—was sure to make Tarzan all the prouder. Tarzan seemed to loathe the boy on sight, quite possibly, it struck me, because the overgrown vandal saw bits of himself in Bobby, one of the more jagged thorns stuck in the neighborhood's troubled north side. There wasn't much difference, it seemed, between destroying others and destroying oneself, no matter if the destruction was disguised as fun, done in the name of having a really good time. In fact the leap (if a leap it was) seemed a perfectly logical one.

But there was another, self-preservative motivation for bragging to Tarzan about winning the hand—if only the hand—of quick-fisted Tina Garzone: I was going to need all the protection I could get once the proverbial shit hit the fan and Bobby, who rarely missed an opportunity to get creative, hauled off and hit me with them both.

For once, Tarzan wasn't home. Or if he was home, he didn't want to be bothered. The front-bedroom air conditioner was on, but that meant nothing; Tarzan liked to sleep with it "cold as the Cold War" and often left it running all day. I banged heartily on the door, as befitting a man who'd recently engaged in an illicit activity with the girl of his dreams, but to no avail. The shades stayed drawn, the lights remained dimmed. The celebration would have to wait.

Back at home, I found my mother out back hanging the wash. Or rather she *had* been hanging the wash—at the moment she wasn't doing anything but clutching a handful of clothespins and staring down at the plastic basket of damp bed sheets. She looked frazzled, which she rarely did, preoccupied by something far more daunting or dangerous than her next household chore. Her hair was half-undone, the hint of barely-there lipstick she favored colored like a full-blown clue.

"Hi, Mom" I said, coming up behind her and causing her to jump. "What's wrong?"

"Jesus, Sam. Nothing's wrong. Why?" My mother had always professed to hating liars. But perhaps this hatred stemmed from a secret jealousy of wool-pulling fabricators, most of whom she deemed sneaky and self-absorbed. It seemed unlikely, but perhaps she hated liars because she herself had never been any good at telling lies, and as a result got away with nothing. (Just what my mother might have to get away with, I couldn't begin to fathom.) She prided herself on being an honest woman, so much so that once when I'd asked her point-blank whether she believed in Santa, she hedged her bets by professing to believe in St. Nick instead. I gladly accepted her answer. I was six at the time, and still under the impression Santa and Saint Nick were one and the same person.

"Who were you talking to?" I asked.

"Huh? When?"

"Just now," I said. "I thought I heard you talking to someone."

"Oh, just myself," she said, and it's true, Deanna Hayes often talked aloud to herself, especially when something was upsetting her. Which begged the question: Who or what was upsetting my mother?

"Now I know," she went on, even though by now my attention had been drawn away from the perfectly plausible story she was admirably concocting, not without perspiration and a too-wide smile, on the spot. "Mrs. Zinni was out back a minute ago. You probably heard me talking to her."

I glanced at the back of feeble Mrs. Zinni's house, which looked empty, abandoned, and fortified against junkies, thieves and would-be squatters with any number of shuttered windows and thumb-thick, double-lock deadbolts. Of course, such precautions didn't necessarily mean that Mrs. Zinni wasn't at home. In fact just the opposite.

So in theory my mother could've been telling the truth. The telltale tortoiseshell Wayfarers, however, implied otherwise.

"Whose are these?" I said, heading over to the picnic table and picking up the sunglasses. I could answer my own question, of course. I put them on without smiling and caught an unwelcome whiff of Polo cologne. The scent wasn't so different from a smack in the face.

My mother shrugged. She looked all of ten years old. "Maybe they're your Dad's."

I whisked them off and made a show of examining the shades. "Dad's are all black," I said. "Besides, his have that dorky day-glo cord to keep them around his neck."

"Maybe he bought new ones," my mother said, her flushed face partially obscured by a billowing pillowcase. She'd nonchalantly begun hanging the remainder of wet sheets, probably hoping that her son, disinclined like all teenage boys to partake in domestic chores, would make himself scarce out of fear of being put to work.

I put the sunglasses back on and stared at her; it was suddenly hard to look at my mother otherwise. "Yeah, maybe," I relented. I brushed past her and headed for the gate, which stood ajar as if in preparation for my rather dramatic exit.

"Sam! Where are you going?"

"I'm going to wear these for a while," I called over my shoulder, snidely adding, "I don't think Dad will mind."

I didn't know what I'd expected—4-D, X-ray vision, the ability to see everything and everyone as little more than pawns to be manipulated in defense of an imposing but far from invulnerable concrete jungle king—but the green-tinted view from behind Tarzan's trademark sunglasses was disappointingly prosaic, boring even. Richtown and its inhabitants looked no kinder or cooler—or for that matter crueler—than from behind my own fold-up Serengetis. Despite what the preening, pretentious salespeople over at Le Carousel in The Gallery would have their customers believe, the clothes did not, after all, make the man. Wherever Tarzan got his shameless and storied chutzpah from, it wasn't his beloved Ray-Bans.

This time I didn't bother knocking. Rather, I opened the storm door and turned the knob; it was unlocked. I poked my head in, went inside.

"Hello?" I called, conscious of the fact that over the last few weeks I'd never spoken the man's name aloud to his face. Calling out for Johnny seemed strange, if not impossible. But I couldn't very well shout for Tarzan.

I found the TV on, the raucous tail-end of a mid-morning game show: bikini-clad spokes-models mooning over a gleaming red sports car.

"Anybody home?"

This was the part where the facemask-sporting axe-murderer lunged, or the chair-stacking poltergeist appeared, or the ghost of Millie Paradise's long-dead sister Lucia demanded, in mellifluous, angry Italian, that I leave the premises at once or be cursed with the kind of old-world evil eye that no dangling *cornicello*, no matter how virile, could cure.

I moved to the kitchen, where I found an old shoebox on the table alongside a half-eaten Tastykake and an empty, fist-crushed can of Bud. I wasn't a snoop by nature—in some respects, particularly where my parents were concerned, I was an anti-snoop, an ostrich walking around with its head stuck in a bucket of sand—but I was a born voyeur. Some photographs littered the far side of the kitchen table, their scattered formation seeming to spell out—rather than, say, GOOD EATS or GO AWAY—my very own name.

The top, flash-heavy photo was bright at its center but discolored at the edges, like a certain brand of tea-cookie my mother lately favored. It was a picture of a girl in a red one-piece bathing suit, more modest than strictly necessary, stretched out on the beach. She looked oddly familiar, this pretty, blonde-haired, blunt-nosed person who couldn't have been much older in the photo than I was now. It took me a minute to realize why: she was my mother, of course, in miniature form, a decade or so earlier, in the midst of catching some much-needed rays. Turning over the photo only confirmed my suspicion: there, in faded black ink, some impressively steady hand had printed *D.D., Wildwood, summer '67.*

I peered into the box and saw that it was in fact full of old photos of my mother: more on the beach, in that prim red swimsuit, smiling into the sun; a few on the boardwalk, posing with another girl and a pink, oversized giraffe; standing flamingo-style atop a pylon, blank-faced and stiff as the Statue of Liberty. I also found a lock of golden hair and a small sheaf of loose leaf letters, bound, oddly, by a ratty scapular, its dour, postage stamp saints faded beyond recognition.

I pulled one letter free and started to read:

> *Dear Johnny, I had tons of fun with you this past weekend down the shore. And your "friend" Maggie was quite the party girl. Let's hope she lives to see 1968. But thanks to you now I've got this awful shoulder burn no amount of Noxema will soothe. (I told you not all Italian girls tan!!) I saw you drooling over Betty McNally at Chet's the other day. I don't really mind. (I'd probably drool over her too if I were a boy. Subtlety is not her strong suit. And you know she thinks she's Mamie Van Doren!) If you're trying to make me jealous, it won't work. I told you before I'm not interested in being your girlfriend. So drool all you want. More than drool. I won't punish you for it. I meant it when I said I wasn't like any girl you'd ever met. D.*

Another read, simply, cryptically, *Consider yourself defiled.* And yet another:

Dear Johnny, I don't know why you keep showing up at my mother's house like that. You won't win either of us over that way. What happened between us shouldn't have. I'm not blaming you. Or maybe I am blaming you, blaming us both. I don't know. What I do know is that it's over between us. I'm with Gabriel now, and probably will be for a long, long time. You were never in it for the long haul anyway, admit it. And to be honest, neither was I. I'm sorry if that's hard for you to hear. But boys like you need to hear it. Please stop calling. And please stop "dropping by." I'm asking you nicely. If my father has to ask you, he won't be so nice...

"Lose something?"

I turned and found Tarzan standing behind me. He clutched a small brown bag of groceries in one hand. The man's other hand, I couldn't help noticing, hung at his side in the déclassé default form of a fist.

I put down the letter and slowly moved away from the table as though backing away from a teeth-baring attack dog. The box was private property, whether or not it contained mysterious images of my mother. Plus, I was trespassing; Tarzan's lair was off-limits despite his professed open-door policy. Neighbor or no neighbor, friend or no friend, I'd crossed a line. I now understood, for perhaps the first time during our brief, near-instantaneous acquaintance, how the man was adamant about calling the shots. The stories he told had passed through his own censorship bureau, the glimpses into his life were all preapproved. Like any well-oiled propaganda machine, Tarzan controlled the spin. He wouldn't look kindly on this breach of protocol, this mutinous attempt to topple his regime.

"I was going to ask you the same thing," I said, brandishing the tortoiseshell shades. Tarzan didn't say anything right away. I hadn't realized how accustomed I'd become to seeing him with sunglasses on. Looking at him now was akin to catching JR Ewing without his Stetson or Mr. T without his turtleneck of gold chains—the man seemed less himself, or at least less of the person I imagined him to be. Which made calling him out easier than either of us expected.

"Thanks, cuz," he said, reaching for the shades. What could I do but hand them over? "They weren't cheap."

"No? They sell them up and down the Avenue for $2.99."

Tarzan smiled broadly now, and I was surprised to see him blush a little, despite the tan. He cleaned the lenses with the hem of his homemade muscle shirt and returned them to their rightful place atop his slightly bent, sun-tinted nose.

"What were you doing in my yard?" I said, surprising myself.

"What are you doing in my house?" he countered, fielding my question as deftly as a first base Golden Glove winner.

"The door was open," I said.

Tarzan smiled at this. "The door was *unlocked*, Buddy. It's never open." He put down the groceries and scooped up his secret souvenirs. "Besides, who says I was in your yard?"

"Where do you think I found *those*?" I said, pointing at the eye-wear as though identifying an odious con-man defendant in a court of law.

"Beats me. For all I know a pigeon coulda carried them off while I was asleep out back."

I stared at him. "A pigeon."

Tarzan didn't avert his gaze. "For all I know."

"My Mom said you came over," I lied. I was surrounded by fictions and fabrications and tall tales of varying heights. Why should I be the only one stuck telling the truth?

Tarzan's big, Cro-Magnon brow collapsed like the army surplus cots Geno and I slept on when we crashed at our Nona's. "Oh," he said. Even with green-tinged plastic clouding his eyes there was no hiding his disappointment. He'd been betrayed; apparently it was a new experience for him. "I thought we agreed to keep it a secret," he said under his breath.

"So it's true!" I shouted. "You were there! You're putting the moves on my Mom!"

"Hey, calm done, cuz. I didn't put the moves on nobody."

"Liar!"

At the sound of the offending word, Tarzan's hand thumped against his chest as though a perfect shot had been fired from the roof of the public school across the street. He even appeared to stagger backwards. "Buddy, I may be a lot of things..." he said, trailing off. "You think you got all the answers." He shook his head and hesitated before adding, "It was your mom who put the moves on *me*, if you want to know the truth."

"Yeah, right. You expect me to believe that?"

"Not now," he said. "I mean before, back when we were kids." He moved toward the table and the shoebox of tiny, younger Deannas. "You don't have to take my word for it. You can see for yourself."

"So you and my mom..."

"Dated, Buddy. We dated."

"What about my dad?"

There was a clamor outside, a kennel-like cacophony of barking dogs. Kids were running up and down the alley, making January and Gigi and Schmidty go wild. Tarzan looked away, in the direction of the noise. "Deanna dumped me for your dad," he said, and smiled.

As unlikely as this sounded, I could see he was telling the truth. Besides, I'd just read as much, in what I presumed to be my mother's own hand. But having dated and been dumped by my mother back before she *was* my mother was one thing. "So what were you doing in my yard?"

"I just stopped by to say hello."

"Bullshit."

"Look, I don't know what I was doing over there. I guess I was just sick of being over here." He sighed, and I watched the man's face darken like a storm-ready sky. I might've been able to sympathize, if the object of Tarzan's affection, in this case at least, hadn't been my very married mother. Didn't he have enough women at his disposal? And even if he didn't, couldn't the likes of Cyndi keep him satisfied? Maybe, for a man like Tarzan, when it came to the opposite sex, satiety wasn't an option. Maybe the guy would always be hungry, despite any halfhearted attempts at diet and exercise. "Either way, it's none of your goddamn business," he grunted.

"Stay out of my yard," I warned.

"Or what?" Tarzan laughed. "You'll call the cops? Or better yet, rat me out to Quick Draw McGraw?"

Before I knew what was happening, I had lunged toward the cardboard box of mementos and knocked them over, scattering pictures of my teenage mother all over Millie's immaculate kitchen floor. I tried to rush past Tarzan but he barred my way. "Buddy, wait..." He put his big primitive palm on my shoulder and attempted a squeeze; for the first time I recoiled from Tarzan's touch as though from the snout of a snapping dog.

"Fuck off," I said. I stalked through the house and stormed through the appropriately named door, as a thunderclap of aluminum punctuated my exit.

Back at home, my mother was stretched out on the couch with a damp washcloth, like some DIY superhero mask, over her eyes. This was the headache remedy she deferred to most—she was suspicious of most medications, and "popped pills" only as a last resort—though it hardly ever seemed to work. I'd thought I could sneak into the house and up the stairs without her noticing, or at least without her making a point of noticing. I'd thought wrong.

"Sammartino," she said without rising, when I was halfway up the creaky, uncarpeted stairs. "Come over here."

"I have to use the bathroom," I lied. Apparently my honesty-loving mother was right—the more untruths you told, the easier it became to just keep on telling them. Lying was so easy, it's a wonder I hadn't formed the habit sooner.

"Hold it in," she said, and took the washcloth off her face. Her pretty blue eyes were ringed with red, as though she'd just stepped out of Celucci's chlorine-deficient public pool. Her pale complexion and damp hairline, wet from the washcloth, also helped to give her the look of a woman who'd just spent a considerable amount of time and energy exerting herself. "I need to talk to you."

"Can't it wait? I really gotta go."

She regarded me for what felt like a very long time. If this really had been a bathroom emergency, the contents of my thinly lined stomach would've been running down my leg by now. "Fine," she said finally. "Go. We'll talk later, if that's what you want."

For once my terse, C.I.A.-perceptive mother was mistaken. What I really wanted was not to have to have this talk at all, not to have stumbled upon whatever ill-advised bond she'd formed (or re-formed) with the greedy gorilla-man crashing at Millie Paradise's homey, hermetic pad next door.

Even though I knew that my mother knew I was lying, even though I hadn't eaten anything in hours and my stomach felt the opposite of full, I went into the bathroom anyway and sat down on the toilet. After a respectable length of time had passed, I rustled the toilet paper and flushed, twice, for good measure. Then I got up, made a Broadway production out of washing my hands and went downstairs.

It turned out this elaborate bathroom pantomime was in vain. My mother was asleep on the couch and snoring loudly, which I couldn't remember ever having heard her do before. (My dad was the snorer, the sneezer, the not-so-secret passer of gas.) I considered waking her and squirming through our little talk. I even sat down next to her and peeled back a corner of the washcloth, feeling a little like a grave robber peeking beneath a death shroud. "Ma," I said softly. And then for some reason: "Deanna." But when neither woman woke up right away, I lost my nerve. I left the house again, headed who knows where, but taking great care to lock the door behind me.

"That, like, seriously sucks," Natalie said, when I told her about Tarzan's shoebox full of photos, and my suspicions about him hanging out with my mom.

"Gee thanks. I feel better already."

"Hey, look on the bright side."

I gave her a look. I had trouble taking her seriously in her new *E.T.* T-shirt and dopey high-top Chucks. What had happened to my flirty schoolyard fiancée? I knew exactly what had happened. I'd blown it. The engagement was off.

"We have Otter Pops," Natalie said brightly.

"Flavor?" I murmured, not wanting to let on that the prospect of sucking on a plastic sleeve of flavored ice had cheered me considerably.

"Louie-Bloo Raspberry."

"Perfect," I said.

To my surprise, Natalie leaned over and kissed me on the cheek. It bore little resemblance to the kiss I'd given her the previous week—to say nothing of my surreal story-time with Tina Garzone—but in some ways I preferred it to our schoolyard smooch. I hadn't seen it coming.

"You're different," Natalie said before heading to the kitchen.

"No I'm not."

She looked at me for longer than I was used to being looked at by anybody except my mother.

"Sure you are," Natalie said. "But different is okay."

She left me alone on the slippery leather sofa in front of the impressive TV, watching some beanpole in a striped T-shirt and gold shoes sashay around an empty classroom. The couch was about the size of a rowboat and fire engine-red. Natalie's mom had bought it on an impulse, the way some people make check-out lane purchases of fashion magazines or tubs of bubble gum.

"We're all out of Louie-Bloo," Natalie called from the kitchen. "It's Strawberry Short Kook or Sir Isaac Lime."

"Sir Isaac," I said, stifling a smile.

"Your dad could've thought up characters like these,"

Natalie said, handing me my second treat of the afternoon.

"Yeah," I said. "Only he didn't." I sucked my stick-less Popsicle.

Natalie turned toward the TV, where she was confronted with the same beanpole, the same classroom, only now it was full of heavily made-up women in lingerie. She wielded the red ice pop like a mini-lightsaber. "If I see this ridiculous video *one more time*…"

"Shut it off," I said. "Or change the channel. I don't care."

At first Natalie looked mildly offended, like I'd asked her to disrobe so that I could try on her cherished *E.T.* shirt. She'd gone to see the movie without me, though I didn't dare ask with whom.

"I wouldn't want to, like, *deprive* you," she said, her eyes wide and glued to the set.

Natalie had put on MTV ostensibly to make me feel better, but the truth was MTV was always on at Natalie's house, at least whenever her dad wasn't home and watching the news. We sat there, mere inches away from each other, our naked thighs practically touching, our eyes, at least, fixated on what seemed an endless parade of music videos interspersed by ads of shameless self-promotion. Save for the bubbly pop music and the suggestive sounds made by our mouths—the slurping and sucking and occasional finger-lick—the house was quiet. *We* were quiet, our brains shutting down, our overtaxed consciousness reduced to the tiny blip that appeared when the TV was turned off.

I moved a hand, tentatively, to Natalie's knee.

"Let's go out," she said, lunging for the remote and aiming it, as though her life depended on it, at the florid, flickering screen.

"Wait," I said, as the TV exploded with sound.

A search party of spotlights roved the stage as though combing the night sky for a hijacked aircraft or U.F.O. When the lights finally came up, they revealed a band unlike any I had ever seen: a black guy in a leather vest on bass; a mustachioed man in a suit on drums; another guy sporting a Japanese bandanna on guitar; a white dude in sunglasses and hospital scrubs on keyboards. Two women were positioned at a second keyboard, standing closer than I had ever dreamed two women could stand, one in a black bustier and fishnet thigh-highs, the other in what looked to be a purple prom gown with the sides cut out. Tilted rakishly atop the former's platinum locks was what looked to be an airline pilot's cap, as though she'd just become a prestigious member of the mile-high club and was cockily brandishing her clout.

Considering they hardly moved—or even so much as altered their facial expressions as they lip-sync their part—the women somehow managed to be sexier than the entire bevy of sluttish schoolgirls inhabiting the previous video. I would've traded bopping around that soft-porn schoolroom with a dozen girls-next-door in exchange for five minutes on stage with this kinky keyboard duo.

"*This?*" Natalie said, unable or unwilling to hide her disdain. She wrinkled her nose like a varmint sniffing out a suspicious windfall of food. "This guy, like, seriously skeeves me."

She was referring to the spry, considerably coiffed lead singer, who, despite toting a guitar and sporting a Technicolor trench coat seemingly made of cellophane, had by now slid down a fireman's pole and taken his enviable position at the main mic.

"Really?" I said, genuinely confused. "What skeeves you

about him?"

"What *doesn't* skeeve me about him. The greasy hair. The runaway mustache. The woolly chest." She shuddered. "Somebody needs to introduce that boy to Mr. Gillette." She rose to go, but stood watching along with me for most of the video. "He looks Puerto Rican," she observed. "Is he Puerto Rican?"

"Dunno," I admitted. "Does it matter?"

Natalie shrugged. "My dad says a black will try to scare you, but a Puerto Rican means business."

"Your dad's a little racist."

"That's like saying someone's a little pregnant."

"Fine," I said. "He's a lot racist."

This made Natalie smile. "Maybe," she said. "But he's right about one thing."

I didn't have to meet her gaze to know that Natalie was vying for my attention along with the purple-clad man on the screen. The man on TV was winning. "Oh yeah?" I said without looking at her. "What's that?"

"Boys are only after one thing."

I pretended to think this over. "Otter Pops," I said.

This time Natalie smiled somehow without smiling. It was a neat trick. "Read any good books lately?"

"No, why?" I asked.

"No reason," she said, heading for the stairs.

"Where are you going?"

Natalie turned and gave me the sort of look certain teachers were inclined to give me, as it dawned on them that for once they'd asked Sammartino Hayes a question for which he did not have a pat answer. "The library," she said, as if it were obvious. "The late fees are pretty steep, and Mrs. Dunbar doesn't know *Catch-22* from *The Catcher in the Rye*. But I hear the floorshow can't be beat."

I wandered aimlessly around Richtown for hours, trying to clear my head, taking in the steaming, early-summer sights, such as they were. Natalie hadn't kicked me out, exactly, but I'd learned firsthand from my dad how to tell when I'd worn out my welcome. Her charity only went so far. Feeling every inch the pauper, I figured it best to continue my begging elsewhere.

By the time the sun began to set, I found myself strolling down a cobblestone side street—a glorified alley, really—that bordered the railroad. Hardscrabble was the word that immediately came to mind, and in a neighborhood as marginalized as Richtown, that was saying something. Whether or not my head was willing to admit it just yet, my heart, as usual, knew the score, and had shrewdly enlisted the help of my feet on the sly. That's how I ended up faced with the pale, impenetrable dwelling that housed inscrutable Tina Garzone.

Tina's house was dark, closed-up, seemingly empty. It looked abandoned, as though who- or whatever once inhabited it had fled the scene long ago, after having taken great pains to secure it by force. It was an unremarkable whitewashed row house, the spitting image of its unassuming brethren on the street. In fact the only notable thing about chez Garzone, the one telltale characteristic, like a chipped tooth or lazy eye, that set it apart from its more or less identical siblings, was that it lacked a front stoop. The steps—or what was left of them—were nothing more than a minor pile of rubble. They looked as though someone had set off a low-grade homemade bomb beneath them, a bomb that may or may not have done its job. The iron pipe railing, though, was still standing, holding fast to a slab of concrete like a drowning man clinging to a buoyant piece of debris.

Tina's street was deserted, not a single stoop-sitter or corner-loiterer or idling automobile anywhere to be found. Unsure of what to do or even what, exactly, I was doing here, I stared at the impassive façade of Tina's house until, almost by sheer will, a light flashed on in a second story window. I would've jumped for joy had I not been paralyzed with fear—fear of what I might do next, having come this far without thinking ahead. Who was this impulsive person masquerading as Sammartino Hayes, son of Gabriel, bet-hedger extraordinaire? My heart having hypnotized my feet into leading me here was one thing—after all, feet were far from free thinkers, and notoriously weak-willed. But what would happen if my heart succeeded in working its hormone-fueled voodoo on my hands or eyes or mouth? What then? At the moment I just stood there, like some poorly positioned peeping Tom, not so much angling for a better view as waiting for Tina to enter my possibly illegal field of vision.

"See anything good?" a shadowy, cigarette-smoking figure inquired as it passed, startling me out of my reverie.

"What? No, I was just…"

"You were just what?" the shadow wanted to know. When it stopped and turned, thrusting its face into the lamplight, I saw that it belonged to the one person in the world I least wanted to see, barring perhaps Tina Garzone herself, albeit for vastly different reasons.

"You were just spying on my girlfriend," Bobby accused, flicking his stinky cigarette and, taking hold of my T-shirt, drawing me close. "So I repeat—*see anything good?*"

How best to answer? A "yes" meant that I'd seen too much, a "no" that there wasn't much to see. Either way, Bobby would be offended. But there were levels of offense, no? Levels, it struck me, which corresponded to the degree of brutality to the beating coming my way.

"I just got here," I said, happy to be telling the truth.

"Yeah," Bobby said. "Me too."

I wasn't sure what Bobby meant by this, but I sure didn't like the way he'd said it. The bully's tone implied one of us was lying, and not very convincingly at that. "I gotta go," I said. "I'm late as it is."

"Go?" Bobby asked, barring my way. "Like you said, you just got here. Stay awhile." He glanced up at the lighted window. "Looks like the show's about to begin."

It would've been a tempting offer, had I been able to take Bobby seriously. And who knows, maybe the kid would actually get off on allowing me to watch his girlfriend undress for bed. Maybe Bobby made a habit of escorting unsuspecting victims here before blackening their offending eyes or knocking their teeth down their throats. Sort of like a final request before the firing squad lets loose. That made more sense than brotherly male bonding.

"I'm already late," I told him again, making the mistake of prissily tapping my Swatch.

Bobby tilted his head as if appraising the preppy accessory. "Cool watch," he said, seeming to mean it. He looked at me. "Hand it over."

"What?" I couldn't help laughing.

Bobby moved a step closer, his rank tobacco breath stinging my eyes. "Give me the watch," he said, "and I'll think twice about giving you a beating."

"I can't give it to you. It was a birthday present. My parents would kill me."

"You mean that metaphorically," Bobby said, surprising me. "What are you late for, exactly?" I started to speak, but Bobby held up a hand. "No, wait, lemme guess," he said, setting me up for the punch line. "Your library books are overdue."

So my little secret had gotten out. There was a leak in Richtown Library, a leak to rival that of the Coles' ravaged kitchen, a leak that no amount of roofing tar or plumbing solder could contain. This particular leak lived in a stoopless house on Seltzer Street and at this very moment was more than likely camped by her bedroom window, a sadistic grin on her face and an enviable bowl of popcorn in her lap, gaily anticipating the bloodbath about to take place in the desolate street below.

I decided, under the circumstances, to laugh it off. "Ha," I said, implying *Yeah, right. That's a good one.* In my defense, I wasn't carrying any books. Plus, nobody in his right mind would suggest that the library stayed open past five, not even a guy like Bobby, who'd never set foot in the place.

"Guess what I heard," Bobby said.

I just shrugged. It was best to treat most of the questions posed by Bobby McShane as rhetorical ones.

Bobby waited a beat. The boy really did have expert timing. "I heard you got sucked off in Richtown library, and let spooky Mrs. Dumbbell watch."

"No! She's lying," I blurted. "It was just a hand-job."

The smile that spread like a forest fire across Bobby's illuminated face told me I'd said too much way too soon. "And here I thought all you guys did was kiss."

The sinking feeling in my stomach superseded my spinning head.

"Where's your bodyguard?" Bobby said, glancing over his shoulder, trying not to look nervous.

"My what?"

"Y'know," he said, miming a muscleman. "Big bad Johnny Bigshot," he said in a low, lunkhead voice. He eyed me suspiciously. "You guys aren't really cousins, are you?"

I could've lied. It might not have helped me much, but it sure couldn't have hurt. Instead I heard myself telling Bobby the truth.

"I didn't think so," he sneered. "You both got big thick heads. But other than that there's no real resemblance."

I didn't know what Bobby was waiting for, why it was taking him so long to kick my ass. Maybe he didn't believe I'd actually be stupid enough to be out on my own without my "bodyguard" lurking nearby, and was expecting the wild jungle animal to pounce the second he laid a finger on me. Or maybe—and this made more sense—Bobby McShane simply enjoyed torturing smaller, weaker creatures. I'd witnessed firsthand his sadistic "experiments" on pigeons and squirrels. Imagine the special brand of torture he'd have in store for someone who actually deserved to be punished, someone ten times that size. All I really knew was this: The more Bobby postponed my pummeling, the more I wanted it over and done with. Perhaps foolishly, I told him so.

"Yeah, you're right," admitted Bobby, dramatically cracking his knuckles. He moved toward me; to both our surprise, I stood my ground. Not out of courage or defiance or futility, even, but out of a sense of rough justice. We both knew I was guilty, and deserved whatever super-size knuckle sandwich Bobby served up. "What am I waiting for?" Bobby said, all but salivating. For once his jumble-puzzle of a face looked strangely, satisfyingly solved. "No time like the present," he said.

"Holy Mother of God," my mother said when I came downstairs in the morning. I hadn't had much trouble sneaking back into the house after my run-in with Bobby, seeing as how my parents were quietly arguing behind their bedroom door. I doubt they would've picked up on my need for first aid had I left a trail of blood and wayward teeth from the front step to my bedroom door. "Not you too."

My mother was sitting beside my dad, who, still dressed in his postal uniform, lay half-sprawled on the couch, where he looked to have spent the night—his shoes were tumbled beside him on the floor, along with a large container of aspirin and a near-empty glass of water. She held a wet washrag up to his face, so it wasn't until she took it away that I saw the man had the same problem his son had—we'd both come home with horribly split lips and matching black eyes.

"Are these damn things contagious, or what?" my mother wanted to know. "Come here."

I did as I was told.

"What happened to you?" my dad asked, a ripple of mild amusement flickering across his face despite his obvious concern.

I shrugged.

"The apple doesn't fall far from the tree," my mother said. "That's what happened."

"And inevitably gets bruised when it hits the ground," my dad said, trying for a joke.

"Well at least *he's* a kid," said my mother, examining my swollen, discolored eye. She took the rag from her husband and placed it on her son's face. "What kind of grown man gets into a fistfight?"

"Fight? What fight?" Geno said, barreling down the stairs. He stopped dead in his tracks. "Holy crap," he said, gaping at the twin shiners. "Did you guys beat each other up?"

"It wasn't a fight, exactly," my dad said, scowling at Geno and pulling himself up to a sitting position. He looked like a different man, less like our father than some vagrant who'd stumbled in off the street and bedded down on our swaybacked sofa. I'd never seen him with as much as a bloody nose. An ingrown toenail, maybe; a seasonal cold sore. The odd nick from shaving. But nothing like this. The bruise, like his work clothes, just didn't suit him. Some guys in Richtown looked naked without a black eye or broken nose or perennial fat lip: the more banged up the better. With my dad it was just the opposite. He looked lost and vulnerable, as though someone hadn't just rearranged his face but systematically altered his genes, so that he was borderline unrecognizable. He turned his ruined eye my way and caught me staring. "The guy's fist didn't stand a chance against my face," he smiled.

"Who was it?" Geno asked.

"Couple of punks," my dad said, glancing at the floor. "I didn't get a good look at their faces."

"What if they come back?" Geno said. "We gotta be ready for them." He went to the hall closet and pulled from it an unused baseball bat, smooth and shining as Cyndi's bare legs, and potentially as lethal.

"They won't be coming back, Geno," droned my dad. "Put the bat away."

"How do you know? Maybe it's the same gang that got Jimmy. Maybe they're after all of us. Maybe they went to get friends…"

"See that?" my mother said, more than annoyed. "See where violence gets you?"

"They weren't Puerto Rican, Geno. Not that it matters."

But my brother was too busy practicing his ninja moves to pay much attention.

"I'll trade you that bat for some breakfast," my mother said to him.

"Pancakes?" Geno asked, wielding the pristine Louisville Slugger like a sword as he trailed our mother to the kitchen. In his best Mr. T voice, I heard my little brother say, "I pity the fool that messes with the Hayes family again! I pity the fool!" But his hotheadedness only lasted for so long. In the end even he, like the other tepid male members of his tribe, proved to be more lover than fighter, and couldn't resist relinquishing his makeshift weapon with Aunt Jemima giving him the laser-eyes.

My dad regarded his firstborn's wounds. "We make quite a pair," he said, pulling me close. "Does it hurt?"

"Only when I…see."

This made him laugh. "I know what you mean."

"Dad, what really happened?" I said. "Who beat you up?"

"You first," he said.

But if I told him about Jimmy, I'd have to tell him about Tina. And telling my dad about Tina was not an option.

"It's no biggie," I said, though of course the opposite was true.

My dad nodded and glanced toward the kitchen, where the rest of his family was busy preparing a healing meal of sponge-like hotcakes. We seemed to have come to an understanding, as two hapless street fighters if not father and son. "Remember what happened to Adam and Eve?" he said.

I nodded. "They ate the fruit of the Tree of Knowledge because they wanted to know everything, like God."

"Exactly."

I didn't get it. "Exactly what?"

My dad smiled widely, wincing because of his blasted lip.

"Sometimes a little mystery is a good thing," he said.

The noon hour came and went without a sound from our displaced neighbor. Ditto the next day, and the day after that. A week went by before I realized that, wherever Tarzan was, he likely wasn't coming back.

"Shit," Tina said, seemingly transfixed by the glob of hypnotic hues circling my ruined right eye. "He really can hit."

"Tell me something I don't know."

Tina smiled, more out of embarrassment than her trademark sadism. "Sorry." She pulled a face. "You have to admit you had it coming."

"But you get off scot-free," I said, more snidely than I'd intended. "Because you're a girl."

"Oh, Sammy," Tina sighed, sounding sixty rather than sixteen. "Girls never get off scot-free. The sooner you learn that lesson the better."

I was as shocked as anybody to find Tina Garzone outside my front door, looking less like a heartless schoolyard vixen than a teenage girl in trouble. But I'd come to distrust Tina, seeing as how my dealings with her tended to end in near-hospitalization. Self-preservation prompted me to half-close the door. Slamming and locking it behind me was not an option "What do you want?"

Tina looked mildly amused. "Two things. First, to tell you Bobby's in the hospital."

"What? Why?" The door opened slightly, seemingly of its own volition.

"Someone jumped him the other night. Knocked out a few teeth. Broke his leg in two places. It's pretty bad." Tina eyed me accusingly. "You wouldn't happen to know anything about it, would you? I mean, this is the first you're hearing about it, right?"

"Me? What would I know?"

Tina shrugged. "Dunno. Bobby says it was a gang of Puerto Ricans. But if you ask me, these mystery spics have been getting a pretty bad rap lately."

I didn't follow. I didn't have trouble buying that in his relatively brief existence Bobby McShane had made mortal enemies all across the Tri-State area, enemies of all different cuts and colors, a few of whom had lately taken some small measure of revenge. But this particular scenario didn't appear to be the one Tina was selling, or attempting to sell, having brought it down from a high shelf and affixed to it a rather pricey sales tag.

"So who, then?" I said. For once I didn't like the way she was looking at me. "You think *I* beat up Bobby McShane?" I was at once flattered and appalled, which pretty much summed up the effect that any attention Tina Garzone paid me had on me.

"Get real. You couldn't beat an egg." She stared me down. "But your lunatic bodyguard could, one-handed."

I was flabbergasted. No way Tarzan did this. Did she really think he'd stoop so low as to put a teenager, a boy half his size, in the hospital?

"I don't have a bodyguard."

"Bodyguard, butt buddy, whatever you want to call him." Her color rising, Tina put her hands on her considerable hips. "You know who I mean. Johnny-Fucking-Purgatory. Your dad-away-from-dad."

"No way," I said. "Why would he even do that?"

"Connect the dots," Tina said. "He hates Bobby. But you, you're the golden boy, the chosen child, for whatever fucked up reason."

She had a point. Tarzan certainly wouldn't need an excuse to put a little fear into Bobby McShane. And despite their falling out, I could see how Bobby's using me as a punching bag would boil the man's blood, might even fan the ravenous, self-destructive fire burning in the furnace of his heart. But I couldn't condemn Tarzan without better evidence than Tina's testimony, plausibly and prettily delivered though it may be.

"What's two?" I said, changing the subject.

"Huh?"

"You said you came here for two things. So what's two?"

Tina, clearly miffed that I wouldn't be siding with her against Tarzan, peered down the street as though expecting reinforcements. But the street was empty. I pitied her in that moment, but only briefly. It was hard to pity a girl who looked and smelled and sounded like Tina Garzone. "My Shakespeare," she huffed.

I ducked into the house and darted up the stairs. I retrieved the cloth-bound copy of *Othello* from where I'd kept it, black eye or no black eye, tucked beneath my pillow like a lost tooth for which I expected, some magical night, to be paid.

"Here," I said, handing the book to Tina.

"Thanks," she said, sounding anything but thankful. She looked it over, as though inspecting it for fingerprints or saliva stains, or worse. She headed down the stairs but stopped and turned back to me as she reached the pavement. Her sundae of sticky, hot fudge-black hair teetered slightly, and seemed to melt a bit in the warm breeze. *What doesn't bend, breaks,* I thought. "Have you ever read *Othello*?" asked Tina, for once not seeming to know the answer ahead of time.

I had no choice but to shake my head no. It killed me to

make that negative gesture, seeing as how doing so could only serve to disappoint my unlikely visitor.

"That's a shame," Tina said, moving down the long, lonely block. "It's all about trust."

I walked in on Bobby watching *Another Day in Our Turning World*, or some such daytime soap. At first I wasn't even sure it was Bobby, what with part of his face taped up and the other part swollen like one of the kid's infamous piss-filled "water" balloons. The patient glanced my way as I entered the room but violently shushed me when I said hello, for fear of missing some ridiculous revelation or catty slur.

"That Whitney McVeigh is hotter than Satan's Hibachi," Bobby finally said, though clearly not by way of starting a conversation.

"What happened?" I said, ignoring the TV. "Who did this to you?"

Bobby wouldn't tear his eyes off the TV, not if Whitney McVeigh and her cave-like cleavage had anything to say about it. The broken boy had a hand behind his head, but that wasn't the one that worried me. The hand that worried me was shoved beneath the thin hospital sheet, foraging like some nocturnal forest-dwelling mammal between Bobby's legs. "Who do you think?" he snorted. "Goddamn spics."

Suspiciously endowed Whitney McVeigh pulled a pearl-handled gun on her rival or mother or coke-dealer and the show broke for a commercial—a speed-talking mustachioed man hawking Federal Express. Bobby motioned for me to sit. But I didn't plan on staying long, and sitting this close to Bobby McShane would put me in a vulnerable position, even with the kid flat on his back and his leg in a cast. "Are you sure? About the Puerto Ricans?"

Bobby took a long time answering. Either he was unsure how best to answer, or he was truly engrossed by the jaunty Coca-Cola ad flickering across the screen. He looked bad. Bobby, of course, always looked bad, which may help explain why Tina always looked heartbreakingly good—somebody had to pick up the slack. I'd always had trouble meeting the kid's eyes. But this was different. It was harder than usual to actually locate Bobby's eyes; they no longer seemed to be where you expected them to be, namely just under his forehead, on either side of his potato nose. "I'm going to rearrange your face" was a favorite metaphor employed by many a Richtown tough, Bobby McShane not least among them. But here Bobby's face actually looked rearranged, like someone had gotten fed-up with its layout and suddenly decided to experiment with the placement of his features, not unlike the way my mother would periodically rearrange the living room furniture.

"Y'know, it's kinda hard to forget a guy's face when he's threatening you with a baseball bat." He looked at me. "Not bad," he said, apprizing the still-impressive shiner. "I still got it."

"I don't think I believe you."

"Believe what, boner?"

"It's all right," I said. "You're just a kid. It's okay to be scared."

"Scared?" he spat. I may as well have called him queer. "Scared of what, dickwad?"

I shrugged and muttered, "Scared to tell me the truth, I guess."

"I just told you the truth. Are you deaf now as well as dickless? A bunch of spics caught me coming out of Val's and asked me if I wanted to join them for nine innings under the highway. They apparently lost their baseball, and thought I would make a half-decent substitute." He glared at his reluctant visitor. "What, do you have a better explanation?"

But I didn't have a better explanation, at least not one I was prepared to offer Bobby. If he wanted to blame the "mystery spics," Richtown's summertime bugaboo, so be it.

"I didn't think so," sneered Bobby. He fished for the remote and turned up the volume on the TV.

"I have to go," I said.

"Good idea."

I was almost through the door when Bobby called me back.

"Hey, Sammy, will you do me a favor?"

I turned, surprised that for once Bobby had used my real name. I expected the bedridden boy to ask me to draw the curtain or fetch him some chocolate-covered contraband from the vending machine down the hall. Knowing Bobby, it wasn't beyond him to ask me to empty his bedpan. "Sure."

I was greeted by the same wolfish grin that devoured the Gingerbread Man and worried Little Red Riding Hood and skulked outside the front doors of the Three Little Pigs.

"Try not to get jerked off by my girlfriend while I'm on the DL," he said.

He came back, of course. They say criminals always return to the scene of their crimes, and Tarzan was no exception. I was out back again when, rather than a yodel, I heard an overplayed pop song blaring from a car stereo on the other side of the cinderblock wall.

I opened the gate and found Tarzan, in a bowling shirt and cut-off jeans, loading what looked to be Millie Paradise's TV into the trunk of his idling Trans Am.

"Hey, Buddy!" he said, as though we'd raised hell together in high school and this was our long-awaited reunion.

"Hey," I said, nonchalant as you please. "What are you doing?"

Tarzan charged into the house and emerged a few seconds later with a toaster-oven the size of a couch cushion. He went to the car and, deeming the trunk too full, proceeded to shove the oversized appliance into the back seat beside an odd assortment of what I took to be his irreversibly ill mother's filched belongings.

"Leaving," he said, without slowing down. He was obviously in a great hurry, and it occurred to me that I'd never seen him this way. I wasn't sure why, but watching Tarzan rush back and forth, up and down, in and out, unsettled me. It didn't seem natural. Whether Tarzan was running to someone or running away, the very act of running just didn't suit him. A fish had more business riding a bicycle. I had more business courting uncourtly Tina Garzone.

"Are you stealing this stuff?" I said, hoping to slow him down.

Tarzan didn't flinch. "You can't steal what you already own, cuz. But I know how it looks, so I'll let that uncharitable comment slide." Back into the house he dove. When he returned, he was cradling a set of china in his arms, which he'd swaddled like a newborn in a red-checkered dishtowel.

"Where have you been, anyway?"

"Busy," was all he said, tucking in the dishes on the floor

behind the passenger seat. He sprang up the stairs, closed the front door and locked up the house.

"You could've said goodbye."

This stopped him, but only for a moment. "Goodbye," he said, deadpan.

"I meant the first time."

Tarzan pulled a face and consulted his wrist, a gesture I'd witnessed I don't know how many times. But for once he wasn't being an impatient smart-ass, he really was wearing a watch, which seemed to signal that this time he might actually have some place to be, an appointment he couldn't afford to miss. Whether that place was Millie's sister's house or Sleepy Jean's apartment or some ramshackle pawnshop in-between was anybody's guess, including mine. Suddenly I felt like anybody, like any *Buddy*. I sure didn't feel like this guy's friend.

"Look, I'm no good with goodbyes," Tarzan said. "Besides, chances are I'll be back. I've got Richtown blood. But I made the fatal mistake of overestimating the old neighborhood's…*allure*, if you know what I mean."

I didn't have a clue as to what he meant, and told him so.

"It's high time I took a little vacation," he said, by way of an explanation. "All work and no play…" he trailed off.

Work? What did he know about work? Between his sporadic roofing job and the odd car repair, Tarzan hardly worked at all. I didn't know how he made his money, never bothered to ask, perhaps because I was afraid of the answer.

"Hey," he continued, "how long did you think a guy like me could last around here, anyway? Cooped up in a row house like some animal at the zoo. I was raised here, remember, reared on pizza and pound cake and kielbasa, just like you. I outgrew Richtown a long time ago, cuz. It just took me a while to realize it." He leaned in close. "Get out while you can, that's my parting advice."

"You beat up my dad," I blurted.

This stopped Tarzan in his tracks. "There are two sides to every story, Buddy," he said, glaring at me. "At least two sides. Usually more."

"Oh yeah?" I said. "And what about Bobby?"

Tarzan didn't say anything right away. By the time he finished swiveling the toothpick around his mouth as though his tongue were nervously pacing his lower palate, I had my answer, or thought I had.

"Well, if I did do it—and I'm not saying I did—what does it matter? The kid had it coming. Bottom line, Bobby McShane's still an asshole."

"He's in traction!" I accused, losing it. "He may never walk again!"

Tarzan waved away the notion of Bobby McShane's lameness with the same gesture I'd seen him use to shoo a pesky bee away from his beer. His insensitivity surprised me. "Mark my words," he said, all but ignoring me, "McShame will survive. Like I said, the kid's an asshole. And years from now, when he's married to a meth-head and managing a Wawa and has five or six creepy, lice-ridden kids of his own, he'll still be an asshole." He gave me a look to see if I was paying attention. "Once an asshole always an asshole. Law of the Jungle # 9."

"I gotta go," I said, turning to do just that.

Tarzan cranked up the radio and peeled away from the curb with his carload of outmoded house-wares, on the road to ruin or rebirth, whichever came first. No real good-bye, no good luck. Not so much as a trademark jungle yodel for the road.

I don't know what I was thinking as I climbed the stairs leading to my bedroom and ducked through the open window to the kitchen roof. The sky was blinding, near colorless, more white than blue. Squinting through the haze, I saw halved pimple balls and broiled sneakers and melted Shatterproof soda bottles. I spotted the blur of my little brother making stick drawings in the dirt of the baseball diamond where Jimmy Duncan had met his tragic, untimely end. When an unlikely breeze blew a whiff of rotting trash and steaming dog shit and burnt tar my way, I nearly went back inside.

Instead I took a step closer to the edge, and slowly began to beat my fists against my hairless, hollow chest. It felt good, the sheer primitive physicality of the gesture, and even though it was scorching, the sun roasting my white skin like a marshmallow, I was tempted to stay that way, above the so-called asphalt jungle, drumming a soft tattoo against my burgeoning body for the remainder of the heat wave.

Old Mrs. Zinni, catty-corner across the ally, stood at her kitchen sink washing dishes, and when she spotted me standing there, shirtless, surveying the working-class squalor, she let out a tiny, European scream. In a flash the old woman appeared at her back door in a garish housecoat and yellow rubber gloves. "Sammartino!" she cried. "Get down! You pazzo, or what? You a-going to fall!"

I mimed for her to shush before my parents, who were arguing in the kitchen below, heard her and stopped me.

"Pazzo!" declared Mrs. Zinni, throwing up her hands. She punctuated her assessment of my mental health with the slamming of her back door.

Self-conscious kid that I was, even with no one watching

I had trouble conjuring the right sound, or any sound at all, really, other than the most tentative and strangled of yelps, more whimpering chimp than roaring gorilla-man. I closed my eyes in an effort to concentrate. I thought of Tarzan, how he would've done it, how he must've felt every day of his life, unleashing that kind of power, how his yodel was more a cry for help than a call to action, and how nobody, including me, had heard him right in the end. I thought about kissing Nat Queen Cole, how terrific and short-lived that was, and how I desperately wanted to do it again, if only she'd let me. I thought of my mother, how beside herself with grief she would be if I fell, how beside herself with grief she already seemed, as though someone or something was dying or had died. Nothing came. Then I thought of my dad, the diehard, the dreamer, what he was doing with his life, or not doing, the many sacrifices he was making, and making for me. I thought of all those undrawn cartoons. And the thought stirred an emotion in him that, many years later, I still don't have a name for.

So I let go. I opened my mouth and, almost by accident, out poured the purest, animal-rousing battle cry my spaghetti-tender vocal chords were capable of producing.

Afterwards, I climbed back through my bedroom window and headed downstairs as though nothing had happened. A glance in the living room mirror revealed the same scrawny, pathetically pale kid I'd always been. But a kid who couldn't help feeling, for the first time in his life and possibly the last, like some newly crowned King of the Apes.

I'm all about the pyrotechnics.

Dream Girl

Aislinn pulled on her T-shirt and blew out the few candles that remained burning along the wide, paint-flaking windowsill. It was a sweltering summer afternoon—the third day running to hit the nineties—and still Sara had insisted on lighting candles. "It smells like Cracker Jacks in here," she'd said, sniffing the air suspiciously, wearing that infamous scowl of hers like a facemask. "Cracker Jacks and cat piss, with—what—a splash of Listerine?" Sara's sense of smell was legendary among their small circle of friends. She could correctly identify a perfume from clear across a crowded bar. Not that many of them even bothered with perfume. Often they camped it up with self-parodic fixative-sprayed wrists, a dab of linseed oil behind each ear. They were art students, after all. That was image enough.

Aislinn folded the bed back into a couch and realized with a pang that she was as confused as a futon. She hadn't really expected Sara to appreciate or understand—or even respect—her period of self-imposed celibacy. But neither had she counted on the woman waging an all-out war; Sara had used every weapon in her sizeable sexual arsenal, from propagandized pillow talk to the twin atom bombs of her eyes, to recapture a small but strategic piece of land that, arguably, had never belonged to her in the first place.

Aislinn went to the freezer and reached for an Otter Pop—her favorite, Little Orphan Orange. Sara had bought a case of them at a bulk-rate food warehouse somewhere in South Jersey. When she was a kid, Aislinn's summer diet seemed to consist of nothing but flavored frozen water: ink-soaked Sno Cones the texture of rock salt; art deco rocket pops of red, white and blue; paper tubs of Italian water ice and their primitive wooden spoons. The cartoon clique of Otters, though, had always been her favorite; they were worthy of their own Saturday morning show.

Back then, once Aislinn had finished sucking the last of the fruit-flavored ice from their plastic packets, she'd slip the empty tubes onto her fingers and put on a sticky puppet show for her brother, drops of iridescent juice streaming down her slender fingers, some traversing her wrists and making it as far as her elbows. She'd done the same for Sara (who tended to lick her clean). In fact when Aislinn first told Sara that she would not, after all, be moving in with her in the fall, it was Alexander the Grape who broke the bad news. Aislinn wasn't fond of disappointing people, even though disappointing people appeared to be her forte.

The person Aislinn managed to disappoint most often, and usually without even trying, was her mother. Agatha O'Connor would have something to say about her daughter's decision to leave school, for sure. And contrary to her conveniently dismissive It's-A-Mom-Thang-You-Wouldn't-Understand posturing, Aislinn knew why. Aggie was adamant about her children knowing exactly what—and who—they wanted (needless to say, she knew nothing about Sara). She'd wasted her own youth on a man whose name, for all they now seemed to have in common, she could just as well have drawn from a hat. Aislinn's parents hadn't divorced when she was twelve, but to hear her mother tell it, they'd come "thrillingly close." These days Aggie appeared in a mad rush to make up for lost time: often she materialized, wild-eyed and winded, with merely the upper half of her mouth smeared with some age-inappropriate shade of lipstick, one lone eye dusted with shadow. It wasn't completely unheard of for Aggie to neglect to brush her chemically enhanced thundercloud of hair. She'd also been known to confuse her shoes, mistaking, in the human cyclone of her haste, a black flat for a pump of navy blue.

Aislinn could deal with her mother's self-styled aberrations of fashion, even if they did tend to throw the entire composition off—*way* off. The real problem was that her mother's recent influx of nervous energy, precipitated by her realization that she had nearly ruined her life and was now, at forty-nine, quickly running out of time to salvage it, didn't only manifest itself in personal hygiene. It also dictated Aggie's behavior, especially in relation to her children, genetic victims of the woman's own inde-cisiveness and well-hashed life-defining mistakes. It killed Aggie that her kids were squandering precious youth by pursuing unrealistic goals, not taking anything seriously, bouncing between majors—in short, if not exactly chasing dreams, trailing them at a safe distance, so as not to scare them away. Aislinn's mother maintained that it had taken her years to determine exactly what she wanted, and now it was too late. But that sorry fact hadn't stopped her from behaving like it wasn't.

Aislinn finished the iridescent Otter Pop and chucked Little Orphan Orange—who no longer looked so vibrant —in the trash. She almost apologized.

Sara had come by ostensibly to retrieve Walter Ego's *Proto-Indo-European Vibe.* She claimed she couldn't paint without it. Music was essential to the creation of Sara's art; it was a catalyst for what she produced on canvas. (Sara often claimed to lack imagination, but Aislinn disagreed. Still, rarely had she seen Sara work without her trusty iPod, and the benefit of a garage band shouting mantras or some self-proclaimed pixie cooing encouraging words in her ears.) But even more than music and making art, Sara thrived on sex. For Sara sex was sustenance. There was simply no other word for it. She insisted on getting off once a day, and preferably not at her own hand. It was no accident, then, that she'd shown up at Aislinn's wearing a plain Hanes tank top. Sara was well aware of Aislinn's weaknesses and often made no bones about preying upon them. They both agreed that there was nothing sexier—perhaps nothing more subversive—than a woman in a wife-beater, especially a woman with Sara's sinewy arms and strong, elegantly tapered back. Sara cracked her knuckles, flexing every muscle along her taut, perennially tanned arms. They hit the futon in no time flat.

"Three weeks," Sara said, once they were through. She consulted what Aislinn called her Batwatch, a cross between a doorknob and a dial of birth control pills. "Three weeks and, look, record time. I've still got the touch."

For all her in-yo'-face sexual prowess and kamikaze resolve, Aislinn knew that Sara's ego was as fragile as blown glass; this was one of the things Aislinn liked most about ˙her, the contrast between the gruff, grown-up exterior and the needy little girl cowering inside. Sara couldn't get it through her head that the prolonged break-up had nothing to do with waning physical attraction or sexual incompatibility. In fact it had nothing to do with Sara, as a lover, at all.

"I'm not leaving you for another girl."

"That's what worries me," Sara said. To her increasing anxiety, Aislinn still hadn't sworn off men.

"I'm not leaving you for anyone," scolded Aislinn. "So quit acting like I am."

Sara sighed her inimitable Sara-sigh. "I hate this."

"So do I," Aislinn half lied; after all, a measure of comfort could be found in control.

"Then don't do it," Sara said. "I mean, it's your choice." She stroked Aislinn's wealth of red hair. "Choose me." With her free hand Sara reached for a ribbed bottle of water. Aislinn watched her drink. "I'm sorry," she said after a moment. "I have to stop pressuring you."

"You have to get that self-portrait started, is what you have to do." Aislinn, like her mother, could change subjects faster than a NASCAR champ could change lanes.

Sara sat up, began rooting around for her clothes. "This is such bullshit. What kind of sadist gives out assignments over the summer?"

"You've got something better to do than make art?" It was a rhetorical question.

"Other people's art? Fuck yeah. Definitely." Sara found her pack of cigarettes, lit one up. "How's yours coming?"

It was one of those lame, masturbatory exercises the semantics of which art teachers stayed up late tweaking: *Paint yourself as others perceive you.* Talk about pointless. Aislinn had no idea how others perceived her, and nor did she care. She had no intention of completing the assignment, but she couldn't tell Sara that, not yet. "Fini," she said with a flourish.

"Bitch." Sara took a drag, expelled a perfect stream of smoke. She looked like an ad for something—not perfume, or cigarettes, or even sex. Aislinn couldn't put her finger on exactly what. Reluctantly she followed Sara's gaze and saw that the sky was clouding over. It was the color of Aggie's infamous mushroom soup.

Sara checked her watch for real.

"In a hurry?" asked Aislinn.

"No." Then, after a beat, "Well, okay. I guess so." She met Aislinn's gaze. "Look, I'll be honest."

"For once."

Sara didn't smile. "The truth is, I kinda have a date."

Aislinn tried to hide her surprise even as she felt her eyes widen, her brow furrow, her jaw slowly lower like a drawbridge. She knew she looked like a parody of her mother now, whose exaggerated features had always struck her only daughter as cartoonish, slap-dash. "Kind of?"

"Let me explain—"

"What's to explain?" Aislinn cut her off. "You have a date. You come over here, fuck me knowing full well I've been trying like crazy not to get fucked, in every sense of the word, and then tell me you're fucking someone else." She shrugged. "Crystal clear."

Sara frowned. "We are so not fucking."

"*What?*"

"Myself and...this other person, I mean. We haven't slept together."

"Yet."

Sara guffawed. "You're a trip, Linn. I mean really. You've dumped me how many times now? No one's ever dumped me in my life! Ever. Then you say you'll see me, but no sex. *No sex.* And you know how I am, you know I've got *needs*—"

"Oh, I know."

"Well what do you expect? What is it you want from me, anyway? Do you even know?"

Good questions, all, thought Aislinn. Which meant they deserved even better answers.

"Yes," Aislinn began, getting both their hopes up. She paused, unsure of how best to proceed. "I want to know her name."

Aislinn *really* didn't want to hear Sara say the words Josie Scarpone, even though every sound in the room, from the humming fridge to the ticking clock to the rapid beating of Aislinn's own increasingly conflicted heart, seemed to count off the syllables of the self-consciously street-tough name.

"It's nobody you know," Sara said. "Just some girl." She took Aislinn's hand. "I'm not telling you her name."

She was downplaying the intensity of this new attraction, but Aislinn had her doubts. Sara wasn't as stolid as she looked. Plus, she was big on affected indifference and prone to hilarious understatements (she'd described the one and only time she ever had a multiple orgasm—three in a row—as "fun").

Sara shrugged. "She asked me to the fireworks and I said yes." She leaned in close, working the sweetness angle. It usually worked, even when she smelled less like linseed oil and more like a carton of Luckies. Or was it the other way around? "I said yes to her, but I wouldn't say no to you," she cooed.

Aislinn knew that Sara falling for another woman was the only foolproof way of ending the relationship. She tried convincing herself that it was a good thing her semi-ex-girlfriend had a date (although it didn't help matters that what Sara considered a date, the legislators of more than a few states in the Bible belt would consider grounds for incarceration). She knew that without the intercession of Josie Scarpone or Becca Brownstein or the Rastafarian woman who waxed the floors of Royer Hall, Sara would never take no for an answer. And, despite her insufferable flip-flopping, no was the very answer Aislinn was intent on giving her.

Still, the thought of Sara falling hard for someone else, and so soon, was unbearable; for over a year now the two of them had seemed to defy gravity.

Aislinn glared at her, but not without love. "This sucks."

"I know. I'm sorry."

"Plus you and your needs need some serious help." Aislinn screwed up her face; she was giving in.

"No argument there." Sara reached for the ashtray—*her* ashtray, a plastic mug molded in the likeness of the Nestlé Quik bunny—and toppled it in the process. "Shit. Sorry again." She regarded Aislinn. "I do more apologizing in this apartment."

"That's okay. Penitence becomes you."

Sara made a kissy face, then got up and quickly pulled on her clothes—jeans, tank top, bad-ass motorcycle boots; she never wore shorts of any kind, though slinky dresses and leather skirts were not unheard of, reserved for those occasions when she felt the need to make a very specific kind of statement. "Text me when you get to the fountain," Sara said. "It's going to be mobbed, so get there early. I can't sarcastically oooh and ahhh all night in unison with a relative stranger."

"It wouldn't be the first time," Aislinn quipped.

Ignoring the joke, Sara leaned over and administered the kind of kiss intended to fill the void in her absence. "Don't be late, Linn," she said. "I'm all about the pyrotechnics."

It wasn't anything Aislinn had ever expected to happen, although Sara had often factored into her reveries as the one girl at Monroe she could see getting close to, closer than she'd ever gotten to any girl. But aside from having survived a grueling Intro to Anatomy class their freshman year, Aislinn hadn't known Sara very well. That is to say, she'd known pretty much what everyone knew: Sara was a favorite of one of the design teachers, a rather sad-looking woman with pendulous breasts and an inordinate fondness for paisley. It was an open secret that they were an item, although the administration at Monroe claimed to frown upon student-teacher sexcapades. Of course Aislinn had found Sara attractive—who didn't? But Aislinn had her pegged as a sheep in wolf's clothing, the kind of woman whose very demeanor was engineered to discourage, if not scare off, people who weren't worthy of her time. When Sara began skulking around Aislinn's studio, making small talk and bringing her various things to eat from the lunch trucks camped along the curb—soft pretzels, cellophaned Tastykakes, Cubist fruit salads—she had more reason than most to consider exactly what is was about Sara Stefano she found so appealing. Aislinn liked the way Sara's jet-black hair, choppy on top but shaved smooth as velour in back, accentuated her strong jaw; she liked the set, slightly drawn mouth and the square-tipped "ski jump" nose; she liked the subtle way Sara's nostrils flared when she concentrated on a painting or—as she soon learned—reached orgasm. And those eyes. Sara had narrow, criminally beautiful caramel brown eyes. They were sympathetic and smoldering at the same time, like those of a woman perpetually on the verge of coming. The eyes of both hunter and prey.

They'd both been drinking gin, which Aislinn was unused to, and attempting, without much grace, to step dance to the closing fiddle of Sinéad O'Connor's "I Am Stretched on Your Grave" at Spring Fling (Aislinn later learned that Sara herself had been responsible for the playlist, and that it was no accident they'd ended up dancing to a song by an artist who shared Aislinn's surname). Drunk and exhausted, they fell to the floor, setting off a chain reaction of tumbling dancers. The short version is that Sara accompanied Aislinn to the bathroom and tried sticking her tongue down her new friend's throat. At first Aislinn resisted, although what had stopped her was the sheer shock of the surprise attack, not a lack of desire. She soon warmed to the idea of having Sara's tongue in her mouth and, an hour later, lapping gently between her legs; back at Sara's, powerless against the gin as well as against that hungry, hell-bent look in Sara's eye, Aislinn was happy to let her new lover lead, if only until she was able to get a feel for the dance, to learn these few unfamiliar, though oddly ingenuous steps. Sara had fumbled with the straps of Aislinn's overalls so long that finally she'd had to pitch in and help. Wracked by the giggles, they teetered there like that—neither fully clothed nor naked enough to get much done—for what seemed like days. Eventually they collapsed onto the mattress, a laughing tangle of hair and interlocked half-clothed limbs.

Aislinn exited the shower and pulled on her jade silk robe—a lavish, misguided present from Aggie that Sara said made her look like something out of Fitzgerald—and plopped down on her schizophrenic sofa. She plunged her hands into the pockets and felt something crinkle. Aislinn knew without looking that it was the latest of Sara's many "presents," part of a Keats poem copied ransom note-style, in squares of mismatched print, and embellished with scrawls of conté crayon. She'd given it to her three weeks before, the second time Aislinn had tried to break it off. Like most of Sara's presents—the Otter Pops, the femme-friendly bumper stickers, the raving purple sunflowers—it was as much an indictment as it was homage.

> *I met a lady in the meads,*
> *Full beautiful, a fairy's child;*
> *Her hair was long, her foot was light,*
> *And her eyes were wild.*

Aislinn didn't think her eyes particularly wild. If anything they were too small, set too close together. But her hair did reach down to the small of her back. And she had an awkward, unintentional habit of catching people off guard.

When she got to the stanza about the "elfin grot," she was reminded of the storage room on the fifth floor of the studio building, where for the first few months of their courtship she and Sara had met secretly. They'd scoured the building for a private place, and Aislinn knew that Sara had deemed it a kind of sanctification of their union when finally they found one. It wasn't that they were so different, or what they were doing so odd. Still, Aislinn wasn't ready just yet to join the proudly swelling ranks, to tout her newfound sexuality as many in the college—students and faculty alike—seemed intent on doing. Because they both had roommates, and because the studios themselves were anything but private, she'd insisted that they find a neutral meeting place and made Sara swear, to the best of her ability, to keep what they were doing quiet.

"Well, I'll try," Sara had said, sounding as unconvincing as she could. "But it won't be easy. You're pretty hot stuff."

They were seated at Sara's enormous worktable, which was strewn with snail-like tubes of oils and thumbnail swatches of pre-treated canvas. Aislinn stuck out her tongue. Sara lunged across the table and tried to catch it between her teeth.

"Careful," warned Aislinn, nodding to her left. Sara's shaven-headed roommate and some disposable boy-toy were getting busy in the bedroom.

"Please," she said, a mischievous glint in her eye. "They're too busy knockin' boots to care about us. Listen."

The sound of muffled groans and a creaking box spring came from April's bedroom.

"Nice work," Sara said. "If you can get it."

"You get your fair share," Aislinn countered, a faint smile gracing her lips.

"I'm a greedy girl," Sara coolly informed her, slowly shaking her head. Her gaze was unwavering. "I want more."

When they first found it, the door to the grot was fastened with a plastic-coated bicycle chain, but Sara was undeterred. She knew how to pick a lock as well as how to forge a signature, hot wire a car. In fact, it was Sara's talent for minor criminal activity that, even more than her talent for painting, had impressed Aislinn, a suburban goody two-shoes who only ever crossed at the corner.

They met often after that, three or four times a week. "Meet me at the grot," Sara would whisper on her way out of Mr. Vine's required English course, a battered Norton anthology tucked under one arm like a weathered pigskin. And there in the dark, the jaggedly stacked desks and jutting easels really had taken on the appearance of rocks, the two naked girls stretched out on a flannel army blanket, love-drunk bacchanals.

From the windows of the grot they could see the streetlights lining Ben Franklin Parkway, and above them the huge, neon emblem of the Blue Cross building, like something out of the Book of Revelation burning a hole in the night. During storms, those lights were their stars, that cross their moon. They explicated *The Waste Land*, and fed each other snacks, and fucked under its glow, their bodies tinted, or so they imagined, with a bluish sheen. Sara always insisted she would paint Aislinn in that light, though she never had.

After a while word got out. It was a small school, and Sara wasn't the best secret-keeper on campus. But by then Aislinn no longer cared. For a long time, all she had really cared about was Sara. And caring had rendered the grot obsolete.

> *I saw pale kings, and princes too,*
> *Pale warriors, death pale were they all;*
> *They cried—"La belle dame sans merci*
> *Hath thee in thrall!"*
>
> *I saw their starv'd lips in the gloam*
> *With horrid warning gaped wide,*
> *And I awoke and found me here*
> *On the cold hill's side.*
>
> *And this is why I sojourn here,*
> *Alone and palely loitering,*
> *Though the sedge is wither'd from the lake,*
> *And no birds sing.*

Aislinn found it increasingly hard to ignore how other women continually caught Sara's eye; in fact Sara often made a show of it, going out of her way to crane her neck at the sight of a luminous head of hair or svelte swiveling hips. But having few illusions about Sara didn't afford Aislinn any sort of magical power. It couldn't even keep her from getting hurt. Sara liked to argue that Aislinn, as a bisexual woman—if that was even the right word—was a liability for her: "Double the temptation. Twice as many reasons to cheat." But Aislinn wasn't a cheater. And she certainly didn't feel like she had the upper hand, least of all when standing next to Sara (or even lying head-to-toe in bed). If anything she felt weak as a wedding cocktail. Of course that was part of the attraction, and part of what irked Aislinn so. The problem was that Sara liked to make a Broadway production out of being in her lover's thrall. Aislinn the Temptress, Aislinn the Femme Fatale, Aislinn the Seducer of Unsuspecting Painting Majors. At times Aislinn wondered which version Sara preferred, the novice she'd seduced at Spring Fling or the wily vixen she'd all but willed into being. Apparently there were two Lovely Ladies without Pity wreaking havoc in this relationship, but the poem wasn't big enough for them both.

Aislinn took an ineffectual towel to her mass of sopping hair and dressed quickly, pulling on a gesso-stained work shirt and a pair of cargo shorts. Carol would be coming in any minute and Aislinn was in no mood for chitchat. Besides, her roommate was an intuitive girl who always seemed to have one ear cocked toward other people's problems. One look at Aislinn and she would know what was up. And not even Aislinn knew, exactly, what was up.

It'd been months since Aislinn had been to the grot, and for the first time she felt a twinge of ignominy as she picked the lock and slipped inside. She wasn't sure what had prompted her to come here, or what she hoped to find. She half expected to find Sara, munching on popcorn or an order of Curly fries from the cafeteria, a smiling I-told-you-so spread across her frustratingly seductive mouth.

It was musty and surprisingly cool inside, welcome relief from the stifling, record-high heat. Everything was just as Aislinn remembered it: desks carelessly thrown together, piled every which way; boxes of acrylic and tempera paint stacked to the ceiling; massive reams of newsprint tucked into a corner like some scrolled ancient text. Sweaty and sleep-deprived, she sat down under the open window and peered out at the gray, late-afternoon sky. Typical Philly Fourth of July: it started to rain.

Aislinn leaned her wet head against the folded crook of an arm and watched the gray overcast sky fade to black.

In her dream, Sara was insisting that she get a tattoo, which was weird, considering she didn't have any of her own. "Why should I?" asked Aislinn. "You can't make me." "All the Monroe girls have at least one," said Sara. "Josie's got *five*, one on her back, one on her arm, one on each shoulder blade, a full set of wings." She lowered her voice. "I can't tell you where the fifth one is." "*You* don't have any tattoos," Aislinn countered. "Oh, don't I?" Sara tore off her tank, revealing a silk-screened Warhol portrait of Aislinn, but Aislinn circa 1997, as a first grader, in pigtails and thick-rimmed glasses. Broken and bare-chested, Sara was suddenly on the verge of madness, cryptically pleading with her girlfriend, "Tell me what the thunder said before you go, tell me what the thunder said before you go..." "I'm not going anywhere," Aislinn said. "Liar!" accused Sara. She was livid. She grabbed Aislinn by her long red hair as she tried to run away. "Liar, liar, snatch on fire! *Tell me what the goddamn thunder said before you go!*" But Aislinn couldn't help her; she'd no idea what Sara was even talking about. "I always cover my ears!" she futilely cried...

Aislinn awoke to a muffled boom reverberating around the storage room. She went to the window just in time to catch a trickle of white light dart over the Art Museum and watched as it burst into a myriad of glitter-trailing spangles. These were Aislinn's favorite, the shy, near-silent fireworks that didn't so much explode as peter out and pop. Of course Sara preferred the blockbusters.

Sara!

Rushing to get up, Aislinn tripped over her own feet and hit the floor hard. A barrage of rapid-fire showstoppers lit up the night sky with a wash of apocalyptic color. Then, just like that, the show was over, and the sky filled only with smoke.

The thought of Sara settling for a Josie Scarpone consolation prize left Aislinn feeling like a flattened tin can. She pushed the image away, preferring to picture Sara alone among the throngs of families jamming the Parkway, searching the crowd for signs of her iridescent hair, all sorts of disasters—everything from a slip in the shower to an abduction and rape—flashing through her excitable girlfriend's mind. Aislinn saw the crowd dispersing, a circle of emptiness widening around Sara and Sara, like some spot-lit, heartbroken tenor, pining for her "dream girl," for that's what "Aislinn" meant, Sara had been quick to point out their first night together: "dream." "And yours?" Aislinn asked. Sara had straightened her back and delicately cleared her throat before answering. "Princess," she said in an affected tone. "Wow," laughed Aislinn, "talk about a self-fulfilling prophecy."

Aislinn got to her feet and thumbed her nose at the makeshift moon, visible now on the other side of the smokeless sky. She stood there a moment longer than she needed to, regarding her own reflection in an unwashed window. The translucent young woman who returned her gaze both was and wasn't Aislinn O'Connor, such as the world knew her. She felt simultaneously crowded and alone, like a person in a packed elevator. She didn't know which way she was moving, or which floor was hers. She could barely even see the tiny lighted numbers, for all the bodies blocking her view. One thing was clear: The ghostly girl in the grimy black glass wasn't especially impressed by what she saw.

O what can ail thee, knight at arms, alone and palely loitering?

Aislinn slipped out of the storage room without stopping to lock the door behind her. She took the stairs two at a time, feeling lighter by the moment. By the time she reached her apartment she'd be nearly invisible. And when Sara called the next day, feeling guilty about her inevitable betrayal but also somehow vindicated, Aislinn, her dream girl, would be nothing but air.

They get high on hospitality.

Party People

"I don't get it," Arty says, handing his mom a stack of retro metallic cups that will be borderline untouchable in ten minutes' time, baked like bread by the searing August sun. "If this is a housewarming party, why are we celebrating the death of a pop star?"

"Honoring, love, not celebrating," his mom says.

"Commemorating," Arty's dad chimes in. Arty didn't see him there, stringing paper lanterns through some of the trees nearest the house. His dad's behind schedule and it shows: his forehead glistens with sweat, and there are twin patches of dampness beneath the short sleeves of his checked broadcloth shirt. His longish wavy hair, which can best be described as controlled chaos, really does look chaotic for once. His pale blue eyes are not kind.

"The impact Elvis Presley had on popular music is immeasurable," he says, and Arty can hear it coming: Professor Voice. It may work on his dad's tittering, top-heavy undergrads, but it no longer works on Arty. "Every band worth listening to over the last twenty-five years has covered Elvis's songs, or at least name-dropped him in their own. His home's practically a national monument. His likeness made it onto a stamp. He may be bigger in death than he ever was in life, which is all any of us wants." He smirks knowingly at Arty, which the boy can't stand.

229

"That warrants a little back yard barbecue, don't you think?"

Ah, but this is no mere back yard barbecue. No party Arty's parents throw will ever be described as an *intimate gathering*. Certain words, like *potluck* or *BYOB*, will never appear on their invitations. They're always trying to outdo themselves, which isn't the easiest or smartest thing to do, considering what little money they once had in the form of his dad's advance has been devoured by the purchasing of McCracken Manor. Arty's parents have never tried to keep their financial woes secret from their only child. But a teensy bit more old-school parental mystery wouldn't kill him.

Arty follows his mom back into the kitchen, where she has a mound of peeled and sliced bananas waiting to be stuffed into peanut butter sandwiches and fried. She's yet to breathe a single word to her husband today, or at least one that Arty has overheard. The tension is so thick Arty could dip crudités in it. Which makes cutting out felt triangles—imitation mutton chop sideburns for all the guests to wear—seem even more absurd than it is, if that's possible.

"You guys don't even like Elvis," Arty reminds her.

"We like music," she says noncommittally, and begins slathering a stack of sliced bread with butter. "All kinds. You know that. We don't discriminate."

This is true. Lately his mom has been listening to gut-wrenching Appalachian stuff, his dad to music that sounds like nothing so much as a multi-car pile-up.

Still, Arty's parents are not Elvis fans. His dad does a passable, toddy-fueled rendition of "Blue Christmas" once a year, complete with his mom on ooh-ooh backing vocals, Arty on synchronized eye rolls. But of the gazillion CDs they own—not to mention the wall of milk crates full of outdated cassettes and shrink-wrapped, out-of-print vinyl—there's not one by the Tupelo boy wonder with the seal-slick hair. The closest thing they have to an Elvis record isn't an Elvis record at all, although his baby-faced likeness appears on the Smiths 12" sleeve, a sepia portrait of the supposed King in his Sunday best, sporting a rather un-rock-n-roll Orville Redenbacher bow tie.

"What are all these bananas for anyway?" asks Arty, even though he already knows. He wants to hear her say it.

"Sandwiches," his mom says, like it's the most natural thing in the world.

"Fried *peanut butter* and *banana* sandwiches," Arty says, hoping she'll realize how strange it sounds, how idiotic it is to serve this odd concoction to their unsuspecting guests.

"The King's favorite," she confirms, sounding alarmingly like a loyal subject.

Arty sits at the kitchen table and sneaks a peek at the guest list. He skips over to the M's and finds a big question mark after the name Celine Murphy. Arty can't ask his mom what the question mark means. She already thinks he has a crush on Naima Murphy. In fact everyone thinks Arty has a crush on Naima, including Naima herself. She certainly doesn't look like any girl Arty has ever known—or, he dimly suspects, like any girl he will ever know. Her skin resembles the creamy inside of a Peanut Butter Cup. Her eyes are the color of the burnt caramel he made with his chemistry set a few years back. Her hair's a loosened bundle of double-stranded DNA. Sometimes Arty thinks about touching Naima's hair. He imagines the texture is not unlike that of a cotton-covered mattress spring, or fuzzy caterpillar.

The Murphys divorced last year. The McCrackens haven't seen McCoy Murphy since, which is a shame, because he used to bring his guitar over to their old house sometimes and stage these mock-serious sing-alongs. He got remarried last month, to everyone's surprise. As far as Arty can tell, nobody from the old neighborhood was invited.

McCracken Manor sits high up on a hill, overlooking a sorry excuse for a creek, complete with a wooden footbridge leading to a not-quite-plumb Home Depot gazebo. It's got a mudroom bigger than Arty's uncle's studio apartment and a detached garage the size of their first house in the city. "The perfect party house," his dad proclaimed the day they made settlement. He held up his hands, the tips of his thumbs touching, like a cliché of a movie director framing a scene. "I see all-night pig roasts and elaborate costume balls. I see neighborhood-wide water balloon fights and bonfire sing-alongs." His dad turned to his mom, his left hand tenderly caressing her shoulder, and Arty swears there were tears pooled in the corners of the man's long lashed, too-blue eyes.

If Arty's dad hadn't just published his first book, they'd still be holed up in a trendy but undeniably ugly part of the city rather than suddenly set free here in the 'burbs. It's not what you could call ugly here, though it's far from pretty. Plain Jane's more like it. The McCrackens' new neighborhood is the geographic equivalent of a Wonder Bread sandwich, with the ethnic-toned crusts cut off.

The house is big, but the party promises to be bigger. It has the feel of a finale, though Arty isn't sure why. Maybe it's the heat, which is borderline unbearable, even here in Shadyville, USA. Or maybe it's the fact that his parents haven't been talking much lately, to say nothing of squeezing each other's knees or rubbing each other's feet like they're famous for. It used to drive him nuts, all that touching. "Touchy" and "Feely" he called them, right to their faces. His dad would smirk, his mom would blush, and Arty would feel like the adult, catching a couple of teenagers playing footsies under the table.

Lately, though, Arty's parents have kept their hands to themselves. But apparently marital discord is no reason not to be social. They've always been addicted to throwing parties. It's like they get high on hospitality. At least his mom does; she's a born hostess. Arty has never seen her happier than when she's presenting a hungry guest with a loaded tray of hors d'oeuvres or topping off a half-full glass of tepid red wine. She's got the same blissful smile plastered across her pretty painted mouth at the beginning of the night, when the first guests arrive, that she has at party's end, while loading a plastic bag with lumps of molded tinfoil for lunch the next day or, more likely, the long ride home. Arty's dad, the covertly ethnic English professor, is a tougher read. He's *Ulysses*-era Joyce to his wife's Judy Blume. A compulsive list-maker, he's a master of planning and preparation. Once, for an English Department party a few years back, he burned a disc of "English major music"—bands named for famous writers (Rainer Maria, Cocteau Twins, Blake Babies) or songs with titles that reference authors ("Hey Jack Kerouac," "Shakespeare's Sister," "Don't Stand So Close to Me") or their works ("Wuthering Heights," "Bananafishbones"). If the devil's in the details, Lucifer should be summoning Arty's dad any day now to plan his next Halloween party.

Yet once the party's off and running, the man can seem mopey and distracted, or scatterbrained, or just plain bored. That's when lovely, smiley-faced Renee takes over. She picks up what she once referred to as the "Stan slack." And they work well together—in this vein. As party planners, at least, Arty's parents make a great team.

Jake Murphy bounds over to where Arty is scrunched inside the tire swing, trying to avoid him. This may seem rude, considering that, technically, Arty is Jake's host. Arty's dad has lectured him in the past on not avoiding Jake, helpfully pointing out how childish and beneath Arty such behavior is. To hear his dad tell it, there's more to throwing a good party than serving watermelon-shaped ice cream cake or tapping a silver barrel of cheap beer. For one, there's *theme*. Anybody can zip over to the nearest Good Time Charlie's and grab a bunch of goofy hats, plastic cutlery and crimped foil balloons. Any DIY dweeb can manage a beer-soaked barbecue. There's no originality in that, and for Arty's dad, originality is key. Try cutting out homemade snowflakes for Winter Solstice till your fingers are red and blistered ("No two can be alike"). Try feeding people in honor of Bloomsday (menu tip: seedcake's more popular than pan-fried kidneys). The McCrackens have celebrated Candlemas, though they're not Christian. They've dressed a neighbor's guinea pig in top hat and tails and passed him off as Punxsutawney Phil. It's bizarre. Arty's parents actually study the calendar for creative excuses to entertain. Failing that, they make up their own holidays: First Snowfall is a big one; so is Last Night on Earth, which is always held on the latest bogus doomsday to infest the Net. Then there's today, August 16th, the Day the King Died. Exactly thirty-five years ago today—the same day his parents chose to have a housewarming party—the world lost its sneering, hip swiveling, majestically coiffed monarch of rock-n-roll.

Jake trips over a tree root and nearly topples a pyramid of jelly donuts. He gets up laughing and doesn't even think to brush himself off. He's a born daredevil; the many bumps and bruises—to say nothing of the broken nose, two broken arms and dislocated shoulder bone—his lanky body has suffered over the years have done little to wise him up or slow him down. Once, back when he was three, he climbed onto an armchair and scaled a radiator cover just to get a better look at the scented candle burning on the windowsill. Mrs. Murphy joked about her son being a budding pyromaniac, but Arty's dad, who tends to be suspicious of small children, has always privately maintained that Jake was trying to burn his humble row house to the ground.

Arty, too, wonders about Jake. He never means any harm. But harm is pretty much all the kid has to offer.

"Hey Arty," Jake calls, a foot from his face. "What're you doing?"

"Shaving my legs," Arty quips, but sarcasm is wasted on Jake. "And my frenemies call me Arturo."

Jake regards his pocket-heavy cargo pants and shrugs. "Want to kick the ball around?"

"What ball?"

He shrugs again. Jake without the shrug is like Kanye West without the crotch grab, a Kardashian sister without mascara. Or Mrs. Murphy without the smirk. "Any ball."

"I don't have any balls," Arty says, and instantly regrets it.

Jake giggles. "Wait till my sister hears that."

Arty gives him the gas face and proceeds to ignore him. No one likes being ignored, but Jake really can't handle it.

It's his weak spot, and Arty works on it like a boxer battering his opponent's bleeding eye. It's almost as if Jake's worried he'd cease to exist without someone to annoy.

"I've got a Frisbee in the car," Jake says, adding, "It's supposed to glow in the dark."

Arty helpfully points out that it won't be dark for a few hours yet.

"My mom brought horseshoes."

Arty peers over Jake's shoulder and watches Mrs. Murphy kiss his parents hello. She hands Arty's mom a bowl of something covered with wax paper and secured with a red rubber band—her disgusting ambrosia, he bets—and his dad a jug of cheap red wine. Arty looks from them back to the Forrester, but no sign of Naima. Jake reads his mind and informs Arty that Naima had a fight with her mom on the way over.

"About what?"

"How should I know?" He's serious.

"You were in the car, weren't you?"

Jake shrugs a third time and it irritates Arty so much that he can't help mimicking the kid.

"I don't even listen to them half the time," Jake says. "It's girl stuff, mostly. Naima wanted my mom to turn the car around and drop her back at home."

"Really."

"Yeah, but my mom said it was rude to accept an invitation and then not show up."

Only Arty knew that Mrs. Murphy had never officially accepted the invitation. It seemed she liked to keep both his parents guessing. It was part of her allure.

"So," Arty asks, trying not to sound desperate. "What did your sister say?"

That does it. Jake flashes a bona-fide pumpkin grin Arty wouldn't mind waiting the full ten weeks until Halloween to witness. "She said *she* didn't accept any invitation, and since when did our family care a rat's ass about what's rude."

"P.Y.T." booms over the sound system—Stan is getting away with a little old-school Michael Jackson, since he was married to the King's daughter for about a week—and instinctively Arty's body starts to move. He scoots out of the tire ring and improvises a dead-on MJ leg twist, much to Jake's amusement. Arty has always been a dancer. His parents claim that he was dancing even before he was walking, but then his parents have a habit of making stuff up.

"Do the moonwalk," Jake says, and Arty does, albeit imperfectly—it's not easy to glide on grass. But it feels good to make Jake laugh.

"Wow," he says, "I wish I could move like that."

Jake Murphy will never move like this. Unless he has a whole team of people, a dance floor pit crew, do the moving for him.

Arty drops to the ground and begins to break dance, spinning like some mechanical toy. He stops stock-still, strikes a pose and flips up onto his feet. He hears Jake clapping, but when he looks Jake's way, he sees that the boy's hands are stuffed into his mouth-like pockets. His jack-o'-lantern grin appears to have doubled in size.

Arty turns and finds Naima standing there in a stiff lemon-yellow sundress, something some silver screen gamine might've worn to a lavish garden party back when their ghost of honor was topping the charts. Her wild hair is reined into a ponytail, of sorts, by a wide purple rubber band. Blue suede Pumas, big as tissue boxes, encase her feet.

"Time for a jelly doughnut." Jake takes off.

"Where are you going?" Arty hollers at his back, to no avail. Naima's looking through Arty as though he's a dirty window, squinting to see if there's anything interesting on the other side.

"Since when did you and Captain Klutz become such pals?"

"We're not *pals*," Arty says. "The kid just happens to know quality moves when he sees them."

Naima smiles, which, Arty has to admit, isn't her best look. By contrast her frowns are devastating, and when she scowls he can actually feel the backs of his knees begin to sweat. But because she's smiling at him, at something he said, Arty finds himself wishing she'd never stop.

She gets in his face. "So when are you going to show *me* some quality moves, playa?"

Arty steps back. He should probably say something like *Right here, right now, ever done it on a tire swing, bay-bee?* and call Naima's bluff. Or at least follow his dad's example and feign indifference. But he's already on the defensive, and instead of mellow or sleazy or smooth, he goes for confrontational, and blurts "I heard you wanted to leave before you even got here."

Naima doesn't flinch. "You heard right," she says, and her face, for all its adolescent softness, now seems coated with a sheen of dried wax. She could guard a hockey net with a face like that. Or run for office.

"You don't like it here?"

"I don't like my mother here," Naima said. "And I'm not too crazy about your dad either."

"My dad?"

Naima waits a beat before answering. She crosses her bare brown arms over her meager chest and, freak that he is, Arty has the inexplicable urge to kiss her elbows.

"He calls our house," she says, as if this explains anything.

"So? They're old friends."

Naima snorts.

"I'm sure they have lots to talk about," Arty says, hoping that talk is all they do.

"All I know is, I hear my mom on the phone late at night, every night, laughing. My dad sure never made her laugh like that. Not that I can remember, anyway."

As if on cue, they hear Mrs. Murphy's cackle from clear across the lawn. And sure enough there's Stan, doing his impression of a man in a singles' bar, not a care in the world, to say nothing of a wife and kid and one ridiculous mortgage payment. Arty scans the yard for Renee, but she's nowhere to be seen.

"It could be anybody," Arty offers, knowing full well it isn't.

"Keep an eye on them for me," Naima says, walking away from him, the party, the great, gratuitous house.

"Why? Where are you going?"

"I need time to think," she says without turning around.

"Think? About what?"

This stops her. Even before Naima turns to face him, Arty can tell from the position of her feet and the set of her shoulders and the tilt of her semi-dreadlocked head that he's going to regret asking this last question. When finally she deigns to look him in the eye, it's with utter and undisguised contempt. "About whether to break up your parents' marriage, *Arturo*," she says and stalks away.

With Naima gone, Arty tries to sneak around to the front of the house, but his dad catches him and calls him over to the barbecue pit where he's still holding court with Naima's mom.

"Say hello to Mrs. Murphy," Stan advises.

"Hello, Mrs. Murphy," Arty chirps.

"Naima's here," Mrs. Murphy says by way of hello.

Stan shoots Mrs. Murphy a knowing look Arty does not like. It's an adult look, a conspiratorial *Do you know what I know?* Arty's about to blow their minds by denouncing the tawny-skinned minx and denying any feelings for her whatsoever when his mom appears, a brick of cartoon-festooned juice boxes in hand.

"We're running low on sandwiches," she lies, insinuating herself between the close-talking college buddies.

"We've got plenty," Stan says, without checking, and waves gaily to the Bennetts, who are making goo-goo eyes in response to the size of the new house.

"Good thing I brought my cell phone," calls Martin Bennett, who teaches Modern British Literature at Stan's school. "A guy could get lost in a place like this."

Mr. Bennett shakes Stan's hand, kisses Renee's cheek, and—no stranger himself to ill-timed marital frisson—steers his third, much younger wife toward the tin washtub of beer.

Renee's gaze is unwavering. "Humor me," she says to her husband. "For once."

Something in her voice strikes a chord with Arty's dad, because he humbly does as he's told. But when he goes into the house to fetch more food, Mrs. Murphy goes too. Everyone notices this, or so it seems. Renee, in particular, is paying very close attention. After a minute Arty snaps his fingers in front of her face and she passes him a juice box.

He's a little old to be getting all worked up over a tiny carton of fruit punch, but he smiles at her anyway and takes it. After all, this isn't the first time they don't have this conversation.

"Did Elvis drink juice boxes?" he asks, trying to distract her, more for her own sake than his dad's.

"When he was a boy," she says distractedly.

"Wasn't he a boy, like, in the thirties or something? I don't think they even had juice boxes back then."

His mom glares at him. It's not a look Arty is used to, coming from her. Stan pretends to be the stern one, the taskmaster, Inventor of the Parental Glare. Truth is, both of Arty's parents are unusually soft touches. "Just drink it," she says.

Arty drinks. He watches his mom watch the back door.

Stan and Mrs. Murphy are gone a long time. Arty can see his mom fighting back the urge to go in after them. He sees her fighting and losing, every time.

"Do me a favor, kiddo," she says finally. "Run inside and see what's keeping your dad."

The second-to-last thing in the world Arty wants to do is run in and see what's keeping his dad. The last thing he wants to do is disappoint his mom.

It's not so bad. He finds them in Stan's office, talking about books. Mrs. Murphy has a garish yellow paperback pressed against her chest as though she's breastfeeding a newborn. He's still going to have to lie to Renee, though. For Stan, lending a woman a book is one step removed from sticking his tongue in her mouth.

"Hey, Mr. Bojangles," his dad says when he sees Arty. "I'm just lending Mrs. Murphy some Roth," he explains, though nobody asked him. "What's your mother up to?"

"Nothing," he says. "Just hanging out."

"Really," he laughs. "I'd like to see that. It's been a long time since your mom's just 'hung out,'" he says, eyeing Mrs. Murphy. "Maybe I should stop her before she hurts herself." He laughs again, one-part seagull, two-parts clogged vacuum cleaner, and suddenly Arty hates the man with all his heart.

"Have you seen Naima?" Mrs. Murphy asks. "I know I brought her here, because she made a point of telling me how much she despises me on her way out of the car."

"No," Arty lies.

It's a little hard to take: Celine Murphy, Concerned Parent. As far as Arty can tell, she's always maintained a strict hands-off policy with her kids. Witness Naima's headstrong independence, Jake's incurable habit of getting hurt.

Arty's dad gives him a look. "You wouldn't be stretching the truth here, would you sport?"

Arty hears the creepy hyena cackle that opens Michael Jackson's "Off the Wall" playing outside. It occurs to him that this could be his dad's theme song: all that stuff about hiding your inhibitions and doing foolish things before you get too old. The old carpe diem motif. Like Prof. McCracken's wide-eyed undergraduates, Arty knows all about it. "Seize the day," his dad routinely cries on his way out the door in the morning. "Did you seize the day today?" he asks his son over dinner. "Please, oh please, tell me you seized the day." Arty never knows what to say, exactly. At thirteen, sky diving with a bevy of supermodels is out of the question, starting his own reality show, not an option. Still, he always gets the impression his dad expects more.

"No," Arty says again, making a point of not looking away. What Arty doesn't tell him is that he wishes he could stretch the truth. If he were older, or smarter, or more his father's son, he'd twist the truth into a goddamn pretzel.

"Naima's going through a tough time," his dad ostensibly tells Arty, though he keeps an eye on Mrs. Murphy. "Her father's wedding must've really hit her hard."

"Little Miss Camouflage, I call her," says Mrs. Murphy. "For a girl who sticks out like a sore thumb, she's become awfully good at blending in. I'll be in the middle of a conversation with her and the next thing I know—poof!—she's all but disappeared." Mrs. Murphy's laugh is not a normal laugh, not a knock-knock joke or soda commercial laugh. It saddens and scares Arty a little. It sounds a lot like the end of something.

Outside, Arty's mom is slumped in a madras lawn chair looking very much like she doesn't want to be bothered. Considering she's the hostess of this ill-timed shindig, this is a problem. There are scores of silly, sideburned people milling around her, trying to respect her space. But there's just something about the one miserable person at a party that's inherently irresistible to the liberally buzzed and happy-go-lucky. She looks pathetic and she knows it. She looks like she's given up. Arty wants to breathe new life into her, not unlike the way she once breathed life into him the time he nearly drowned at a tragically unsupervised public pool.

"Well?" she says without looking up. "Give it to me straight."

"They're looking for Naima."

His mom shoots him a look.

"She's kind of disappeared."

To his surprise, Renee's eternally sad eyes do not widen. She doesn't jump up from her Easter basket chaise and begin phoning 9-1-1. Instead she just sits there, unconsciously worrying the tattered edge of the chair's webbing like a preschooler picking at a scab.

"Lucky girl," she says.

By the time the paper lanterns have begun to hum with color and Jake has proceeded to maim a number of remarkably unfazed partygoers with his Frisbee, Renee is drunk and Stan has retreated to the dark uppermost floor of his unassailable new house, from where, his son can only assume, he's perched on an as-yet-unopened box of books, watching them all. Arty wants to but hasn't gone looking for Naima, mostly because he knows she doesn't want to be found. Dusk somehow belongs to Naima, a girl who often seems heartbreakingly in-between. Something tells Arty he couldn't find her now even if she began cackling like her mother and dared him to follow the sound.

"Ow!" yelps Arty. There's a sudden, sharp pain at the back of his head.

"*Sor*-ry," Jake calls from clear across the yard. Embarrassed, Arty suppresses an urge to toss the glowing UFO in the creek and instead wings it back at Jake, half-hoping to slice off the kid's head. To his surprise, Jake adroitly catches the Frisbee and quickly hurls it back. His return throw's a bit high, but Arty catches it too, a split second before it decapitates ancient Mrs. Josephine, an old neighbor from the old neighborhood whose first name, for some odd reason, has always supplanted her last. Arty laughs despite himself, mimes *Phew! That was close.* He catches himself having fun. With Jake. Someone must've spiked the Blue Hawaiian punch.

Arty's stomach begins to rumble and he realizes he hasn't had anything to eat. "Time," he says to Jake, and heads for the buffet.

He's reluctantly munching on a cold peanut butter and banana sandwich—which isn't half bad—when his mom appears, an army-green backpack thrown over both shoulders. His dad trails after her at what seems an insultingly safe distance, his mutton-chop sideburns guiltily askew.

"Arturo," she says to him, flushed, distracted, pausing in her haste. "Give me a kiss, huh."

"What's going on?" He looks from his mom to his dad and back again, his mouth full of buttery banana mush.

Some of the guests, sensing a show, have formed an imperfect little circle around their pathetic excuse for a family. Arty feels them slowly closing in, the sweaty, half-soused party people and ruddy-faced Elvis rejects, not unlike the flesh-hungry zombies in the "Thriller" video.

"I'm leaving," his mom says finally, more, it seems, to the expectant, disappointed crowd than to Arty. "I need to get away for a while." She shoots a dark look at her husband. "At least until certain people learn to keep their hands to themselves."

"I told you, Celine banged her head on the bathroom jamb," his dad lamely explains. "I was only feeling for a bump."

"You're such a lousy liar, Stan," spits Arty's mom, as if this is a bad thing. "You should've just claimed to be searching for head lice. That I might actually *believe*."

Arty's feeling nauseous and confused, the fried banana paste catching in his throat. "But you can't leave," he protests. "You have to stay. You have to help us look for Naima."

"Don't be silly," snorts his mom. Arty gets the feeling she's really directing this admonishment to his dad, or to

Mrs. Murphy, who's exited the house and is now within earshot. "Get over Naima. She's smooching with Bobby Lewis in the big oak tree."

Bobby Lewis? Who the hell is Bobby Lewis?

His mom reads his face like a billboard. She places a warm hand, tenderly, against his cheek. "Our neighbor, babe. We invited him, of course." She takes her hand away and leans in close. "I'm just going to Gram's," she whispers, kissing him goodbye. Her breath reeks of the "King of Beers" his dad couldn't resist serving. "Be good while I'm gone."

Arty watches his mom stagger down the hill toward her car, thinking of her unofficial theme song. He knows it by heart, of course, the way kids with moms named Barbara Ann or Billie Jean or Ruby Tuesday know those songs seemingly penned for the most important women in their lives. His dad's fond of breaking into the chorus whenever she leaves for work in the morning, or runs an errand, or stomps upstairs in a huff. But no one who witnesses her inevitable, awkward departure—including her foolish, music-fueled husband—feels much like singing now.

Arty glances at Mrs. Murphy, who catches and holds his gaze. It's hard to read her eyes behind the dorky, unfeminine glasses, but her thin lips part as if she's about to say something, to offer an apology, maybe. Whatever she has to say, Arty doesn't hang around long enough to hear it. Instead he goes looking for Naima.

His mom's right: On the other side of the gazebo he finds Naima sitting in a tree with some kid he doesn't recognize, a kid apparently named Bobby Lewis. Whether they've been "smooching" is hard to tell. Bobby's got his arm around Naima's shoulder, that's for sure. But Naima isn't facing him—to her credit, she's facing the other way.

"Hey, Little Miss Camouflage," Arty says.

Naima turns, and he catches her looking surprised for a second. "Don't call me that," she says.

"I'm Bobby," the neighbor says. He's got an inverted felt triangle stuck on his chin like a goatee. His takes a swig of underpriced beer. "This is some whack party."

Arty says nothing. The kid still has his arm around Naima, and he's about three seconds from scaling the trunk of the tree—*his* tree—and removing it for him. Bodily, if necessary.

"What are you even doing up there?" Arty says. "Last I heard you were afraid of heights."

Once, when they were kids, he and Naima scaled a park tree half the size of this one. But when they got to the top she refused to come down. Arty didn't care; he could've stayed up there with Naima all day, and on into the night. For a while it was paradise, their own private Eden in the sky. Then their collective parents came looking for them and Naima got even more scared, too scared to move. Mr. Murphy had to come up after her and convince his terrified daughter to climb upon his back and wrap her arms around his neck, her legs around his waist. They resembled a couple of koalas lowering themselves through the leaves. As frightened as Naima was, Arty remembers catching her smile.

Naima blushes. "I'm over it," she says, making sure it sounds a lot like "I'm over *you*." "Where's your mom going?"

He shrugs. "To visit my grandmother."

"In the middle of her *party*?"

"It's an emergency."

Naima's face drains of color. "Oh."

"Not that kind of emergency. She just needs some time away from my dad."

Naima smirks, and for the first time Arty sees how she resembles her mother in spite of the dark skin and lavish hair. They look at each other for a long time, and keep looking. For all Arty knows, hours, days, weeks are flying by.

Finally Naima says, "This is where you say my mom's looking for me, and I have to come down."

"I like your hair," he tells her. It just sort of comes out.

Naima knits her brow and regards him sideways, suppressing one moon-rivaling smile. "Thanks," she says.

"I've always wanted to touch it," Arty admits, mostly because he has to. He doesn't have a choice.

Bobby Lewis begins to laugh. The noise startles Arty; he's forgotten the kid is even here. He feels like a cocky, presumptuous batter who's lazily rounded first, only to find that the leftfielder has made a stupendous play and superhumanly supplied the second baseman with the ball. Bobby grins evilly and toys with Naima's dreads, just to get on Arty's nerves.

Arty can't look at him, can't look at *them* like that, so he turns and heads back to what's left of the party, where the music has stopped and people are protesting that his mom can't drive in her condition and her car sounds like it's about to explode right there in the driveway. Or implode. Whichever is worse.

Arty doesn't realize it at first, but by the time he reaches the gazebo he's searching for a sizeable rock with which to knock smug Bobby Lewis out of his tree. He bounds up the steps and begins crossing the poorly planked floor when he hears Bobby holler *Hey, wait. Where are you going?*

He keeps walking, ignoring the boy's taunts, until he feels a hand grip his shoulder.

Arty turns. Naima has let her tightly bound hair down, or out. She holds out a tangled lock of it for him to sample. She's still smiling but she's shivering too on this muggy August night, and there's something strange going on behind her eyes, something that makes Arty think of that nerdy sepia portrait of poor Elvis Presley, the sweet, un-kingly image that never made it onto a stamp.

Arty takes the dreadlock between thumb and forefinger like he's appraising the fabric of an expensive suit rather than a strand of matted human hair. It's smooth and rough at the same time, like steel wool or a cat's tongue. He's reluctant to let go.

"Okay, that's enough," Naima tells him, blushing now despite herself. She doesn't make a move to stop him. "This is getting weird."

"You're right," Arty says, his hand trembling slightly as he continues to stroke Naima's hair. "It *is* weird."

But with the car convulsing in the drive and the King's party grinding to a halt and his parents' marriage finally falling apart, it feels like the most natural thing in the world.

Ding-ding-ding.

The Front

"Aren't you a little old for dolls?" the barefoot girl said, plopping onto Ken's front seat as if she owned it. She tossed her canvas sneakers like an offhand comment over a speckled shoulder and smiled. Her smile resembled Ellen's, or what Ken could remember of it, back when his wife still considered smiling a personal strength to be reckoned with rather than a weakness to be exploited. Now whenever Ellen caught herself grinning she quickly clamped shut her mouth, no doubt fearful of letting slip the coveted key to her heart she kept tucked, like some wily escape artist, beneath her tongue.

"Dolls?" Ken asked, pulling away from the curb.

The girl tapped his mirror and shoved her portfolio protectively between her legs.

Ken glanced in his rear-view at the loveable red monster sprawled, pieta-style, across his son's car seat. It was currently Jamie's favorite. He was miffed that Ellen had forgotten to retrieve it from the truck; the Muppet, perhaps more than the man, would be missed.

"Are you kidding? Elmo's a babe magnet," Ken said, then immediately wished he hadn't. He wasn't a kid anymore. Much like a pair of low-slung skinny jeans, slang suddenly seemed tailor-made for people half his age.

"Ha, more like a baby magnet," the girl gamely shot back. With a deft finger-flick, she adjusted a stray bra strap that had slipped out from under her top.

She was dressed predictably, in a black razor-back tank and a pair of those ubiquitous cargo shorts everyone was wearing—members, Ken inwardly scoffed, of some privileged, Gap-funded militia. Years ago, while riding the subway to school, he'd been harassed by a homeless guy for toting a military satchel and wearing a Bono-inspired beret (it was the eighties, Cold War chic at its peak). Back then the only places you could find clothes like these were at army surplus stores. Now the same clothes were mass-marketed by specialty shops with interactive websites and glossy mail order catalogues. Every suburban princess and prep school skate rat owned multiple pairs of cargos, none of which had been bought secondhand.

"So, where are we headed?"

"You tell me," Ken said.

"Hey, you picked *me* up, remember?" the girl said. "You're the man with the plan." She turned toward the window. "It's not like I even need a ride."

This last comment confused Ken. He'd spotted her strolling along busy Hammond Road as if it were a stretch of pristine private beach, shoeless and apparently singing to herself, though the telltale dangling white wire—pure genius, from a marketing if not an aesthetic standpoint—was nowhere to be seen. Her bare feet, even more than her red hair or cumbersome art school prop, intrigued Ken, a man whose curiosity wasn't all that difficult to pique.

"I thought you were hitching," he said.

"And I thought *you* were looking for a friend."

Ken just stared.

"Okay," she said, "just so you know, first rule of picking up hitchhikers—not that I was hitchhiking—is it helps to have a game plan."

Ken wasn't in the habit of picking up hitchhikers. In the movies hitchers always seemed relieved and grateful that someone had stopped (especially those, he couldn't help thinking, with butcher knives stashed in their backpacks—or pleather portfolios). But this girl didn't seem grateful. If anything, she behaved as though she were doing Ken a favor by allowing him to give her a lift.

"You're new at this, aren't you?"

"At what? Helping someone out?" he said. "No, actually I do nice things for weird people all the time."

The girl snorted. "Fantabulous. I'm riding shotgun with Scout Master Bob."

Ken slowed for a stop sign and shot a disapproving glance her way.

"I'm out of here," she said, tugging at the door handle.

"Are you crazy, we're still moving!"

"I'm nobody's merit badge," she said.

"Close the door." Even through the black plastic of her glamourpuss shades Ken could feel her glare at him. "*Please.*"

She did as he asked. "You can't keep me here against my will," she said. "It's called kidnapping. It's kinda against the law."

Ken stopped the truck. With a mix of derision and wonder, he regarded the strange young woman seated cross-legged on his passenger seat. Her arms were fleshy, her ankles a bit thick. She wasn't exactly chubby, just soft in some of the places Ken preferred women hard. (Ellen, by comparison, was rail-thin, with surprisingly strong limbs but no real curves to speak of.) Her shoulders and upper arms were peppered with freckles and fawn-colored moles—just like his mother's. Ken's father used to call them beauty marks, back when he still cared enough to maintain at least a semblance of marital harmony. Of course that was long before the split, before Ken's mother had found an envelope full of tenderly inscribed Polaroids of one of her husband's "kids," a Japanese exchange student with a suggestively pierced tongue, de rigueur for women under twenty-five. At the start of every new semester it was his father's habit to take pictures of all his students, ostensibly for his records; photographing coeds in their skivvies, however, was frowned upon all around. When one morning over a heaping bowl of Froot Loops Ken's mother confronted him with the photos and suggested that, rather than the "A" this Miki was sure to get, an "X" would be more appropriate, Ken's father accused his wife of being old.

If moles were truly marks of beauty, thought Ken, this girl would be a veritable Helen of Troy.

"Go ahead," he said.

"What?"

"Jump, if you want. Nobody's keeping you here. You're certainly not being kidnapped. I was just trying to save you from a broken arm, or worse."

"My hero," she muttered from beneath her inferno of curls.

Normally Ken was slow to anger, but this girl had him on the defensive in no time flat (shattering Ellen's longstanding record). "Do you live anywhere near here?" he asked.

"Sure," she squealed, suddenly animated. "Want to meet the 'rents?"

"No thanks," he said, his tone implying that if she was the apple, he'd hate to meet the tree.

"I'll say I found you on the street, like any other stray. We'll convince them you've got amnesia, or banana fever, or both. I'll keep you in my room, in a big cage my Dad will fashion from wooden shims and chicken wire. When the coast is clear I'll let you into my bed—but just to cuddle, no funny stuff. I'm saving myself for Walter Ego."

Waiting to have his hair cut, Ken had read an article on Walter Ego in *Newsweek*, which described the guy as an "underground pop sensation," whatever that meant. He didn't care much for the man's music, though, or what he'd heard of it. It was sugary discordant stuff, undergraduate poetry set to the tune of a hundred different wind-up toys.

"Better him than me."

"Or we can play it another way," she said, ignoring him. "I'll sit on your lap and toy with what's left of your hair, introduce you as Mr. Mid-life Crisis. Over dinner we'll tell them you've knocked me up, even though we took every precaution." She turned to face him. "Okay, let's get our stories straight. The wedding's in, what, October? Lots of mums and pumpkin centerpieces. Ooh, and a crown of colorful leaves in my hair."

"I'm already married," Ken said, flashing his wedding band, even though she couldn't have been serious. "And not exactly middle-aged."

"And this is no crisis, right?"

He eyed her suspiciously. "Right."

"Then take me home, stay for dinner. Thursday's Tex-Mex night. *Yo quiero Taco Bell.*"

Even if Ken were inclined to call this girl's rather colorful bluff, Thursday was out. Thursday nights he had a standing date with Ellen. He didn't like it, but they'd turned into one of those sad, clichéd couples forced to make appointments to be intimate. Of course most of it had to do with their schedules—Ken was home with Jamie during the day while Ellen raked in the big bucks defending high-profile clients for a prestigious Center City law firm. Three nights a week no sooner had she walked in the door than he was out it, on his way to the design course he taught at the local community college. Weekends there was family and, with Ellen's career on the rise, an inflating circle of colleagues to entertain. (Ellen's organizational skills coupled with Ken's "sense of play" made them peerless entertainers; think Martha Stewart meets the Cat in the Hat.) But more often than not Ellen brought work home with her. With what little time they had left over, they tended to fight, namely about family, the inflating circle of colleagues, Ellen bringing work home with her.

Then there was the flagging attraction, at least on Ellen's part. Or so he imagined. Ken had no problem with being a stay-at-home dad. In fact he enjoyed it. It was other people, including his driven, secretly traditional wife, who appeared to have a problem with his decidedly untraditional role. A self-proclaimed New Woman through and through, Ellen nonetheless had a conservative streak as thin yet as vital as a jugular vein. It was simple: Ellen made much more money, got amazing benefits to boot. Ken, as an adjunct, was considered part-time help. Of course, Ellen had known this all along; it was her idea that Ken not pursue a full-time position while Jamie was small, rather than ship him off to daycare. Something in her recent behavior, however, suggested that she was unhappy with the current arrangement. Nothing blatant, but it was there, Ken could feel it. Ellen was a lousy actress.

Yet she was masterful at placing blame. Not coincidentally, the person she blamed for most of whatever was wrong with her life was Ken (her mother was a close second; her father she adored). Above and beyond everything else, though, Ellen blamed Ken for having wasted his time pursuing an arts degree, when he could've majored in something much more practical, like accounting (he had a phenomenal head for figures, considering his "unhealthy preoccupation" with the visual arts). Still, Ken knew that Ellen was content, if not secretly thrilled, with being the breadwinner; maternal was not a word that would appear in a top ten list of adjectives describing his wife. He didn't like to think so, but Ken suspected Ellen had given birth to Jamie out of a sense of duty more than anything else, or some twisted need to prove to herself and everyone else that she could do/have it all. And now that her career was taking off, Ellen was available—for diaper changes, for baths, for a simple bedtime story—less and less often. As ludicrous as it seemed, Ken couldn't shake the notion that he and his adorable little boy were systematically being left behind.

"I had Taco Bell for lunch," he lied. "But thanks for the invite."

The girl smiled, genuinely this time.

Ken started the car. "I still don't know where we're going."

"Want to see something?" she said, apropos of nothing.

Before he could answer she'd lifted her tank top just high enough to reveal three scabrous, calligraphic words inked onto her unfirm tummy. "Sanskrit," she said in response to Ken's pained expression. "It's poetry."

"What's it say?"

"Well, loosely translated it says 'I'm with stupid.'" She cracked up. "Just kidding. I can't tell you what it says. I mean, *I* know what it says, but I'm not sure I want *you* to know, you know? It's healthy to have a few secrets."

Ken nodded, but his own take on having secrets varied according to the nature of the secret, who was doing the secret keeping, and from whom. He considered himself an honest person, more or less. But the second this girl set a bare foot inside his truck, he knew he would not tell Ellen about it. How healthy was that?

They drove along in silence. Ken considered stopping to pick up the sack of Science Diet his aging tabby so anxiously awaited or the *Blue's Clues* video Jamie couldn't seem to live without. But under this girl's gaze, he knew he would be robbed of the flash of satisfaction he normally derived from completing such minor, mindless tasks. With her eyes on him, his simple errands would feel more like embarrassing chores.

Ken turned and caught the girl peering down her top at her healing tummy-text. "My babysitter's got a tattoo," he offered.

"Really."

"Cleopatra's asp, or so I'm told. Looks more like a night crawler to me."

"Where?"

"Where what?"

She faced him. "Where on babysitter's *person* is said tattoo?"

"Oh, her ankle," Ken said, simultaneously irked and flattered by the implication. "In plain sight."

Kristy the babysitter was an effortlessly pretty girl with hair the color of crème brulee and the length of leg that separates runway models from the rest of the world's beautiful women; a senior in high school, she was almost as tall as he was. Kristy had a lot going for her, especially from a thirty-nine-year-old man's point of view. At seventeen, though, Ken wouldn't have been nearly as enamored of her. There was nothing mysterious or problematic about Kristy, at least not that he could tell. Back then, Ken had preferred difficult, unknowable girls, girls who kept him guessing, girls who felt a burning need to distinguish themselves from the unimpressive pack via half-shaved heads or threatening footwear or truly bizarre behavior, one of whom had carried a dead baby bird around in her tackle box for a week.

"My point," he continued, "is that she's got this tattoo, this permanent, consciously badass *picture* on her skin, but she's also got a lead position in the church choir and a full scholarship to Penn."

"Yay for babysitter."

He wasn't getting through; flustered, he fell back onto the plush comfort of clichés. "You can't judge a book."

She made a show of surveying the interior of his truck. "Apparently not."

"Meaning?"

"Well, Father of the Year you ain't," she said. "Despite the front."

Ken suppressed the urge to take a wild turn and watch her tumble into the street. "Do you even have a name?" he blurted.

"Yep. I've got lots of names, actually." She began reciting a long list of aliases, some of which had been cribbed from pop culture (cereal boxes, *Buffy* reruns, a phenomenally popular Walter Ego song), others Ken couldn't even pronounce let alone recognize. "My screen name's Dago Red, but don't tell my dad." Then, adopting a mock-academic tone, "But the one I prefer, by and large, to all others is *La Belle Dame sans Merci*." Her accent was dead-on.

"Wow," said Ken, softening.

"You can call me Mercy for short." She ditched the Jackie O's. Her bright round eyes reminded Ken of the lemurs on *Zoboomafoo*, another goldmine kiddie show his son was hooked on. Rather formally, she extended a hand. It seemed like a challenge.

Ken let her hand hang in the air between them for a beat longer than was customary. Something told him not to do it, not to align himself with this strange young woman any more than he already had, *if* he already had.

"I'm Ken," he said, shrugging and shaking her hand. It was warm and clammy, calloused in places. It sort of turned him on.

"No shit," Mercy giggled.

Twenty minutes later, Ken had been circling the same strip mall, trying without much luck to trick Mercy into revealing a street address or the name of a development he might recognize. But Mercy wasn't ready, as she put it, to divulge such privileged information. She wasn't in a hurry. She claimed to have nothing better to do.

Ken, by contrast, had lots to do, and less and less time in which to do it. After all, Ellen was home alone with their two-year-old son. He needed to get back.

"So, you're an artist," he said, apropos of the portfolio. It was big and beat-up, the size of a kitchen table, festooned with fem-friendly slogans like *Grrrl Power* and *Babe on Board*.

Mercy snorted. "'Fraid not."

"You're in school, though."

She nodded. "Monroe."

"Wow," said Ken, impressed. Monroe was an all-girls art

college in the city. From what he'd heard over the years, the exorbitant tuition was almost justified by its stellar reputation. Or was it the other way around? He'd known a girl or two, back when he himself was in college, who'd attended Monroe, self-absorbed urban aesthetes with a penchant for pseudo-philosophical discourse. Or so they'd seemed at the time. In retrospect these same girls didn't seem self-absorbed so much as just plain scared. Scared of what, exactly, Ken still wasn't sure. But at thirty-nine, he thought he had an inkling.

"Not bad," he said.

"Not good either," Mercy countered. "I just dropped out."

"Really? Why?"

"Other plans," she said vaguely, shifting in her seat.

Frustrated, Ken said, "These other plans of yours, would they happen to involve going home, preferably within the next ten to fifteen minutes?"

Mercy stared him down, which had to be a kind of hollow victory, considering how Ken had to keep his eyes on the road. "No way, uh-uh. They did, at first, when I got off the train. But not now." She paused for dramatic effect. "Now that I have you." Out of the corner of his eye Ken saw her make a kissy face at him.

"I can't drive in circles forever. I'm low on gas, and I refuse to fill up just so I can schlep you around for who knows how long. I've got a life to lead, you know? A wife, a child?"

"And one on the way."

Ken gaped. He hadn't mentioned Ellen's pregnancy scare. Why would he?

"How do you know about that?"

Mercy stared catatonically through the windshield. "I...have...a gift," she intoned, à la M. Night Shyamalan. She eyed him playfully, unable to contain her mirth. "Oh, come on," she guffawed, "there's nothing extrasensory about it. You just fit the profile. I'd say you're about due for another. How old's what's-his-name?"

"Jamie."

"How old is Jamie? Three?"

"Two and a half."

"See." She patted him consolingly on the thigh; although he jumped, her touch wasn't unwelcome. "Relax. You're not such an enigma, Ken. None of us is. Try as we might." Mercy frowned. "But don't look so glum. The Unknown's overrated. So I'll come clean and quit jerking you around. I'm not going home, okay. You can drop me at the nearest motel. There's a place off McAlister, not far from St. Clare's. I need to be alone."

Mercy began fiddling with the radio, settling, ultimately, on what sounded like the eighties station. This is what it means to get old, thought Ken: bizarre college girls intuit more about your own life than you do, and commercial radio appropriates the music of your youth. "Raspberry Beret" was on, the part about the clouds and the girl mixing, funnily enough.

"Are you sure?" he asked. Suddenly it was very important that he see her home safely. "What's wrong with where you live, with your family?"

Ignoring him, Mercy popped open the glove compartment, began rummaging brazenly through its contents. Disappointed, apparently, not to find a pet tarantula or a severed hand, she pulled a face and had started to close the door when something caught her eye, something that made her smile.

"What's this?" she said, dangling a sandwich bag by two fingers. In one corner of the plastic pouch was a tiny triangle of ground-up green.

Truth be told, Ken didn't know. That is, he knew what it was, just not how it had gotten there. There was only one logical explanation, of course. Before Jamie was born, he and Ellen had gotten high on a weekly basis. It was one of the things he'd found most attractive about her: the straight-laced woman's ability to let loose, her talent for surprising him. Now Ellen's talent seemed to be for keeping secrets, for concealing rather than revealing. Ken couldn't help but see the weed as another warning sign on the road to matrimonial ruin.

Mercy was all teeth. "I take it back," she said. "You *are* an enigma." She broke the seal and took a whiff.

Ken suppressed a smile, secretly pleased that he had managed to impress Mercy to this small extent, even though, technically, it was Ellen who'd impressed her, not him. But he wasn't above taking the credit. Vaguely, he wondered when impressing this girl had become a priority.

Mercy switched off the radio, silencing a raspy Rod Stewart ballad for the good of all humankind. She fished around in a pocket of her silly-looking shorts, which swallowed half her arm, until she produced a strange, ancient lighter, apparently made of brass.

"I don't have any paper," Ken informed her, one eye on Mercy, the other on the road and the encroaching storm. Giving a girl a lift was one thing; getting high with her was quite another. Ellen, for one, would not approve. Then again, maybe she would. Ken had no idea.

Mercy cleared her throat. "Enter: Former Art Student." Her arm disappeared again. "Allow me."

"Hold on," he said, surveying the crass consumer

landscape. He settled for the parking lot of a nearby Arby's and headed straight for a herd of elephantine Dumpsters.

"Perfect," Mercy sniggered. "I always get *mad* munchies."

When she was finished rolling the joint, Mercy studied her handiwork. She turned to Ken. "It's your stash," she said, proffering him the tightly twisted cigarette. "Do the honors."

Ken lipped the joint as Mercy lit it. He took a tentative drag and could tell right away that this was no ordinary street weed. The person supplying Ellen's stash was getting top dollar.

"It's going to storm," Ken said, passing the joint to Mercy.

Mercy took a hungry drag, held the drug in her lungs, exhaled. She passed it back to Ken, pushed her seat back and sat staring through the windshield, flicking her antique lighter. "Rain, rain, come and stay, don't come back some other day, make it wet and make it gray, rain, rain, come and stay." As if on cue, there was a terrific crash of thunder and Mercy jumped, dropping the lit lighter in her lap.

"Christ!" yelped Ken. "Watch it. Leather seats aren't cheap."

"Relax, Mr. Materialism." Mercy checked her shorts for burns. "You're one paranoid android. Clothes like these are practically fire proof." She smirked. "Besides, self-immolation's not my style."

"Oh, no?"

"Uh-uh. I prefer a warm bath and a sharp razor blade to a can of kerosene." Mercy pantomimed the slitting of wrists, accompanied, with convincing realism, by bugging eyes and lolling tongue. Resurrected, she hung her right arm out of the open window and, after checking unsuccessfully for rain, beat a secret rhythm on the door of the Escalade. "Only with bubbles. As far as I know, nobody's ever done it with bubbles. See, I strive for originality. Most suicides tend to take death *very* seriously."

"What are you saying?"

Avoiding Ken's gaze, Mercy reached between her legs and tapped the side of her portfolio for good measure.

Again Ken was confused. Either the weed was even stronger than he'd thought or Mercy was being evasive. "You've decided to suffocate yourself with that thing instead?"

Mercy shot him the same look, he supposed, that she gave people who asked her to explain her art. It was a look he himself had been fond of subjecting older people to, back when he too was the only person in the world who had a clue.

Slowly Mercy unzipped the large black envelope and from it extracted a large utility knife, the word *X-Acto* printed neatly on its side. With her thumb she slid a small black button back and forth, causing a triangular blade to appear, disappear, appear again, like a dorsal fin surfacing and stealthily going under.

The rain began to fall.

"So you really are planning on slitting your wrists," Ken said, finally getting the hint.

"Ding-ding-ding." Mercy gestured to the prominent brand name like a game show spokesmodel with a sick sense of humor. "*X*-actly," she beamed.

They sat in relative silence, listening to the wind whipping through the anemic, evenly spaced trees and watching the rain bounce, like a troupe of Lilliputian step dancers, off the hood of his "glorified pickup." Mercy's revelation had proved to be one major conversation killer. She hadn't breathed a sarcastic comment or so much as sneered at some private epiphany for a good ten minutes.

Finally she began rooting around her portfolio and pulled out what appeared to be a watercolor sketchpad, the once-wet pages rustling like dried leaves beneath her paint-stained fingers.

"May I see it?" Ken asked after a while, simply to fill the quiet car with sound.

Mercy closed the book. She looked genuinely surprised. "I hardly know you."

Ken recalled the time, his sophomore year of high school, when he was caught going through Trudy Lim's sketchpad without her permission—a transgression he now understood to be the artistic equivalent of a panty raid. Trudy was the kind of girl who wore a leopard print cloak over her flannel shirt and black jeans, the kind of girl who used JELL-O for hair gel. The kind of girl who was kind of amazing, Ken thought with a pang. He'd had a horrible crush on her, and had managed to delude himself into thinking she liked him too. (She'd lent him a dubbed cassette once, with songs by bands like The Jesus and Mary Chain, Dead Kennedys, The Cure. It wasn't quite the same thing as having *made* him a mix tape, but still.) But Trudy turned out to be an intensely private teen. "Hands off," she'd snapped, snatching up the black book of amoebic ink doodles and charcoal nudes as if she were retrieving a frilly pair of Calvin Kleins. She'd rarely spoken to Ken after that, which of course only intensified his feelings for her. To this day he was half in love with her, or at least the secretive, snotty young woman she purported to be.

"I studied art once," he confessed.

"Really," Mercy said, wholly unimpressed.

"I've got a pretty good eye, too. I could give you some feedback, maybe, if you're interested. Let you know what I think."

Mercy stuck her tongue out at him. Then, in a bad British accent, "I don't give a monkey's rump what you think."

"Of course you don't," Ken said, a bit defensively. "I didn't, either, when I was your age. But I should've. I should've paid better attention. I should've done a lot of things I didn't do, and so should you."

He was thinking of the person he used to be, and what had happened to him, happened to his Dream. The answer was nothing. Nothing had happened. Ken simply decided, all on his own and without much fanfare, to abandon it, to systematically squander whatever talent he might've possessed by paying his Dream very little attention, and then ignoring it completely. It worked like a charm.

The next thing Ken knew he was engaged to a pretty, practical woman who made no bones about preferring a gainfully employed anything to a struggling would-be. And who could blame her?

"Coulda, shoulda, woulda," Mercy crooned.

"I got scared," Ken admitted, though he hadn't intended to.

Mercy opened her mouth, presumably to say something smart, but closed it again without comment. She looked away. "Do *I* scare you?"

Ken didn't know how best to answer; he wasn't sure he rightly understood the question. "I want to help," he said, unclear even himself as to how or why.

Mercy swung around and glared at him as if he'd yanked her hair. Her bottle green eyes were cruel and accusatory. "Help? This isn't about help. I'm so beyond help, Ken, you have no idea." Her face changed, her features softened.

"But there is something you can do."

Ken resisted the urge to turn on the wipers. They could've been stalled in a car wash, it was raining so hard.

Mercy found a pencil and scrawled something across one of the miniature paintings in her sketchpad. She tore out the page, folded it in half, then folded it once more. She wrote an address on the outside and, in lieu of a wax seal, affixed the seam with a gray blob of something resembling dirty chewing gum. A kneaded eraser, Ken realized.

She handed him the imperfect square of paper.

"What's this?" he said.

"Call it a visual aid."

"For me?"

"No, no, no. You're not to break the seal." Mercy smirked.

Ken read the address, which he recognized as being more than a few miles down Noble Road, on the other side of the mall. "Who lives here? In Elysian Fields."

Mercy waved him away. "Nobody you know. Nobody worth knowing." She cackled sadistically. "In fact that's practically our family motto, what it says on our coat of arms: *Nobody you know, nobody worth knowing.* Only, y'know, in Latin."

Ken handed back the paper. "I think I know what this is. I'm sorry, but I can't do it."

She regarded him evenly. "Can't or won't?"

He shrugged. "Take your pick. I don't want any part of this."

In one fluid motion, Mercy peeled off her tank top and pressed herself against him, or rather what would've been against him, had Ken not recoiled from her in something very much resembling horror. Her torso was splattered with a galaxy of freckles and more of those presumptuous beauty marks. Housed in a modest gray sports bra, her breasts looked like nothing so much as a pair of speckled dinosaur eggs.

Again Ken read the cryptic, calligraphic words etched onto her stomach without comprehending a single syllable.

"Put that back on," he panicked, tossing the tank top her way.

"I gross you out that much, huh." She leaned a little closer.

"It's not that."

"Then what? 'I want to help you,'" she mimicked, climbing onto his lap. "It sure *feels* like you could use a little help."

"Come on, get off."

"I'm *trying*," she laughed.

"I mean it," said Ken. "Go over there."

"Geez," she whined, "this coming from the Marquis DeSuburbia." Ignoring his instruction, she unhooked her bra.

Ken could feel his ears burning red. It was a reflex he'd always tried, without much luck, to suppress, especially in front of consciously unselfconscious people like Mercy. *What's wrong with this picture?* he thought. Mercy was the one who was half naked, her breasts, big and indifferent, regarding him like the billboard eyes of Doctor T. J. Eckleberg. Yet he was the one blushing.

Slowly, almost methodically, Mercy began grinding him, pushing her sizeable hips into his own. It was a bit painful at first, but soon felt good. Better, at least, than it should've felt, considering Ken was a married man and Mercy apparently suicidal. She clutched his headrest for leverage; loose-haired and lemur-eyed, she stared him down. It was as if they were paralyzed from the waist up. They didn't hug, they didn't kiss. They barely touched at all. Yet, in another sense, all they did was touch, their clothed bodies bucking and rubbing like two giant sticks seconds from starting a fire.

The rain beat against the windshield like a battalion of crazed birds.

"You owe me," Mercy whispered when Ken was through.

He was breathless, sticky, more than a little disoriented. "What? I don't believe you."

She draped her bare arms over his shoulders. "Correction: You *won't* believe me. That's not the same thing."

Ken took hold of her by her upper arms and, as if handling precious cargo—a neighbor's newborn, perhaps, or a record-breaking soap bubble—eased Mercy off of his lap and onto the passenger seat beside him. There was a damp stain on his shorts; if it didn't dry in time, it would be hard to explain. "I have to get back," he said, still flustered. "I've got things to do."

He knew it wasn't his finest moment, but what choice did he have?

"So get back," Mercy sneered, pulling on her shirt; her bra she stuffed in her pocket. "Get back to your wife and your kid and your wet dream Ivy League babysitter. Get back to Olive Garden and Reality TV. Get back to your *dog*. Take your ego stroking, ozone choking SUV and go. But know this," she said, suddenly intense, wild-eyed; Ken half expected her to grab him by the collar. "You're nothing without me, and I'm gone."

She burst into tears.

Ken was slow to respond. A crying woman had never elicited from him the traditional response. Besides, Ellen hardly ever cried, and he was unused to being tender. He placed a hand, tentatively, on Mercy's shoulder. It appeared to be enough.

"Forget it," she said, drying her eyes with a fiery shammy of hair. "I mean it. Please, just forget...everything."

Ken would've liked nothing more than to reassure her, to take Mercy by the hand and convince her that everything would be okay. But he didn't know this for a fact, and lying to the girl seemed far worse than letting her go.

Mercy pushed open the car door, letting in a baby squall of Indian summer rain. She lunged toward Ken and kissed him hard, catching the corner of his mouth. Her breath reeked of pot, of course, but there was something else he couldn't quite identify, a vaguely metallic taste mingled with the residual salt of her tears. "Consider yourself absolved," she said, making a revised Sign of the Cross. She slid across the passenger seat and out of the SUV, raising the portfolio over her head as a shield against the stinging rain.

Ken sat motionless for a long time listening to water pelt his big, ridiculous truck. Ellen wouldn't go for it, but he'd resolved to trade it in for something a lot less practical, something funky and not brand-new, with a modicum of style. The kind of car a former art student could respect.

He glanced in his rear-view and saw that Elmo's gaze was upon him, Mercy's cheap red sneakers piled cozily in the Muppet's lap like a tableau of a parent protecting its young. Would she go through with it? Would Mercy really make her way to some anonymous rented room and spend the evening draining the life from her soft, speckled body? It was anybody's guess, least of all Ken's.

He peered through the rain-dappled windshield in the direction of Mercy's development and started the truck.

Most of the storm's violence had abated, the sky's massive temper tantrum nearly run its course. It wasn't over—there were distant grumblings even now, and bouts of wild weather semi-forecasted for the long week ahead. But the worst of it, he supposed, had passed.

Suspend your disbelief, for once.

Bloodsucker

Stevie was a mere few feet from the register when a toddler sporting a full-head werewolf mask wandered into his path, tempting him to reconsider his last-minute costume choice. The kid had the right idea. Werewolves were more Stevie's style. The furred face, the torn clothes, the shameless, hair-raising howling at the moon. Werewolves didn't put on airs. Werewolves didn't let you use the phone, knowing full well the line was dead. Werewolves didn't make polite chitchat over the turtle soup only to sink their incisors into the necks of their dinner guests the first chance they got. Still, if it was said of men with beards that they couldn't be trusted, what to make of a moon-mad half-man covered head to foot in synthetic fur?

"Oh yeah," said a lilting male voice behind him. "I totally see you in that." Stevie turned away from the pint-sized Lycan and found himself face-to-face with a college-age sales-boy in sleeveless mesh T-shirt and pink feather boa, robustly confirming what he, Stevie, dimly suspected but up until this point had merely hoped was true: that at forty-two he'd finally make a convincing vampire. He was still a big-boned man, but he'd lost most of the weight that had plagued him for so long, like some inflatable pool float he couldn't slip out of, forcing him to steer clear of clingy silk-cashmere sweaters and hieroglyphic-stitched low-riding jeans.

"Think so?"

"Totally," repeated the budding transvestite. He was a good-looking kid whose sharp, feline features were highlighted by a conspicuous sheen of meticulously applied make-up. But the boy's face could've been magnetic, considering all the metal sticking out of it. Shrapnel, thought Stevie, a casualty of some invisibly hip, trans-campus war. "Besides, nothing says Halloween quite like the Prince of Darkness, n'est-ce pas?" He laughed aloud, revealing a tongue punctured by multiple balls of bright, saliva-slick silver. Used to be kids did anything to keep metal out of their mouths in the way of braces. Now they were all too eager to shove the stuff in. "Halloween without Count Dracula is like Christmas without Santa, or the Fourth without fireworks." He shrugged a shoulder and yawned. "Can't be done." He laughed again, this time without much sound, and stuck out a hand notable for its disconcerting smoothness and black-shellacked fingernails. "I'm Frederick," he said.

"I'm sold," said Stevie.

"Good one," Frederick said, withdrawing the hand. "You're lucky to even get a vampire costume, with all the Robert Pattinson wannabes running rampant."

"I was thinking more along the lines of *True Blood*."

"True dat. By the way, toothpaste tubes of corn syrup are two-for-one. "

"I'm good, thanks."

"We've got buckets of rubber eyeballs—they look like the real thing. Let's see, Styrofoam bones, talking tomb stones, cans of spray-on spider webs from the makers of Crazy String."

"Just the costume, I think."

"Suit yourself," Frederick said, smiling at the pun. He took the costume from Stevie and led him to the checkout counter, where he was greeted by a sign that read NEXT CADAVER PLEASE. The buxom girl behind the register had a series of X's and O's and dotted lines scrawled across her face and down her neck and over her considerable cleavage, as though she were a page in a playbook. She was avidly clicking the buttons on her cell phone, sending an urgent text message, no doubt, about the abundance of creeper dads and their obsession with making sustained eye contact. She caught Stevie staring and rolled her own expertly painted eyes.

"Hey, Penny Pre-Op," Frederick said. "Do me a solid and give Spike here the much-coveted friends and family discount."

Penny snapped shut her phone and looked Stevie over doubtfully. "He a friend or a family?" she snorted.

"What's it to you?"

"You can't keep giving discounts to guys you want to blow, Freddy."

Frederick showed her a mirthless smile. "Says who?"

"Whoa," interjected Stevie, "back up a minute."

"Unbelievable," Penny said, shaking her garishly painted head. "Third time today."

"Where's your manager's badge, Penny?" Frederick asked her. "Hm? Could it be you left your manager's badge at home today? Or could it be that, unlike me—and despite your insistence on questioning my truly wicked retail acumen—you are not in fact a manager at this or any other Halloween Dreamz location?"

"You're an assistant manager," corrected Penny.

"Operative word being—read my lips—*man-a-ger.*"

"The discount isn't necessary," Stevie said, checking his watch. He wanted to be home in time to have dinner and apply his make-up before driving the twenty-odd miles over to Miranda's. "I'm happy to pay full price."

"I bet you are," said Frederick, with more than a tinge of blue coloring his tone. He leaned in close and stage-whispered, "Penny's famous for turning customers to stone even when she's *not* on the rag, so do yourself a favor and forget to make eye contact. You'll live longer."

Having delivered this friendly advice, Frederick sauntered over to a manhandled display of select dismemberments. Stevie watched him listlessly fondle the huge rubber boobs and restack the gleaming plastic asses.

Even as a kid, Stevie had seemed to realize he lacked the dramatic bone structure and smoldering Old World charm necessary to pass himself off as a convincing Count Dracula. This despite the avid protestations of a mother who'd always seemed overly smitten with the svelte, suave, Vitalis-drenched undead. Every October without fail, Stevie's mother happily supplied her only child with the fake teeth, peaked wig and high-collared cape of a shamelessly store-bought bloodsucker. He humored her, of course, silently suffering her ministrations before the bathroom mirror while she smeared a fragrant pallor—half water, half Johnson's baby powder—onto his face with her fingers, or daubed burnt cork round his eyes. Her efforts invariably were in vain. Stevie would make it as far as the front door, perhaps, before loosening his retooled superhero cape and coughing his fanged dentures into his hand. He'd end up hitting the street hidden beneath a sheet or behind a rubber mask—any costume whose success didn't depend so heavily on his ability to fool people into

believing he was as exotic as Bela Lugosi, or creepy as
Barnabas Collins, or cool as David Bowie.

But fooling people, according to Stevie's failed-actress
mother, was what Halloween was all about.

"Tell me, what's the point of giving yourself a role to
play if you're only going to play it halfway?"

"Candy, Mom," Stevie had said, stone-faced, as if
informing her he hadn't yet learned how to fly. "Candy is
the point."

She dismissed the idea with an impatient wave, as if
directing a bad smell away from her overly sensitive nose.

"Nonsense. The point is *transformation*, the point is pure
and instant *change*."

But Stevie was just a kid, and didn't see the rather adult
benefits of a holiday devoted to the idea of reinvention.
Change would come in droves whether he liked it or not,
everybody said so. Where pillowcases of free candy were
concerned, there were no such guarantees.

Not for the first time, Stevie wished he could smack the
man hamming it up on the "Prince of Darkness"
cardboard packaging. This wasn't a costume so much as a
flimsy disguise, one step up from a Lone Ranger mask or
Groucho glasses. But Stevie needed more than a disguise,
he needed to go incognito, deep undercover; for once he
couldn't afford to be recognized. He lamented the fact that
nobody wore actual costumes anymore. And because
nobody wore costumes, quality costume shops were hard
to come by. Now these shoddy, fly-by-night seasonal
warehouses were the norm, hastily assembled emporiums
of mass-produced ghouls and gore. Stevie recognized
convenience as the real killer. Like their banking and their
medication and their meals, Americans craved convenience; they wanted to be in and out of the Halloween

shop, wanted to get this holiday over and done with and on to the next one (and so on and so on, all through the year, on to their graves). What's so great about originality anyway? Who had time to break out the spray paint or sewing machine and get *creative*?

One moment it was a discount furniture or cell phone store, the next—*abracadabra, presto-change-o!*—it was Halloween Dreamz, retailers specializing in plastic pitchforks, pirate hooks and samurai swords; fright wigs and fishnet stockings; rubber rats and bats and spiders big as your fist. The location Stevie was currently driving away from had been a discount lingerie store in its former incarnation, something called Kiss-N-Tell or Hide-N-Seek or some such liberally hyphenated linguistic inanity heavy on the innuendo. As a testament to this sad fact, the racks were loaded with the sort of sheer, barely-there unmentionables that had less to do with a coven of lascivious witches than with a whole other breed of spell-inducing ladies of the evening.

But what Stevie objected to even more than the outlandish prices or desperate, dubious undergarments was the preponderance of gore. For him, there had always been a marked difference between spooky and scary. Severed heads and limbs, served up on a slab of Styrofoam and stuffed under Saran wrap meant to resemble supermarket meat, had Stevie pining for the days of implied violence, of the kind of horror that might be but never was. Subtlety had gone out the window. The stock was over-the-top, in your face, X-treme Halloween. As if a night dedicated to the risen dead weren't extreme enough.

Stevie had met Miranda years ago on Halloween, working in a kind of catch-all costume shop in Bucks County.

Bananafishbones was the kind of place that specialized in outlandish vintage apparel and overpriced pop culture collectibles, many of which Stevie was certain he had boxed up, still, in his mother's cramped basement down in South Philly. It was as if a truck filled with the contents of a dozen quirky families' attics had backed up to the stockroom and dumped its outdated, questionable cargo. The shop itself was a kind of microcosm for the entire town, which managed to be quaint and progressive, provincial and worldly, antiquated but undeniably hip all at the same time. Miranda had been thirty-five at the time, a college dropout, frustrated clothing designer and lapsed Wiccan. Stevie was a bit younger but teaching creative writing at a liberal arts college across the river, living with another adjunct professor in half of a rented Victorian. His first book of stories had just come out, to decidedly mixed reviews. He told himself that even a mediocre book was better than no book at all. He was all puffed up with his own importance, and looking to float away on it for a time while everyone down below pointed and waved and wagered on whether he'd ever again touch ground. Settling down in any sense was the furthest thing from his mind.

Entering the shop, he'd been struck by Miranda's skewed beauty almost as much as by the sickly-sweet smell of marijuana that permeated the store as pervasively as skunk musk. She had a pert ski-jump nose and wildly expressive too-blue eyes. Her hair blazed with the color of the felled maple leaves coating the front stoop like decoupage. But her lips were thin as bobby pins, and her forehead two fingers too high, which gave her the wooden, slightly daft look of a marionette. Big brown freckles littered her skin like confetti in the wake of a parade.

"Can I help you?" Miranda asked when she caught him staring.

Cautiously, he approached the counter. "Can I get a hit?" he said, trying to be funny.

"Excuse me?"

"The weed," he said, all but waggling his eyebrows, "I can smell it."

Miranda shifted on her stool but her expression didn't change. "I don't smell anything," she said.

Stevie looked aghast; his mother had taught him how. "Really?" he said. "Then you paid way too much for that nose job."

He regretted saying it as soon as the words left his mouth. But her nose really was a little too perfect to be believed. He wanted to tap on it like a table, just to prove it wasn't drawn on.

"Seriously, is there something I can help you with?" she said, to her credit sounding more amused than annoyed. "Maybe something for sale, that you can't actually smell?"

Stevie knew a parting stage direction when he heard one, but he wasn't ready to leave just yet. He wasn't sure he *could* leave, truth be told. He quickly scanned the shop and his eyes alighted on the replica of a wolfman doll beloved by a certain boy vampire in a sixties television show.

"How much is this?" he said, handing it over.

The girl examined the toy as if it were Stevie's to sell. "Fifty bucks," she said.

"I'm in the wrong business," scoffed Stevie.

She shrugged and suavely stowed the plush wolfman beneath the counter. "What sort of business are you in?"

"I'm a writer," he said, and for the first time since officially becoming one he felt slightly foolish.

"Hey, Miranda," a scratchy male voice called from the back of the shop. "Okay if I cut out an hour early?"

"Hot date, Neal?" inquired Miranda.

"You know it," Neal replied.

"What time does the shop close?" Stevie asked Miranda.

"That depends on what kind of writer you are."

He could see she didn't believe him; she thought this business about being a writer was just a line (it was and it wasn't). "How about I come back tomorrow and drop off a copy of my book."

"Yeah, right."

"Honest," he said, sounding all of ten years old.

"I doubt there's an honest bone in your body," Miranda said, making a show of looking him over. "But I'll be here till nine tomorrow night, just in case you're capable of surprising me."

"I'd almost given up hope," Miranda said when Stevie arrived the next night, middling story collection in hand.

"Do men typically stand you up?"

She shot him a look he'd never dream of dodging. "Men around here don't typically do anything," she said. "That's part of the problem."

"You're a conventional girl, beneath the spiked dog collar and Barbarella boots."

Miranda seemed to consider this assessment and find it not far from the truth. "Let's just say I've dated three different guys over the last six months, and at some point every one of them asked to borrow my make-up."

"I don't wear much make-up," admitted Stevie.

"That's a plus."

"I'd make a horrendous woman."

Miranda laughed. "Music to my ears."

She took the book from Stevie and scanned the blurbs, such as they were. "Wow," she said finally, handing back his life's work. "A real-live author. I'm impressed."

"That makes two of us."

"You impress yourself?" Miranda laughed again.

"No, I mean you. You impress me."

She turned the color of strawberry preserves, but was brazen enough to ask Stevie what it was about her that impressed him so.

"Well, aside from the obvious, I'm impressed that you're impressed by a writer. Nobody reads anymore."

Miranda frowned, though whether in sympathy or in protest, Stevie couldn't tell. "So, what's this book of yours about?"

"You," Stevie said without missing a beat. It wasn't a complete lie. "It's all about you."

Miranda's smile stretched her thin lips to obsolescence but her teeth were white and true. "You're a smooth talker, Mr. Author Extraordinaire. How old are you, anyway?"

"Older than I look." Apparently this was true. Everybody was always telling Stevie he could've passed for a younger man. Which he chose to believe gave him a certain amount of license to behave like one.

"I'm no kid," Miranda said.

"No kidding."

She rolled her translucent eyes at that. "Maybe you should save some of that snappy dialogue for your next book."

"I'm already writing it," he said. "This is the part where you agree to be my girlfriend." He hadn't expected to say this—the words had simply tumbled out of his mouth like a series of fanciful clowns from a car.

"Life imitates art, is that the idea?"

"Now there's a scary thought."

"I can think of a scarier one," she said.

"Like what? You not falling head over heels in love with me?" More clowns, bigger and brighter and more reckless than the others. How did they all fit?

"Oh, I'm already falling for you," Miranda said, gamely playing along. "What's scary is what you end up doing to me in your fiction. Or some version of me."

Stevie wisely decided to play dumb and let the matter drop.

"Okay," Miranda said two weeks later, apropos of nothing. They'd paused midway across the steel truss bridge that separated their respective towns to marvel at a charcoal-sketch November sky that seemed inseparable from the stalled charcoal-sketch river below.

"Okay what?" asked Stevie, pulling her close. He buried his face in Miranda's hair and inhaled her wood smoke perfume.

"I'll be your girlfriend," she said.

He searched her eyes for sarcasm and found none. "Well, it sure took you long enough," he said, feeling elated and taken aback and slightly disappointed all at the same time. What Stevie had never admitted to anyone, least of all himself, was that he hadn't been all that anxious for Miranda to give in to him where their romantic status was concerned. Wonderful as she was, he would've been happy to give her a bit more time to decide, had she needed it.

Six months later they were engaged. Six months after that, on the spooky anniversary of their meeting, they were married in the banquet room of a reputedly haunted, colonial-era inn a few blocks away from Bananafishbones.

The bride wore black, of course. The groom, a loopy frozen smile.

"Here, Count Chocula," Stevie's mother had said to him the October he turned thirteen. "Put these on." She handed him a pile of the latest in a long line of vampire paraphernalia and disappeared upstairs while he fiddled with his homework. She returned wearing a dowdy white nightgown her son had never seen before, though she rarely went to bed before midnight and it was barely eight p.m. Her normal mess of hair was piled high atop her head like some nesting water fowl, her striking green eyes raccooned with black.

"What are you waiting for?" she asked when she saw he hadn't moved from the dining room table.

"Tomorrow's Halloween," Stevie said, squinting suspiciously at her outfit. "You're a day early."

"Close enough," she said. "We're going to put on a little pre-holiday play, you and me."

This was nothing new. Stevie was well acquainted with his mother's holiday "plays." She'd had him dress as a leprechaun one St. Patty's Day and skip about the house singing "When Irish Eyes Are Smiling." They'd put on their very own Christmas pageant for years, using an array of stuffed toys as stable animals and a swaddled sofa cushion as a stand-in for the Baby Jesus. Stevie was an official teenager now, and sick of his mother's odd little dramas, if not more generally sick of the person who produced them. "I don't want to put on a play," he told her.

She rolled her kohled eyes and regarded her young son as she might a near-stranger on the street, someone she vaguely recognized from weekly run-ins at the dry cleaner's or supermarket but had zero interest in befriending. Stevie couldn't help noticing how pretty she looked, with her eyes darkened and her throat exposed. "Oh, don't be such a party poop," she said. "Put these on upstairs while I stay down here and set the scene. Come back down looking hungry for blood. But descend the stairs *slowly* and *quietly*. Vampires are famous for their stealth."

Stevie took the stairs one at a time, which wasn't his custom.

Upon his return to the living room, Stevie found the lights dimmed and the secondhand candelabra they'd bought at a flea market in Fairmount aglow with ghostly white tapers. Music was playing softly, but it was music that more closely resembled the death-rattle of dry leaves being scuttled down the street by a breeze. His mother was splayed across the couch as though she'd fainted, her pale arms thrown over her head and her eyes closed. Stevie's instinct, as it so often was in response to his mother's theatrics, was to call 9-1-1. Yet as he approached the couch in his ghoulish get-up and stood over her still-young, apparently slumbering form, Stevie was struck by how expertly she resembled something out of a fairy tale, simultaneously wanton and wan, and by how very different this apparition looked from the corporeal, world-weary woman who helped him with his homework and washed his clothes and cooked his meals. The skill and ease with which his mother could utterly transform herself startled Stevie as it so often had, a boy known to suffer panic attacks at the prospect of having the living room furniture rearranged, or getting his bi-monthly haircut.

He'd been standing there for a good couple of minutes before his mother, wondering about the holdup, popped open a blackened eye and gently elbowed him in the stomach.

"What do I do now?" he muttered through painful plastic teeth.

"You know exactly what to do," whispered his mother, reclosing her eye. "You do the only thing vampires know how to do, hon. You ply your trade. You bite me."

"I'm not going to bite you," Stevie said.

"Why not?"

Stevie could hardly believe he was having this conversation. "You're my mother."

"Wrong," she droned. "At the moment, I'm nothing more to you than a tasty gourmet meal. Think about it: bite me or die. Those are your options."

"Vampires can't die," he said. "They're already dead."

"Call it whatever you want," huffed his mother. "But if they don't suck blood they cease to exist. End of story. And the more *nubile* the victim, the more nutritious the meal."

"So you're, like, the equivalent of a cheeseburger and fries?"

Now both eyes popped open, and the shaming look they leveled at Stevie was not one he enjoyed being the recipient of, not then, not ever. "Not nice," she said.

"Sorry."

"Apology accepted." His mother rearranged her sacrificial posture and closed her eyes again. "C'mon," she hissed, sounding petulant, teenager-ish, "you're ruining the scene. Suspend your disbelief, for once. Sink your teeth in. *Do it.*"

In the end he lost his nerve. Stevie always lost his nerve. Whether it came to giving his mother a hickey or leaving the house on Halloween dressed as she intended, he could only be a disappointment. But better a disappointment than a fool, reasoned Stevie. If the badly accented line *I vant to suck your blood* sounded patently silly being delivered by boys who actually went on dates, how ridiculous would it sound coming from a husky blonde kid who had never so much as held a girl's hand, let alone nibbled, rodent-like, on one's creamy perfumed neck. No, the neighborhood was teeming with natural-born bloodsuckers, lanky, heavy-lidded Lotharios good girls in particular seemed to swoon over, even without plastic fangs protruding from their preternaturally profane mouths and their center-parted hair slicked back.

It was a grim joke, his decision to finally dress as a B-movie bloodsucker, but one that Miranda would certainly appreciate, had Stevie been able to let her in on it. It had been a running joke throughout their failed relationship that artists in general and writers in particular were more or less parasitic creatures that sustained their creative life by sucking the love and energy and, yes, the very soul out of ordinary mortals, especially the luckless few who were closest to them. After all, it was the parasite's loved ones, far more than its peers or editors or creative writing students (and far, *far* more than one seemingly irresistible student, whose last named just happened to be Straw, though who knew, at the time of their awkward coupling that fateful spring day, that she represented the proverbial final one) that had to deal with the abandonment issues and the crippling insecurity and the writer's block on a grueling daily basis.

Even Stevie recognized he'd crossed a line with Elizabeth Straw, a line that had begun as little more than a crack in the pavement and ended up a full-blown San Andreas-grade fault. It hadn't been a question of *if* but of *when*. The funny part was, Stevie hadn't recognized Elizabeth as having Big One potential on the first day of class (or for that matter, on the fortieth). He'd been too distracted by the more obvious beauties, the hair tossers and leg crossers, and the frequency with which they lingered after class, the fruitless way the tried to trip him up by brazenly staring him down. He didn't mind the extra attention, of course, was far more flattered by it than he let on. But there's nothing stealthy about raw beauty: it's about as subtle as a thunderstorm. By contrast Elizabeth Straw had snuck up on Stevie. By the time he'd noticed her at all—really, truly noticed her—it was already too late. Her slightly crooked, caffeine-tinged teeth had long since torn Stevie free of his own life, her lightless gray eyes swallowed him up like a jagged crevasse in the earth's crust.

Stevie hadn't found out about Miranda's pregnancy until it was too late. They'd made reservations at Opal's to celebrate their third wedding anniversary, and he got it into his head to confess to her over dinner. Of course his timing had been terrible. Here he was, reluctant dumper in what was rapidly shaping up to be a dumping ceremony, while Miranda, he later learned, had spent the afternoon dreaming up potential baby names. His wife wasn't by nature a forgiving person (she held a years-long grudge against her twin sister for wearing and ruining her favorite suede ankle boots back when they were fifteen). Still, if it had been a simple matter of clichéd student-teacher infidelity, Miranda might have found it in her un-pardoning heart to forgive him, now that she was pregnant. But the worst of it wasn't what had transpired between Stevie and Lizzie Straw, though he knew Miranda well enough to know she would demand details; her loathing of duplicity smacked of evangelism, and bordered on the masochistic.

The fact of the matter was he couldn't help hurting her. Stevie hated to admit it, but he knew himself fully capable of committing the very same crime again, with Elizabeth, for sure, but also with a swelling host of nameless, faceless women he had yet to meet. A barrage of romantic intimations—a sample of female laughter at the start of a pop song; a waft of cinnamon perfume on the wind; a flash of golden hair in an open-topped car—accosted him on an almost hourly basis. At times he felt downright manhandled, surrounded and bullied by these fleeting sensations like an ornately bespectacled school kid during recess. Oddly, the realization that he should never have married Miranda didn't dawn on Stevie slowly, like late-September sunlight saturating a room—it yanked him into an alley and hit him square on the jaw. Years later he was still seeing stars. He wished they'd go away.

Stevie had waited until after dessert to deliver the news. He saw no reason to ruin their meal, and the last thing he wanted to create, at least figuratively, was a scene. Besides, he was still half hoping he'd chicken out. A voice at one of Stevie's shoulders told him he was doing the honorable thing by coming clean, even if it meant abandoning Miranda and cruelly breaking her heart; another voice at the opposite shoulder said he was a fool to confess, what his wife didn't know wouldn't hurt her, his first priority should be to spare her feelings, not selfishly keep his conscience clear. But which voice represented the angelic in Stevie and which the demonic was impossible to tell.

Miranda didn't cause a scene. In fact there was little in her behavior to suggest that her marriage had just shattered as easily as the shell of her crème brulèe. She rose from the table and insisted on walking the mile and a half back home. But she never showed up at home, and refused to return to the apartment until Stevie moved out, which he did the very next day.

He called her a few weeks later, just to check in. The semester was winding down, and with it Stevie's social calendar: soon his pre-fab audience of rapt undergraduates would be heading home for the holidays. Come the new year, everything could change. Miranda picked up the phone on the first ring, as if expecting his call.

"It's me," he said, sounding for all his forced intimacy like a complete stranger. "How are you?"

"Pregnant," spat Miranda, "that's how I am. Or was."

Stevie was taken aback. He was prepared for unmitigated vitriol but not for emotional blackmail. Half convinced Miranda was bluffing, he asked her what she was talking about.

"I'm talking about how, up until very recently, I was having your baby."

It wasn't impossible. They'd never been overly cautious when it came to unprotected sex. In fact, once they were married, an almost subversive thrill accompanied the notion that sleeping together could result in the creation of a third person. "What do you mean, 'until very recently'? What happened? You lost it?"

"Yeah, Stevie," Miranda cackled, "I lost the baby. There's this big old hole in my pocket I've been meaning to sew. The baby must've slipped on through. I tried retracing my steps, but no luck. Wanna help me post fliers on telephone poles around town?"

It took a minute for his brain to kick in. "You're saying you had a…procedure."

"I'm saying I was pregnant and now I'm not and it's all your fault."

"You should've told me," he said evenly, convinced now that she was telling the truth. "You had no right."

"Fuck *you*, Stevie. I had *every* right. My body, my rules. Besides, we're not a couple anymore. I'm too old for you, remember? I'm a fucking *relic* next to the fresh-faced president of your teenage fan club."

Stevie had nothing to say to that. Even if he could think of something legitimate to contribute to the conversation, once again he was reminded that words wouldn't save their marriage, or reanimate their unborn baby, or banish the likes of lascivious Lizzie Straw. If anything, words were largely to blame for the pathetic mess Stevie had made of his life thus far, the pathetic mess he would continue to make of it. In the end, what good were they?

"Just do me one favor," Miranda said, just before hanging up. "Don't mythologize me. And don't you dare put our unborn baby in a fucking book."

In the end he'd done just that, turning their brief time together, their doomed marriage and the child that wasn't, into an award-winning story. And then, as if to rub Miranda's perfect little nose in it, promptly turned the story into his first novel. Doing so wasn't solely about revenge. Stevie just happened to be one of those writers who wrote from experience; he'd always trafficked in thinly-veiled autobiography. Hadn't his own mother served as the title character in his first published work? The character wasn't what you'd call a flattering one. But then Stevie's mother was a staunch believer in there being no such thing as bad press. Miranda, on the other hand, was an intensely private person with a broken heart and an aborted pregnancy. He should've exercised a little self-control.

"The Abortion Story" Miranda had retitled it the one and only time she called to castigate him for his callousness. That's when all the vampire comparisons began in earnest. "You've become your mother's son after all, Stevie, a monster only she could create. You're a true vampire now, and not some pointy toothed Transylvanian out of an old horror flick. You've fed off me, off my love and my loyalty and my pain, just like you feed off everybody dumb or young enough to call you a friend. That's all we are to you: sustenance, pure and simple. Grist for the fucking fiction mill. Trouble is, the more you feed, the more you crave. It never ends. The living dead, that's you, Stevie. Nobody touches you. In ten years' time you won't have a friend in the world."

And now Miranda's melodramatic prophecy had come to pass. It was true Stevie didn't have many friends, but he was a loner by nature. Losing Miranda had been the worst of it. He'd never quite recovered. Over the last decade Stevie had tried on various occasions to reconcile with her; he'd sent handmade cards at Christmas and her favorite flowers on her birthday and left cryptic messages on her machine on Halloween, their defacto anniversary. But Miranda Burns held grudges—held them longer and more tightly than most people hold their own children. The first few times she'd bothered to respond at all, she'd set Stevie's flimsy olive branches ablaze. Then she stopped responding and Stevie stopped apologizing and, in the time it had taken him to fill two more mediocre books with unsavory characters culled from his own life, somehow they were strangers again.

A month ago, Stevie received a bizarre postcard in the mail. It featured a pen-and-ink drawing of a Victorian-era baby carriage, with a hood segmented like a seahorse and wheels as big as a bicycle's. The flipside read *Did you lose something?* That's it. No signature, no return address. Or rather, the return address was a bogus one: 0001 Cemetery Lane. Home, only a monster aficionado like Stevie would know, to Charles Addams' creepy, eponymous family.

It wasn't much, but it was enough. Stevie often received a smattering of fan mail after a book of his came out—some of it straightforward, some of it not so much—but something told him that wasn't what this was about. It didn't take long for him to track down Miranda. She had a Facebook page like everybody else. All the settings were private, so he couldn't tell for sure whether it was his ex-wife. But the profile pic was promising: a famous black and white portrait of pouting, panda-eyed, shock-haired Siouxsie Sioux. He sent her a message asking point-blank whether she had a child and, if so, whether the kid was his. She could've just said, Sorry, buddy, wrong Miranda Burns. She didn't have to respond at all. Instead she got back to Stevie within the hour:

PRESUMPTUOUS MUCH? SORRY, STEVIE, NO SONS, NO DAUGHTERS, NO PROGENY OF ANY STRIPE. I'M A BARREN WOMAN, BY ALL ACCOUNTS. BUT IT WAS SWEET OF YOU TO ASK. NOW FUCK OFF AND DIE.

He could've taken her word for it. Miranda had always prided herself on how inept she was at telling lies. But Stevie's love life had been far from tantric. As a professional parasite, he'd feasted on his fair share of women in the aftermath of his marriage to Miranda, but nothing like the banquet of literary acolytes of which Elizabeth Straw had seemed but a tantalizing appetizer. Plus, post-Miranda he'd had unprotected sex exactly once, and that, despite or possibly because of the fact that he was now middle-aged, was a mere three years ago. Stevie was no expert on childhood development, but he was pretty sure that even the most precocious of toddlers would be hard-pressed to write a postcard at the tender age of two.

An online search of the White Pages revealed Miranda's most current address. An incorrigible creature of habit, she was living in the very town where Stevie had left her.

The charming, leaf-littered streets were weirdly quiet, considering it was prime-time on Halloween. Stevie expected to be greeted by throngs of miniature monsters, a parade of pirates and princesses and pointy-hat wearing witches. But he hadn't seen a single kid, costumed or not, since turning into Miranda's somnolent, poorly-lit neighborhood. Maybe he was just missing them; maybe the trick-or-treaters zigged one way while Stevie zagged another. Or maybe the haul this year was so good—the lollipops big as 45's and all the chocolate bars full-size and nary a doctor averting apple to be found—that they'd all quickly met their quota and turned in early, and were at this very moment comparing each other's take at candy-strewn kitchen tables all across town.

Stevie coasted by Miranda's house and parked his aging Volvo wagon around the corner, out of sight. His plan had been to insinuate himself among a group of pint-sized panhandlers and their parents, thereby giving the impression that he was an overzealous paterfamilias, one of the "fun" dads who would be dressed as Santa eight weeks hence and went all-out on Halloween. But since there were no kids, there were no dads. He was conspicuously alone, the supposed way he preferred it.

Other than the ceramic bat wind chime they'd bought on what they'd laughingly referred to as their honeymoon—two sleepless nights spent at the haunted inn, screwing and searching for ghosts—he found the house devoid of decoration. You wouldn't have known it was Halloween. You could barely tell, looking at the pumpkin-less front porch, that it was October. He double-checked the address. What had become of Miranda, that she could play fast-and-loose with the change of the seasons, to say nothing of her favorite holiday, this way? What odd illness had infected the mischievous person who'd accompanied Stevie on a prankish Mischief Night raid, bombing the houses of his tweedy English Department colleagues with eggs and shaving cream and Crazy String? What of the flamboyant still-young woman partial to Barbarella boots and dog collars and underwear festooned with Emily the Strange?

Although it was well past eight, it didn't look like any trick-or-treaters would be rallying to help Stevie. He was far from confident in his costume. But he had no choice but to ring the bell himself.

"Good evening," he said in a passable Transylvanian accent to the oddly pretty red-haired girl who answered the door, his daughter.

"Good evening," she repeated, smiling and shaking her head. She had Stevie's nose, that much was clear. "Can I help you?" she asked, knitting her brow.

"Er, trick-or-treat," Stevie said, suddenly realizing he'd neglected to bring a bag. Lamely, he stuck out his hands, a beggar now in every sense of the word.

The birdlike tween looked at him askance. Where was her costume? And why was the tidy, brightly-lit house behind her so quiet, so decidedly un-spooky, on this, the spookiest night of the year?

"I guess you didn't get the memo," she said, sounding just like Miranda.

"Memo?" Stevie said, genuinely confused but unable to abandon the role he was apparently born to play. "Vhat memo?"

The girl's sleeves were rolled, her fingers and lower forearms veined with what looked to Stevie like nothing so much as yellow-orange snot. She clutched a tiny scalpel. Despite the dearth of trick-or-treaters, it heartened Stevie to find that he'd interrupted his daughter in the midst of performing cosmetic surgery on a pumpkin. All was not lost.

"Halloween was yesterday," she said. "You missed it."

"No, no, no," he said, shaking his own head now. "Today, my darling young lady, is Hallo-*veen*." He spread his black cape wide, as though its satiny underside displayed a calendar on which he could confirm the date. "Count Dracula should know."

She shook her head more vigorously now, her coiled, coppery hair, a replica of her mother's, catching and seeming to crystallize the light shed by the tiny foyer chandelier.

"You don't get it. The township decided to celebrate Halloween last night, Saturday, instead of on a school night."

The township? What township? Since when was Halloween in the hands of a township?

"You're a day late," she informed him, sympathetically adding, "That sucks."

Stevie couldn't resist. "No pun intended, eh?"

The girl's expression changed from one of mild amusement to wary suspicion. She wasn't so sure about him anymore. She fiddled dangerously with the scalpel.

"Do I know you?" she said. She squinted at Stevie, and the house behind her seemed to shrink.

"I live avound the corner," he lied to his little girl. "I know your mother." Another lie, of sorts. Had he ever known Miranda?

"Astrid, what's going on down there?" called a female voice from deep inside the house. It was a familiar, oddly bloodless voice, like a song Stevie still knew all the words to though the tune somehow eluded him. "Who's at the door?"

Astrid, thought Stevie. *Perfect.*

"A vampire," their daughter called back, giggling. Then, under her breath: "An *old* vampire."

"A *what?*"

"A confused trick-or-treater."

"Tell them we're fresh out," Miranda said. "Halloween was last night."

Astrid turned to him smiling. "My mom says to tell you Halloween was last night."

"So I heard." He was running out of options. He couldn't very well stand here secretly chatting with his kid until Miranda came down, identified him despite the best efforts of Halloween Dreamz, and called the cops. As it was, he could hardly believe his luck. Here he was, having an exhilarating if fundamentally dishonest conversation with his kid. He felt truly transformed, as though a kindly old witch had taken pity on him and cast this wonderful spell. Kiss the frog and a prince just might materialize. But if Astrid were to lean forward and inexplicably kiss this phony vampire's cheek, would Stevie have the courage to morph into her father? "Oh vell," he sighed, deciding it was in everybody's best interest for him not to break character. "There's alvays next year."

Mistaking the disappointed look on her father's face, Astrid frowned Miranda's lipless frown and said, "Wait here." She put a finger up to her prominent nose and quietly closed the door.

Now was his chance for a clean getaway. Astrid was probably going to get her mother, who would instantly recognize Stevie even with the weight loss and shaved face, even beneath the shellacked hair and deathly pallor and masochist's plastic teeth. But he couldn't move. For the first time he truly felt like a parasite, sucking whatever familial life he could from the dull domestic scene unfolding on the other side of the door. He almost opened it and walked right inside, an ill-advised move that could very well result in jail time. Besides, vampires, he recalled, couldn't enter a home unless they were invited. Even the undead, it seemed, had to abide by certain universal rules.

He was turning on his heel when Astrid reappeared at the door and handed him something.

"Vhat's this?" Stevie said, before giving it a good look.

"Candy," she laughed. "Isn't that why you're here?"

And it *was* candy: Goldenberg's Peanut Chews, of all things. Stevie had been allergic for years.

"Astrid?" came Miranda's voice again, an impatient octave higher than before. "Enough with the pumpkins. You have homework."

"I gotta go," Astrid whispered, glancing over her shoulder. She eyed him one last time. "Are you sure I don't know you?"

Stevie held her gaze, attempting a kind of paternal telepathy. The message he imparted—*I only just met you, but*

I love you more than life—was simplistic and earth-shattering, an everyday miracle in the making. Seeming to sense as much, Astrid squirmed under his scrutiny, for which her father was thankful. "No," was all he said, meaning *No, I'm not sure* not *No, you don't know me.*

"Astrid *Louise!*"

"Sorry, I really gotta go." She smiled goodbye and began to close the door on Stevie's bloodless, barely familiar face.

That's when it happened. She wasn't being careful, and somehow the surgery-sharp carving implement—where had she secreted that damned scalpel?—must've bit into her finger. She lurched as though stung by a kamikaze killer bee, or worse. His little girl.

"Ow!" she yelped.

"Here," Stevie said, instinctively taking hold of Astrid's hand. He had his lips on her finger, was chastely kissing the split digit, before either of them could register what was happening. "There," he said softly, like a real dad that had just dispelled all manner of monster from beneath her frilly, four-poster bed. "All better now."

The shocked expression on Astrid's face made Stevie second-guess the wisdom of planting even a fatherly kiss on this girl to whom he was nothing but a stranger. "Sorry," he stammered, backing away from the door and the dumbstruck features that, suddenly, so closely resembled his own. He offered her what he hoped would be construed as an utterly paternal and unperverted thumbs-up. Then he beat a hasty retreat to his car.

Stevie was inches from the ancient Volvo when Astrid's panicked call for her mother pierced him like a stake through the heart. It was all he could do not to turn round and rush to her aid. But it pleased him how his little girl had come to her senses, how, like her mother, eventually she could be relied upon to recognize a creep and deal with him accordingly. He slid behind the steering wheel feeling more content than he had cause to be, with poisonous candy in his pocket and his child's blood on his tongue. He'd never tasted anything so sweet.

There's nothing secure about it.

Shiner

Gritty, ungodly music manhandles Paul as he climbs the warped stairs leading to Tilda's apartment. He finds her door torn free of its hinges; it lounges in its jamb as casually as a kid on a street corner. Paul considers showing himself in but hangs back and knocks hard on the hollow wood. Tilda claims to be shameless—the girl can transform a common belch into a kind of gastrointestinal aria—but he has no desire to catch her in the midst of that most private of acts: the air-guitar solo.

Tilda appears in the doorway, bubbly and out of breath. She's wearing dingy white overalls and oversized sunglasses. She's sweating, slightly. "Hey," she says without smiling.

Tilda leads Paul over to a big vinyl armchair, instructing him to take a seat with a dismissive wave of her hand. No sooner has he sat down than something cold and wet strikes him in the face. It takes him a second to realize that Tilda has turned suddenly and shot him three times—*bang, bang, bang*—with a translucent red pistol she's filled from the tap. Tilda tosses the toy aside with the carelessness of a true gunslinger and stalks to where he sits, damp and slightly annoyed.

"Thirsty?" she asks, straddling him. She improvises a hip-swivel-rump-wiggle to the desperate beat of the music.

Paul nods. Tilda is halfway through what might be but most likely isn't her first beer of the day. She has no qualms about drinking alone. Tilda has no qualms, period.

"What happened to your door?"

"I painted it," she says. "Kiwi-green is the new black."

"Not that."

Tilda shrugs. "I had a Black Friday black light party last night. Things got a little out of hand." She pulls a face. "You weren't invited," she adds, almost as an afterthought.

"Lucky me."

Tilda bites him on the neck, hard.

"Ow!"

"Oops, sorry," she says. "I forgot—no marks."

Paul watches her slink away. When Tilda stops at the boom box to change the music, he keeps on watching. The overalls leave too much to the imagination. After all, it was Tilda's lithe body—rather than her pretty eyes or practiced street sass—that had floored Paul three months before, at the time of their meeting. He'd just come from class, where Professor Sable had spent half an hour expressing just how "unexciting" Paul's mixed media project was, how generally "misguided" and "ill-conceived" most of his students' mixed media projects were. Paul was in a dark mood. Tilda helped lighten it. As she crisscrossed the café, serving aging creatives their fey, gourmet lunches, it was all he could do to keep from sidling up behind the suicide-blonde server in the synthetic hip-huggers and doubling her over the dessert counter.

Another song kicks in, unrelated to the last. Paul catches the words "kitchen" and "Kentucky" and "Peter Pan."

"So how'd it go?" he asks.

"How do you think it went?" Tilda laughs. She hands him a drink.

Paul shrugs and takes a long pull on his beer. He doesn't really want to discuss Tilda's party. It's not that he feels slighted, exactly, although the courtesy of an invitation—even one of Tilda's flip *come-if-you-want-I-don't-give-a-shit-either-way-whatever* invites—would've been nice. As a rule, Paul doesn't come to Tilda's to talk.

Tilda shifts her weight and nearly empties her painted bottle of Mexican beer. She hasn't taken off the ridiculous sunglasses. "I thought you might show," she admits. "You're an incorrigible creature of habit, in case you haven't noticed." She finishes her drink. "I thought Friday was, like, *our* night. But I guess you couldn't make it, huh. For obvious reasons."

She's referring to Jacqueline. Paul doesn't have the energy to explain that, rather than rolling around his girlfriend's futon, he'd spent a sleepless night in his own bed, wrestling with the news that his father had just been diagnosed with non-Hodgkin lymphoma, news his parents decided to break over Thanksgiving dinner, with his stone-faced paterfamilias being admitted for treatment the very next day. Tilda wouldn't know what to do with such news. *Paul* hardly knows what to do with such news. They've exchanged bodily fluids, but not phone numbers, not emails. They may not be strangers, strictly speaking, but they're far from friends.

Tilda smirks her inimitable Tilda-smirk. She holds Paul's gaze through CD-size lenses of cheap black plastic. "So much for my security deposit," she huffs, apropos of the door. "I hate my friends."

"If it's any consolation, I hate your friends too."

"You don't even know them," she snaps.

"That makes two of us."

Tilda flips him the bird. "You barely know *me*."

Paul considers this comment and is tempted, fleetingly, to respond to it in a mature manner. But despite his sick dad and his demanding girlfriend and his unimpressive GPA, he's decided that mature behavior is grossly overrated.

"Ah, but that's the way I like you—bare."

"Down boy," Tilda says dryly. "First, a toast."

Tilda hands Paul her empty and skips like a schoolgirl over to a ladder leading to a hole in her roof. She glances coyly—or coyly for Tilda—over her shoulder. Consistent with his character, Paul watches her climb.

Tilda's loft is a dilapidated, sporadically furnished space ("broken-in" is her optimistic word for it). She makes no attempt to detract from what she no doubt sees as its starving-artist allure by tidying up: loose change and stale candy are strewn across the rusted retro kitchen table; Hefty bags full of dirty laundry—a bulwark against some encroaching flood—are haphazardly stacked along one wall; a week's worth of dishes teeters like some mythic, ill-planned city in the utility-tub sink. Nothing here matches: the sofa cushions are related only by marriage, and each of the four walls is painted a different, oddly uninviting color. Even the toilet seat, recalls Paul, is too small for its bowl.

As for the ladder, Tilda built it herself from planks of plywood she found in the basement of the building. The circular hole—or hatch, as she calls it—came with the apartment, and had even been cunningly listed in the rental ad as a skylight. She has no idea who made it or what, exactly, it's for. It does let in a fair amount of sunlight, though, and because of this Tilda has positioned her easel directly beneath it. Wishful thinking. When she isn't painting, which forever seems to be the case, she sun-bathes, or skims Anais Nin, or simply sleeps, up on the roof. More than once she's tried to get Paul to join her, claiming, among other things, that he's missing out on one spectacular view. But the view from where Paul sits watching Tilda ascend the ladder is about all the spectacularity he can handle.

Other times Tilda drops the pretext of the scenery and admits, with a bluntness that never fails to surprise Paul, that she wants to fuck him up there on the cool, gritty tarmac, under the moonless, soupy sky.

"I'm an earth sign," Paul reminds her, peering up at Tilda's inverted head from safe within the apartment. She appears glowing, angelic, in the iridescent square of fading light. "Besides, that thing doesn't look very secure."

"That's the whole point," Tilda squeals in disbelief. "There's nothing *secure* about it."

Paul's read somewhere that the poet Frank O'Hara used to keep a fresh sheet of paper rolled in his typewriter at all times. This way, in the middle of the night or arriving home on his lunch hour, he could dash off a few of his breezy, busy poems before falling back to sleep or returning to MoMA, where he worked. Maybe Tilda has the same idea, only with canvas. But O'Hara was a prolific artist, whereas Tilda—

"Let's go," Tilda says, shimmying back down the ladder. "I'm out of beer."

Paul glances at his watch. "I don't have time for a pub crawl," he says.

"No?" Tilda shoots him a knowing smile from behind her Captain Fantastic eyewear. "What do you have time for?"

Paul's due at the hospital soon. Tilda's apartment is only a few blocks away from where his father sits awaiting his first chemo treatment.

"Not a whole lot," he admits.

Paul and his father have never been close. The man always seemed to prefer the company of his freshly doodled cartoons to that of his flesh-and-blood family. Throughout his childhood, Paul had gotten the impression that his father considered his only child a liability—if not exactly a noose around the neck, then an anchor tied to the foot, an irremovable pair of one-size-fits-all cement shoes.

"Then we'll make it a pub *jog*," Tilda says, laughing and pulling Paul toward the door. "A pub sprint. A pub run."

"I'm not even supposed to be here," he blurts.

This stops Tilda in her tracks. "You're never *supposed* to be here," she pronounces.

The truth is, Paul and his father hardly speak to each other on the best of days, so what is he supposed to say to the man on the absolute worst? For all his fluency on the page, for all his skill at communicating his characters' inner life in a few deft strokes, talking seriously or at length to his son proves beyond his father's faculties.

Tilda reaches into a closet and pulls out a puffy down vest. "First rule of seduction: Make her wait. You're an artist. Absence makes the heart grow fodder."

"That's good," Paul says. "I like that. Would that it were true."

"Hold that thought." Tilda ducks into the bathroom. For once she shuts the door.

Paul hears the toilet lid strike the tank and the sound of running water. Monroe appears out of nowhere and begins shamelessly rubbing against his leg. Tilda's kitten is named for the prestigious women's art college that recently rejected her application. When Paul suggested changing the pet's name, Tilda waved away the idea as if it were an airborne bug. "It's still a great school," she argued. "They're probably better off."

Not for the first time Paul fantasizes about throwing over Jacqueline and taking up with Tilda, but quickly reminds himself that doing so would defeat the purpose. Besides, he doesn't relish waking to the sound of gunplay, or barricading Tilda's broken door with the magazine-filled steamer trunk she uses in lieu of a deadbolt. Or taking his meals—weak coffee; frozen pizza; a rare, celebratory bowl of Lucky Charms—with the cockroaches and mice that Tilda, in her infinite boredom, is halfheartedly attempting to train. Squalor is an okay place to visit, but a guy like Paul could never actually live there.

And yet, now that Paul *is* there, he's oddly reluctant to leave. Only part of this reluctance, he realizes, is the result of Jackie's increasing suspicions, or the knowledge that soon he'll have to show his face in his father's unconvincingly cheery hospital room. A bigger part results from the sex. Unlike Jacqueline, whose fleshiness is the physical equivalent of comfort food, Tilda's body seems tailor-made to Paul's specifications: trim and strong-limbed but jarringly curvy where it counts. It's mercifully easy for Paul to lose himself in Tilda's apartment, to drown amid the torrent of deafening indie rock and the waves of filched hospital blankets breaking over her makeshift bed. There's a strong undertow here; it tends to set him adrift.

Tilda exits the bathroom still donning the dime store shades. She checks herself in three variously shaped mirrors hung one atop the other to form a composite full-length.

"Ready," she says, grabbing her keys.

"Do you have stock in Sunglass Hut or something?" Paul says. "It's thirty-five degrees outside. They're calling for snow."

Tilda hesitates, something Paul is unused to seeing her do. "I had a little accident," she says. "At the party." She removes the sunglasses. The skin surrounding her right eye, which she hasn't quite managed to conceal with cover-up, is bluish-green and badly bruised, bee sting-swollen.

"Wow," Paul says.

"For lack of a better term."

"What happened?"

"Trust me," Tilda says, milking the mystery for all it's worth. "You don't want to know."

She's right, he doesn't.

At Skeezy Pete's, Tilda orders some drinks, and the bartender—a big black guy with a shock of yellow hair—makes some requisite cracks about her sunglasses.

"Oooh, there's a celebrity in the house," he coos. "Excuse me, Miss. Can I get your au-to-graph?" Tilda defiantly flashes her shiner. "Damn," the bartender says, slowly shaking his warning signal of a head. "What's the other bitch look like?"

"*He* looks like shit," gloats Tilda.

The bartender gives Paul an apprising look. "Don't let her fool you. She likes it rough."

"Fuck you, James," Tilda says.

"Anytime," James gallantly replies.

"Ditch the shades, will you," Paul tells Tilda. "I feel like part of your entourage."

"What, you're not?" Tilda sticks out her tongue but does as he asks. "You know, everyone who sees this is going to automatically assume you're responsible."

He levels his eyes at Tilda, which given her condition isn't an easy thing to do. "And that's a good thing?"

"It can be," she says, lighting a cigarette. "Depends how you play it."

Paul takes a swig of beer. It's warmer than he expected. "I don't think I could pull it off, the whole Ike Turner-James Brown-Rick James routine."

"Hey, white guys beat women too." Tilda frowns. "And what's routine about it?"

"What I mean is, I don't think anyone would confuse me with a guy like that. In fact, women are always telling me how non-threatening they find me."

"Ha—before or after they pose for your paintings?"

"They mean it as a compliment."

Tilda makes a show of eyeing him critically. "I don't know, I think you've got real potential," she says. "You strike me as an angry-head just waiting to happen."

"I'm a walking time bomb," Paul mock-agrees.

She squints at him. "Nah. More like a dormant volcano."

"Meaning?"

Tilda blows a plume of smoke toward the ceiling, a parody of a looming eruption, and fixes Paul with her Siberian husky eyes: one a perfect, translucent blue orb, the other runny and bloodshot, a broken yolk. She starts to speak, then stops short. Clearly something is on her mind, and Tilda isn't the type of sparring partner to pull punches. "How about I just paint you a picture."

"I don't have all year, Lambchop."

"Don't call me Lambchop," Tilda snaps, squashing her cigarette. "I'm not your fucking *girlfriend*."

Once, coming out of the bathroom, Paul caught Tilda going through his wallet—she claimed to be looking for a condom. Instead she came across a photo of Jacqueline, naked from the waist up, sporting a nappy pair of "Little Bo Peep" lamb's ears. The ears were sort of sexy and fun and very un-Jacqueline, but then that was the point.

"More lame than lamb," snorts Tilda, clearly pleased with the pun.

"You said something about a toast," Paul reminds her.

Tilda is beaming. If she remains self-conscious about her black eye, it doesn't show. In fact she seems almost proud. Poised with a fresh cigarette, a constellation of twinkling lights framing her semi-swollen face like a nimbus, somehow Tilda's bruise suits her. Some women accessorize with jewelry or reading glasses or peek-a-boo tattoos. Tilda, it strikes Paul, accessorizes with pain. Most of the time this pain is merely implied, a festering, poorly hidden sore beneath the Band-Aid of drugs and booze and all-night raves. But here Tilda has taken the next logical step: her black eye is the pain made manifest, for all to see. Not coming clean about its origin can only work in the waif's favor.

Tilda trains her eyes on him, forcing Paul to look away. She raises her beer. "To me," she says. "I'm going back to school."

Officially, Tilda never even started school. But Paul's not about to play semantics with her now.

"Congratulations," he says, tapping the sweaty neck of his bottle against hers. "Where? Taylor? Don't tell me PIA?" Monroe, he knows, is not an option.

Tilda gamely shakes her head. The expression on her face isn't one Paul can remember ever having seen before. "None of the above." She puts her sunglasses back on. "Not even close. I've enrolled in nursing school." She reaches a hand under the table and squeezes his thigh for emphasis. "I'm going to heal the lame."

Paul doesn't say anything right away, partly because it's taking his brain a few moments to download the truly bizarre image of Tilda Harrington, RN. Try as he might, he just can't see Tilda, with her flaking purple nail polish and pronounced nose ring, sporting hospital clogs and teddy bear scrubs. She doesn't even have health insurance.

"Wow," Paul says, flustered. "What about, you know, art?"

"Oh, *him*," Tilda jokes, eyeing him strangely. "Turns out he was a total prick, schtuping my sister the entire time."

"Seriously."

Tilda takes a long time answering, choosing instead to study the eagle on the label of her lager the way most museum-goers pretend to ponder a great work of art. "This is, like, the first good thing I've done for myself," she says. "Ever." She squeezes his thigh again. "Are you mad at me?"

"What? No," Paul half lies. "Why would I be mad?"

Tilda smiles widely. She makes an encouraging kissy face at Paul right before she kicks him under the table.

"Shit!" he yelps.

"How about now?" Tilda asks.

Paul rubs his leg and gives her a look. "Getting there."

While he's busy tending to his leg, Tilda touches the tip of her smoking cigarette to the sleeve of his nylon bomber jacket.

Paul yanks him arm away. "Are you fucking nuts?" He glares at her.

"How about now?" she prompts. "Are you mad now?"

"Yeah, okay," he barks, checking the damage. "I'm a raving lunatic. Satisfied?"

Tilda clinks the bottom of her green bottle against the top of Paul's, causing a surge of foam to spill over and stream down the outside of his barely-touched beer. She drains what's left of her own lager in one long gulp. "Come on," she says, stubbing out her cigarette and rising to go. "Let's go re-channel some of that typical male aggression."

It's windier than Paul expects up on the roof of Tilda's decrepit building, the snow a modern dance dervish of colorless ice crystals. The weather's a minor miracle considering the news-folk predicted it; the pretty fluff coats their hair and clings to their clothes as doggedly as the fake stuff.

Paul was right about the ladder: it's wobbly and worrisome, likely to splinter at any second under his heavily shod feet. He's right about the ladder, but Tilda's right about the view: from this vantage the city seems downright enchanted, a shimmering oasis in an endless sea of unfathomable dark. It's like some private, self-created place Paul's only ever seen on cards postmarked from his restless mind's eye.

Tilda's roof, by contrast, resembles an accident scene; remnants of her recent bash litter the tarmac like the personal effects of the victims of some freakish disaster: cigarette butts and crushed beer cans and spent dime bags coupled with more troublesome items like lost jewelry, the odd discarded sock.

"I'm proud of you," Tilda announces, and despite her efforts to shield it with ridicule, something resembling pride does in fact color her words. "My baby boy's all growns up."

Paul considers admitting to Tilda that, despite the obvious wisdom of her decision, the news that she has thrown over art in favor of a nursing degree doesn't sit well with him. In theory he knows it's a good move for her, but on some level he can't help feeling betrayed. Though just how he could feel betrayed by someone who'd never pledged to him her loyalty in the first place confuses even him.

Tilda wraps a hospital blanket around Paul, bat-like, and bites him on the ear. "You deserve a reward," she says.

They kiss, roughly, the way the bartender claimed Tilda likes it. "Tell me about your eye," Paul says. "For real."

Ignoring him, Tilda loosens Paul's belt and slides a surprisingly warm hand down his pants.

"Seriously," he says. "I'm a big boy, I can take it."

Tilda reaches between his legs. "You're not *that* big," she giggles.

Paul isn't amused. In fact he can feel himself turning against Tilda; the temptation to abuse her somehow takes hold of him as tangibly as drops of frozen water strike his skin. He adjusts his pants and makes an effort to move away from her, then surprises them both by whipping off Tilda's sunglasses and tossing them over the side of the building.

"What the fuck?" Tilda says.

Paul doesn't respond. Tilda's ruined eye has taken him by surprise. Back at the bar, mere inches away and garishly lit, it was all he could do to look Tilda straight-on. But up here on the roof, in the biting cold and semi-dark, Tilda's shiner is doing just that: shining like some evil star in the muted light of an overhead lamp. It's an accident scene Paul is hard-pressed to turn away from.

"Tell me what really happened," Paul says, staring her down. "Pretty-please."

A second cousin to a smile pays a visit to Tilda's plump, perennially chapped lips. She sheds her casual, world-weary voice and slips into a new one, a strapless number with a tawdry slit up the side and fake gemstones scattered like bridge fare across the bodice.

"I already told you you don't want to know," she teases.

"But I do," Paul assures her. He isn't sure why, but he's suddenly desperate to know everything about her, beginning with the story behind her battered eye. "Whatever happened, whoever did this to you, I want you to tell me."

Tilda starts to say something but stops short. "Like you care," she snorts. "Like anybody cares."

Paul wants to convince her but doesn't know how. He can't think straight, what with Tilda's bruise shamelessly gleaming at him like that. The sickening mix of color mesmerizes him, so much so that Paul can't help thinking that if Tilda allowed these deviant hues to dominate her palette, she'd fare better with her art.

"This isn't fun anymore," Tilda says finally, moving toward the hatch. "I'm going back inside."

Paul jumps in front of her. "Not yet," he says, barring her way. "Tell me."

Tilda smirks.

"I mean it," he says. "You're not going anywhere until you tell me."

"Fuck off," she says, trying to push past him.

Paul takes hold of her shoulders and pulls Tilda out of her ratty cocoon. They watch the blanket flutter like a flag of surrender over the side of the building, going the way of the sunglasses.

"Asshole," Tilda hisses.

Paul falls on top of her and forces Tilda to the tarmac, pinning her to the roof. Tilda doesn't fight back; she's incapacitated by a sudden and surprisingly robust fit of giggles.

"What's so funny?" he snaps.

"The volcano," sputters Tilda. "It's finally erupting. Head for the hills!"

From a painterly point of view, there's an odd logic to giving Tilda a second shiner, to countering one grossly overworked side of the canvas, so to speak, with bolder strokes, braver shapes, deeper shadows. The rather rigid laws of composition all but demand it. Tilda, herself, seems tacitly to be giving Paul permission to strike her: her jaw is set and her eyes now closed, all but bracing for the blow.

An ambulance races down Walnut Street, siren blaring. They listen without moving as it rushes headlong through the falling snow, its wailing gang-way filling every side street and vacant lot and abandoned back alley from here to the flurry-dusted Delaware. It's headed, no doubt, to the colorless, too-clean place with which Paul's family is about to become all too familiar.

Paul releases his grip on Tilda and slowly gets to his feet.

"Did I miss something?" Tilda says, confused. "Don't tell me you already shot your load!"

Paul ignores her and heads straight for the hole in the roof.

"Come back here and fight like a metrosexual!"

Without a thought for his safety Paul scampers down the wobbling ladder, jumping the last few rungs in his haste. He maneuvers through the darkened apartment and, moments later, is out on the street.

He hydroplanes most of the way through an inch of wintry fluff and skids to a stop across the street from the hospital. The place is big and brightly lit in a way he should find comforting, but doesn't. *Open 24 hrs* he can't help thinking. *The sickness business is booming.*

Paul considers going inside and facing his father, mutely perhaps, and to nobody's relief more than his own, but facing him nonetheless. He considers cutting out and catching a cab to Jacqueline's, where he can pretend for a little while longer to be the man she believes him to be. He even considers heading back to the litter-strewn roof, where he imagines Tilda sitting cross-legged and catching the season's first snowflakes on the crest of her warm, wet tongue.

Instead Paul begins massaging the skin surrounding his right eye as though plagued by some vague, untreatable pain. A little girl in ladybug boots points and asks her mother what's wrong with him, why's that man rubbing his face that way. As the subtle massage morphs into a full-blown baker's knead, a few more people stop and stare, but no one seems eager to approach him, let alone see if he needs help.

The light changes color half a dozen times while Paul stands outside the big glowing building in the scurf-like snow, all but willing his deceptively smooth skin to blacken and swell.

It's all very chummy and nostalgic and sweetly sad.

Public Displays
of Affectation

"Where's the butterfly?" Damon asks, frisking the barmaid with his wire-rims. "I don't care how bad-ass you are, Drusilla, when it comes to body art, girls always go for the butterfly."

I seriously doubt the woman's name is Drusilla. And given the tattoos that are visible—Jolly Roger beneath knotted belly button; iridescent snake winding around her neck; the word "slut," manly and municipal in FuturaBlack, stamped upon her left shoulder blade—I'm betting against the butterfly. But you never know. Take my boss Gertie, for instance. Nothing about the woman would seem to suggest she'd pay a stranger to etch her flesh with an ink-filled needle. And yet, amazingly, there it is, branding her right ankle for everyone to see: melded male and female symbols, the same idiosyncratic glyph some pint-sized performer from Minneapolis made famous back when I was a boy.

Gertie's running late, so I'm stuck listening to the guys from Accounting give the world-weary barmaid the requisite hard time. They quiz her on imaginary drinks, dare her to show them any and all tattoos not in plain sight. The barmaid's an overly inked woman by anybody's standards. Plus, she's been cursed with what my ex-girlfriend, Melanie, annoyingly referred to as a "rainy day face." As in "Uh-oh, Nathaniel's got his rainy day face on today—look out." She'd break into an uninspired rendition of "You Are My Sunshine" or "Here Comes the Sun," partly to help cheer me up but mostly just to get on my nerves. That's Melanie. Anyway, the barmaid's got this nonexistent chin, and gray circles around her eyes I'm not convinced are the result solely of cosmetics. But I like her mouth, which puts me in mind of something ripe and seed-bearing, and her grown out, shadow-black mullet is just the right mix of straight-from-the-salon and I-don't-give-a-fuck. The guys from Accounting—Damon the Ringleader, Stuart the Lackey, Leon the Clown—aren't big fans of skewed beauty, and it shows. What they *are* big fans of is cleavage. Drusilla knows her audience; she's craftily played to the crowd by stuffing her meager breasts into a Hanes tank top, Boys 8-12.

"Careful lads," I say, hoisting my lager. "I hear she eats men like air."

Damon gives me the gas face. He's not a big guy, but he's in good shape. Still, with his thuggish shaved head and nerdy spectacles, he's a master of mixed signals. "Yeah," he says, grabbing his crotch old-school hip-hop-style, "well tell her I've got a grand-slam breakfast buffet in my pants."

"My hero," I say.

"Hey, I'd bang her once for you, Nate," crows Damon, not without love. Damon is the kind of guy who assumes everyone is getting laid less than he is. It's true that my romantic life has taken some hits lately, beginning with Melanie. It certainly doesn't help matters that my creative life seems to be in a permanent tailspin. The older I get, the more difficult it is to convince myself I'm anything more than a creative hack-for-hire. The problem with being a starving artist, of course, is the starving part. My belly may be full but I'm hungry all the time.

And tired. Much too tied, in fact, for someone whose true vocation would seem to be the creative and sustained shunning of all forms of physical exertion. I get plenty of sleep, upwards of nine hours a night. So why am I tempted to use toothpicks to keep my eyelids open, *Tom & Jerry*-style, at 5:30 in the evening?

"Wake up," Gertie snaps, too close to my ear.

"About time," I say, shamefaced. Gertie expects nothing less than wide-eyed vigilance.

"Tell me about it," she says. "Chino had me on this conference call for over an hour. Who schedules a conference call for 4:30?"

"Chino, looks like."

"And who schedules Happy Hour on a *Tuesday*?" She shoots Damon an accusing look.

"Hey, man," Damon says, "I just put my name in a hat. The powers-that-be told me where and when."

"Tell the powers-that-be to get their shit together." Gertie glances around at the décor, the junior accountants, the sourpuss, possibly French barmaid with the sketchpad skin. "Jesus," she says, horrifically unimpressed.

"Bunch of bozos," I offer.

Gertie cuffs me lightly on the head. "Those bozos are your colleagues." I can't tell if she's serious, which is a problem. Sometimes when we meet face-to-face it's like we're conversing via email, the tone is so tricky to pin down. "Leave it to Chino to be named after a pant." She grins unevenly, and peers down the long, dark hall toward the rest rooms. "Order me a beer, will you," she says, and promptly disappears.

I glance around the bar vaguely hoping to catch sight of

Melanie, or some semblance of Melanie, such as I knew her. A favorite cigarette lighter, say, a whiff of cinnamon-stick perfume. But bars like O'Hooligan's aren't Mel's scene, and lucky for us both never will be. The place is packed with buzz-cut, lower-echelon business-types. The majority of them look to be in their thirties, though their dull demeanor and somber attire point to premature versions of their fathers, or the fathers they would've preferred to have, given the choice. Part of me pities the barmaid having to smile (barely) and serve (dutifully) these junior CPAs their god-awful shots and dishwater domestic beer. Then I remember the woman stands to benefit, at least financially, from all the attention. Happy Hour is a euphemism, less a promise than a dare. These corporate penny pinchers are determined to make a night of it, tossing ragged bills onto the bar as though the tens and twenties pulled from their pockets are personal days they need to either use or lose by night's ever-nearing end.

It takes me a while to get Drusilla to notice me. I don't command attention. I'm quoting Melanie here, a woman whose plump lips and long legs and celestial blonde hair land her modeling gig after modeling gig. They landed her an apartment off Rittenhouse Square that by rights should've gone to somebody with better credit and far more money in the bank. They landed her a new beau named Ezra, of all things. I don't think I'm being spiteful when I say my ex-girlfriend has a lot to offer a guy, on the surface.

I glance over at my esteemed colleagues and find Leon, who is surprisingly limber for a man his size, doing his famed Mr. Roboto-cum-Chicken Dance to early Duran Duran. I don't mind confessing that for a while there in the mid-eighties I had a minor crush on most of the band members, especially Nick Rhodes, who wore more make-up than any girl I knew and seemed at least as strange and aloof as the opposite sex. It'd taken me a few weeks to conclude he *wasn't* the opposite sex.

"Go Leon!" hoots Damon, egging him on. "It's your birthday! You crazy!"

Damon would never let loose and put himself on the line this way, though every indication is he'd like to. He's much too vain. He bills himself as this big-time party boy, but I've been out with him more than a few times now, and more often than not he ends the night sullen and near-silent, staring into his empty tumbler like Narcissus at his own reflection in a pool, only more impressed. I can't help thinking there's something eating at Damon, but maybe that's giving him too much credit. Perhaps the only thing eating him, at least metaphorically, is Janis from HR. Janis is smart and sexy and cool as a cave, the way only blue-collar neighborhood girls can be. But she's also married. I've witnessed firsthand the ironic, shameless way Janis flirts with Damon, and the way he laps it up, a dehydrated man presented with a tepid puddle of rainwater. One look at Damon three seconds after Janis has breezed out of the break room tells me everything either of us needs to know: cool or not, the woman's conservative streak runs as deep as the Delaware.

Gertie returns from the bathroom in a rage.

"He's answering the phone now!"

"What? Who?"

"*Doodle*. I called to check my messages and he picked up."

I shrug. "He probably thinks he's doing you a favor."

"He thinks we're fucking married, is what he thinks." She yawns one of her Olympic yawns and I can practically count the number of cavities. Most yawns are contagious, but I've been doing it so much lately that other people's yawns have little effect on me.

"What did you say?"

"I just hung up," she admits. "He's your friend, Nate. How do I get rid of him?"

"Like all strays," I say. "Stop feeding him."

"But that's just it, I *don't* feed him. The guy survives on tap water and Pop Tarts."

I try to put this delicately, even as "Love Shack" comes on the jukebox. I can't help smiling. "I meant that metaphorically."

Gertie knits her considerable brow. Her look of confusion morphs uncomfortably into one of embarrassment, and then outright anger. "He told you that? That we had sex?"

"Actually, the term Doodle used is 'make love.'" I'm not kidding.

Gertie smiles, but not happily. "He's a liar, okay. I let him stay a few days because I felt sorry for him, but that's it. I'm not saying we didn't hook up that first night, because we did." She takes a gulp of beer, wiping her mouth, like some school kid downing a Yoo-hoo, on her plum-colored sleeve. "Puppy dog eyes or no, I want him gone."

"I'll call him tomorrow."

"Wrong. I've got a meeting first thing tomorrow with Sasha and Saul. *Sasha and Saul*," Gertie snorts. "Why does Finance sound like a Maurice Sendak book?" She takes another swig of beer. "They're looking to cut one of my creatives right after Christmas." She gives me a look I'm not supposed to like. I'm the only creative.

It's not like I haven't heard about the cuts. Rumors have

been circulating for weeks. A number of supposedly expendable positions are being eliminated. I consider what losing my job might mean, weighing the moths in my wallet against the newfound freedom and time on my hands. I can't say I'm not intrigued by the prospect of unemployment. Of course I've got bills to pay, a monthly rent that's already past due. When Melanie moved out a few months back, she generously left me a check to cover her share of the rent through the end of the year. Now the year's almost up and I haven't saved a dime. Finding another roommate, too, is a chore I never got around to completing. I don't relish the prospect of placing an ad in the paper, sharing my space with a stranger. How will I get any work done—creative work, that is, the silk-screened T-shirts and mock book jackets I amuse myself by designing—with some bike messenger blaring music or surly serial waitress camped on the couch in cheap polyester pjs?

"I can't afford not to be on my game," Gertie says. "I need Doodle out of there tonight. I haven't slept a wink."

Gertie's a chronic insomniac anyway, but I decide not to comment on this. Ever since her live-in boyfriend, Amos, left her she's been on edge. In my opinion, on edge is where Gertie feels most at home; she's like a perpetual would-be suicide, a woman who could never bring herself to actually jump but who also can't fathom having to navigate the throngs of schleps bumbling around down here on the ground.

Gertie's my boss, so we're conscious of keeping our friendship respectable. Still, rumors abound. The guys from Accounting, I suspect, are largely to blame for this. Damon in particular seems obsessed with whatever Gertie and I may or may not be doing behind closed doors (and against company policy). Some days I like to feed him misinformation, other days I feel like punching him in the nose. Once, when I knew he was the only one looking, I put my arm around Gertie's waist and whispered sweet nothings in her ear. Literally. I said, "Sweet nothings, sweet nothings, Damon's watching, sweet nothings." Gertie giggled like a pro and pinched my behind.

But that's about it, I'm afraid, for the PDAs. We're card-carrying members of the Mutual Appreciation Society, and most of the affection we feel toward one another—as colleagues, as cohorts, as friends—is merely implied.

Gertie takes another great swallow of beer. "Ready?" she asks, though it's not a question.

"After you," I say, gesturing gallantly toward the door.

Short and solid Damon bars our way. I wouldn't be able to move him any more than I'd be able to move a mailbox, so I don't embarrass myself by trying.

"Where are you lovebirds going?" He smiles and spreads his arms wide, a game show host suggesting *All this could be yours.* "Why the long faces? Haven't you heard? The holidays are upon us. Plus, it's Happy Hour."

"Happy Hour's over," Gertie tersely informs him.

Damon looks at me as if to say *You're going home with* her? *All the half-lit women at your fingertips, and you choose one named* Gertrude?

"Out of the way, Damon," Gertie orders. "Now."

But Damon is no longer paying attention. Janis is coming through the door, but she's not alone. There's a strange, skinny man with her, with whom she appears to be holding hands.

"Sorry we're late." Janis says, by way of hello. She notices our coats and frowns. "You're leaving?"

"Family emergency," Gertie lies. "See you tomorrow."

"Oh. Okay."

I watch Janis and her husband join Stuart and Leon at the bar, who at some point in the evening are sure to be joined by Casper and Lauren and a temp named Rose. It's a familiar if not downright cozy scene. After all, they're young and reasonably attractive and, for the time being anyway, gainfully employed. A vestige of the self-destructive streak I've long since learned to ignore votes to stay.

Gertie tugs me by the scarf, winning the election by a landslide. "C'mon," she says. "You owe me one."

"Do yourself a favor and go home," I whisper to Damon on my way out the door. He appears frozen, borderline catatonic. Of course there's no way he's going home. Like all pointless, classic infatuations, Janis brings out the masochist in him.

"Did you drive?" I ask Gertie once we're out in the cold. The weather is reason enough not to have left the bar. Drusilla's androgynous cotton undershirt is certainly another. Plus, I'm not looking forward to confronting Doodle. Doodle's a little guy, smaller than I am, even smaller than Damon. But we've been semi-friends since we were kids. I get the feeling he's in over his head. Enter yours truly, a man who has yet to master the finer points of the doggie paddle.

"I don't drive," Gertie reminds me. "Cars are coffins on wheels."

"Cab?"

"Don't be a wuss. It's only a few blocks."

The wind cuts through my flimsy winter coat like a scythe. I bought it, against my better judgment, for a small fortune at a shop called Maestro off Rittenhouse Square. What it lacks in weight, of course, it more than makes up for in style: tweed and toggles and a collar that's flamboyantly vampiric. It was Melanie who'd suggested that I buy it, on one of our marathon shopping sprees. "You're not in the Merchant Marine," she'd said, referring to my ancient navy-issue pea coat. The sales-boy giggled. "Nobody mistakes you for post-Columbia Kerouac."

Winter here is typically short-lived but can be merciless for days at a time. Our breath isn't just visible as we march down Walnut Street; it whips across our numb-nosed faces like sea mist, turning to snow before our squinted, watery eyes.

"It's downright Chicagoan out here," I say, feeling wide-awake for the first time today.

"Chicagoan."

"Buffalonian?" I try.

Gertie smiles, and shouts into the wind, "What are you going to say to him, anyway?"

"I don't know," I yell back, mostly because I don't. "Any ideas?"

"9-1-1, that's my idea."

Once a month I have dinner with a few members of the old gang. Most of them are already married, with school-age kids and nondescript single homes in suburban New Jersey. We take turns picking the spot, always in downtown Philly, and more often than not Italian. We eat well, drink a lot of red wine, and talk about the good old days—a bunch of old-timers at the ripe old age of thirty-five. We end the evening with one-armed hugs and tentative plans for next month's dinner. It's all very chummy and nostalgic and sweetly sad. The thing is, three-and-a-half weeks out of every four, I barely think about these guys anymore. To say I miss them would be a gross exaggeration, if not an outright lie.

Last week I took Gertie along. We were out drinking after work, and she got hungry. When I mentioned the dinner, she asked if there would be any single guys in attendance, "just out of curiosity." I told her Brandon was single, but that Brandon was gay. "That's it?" she said, disbelievingly, as though I were holding out. "Well," I admitted, "there's Doodle."

Part of me actually wanted Gertie to meet my oldest friends, or wanted them to meet her. But I never thought she'd fall for any of them, or even so much as exchange phone numbers. Gertie was born in Israel. Her family moved to the States when she was ten. The Silversteins originally settled in Baltimore but eventually relocated to Western Pennsylvania. Like a lot of bright, culture-starved kids, she spent the summer after high school graduation backpacking through Europe with a couple of girlfriends. As a grown woman she's lived in Toronto, Tel Aviv, Barcelona, Dallas, San Diego and now, perhaps anticlimactically, Philadelphia. My friends are predictable, conventionally handsome neighborhood guys. Gertie's an erratic woman of the world.

Of course I'd had ulterior motives for inviting her. I simply couldn't face another heavy Mediterranean meal, washed down with liberal helpings of liquid nostalgia, alone. My logic, I now realize, was the logic of the abuser: If I had to suffer through another regurgitated chapter of this working-class rendition of *Remembrance of Things Past*—with anise biscotti in place of madeleine—so should Gertie.

Needless to say, dinner was a disaster. My friends were not impressed by Gertie, despite her commando-style conversational skills and loosely-buttoned, French-cuffed blouse. Of course, had Gertrude Silverstein been cast more, say, in the mold of Angelina Jolie, I'd still be receiving handwritten thank-you notes and impromptu high-fives. No matter. Brad Pitt, too, was hard to come by at our circular, linen-draped table.

The evening ended with a bored, disappointed Gertie turning up the flame on the gas-lit table lamp so high that her hair momentarily caught fire. It was Doodle who put it out, smothering the life-threatening flame with his slightly stained, massive cloth napkin. Afterwards, Gertie began dropping hints about the cold weather and wondered aloud which of my friends drove what. This surprised me for two reasons: 1) Gertie isn't a hint-dropper; she once read Marvell's "To His Coy Mistress" and faulted the shepherd for not being more direct. 2) She knew I didn't own a car. But then, the hints weren't meant for me. They were meant for the puppy-eyed Rescue Hero with the cartoon name.

I later learned that Doodle ended up staying the night, and then the rest of the weekend. In fact he was still there, passed out on Gertie's sofa, when she'd left for work this morning.

"He's very sweet," was all she said when I pressed her for more intimate details. "It's kind of nice having a man around again."

"Man-child's more like it," I huffed. I wasn't the jealous type, and my interest in Gertie wasn't nearly as epic as, say, Damon's ill-fated obsession with Janis (or even with himself). But something about the situation rubbed me the wrong way. Oh right: it was the fact that my charmless childhood friend, a man who well into his twenties used to phone his mother an hour before we left a dance club to see if the air conditioning was on, had slept with her first.

"I thought he'd have disappeared by now," Gertie whines, half a block from her building. "Y'know, poof!

Presto-change-o. Most guys are such magicians that way. You couldn't find them if you wanted to. Not Doodle." She sighs heavily. "He really needs to be gone. Like, of his own volition."

"Doodle doesn't have much volition," I say.

"Can we call him something other than Doodle? It's a ridiculous nickname."

"It's funny, but I don't even know his real name; we always just called him Doodle."

Gertie looks doubtful, and tightens her scarf. It's gaudy and crocheted, homemade in the worst sense of the word. "Would a swift kick in the ass do the trick?"

"Just throw him out. He won't make a fuss."

"Listen to you, 'He won't make a fuss.'" Gertie spreads her arms wide and turns, slowly, like a talk show makeover showing off her life-altering designer look. "The man's obsessed!" she squeals. "And for obvious reasons! Of course he'll make a fuss!"

Outside Gertie's apartment the wind really kicks up. She reaches into her leather sack of a handbag, digs out her keys and lets us into the building, the foyer of which is brightly lit and warm as a kitchen on Christmas Day. And, like that kitchen, inhabited by a variety of conflicting smells, not all of them identifiably culinary.

"I'll wait down here," Gertie says.

The overheated entranceway has me craving a soft place to lay my head. There's a well-padded package for somebody named Beatrice Fru lying right there on the floor...

"Maybe you should come up too," I say.

"Trust me, it's better this way. If he sees me, he'll just relive his obsession all over again."

This worries me. Gertie's the most confrontational

woman I know. She goes out of her way to make eye contact with the various urban wackos wandering around town. During lunch, she welcomes the chance to castigate wait-staff for imperfect meals or poor service.

"I hope he's not disappointed," I say, realizing that I'm probably the last person Doodle expects to see walking through Gertie's door.

She ignores my comment and nods toward the stairs.

"Wish me luck," I say when she begins checking her mail.

Gertie surprises me by leaning over and kissing me on the cheek. Even given the fact that no one's around and no tongue is involved, this is huge. Gertie's nothing like those theatrical women you see smooching their boyfriends up and down Walnut Street on warm spring days. She loathes PDAs—calls them Public Displays of Affectation. To her mind, there's nothing wrong with professing your love for another human being, so long as you do so in the privacy of your own home, preferably with the shades drawn and the door locked. "You're a lifesaver, Nate."

Gertie lives on the third floor, across from a woman who wanders the halls in an Eagles jersey and tube socks searching for an imaginary cat unimaginatively named Fluffy. Gertie has dubbed the woman Fluff-n-Nutter. I pause outside my friend's door and put my ear up to the wood, which is unexpectedly warm and smells only of paint. I don't hear anything, other than an overly familiar episode of *Seinfeld* emanating from Fluff-n'-Nutter's apartment. Maybe Doodle's asleep, I think, or passed out in a pool of his own vomit. Or maybe he couldn't wait for Gertie to get home, and has decided to spend some quality time with Mrs. Thumb and her four accommodating daughters. These aren't exactly pleasant thoughts, but I let myself into the apartment anyway, sweetly enunciating Doodle's name as though I'm greeting a pet. I don't want to shock him. And I really don't want to catch him with his pants down, figuratively or otherwise.

I conduct a quick search and declare the place empty. I declare this to myself; Gertie is still hiding downstairs. I can't find any signs of Doodle: no Anime basketball sneakers; no overstuffed I Goldberg-issue bomber jacket; no Warholian Pop Tart wrappers on the table or in the trash. He's gone. It's taken a brick wall, but he's finally gotten the hint.

Rather than call for Gertie, I plop down on the sofa and sink into the thing. This is no flimsy, mass-produced futon, it's an antique bear hug of a couch, with loads of overstuffed throw pillows and a plush afghan draped over an arm. Gertie's bed, too, is far from the Scandinavian pallet you might expect to find in a young single person's apartment, but rather part of a cumbersome Deco set sporting large circular mirrors and naked, oddly nipple-less figures reminiscent of Barbie dolls. All of Gertie's furniture, it turns out, is substantial, oversized stuff. I'm impressed. My own glorified closet of an apartment is a veritable showroom of foam, flake-board and tin.

I consider heading downstairs to fetch Gertie and tell her the good news—Doodle is gone and likely won't be back—but I can't bring myself to leave the couch, it's so insanely comfortable. I feel like I haven't sat down in days, though in truth all I do, all day long, is sit. It seems criminal not to kick off my shoes and stretch out for a spell. My silly coat's collar has the makings of a cocoon. My eyes begin to close…

"Nate?" Gertie's voice jars me awake. "What's going on?"

It takes me a second to get things straight in my head: who she is, where I am, why we're here. "He's gone," I say finally. Gertie's silhouette fills the doorway. She looks as if she's afraid to come in, as if the smell of Doodle is thick in the air, and she's debating whether or not she can handle breathing it in.

"What did you say to him?" She approaches me tentatively, as though I'm an animal she's not quite convinced means her no harm. "Did he sneak out the back? I didn't see him come down."

"He was gone before I got here," I answer, just before my lids begin to lower again.

"Nathaniel!" Gertie snaps. "What are you, stoned or something? You can't sleep here."

But it's no use. My eyes are just about shut. I'm paralyzed with fatigue.

"Get up, Nate!" Gertie shouts. "Now!" She tugs so sharply on my leg that my pants start to come down, revealing the waistband of an immaturely patterned pair of silk boxers. A parting gift, as it would turn out, from long-limbed, shortsighted Melanie, latest heartbreaker to hit the Square.

I come to and grab hold of a muscular sofa arm, clinging to it as if for dear life. To look at me you'd think my ship has sunk and all that's keeping me from a watery grave is this bobbing piece of debris.

"Out," Gertie yelps, laughing now despite herself. She gives another pull on my leg and my grip loosens, as do my pants. One more tug and I'm a goner, and she knows it. But just when I think all is lost, Gertie forfeits the game. She drops my leg in apparent disgust and heads off to her bedroom. She resists glancing back over her shoulder, coyly or otherwise.

I sit there, sort of relieved in the semi-dark, adjusting my underwear.

A few minutes later Gertie re-enters the room in white yoga pants and a matching hoodie. She looks like a laidback angel, some hip Pearly Gates PR woman come to sell me on the idea of salvation.

Gertie sits down and regards me suspiciously from her end of the couch. "I can't do this now," she says, and I almost believe her. "It's too soon. Amos has only been gone a few months, and then this Doodle guy—"

"You won't have to do anything," I cut her off.

"Oh no?" She's smiling now, and fidgeting with the drawstring of her heavenly sweatshirt. "What kind of relationship is that?"

"The new kind," I say. "The non-kind. Haven't you heard? No talking. No touching. No sex."

It sounds ludicrous, I know, but I see it all so clearly in my head. I think about the myriad women I've admired and idealized from afar, and how flawless falling in love is, how flawless it's always been, how perfect. I think about Melanie, and how expertly we ruined things, how we couldn't resist dooming our union with that very first kiss.

I'm so engrossed by this blissfully warped vision of the platonic that when Gertie finally gets up to close the apartment door, in effect sealing our fate, it barely registers. Suddenly she's next to me on the couch again, closer than before, maybe too close. I won't look at her for fear of losing concentration. *Do it right*, I tell myself. *Don't ruin things*. It becomes a mantra. And for a few seconds I surprise myself; for the better part of a minute, I excel at ignoring her. But somebody's heart is beating too loudly, much too fast, and the temperature inside the apartment suggests Doodle's left the oven on all day. When I make the rookie mistake of meeting her gaze, I find Gertie's pretty, crooked mouth moving toward mine at a ridiculous clip, warp speed, no time to think or move or do anything but brace myself and take the hit. Seconds from now it'll all be over, *we'll* be over. Months, maybe even years will fly by in the time it takes our once-eager lips to unstick, and then: nothing. Black hole. Full circle. Square one.

We kiss.

Acknowledgments

Special thanks to literary dynamo Marc Schuster, for holding my hand throughout this entire process and never (not once!) tickling my palm. His advice, eagle-eyed editorial skills and general expertise were crucial to the creation of this book.

Thanks to the editors of the magazines in which a few of these stories first appeared, specifically Carla Spataro and Christine Weiser at *Philadelphia Stories*, Barbara Westwood Diehl and Susan Muaddi Darraj at *The Baltimore Review*, and Tim Monaghan at *The Ledge*.

Thanks to everyone who ever gave me feedback on the contents of this book, particularly Liz Moore, Kelly Simmons, Laura Spagnoli, Jim Miller, members of the PS Writers Group and those font worshipping superheroes, the Helveticats.

Thanks to Alyssa Robb, for her photographic eye; thanks to Shay Kretowicz, for her photogenic eyes.

Thanks to Enrico Botta, for bringing Bobo Lazarus to life.

Thanks to my family and friends, especially my parents, for myriad manifestations of love and support.

Thanks to Sebastian, Julian and Alexander, for thinking that writing fiction is cool.

And finally very special thanks to Maureen, who knows firsthand that while writing fiction *is* cool, it's also time-consuming and often frustrating as hell. I owe you big-time.